At the edge of the _____ e
his pursuers. The _____ ir
and beard with grey, filling his eyes _____ g
bitterness that had withered and wrinkled the skin
around them. There was a weapon in his hand, and the
thin set of his mouth told them he meant to use it. For a
moment they felt the terror of him in this place where
neither they nor he had any right to be; for a moment
they were held – and in that moment, with a single
sobbing cry of despair, he turned and ran into the trees.

An Orbit Book

First published in Great Britain in 1991 as an Orbit Book by
Futura, a Division of Macdonald & Co (Publishers) Ltd, London
& Sydney

Reproduced, printed and bound in Great Britain by
BPCC Hazell Books
Aylesbury, Bucks, England
Member of BPCC Ltd.

ISBN 0 7088 8354 0

Orbit Books
A Division of
Macdonald & Co (Publishers) Ltd
Orbit House
1 New Fetter Lane
London EC4A 1AR

A member of Maxwell Macmillan Pergamon Publishing Corporation

THE DRAGON IN
THE STONE

Allan Scott

To my mother, for all reasons

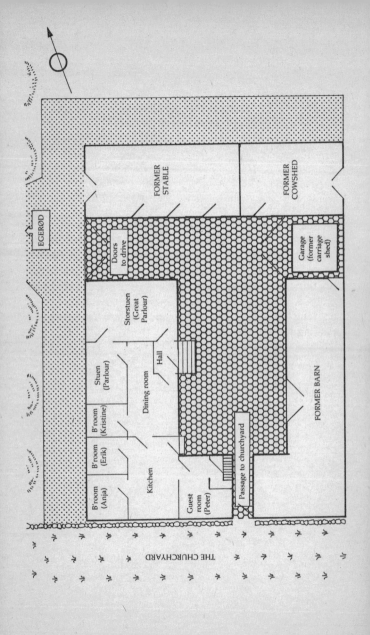

ACKNOWLEDGEMENTS

My thanks to everyone who helped me raise the dragon: to Richard Evans, who gave me the confidence to start; to John Jarrold at Orbit, for his belief in me and in the project, for seeing what I wanted and for helping me achieve it; to Mike Scott Rohan for constant friendship, support, advice and encouragement; to Maggie Noach, agent extraordinary; to my family in Denmark, for their unfailing hospitality, their time and patience during many months of research; to Andrew, Debra and James for opening the door into twilight; and to Rosemary for making it all worthwhile.

I had a dream, which was not all a dream.
The bright sun was extinguished, and the stars
did wander darkling in the eternal space,
Rayless, and pathless, and the icy earth
swung blind and blackening in the moonless air . . .

Byron

CHAPTER
1

Hwær cwom mearg, hwær cwom mago, hwær cwom
*   maððumgyfa?*
Hwær cwom symbla gesetu? Hwær sindon seledreamas?
Eala beorht bune, eala byrnwiga,
Eala þeodnes þrym! Hu seo þrag gewat,
gewat under nihthelm swa heo ne wære!

Where is the horse, and the hero to ride it? Where is
    the giver of gold?
Where are the boards, bedecked for the feast? Where
    are the joys of the hall?
Alas for gold goblets and glorious warriors!
Alas for the princes! They perished in shadow,
Passed into darkness like dreams on the wind ...

The Wanderer (c. 8th century AD)

At the edge of the wood the injured man stopped to face
his pursuers.

The long, wasted years had frosted his hair and beard
with grey, filling his eyes with overflowing bitterness that
had withered and wrinkled the skin around them. There
was a weapon in his hand, and the thin set of his mouth
told them he meant to use it. For a moment they felt the
terror of him in this place where neither they nor he had
any right to be, for a moment they were held – and in that
moment, with a single sobbing cry of despair, he turned
and ran into the trees.

He sought the twilight. He found shadow and the

sweet, warm smell of growth and decay. Birds and animals fled from the rush of his feet through the dead leaves. Darkness whispered to him as the hundred voices of trees and branches answered a westerly breeze, drawing him onward and inward. Ahead, the last bastions of the ancient forest gathered themselves into a tunnel roofed with massive, green-stained branches. Probing creepers trailed their tentacles, seeking him blindly with dark clusters of polished leaves. Brambles and nettles snatched at the bruised flesh behind his torn clothes. What he sought was close, he knew that – but it could not be close enough. He had been mad to stop. Fighting them now would achieve little. A few might die, but nothing else would change, and if he let them kill him all those twilight years would remain as empty and useless as his love.

The strength was draining out of him. Each breath battled to escape his imprisoning ribs; each footfall hammered up his legs, jarring muscles, tearing at ligaments, bruising joints. In the entangling darkness every direction looked the same, and he could not know which was right. Behind him . . .

Behind him there was stillness – a silence that seemed as old as the wood itself. He stopped, listening, clasping his arms around his heaving chest, sinking to his knees as the last strength trickled from his limbs. Even the wind had died, as if the forest were holding its breath.

His pursuers were no longer following him.

He felt no sense of relief or escape. If they had gone, it was because their presence in this ancient place had brought another pursuer out of the twilight, something they feared more than the anger of their leader. It was behind him now, cloaked in silence, hunting him as they could not. It belonged to the arches of the trees, the slow rising of ancient sap, the cycle of a life too long to be measured in the motions of sun and moon. It belonged to the forests that had been once and might be again. It had seen men come, and it would return when they were gone. For a moment he saw, or thought he saw, the green light of its eyes – and he trembled, and once again he ran, knowing that his death followed him ...

Peter Brockman hated cemeteries, and nothing about this one made him feel like changing his mind. If anything, it was worse than most. Even so, it was not the place he disliked – it was the oppressive neatness of it.

The feeling had been with him since the moment he had walked out of his Copenhagen hotel into the cutting edge of a frosty September morning. The clean streets had been full of neat people going to tidy jobs in shiny cars and buses. In Town Hall Square the green copper roofs and spires had gleamed at him through the wintry air, daring him to find water stains. The station concourse had been strangely garbage-free, and the S-train had arrived with irritating punctuality. As its doors swished open, well-groomed Danes had glanced at him with passing interest, then buried themselves between the aseptic white sheets of their morning papers. Even the graffiti were clean. The slogan sprayed on the bus shelter outside Egerød station would have earned straight 'A's in art and handwriting. *Leve kærlighed – befri fantasien.* He grinned, almost despite himself. Back in the sixties a child called Peter Brockman had sprayed the same kind of thing in larger, clumsier letters all over the Berkeley campus.

Long live love. Free the spirit.

He read the other epitaphs. The words – love, God, faith, rest, peace – were only a little stranger in Danish. The freshly-raked gravel, the manicured grass, and the carefully-nurtured flowers gave the impression of a prim and overprotected garden. Brockman felt a pathological urge to tear up the flowers and scatter the gravel, to destroy the tidiness and order that mocked the horror of death.

It took him fifteen minutes to find the stone. It was green with age, but it stood alone in an oblong of gravel behind a well-tended square of flowers.

3

Per Munk, min elskede Mand. Grethe Munk, vor kære Mor. Lille Else, 18 September-24 December 1921 . . .

He hated the flowers. He hated the stone. The names were meaningless marks, nothing to do with him, his mother, or anyone he cared about. He shut his eyes, struggling to remember. *Per Munk, my beloved husband* – his grandfather, the man he had been named for, a sepia portrait with pince-nez and a formal suit, a square-faced, respectable man with a furrowed brow and an expression at the same time stern and compassionate. *Grethe Munk, our dear mother* – a young girl, scarcely free of her puppy-fat, love shining in her eyes for the tall, stiff banker who held her arm so formally. *Little Else* – his mother's twin sister, a bundle of nothing lost in the endless, hand-embroidered folds of her christening robe. Pictures in an album, names on a stone; but somewhere back in time they were real people, people with fears and hopes who loved and quarrelled, bore children and buried them.

He remembered his mother talking about Else, telling him how she had always felt guilty, as if she had taken something that the younger girl needed to stay alive. She had thrown herself at the world with a boundless energy, as if she had two people to live for and just one life to do it in. And then she had died. His father's suddenly empty life had lasted another year. Brockman always felt the old man had died of loneliness.

Little Else. You could've been my mother, in some other world. And now she's with you, wherever you are, and I'm here, and I still don't know why the hell I came. OK, you brought me here. You tell me why.

He opened his eyes, but the answer was a long time coming.

It began with the sky. It was too blue to be real, a frail bubble that had caught and somehow held a fragment of the past: an old church, a churchyard that might be even older, and a thatch-roofed house. Two ancient buildings, clean, whitewashed, cared for and loved by a whole

4

community through a hundred generations or more – and buried in regimented rows between them the men, women, children and babes in arms that had brought them life. Outside, just outside, was a busy city suburb. If you listened hard you could hear the traffic, the murmur of morning shoppers, and the meaningless music of electronic cash registers. Inside, in a world that was somehow more immediate and more real, a cat pattered across the gravel, birds sang in a tree, and the old church clock in its step-gabled tower struck the half hour.

It was half past nine – and Peter Brockman was still alive.

He smiled, here where only the ghosts of a lost time could see it, and wandered into the white, frost-chilled coolness of the church.

It was like walking into the past.

At first, before his eyes adjusted to the more subdued light inside the church, he saw only the shadowy masses of huge, circular columns. Above them, heavy, semi-circular ribs spanned the nave and the aisles – solid, reassuring, and seemingly built to stand till Doomsday. Everything around him spoke of age, of a time so far away as to be almost beyond imagination, a time when simple faith was all that stood between fading light and eternal darkness . . .

But the darkness was an illusion. There were colours among the shadows – red, white and green bands on the great ribs of the vault, and vivid, geometrical patterning on the columns. There were images, too – paintings and frescoes, a tumult of colour exploding out of the shadows. The walls and the vaults they supported were crammed with figures, patterns, foliage and black-letter inscriptions. On the outer wall, a few feet from the floor, a painted battle raged along either side of the church – mail-shirted soldiers, their faces long since worn away, hacking and thrusting with axes, swords and spears. Above them was a procession of robed figures, trees and animals – Old and New Testament seen through the earthy eyes of a Danish peasant. Higher yet, the vaults that spanned the nave sprouted painted flowers, vines and creepers that blossomed into the figures of saints and patriarchs. In a side chapel, harvesters, clerics, nobles and kings linked hands in a whirling, circular dance – but leading them was a hideous, reptilian figure with curved, dagger-sharp teeth bared in a lipless grin. Long, snaking arms tipped with scythe-like claws hung from peaked shoulders rising almost higher than the head. It was the embodiment of Death – but this strange, almost surreal image was unlike anything Brockman had ever seen before.

Automatically he took out his sketchpad, copying the clean lines of the fresco with practised skill. In a long and lonely career he had sketched pottery, sculpture, wall-paintings and artefacts in tropical rain forests, mountain snowfields and desert oases. It was almost second nature. Yet now, for the first time, he felt something stronger than a casual contact with the past. It was as though his own sketches echoed and magnified the designs of the original artist – as though, somehow, he could sense what the man had *wanted* to achieve ...

As he walked slowly towards the high altar, he saw other, even more powerful, paintings in the same style as the battling figures far below. Colours shouted at him – green, red, yellow, brown, scarlet and pale gold. In the first bay a monstrous, flame-like horse with a strange, naked rider battered at a tree, while two figures in a turret shot at it with arrows. In the next a snarling dragon writhed on the long-bladed lance of an almost demonic St George. The knight's grotesque armour and masking helmet seemed to echo the figure of Death in the side chapel. The visor was lifted, and the face below it seemed almost Moorish – dark-skinned, with flashing eyes. The dragon was strangely distorted, with limbs like twisted tree-branches and a face like the storm-battered trunk of a hollow tree. The flowing lines of the painting gave it a ghastly vitality. Beyond, in the last bay, was a peasant

6

Pieta – an aging Mary in a braided robe and a coarse kerchief weeping over a stricken Christ dressed in rough tunic and trousers. For a moment Brockman was curious. These clothes seemed out of keeping with the rest, as if the artist had consciously copied a far older style. Then he saw the eastern wall, and every other thought was driven from his mind.

Staring, Peter Brockman walked forward into the Day of Judgement, beckoned by elaborately armoured devils with bizarre heads and bodies – the demonic visions of Hieronymus Bosch, prefigured in bold, simple and imaginative strokes. The figures were dark and shadowy, each burning with a pallid, blue-white flame. Superficially they were similar, but when he looked more closely each was somehow distinct – almost personalised. The images, and the idea behind them, fascinated him.

It's true. Hell isn't a place. It's something we make for ourselves. And everyone does it their own way . . .

Most medieval artists showed Hell as the gaping mouth of a hideous dragon; here it lay in the shadow of a vast mound that was raised on painted stone columns like those of the church itself. Within, amid twisting spires of sapphire and ruby flame, monsters and miscegenations grappled and tore at the blackened bodies of their victims. On a mountaintop far above, beyond the reach of his creation, a gigantic bearded figure stared down into a wilderness of flame. Beneath the Father's haloed gaze pygmies ran in aimless panic, naked, powerless, searching for somewhere to hide.

And in their midst a woman transfixed on a demonic trident turned her face outward into the church in a final, desperate entreaty . . .

Sarah . . .?

How did he know? How could he know?

The painting was old, so old that many figures were little more than outlines, Picasso nightmares with faces lost in time. It was the lines that spoke to him, the sweeping curves of running legs, upraised arms, heads

7

turned skyward in terror, hearing death on the wind, waiting for fire from heaven. Somehow, seven centuries ago, a man had reached across the years to snatch a vision of hell from the mind of Peter Brockman.

I've been seeing this place wrong. Looking at it the wrong way. Those people out there – my people – they knew about death, the way I know. It's the ones still left who've forgotten.

For the first time, he realised that he had come home.

Outside, the air was still crisp with autumn frost. He stood for a few moments in the shadow of the porch, breathing in the morning, looking at the ordered ranks of his ancestors with their headstones standing to attention either side of the raked gravel path. In the shadow of each stone, white ice-jewels glittered and vanished under the eye of day.

The house was directly opposite. Its side wall ran along the churchyard boundary, pierced by two windows, one clear, one covered with a drawn-down blind like some bizarre eye-patch. They seemed to stare in disbelief at a mound half-buried in tall, uncut grass and capped with a column of grey stone. Brockman grinned. He liked the mound. It cut across the ordered ranks of grave-plots, across the paths, as if it had been there longer than any of them and had no intention of moving now, an ancient giant that had lain down to rest in an age out of time and slept on into a world of pygmies. Now it lay white-haired with dandelion clocks, grizzled with field grass, robed in nettles and wild flowers. At the base of the grey stone that crowned it, a thrush cracked its first catch of the day with a monotonous clicking sound. There was something puzzling about the mound, something else that set it apart from the rest of the churchyard.

Yes. Odd. Even in its deepest shadows there was no hint of last night's frost. Its shape was strange, too – bumps and hollows that hardly seemed natural, making a pattern of light and darkness – a broken pattern that was somehow familiar.

He was running before he knew it, driven by the nightmare he had relived in the church. The distant bang of a car exhaust became shots on a sea breeze. Two great black birds, startled into flight, clattered out of a tree with a sound like distant helicopters. He knew the pattern on the mound because he had seen it before. It was the pattern left by a human being in long grass – the signature of death.

The gravel crunched and rolled underfoot as he ran, like tiny hands tripping him, slowing him. As he reached the mound he stumbled, threshing the grass aside in his fall.

The stranger lay in a huddled ball like a terrified child. His clothes were nothing more than rags, torn and stained. His beard and hair were unkempt, cut through with slashes of grey and white. He stank of old sweat and urine. One clenched hand reached out towards the grey stone above him like an unanswered prayer. He belonged outside a condemned block in uptown New York, in a passage on the London subway – anywhere but the middle of a serene Danish churchyard. For a moment Brockman thought the man was dead, and reached out blindly as he had all those years before, fumbling for the faint beat of a dwindling life.

The pulse was erratic, but it was there. Instinct took over.

First thing is to keep him warm – my jacket, yeah. God it's cold – still, he needs it more than me. No bones broken, far as I can tell. Just exposure, I guess. No – Jesus Christ, that's blood! Looks like they have muggers in this country as well as street cleaners. Eyes OK. No concussion –

The hard grip on his wrist was the last thing he expected. The old man's icy fingers pressed flesh against bone with bruising force. His eyes were wide open, a cold gun-metal blue that held Brockman like a searchlight. The face was intensely aware, alive with knowledge and intelligence. The lips, drawn into a tight rictus of pain, parted just enough for a harsh whisper.

'You! *Get me into the house!*'

The eyes flickered shut. The force went out of the sharp grip around Brockman's wrist. Once again the old man was a pathetic tramp, his face harsh with grime and grey, tangled hair.

So he knows someone. Someone in the house. Maybe he tried to get in last night . . .

Brockman was already on his feet, running towards the single, staring window, hammering on the frame.

Come on. Come on, for Christ's sake!

He hammered again and felt something splinter under his fist. Glass cracked like the flat report of a rifle. A face appeared beyond the window, distorted by the shattered pane, shouting something he couldn't understand. He shouted back.

'There's a man out here! He needs help – he's been attacked!'

The window slammed open, and the glass flew apart under the impact.

'*Hvad fanden laver du her?*'

She was young, pretty, and very angry. More than that he still wasn't calm enough to notice.

'Look, I'm sorry about the damn window but there's an injured man out here – oh Christ, I mean *taler du Engelsk?*'

'*Hvad* . . . yes, I speak English, but . . .?'

'OK, can you come out, right now? I need some help.'

'You are hurt?'

'No, some guy over there,' he gabbled, 'a hobo. I guess he got caught in the frost or something, but he's in bad shape. Looks like somebody mugged him.'

'I'm sorry, but please speak a little slower, or I don't understand. I will come out, *ja?*'

'Yeah, OK.' He took a deep breath, trying to summon up patience he didn't have. Not her fault if she couldn't follow an American accent running at machine-gun speed, especially at half past nine on a cold September morning. 'Sorry. But he looks pretty bad.'

She frowned and nodded. There was a cast to the girl's features – with those almond-shaped eyes and high cheekbones in that broad, triangular face she looked almost oriental, but her hair was all Scandinavian, long and blonde and shining. It bounced as she turned away, and the smell of it was a perfume.

Something about her ... Damn it, Brockman, there's a man dying out there!

He swore softly under his breath, and ran back to the mound.

The man was lying as Brockman had left him. His eyes were squeezed shut against the brilliance of the winter morning, and his hair and beard were spangled with dewdrops. His clothes were stained with dried blood. They had been little more than sacking to begin with, but now they were slashed and torn, revealing half-healed wounds that had been camouflaged by a layer of grime and dirt.

'This is the – hobot, you call him?'

Brockman was momentarily startled. He hadn't heard the girl's approach at all. She wore casual clothes and a pair of thin, tapered slacks that stopped halfway down her calves. He could only think that she must be very cold. She squinted down at the huddled figure on the mound, and Brockman smiled. Vain as well as pretty – ten to one she was nearsighted, and even better odds that she kept her eyeglasses locked away in some drawer inside the house.

'Found him right here.'

'He is OK?'

'For a guy who's damn near dead, he's fine.'

She did not reply. Instead she knelt down next to the man, put a hand under his neck, and pulled up his chin. *Clearing his windpipe. Damn it, I should've thought of that.* Satisfied he was breathing properly, she rolled him onto his side, then checked his pulse against her watch. Pale strands of hair fluttered across her forehead in a sudden breeze, and the trees around the churchyard answered with a low sigh. For a few moments she seemed totally absorbed in her simple examination, but when he saw her face again it was grey, and her upper lip was beaded with sweat.

She has to be a trained nurse. So what's bugging her? Can't be the blood, she'd've seen worse than that. Got to be that she knows him.

'Look, I can see you're upset, but I'd like to know what's going on. Who is this guy? What the hell was he doing here?'

'I have not seen him before. Now take up his feet, OK?' Her face was still pallid with shock, but her voice was harsh and commanding. It set Brockman's teeth on edge. Without waiting for an answer she put her hands under the old man's arms, supporting his head as she lifted him. Brockman shrugged and picked up his ankles.

Why're you lying? You're not even good at it.

Her features were half-veiled now by a curtain of fine, white-blonde hair, but as they walked back towards the house she seemed to be looking resolutely at the ground, avoiding both his face and that of the old man. They came to a heavy wooden door in the churchyard wall, bound with long, iron hinges and studded with square-headed nails. The girl backed against it, pushing it open, and tossed her stray hair to one side as she checked quickly behind her.

'Please hold the door,' she said with brittle crispness, 'or it will hurt him.'

He was almost ready with a wisecrack retort when she turned her head back towards him. Her expression took his breath away. For two years, on the dig in Israel, he had lived on top of people who spent most of their time on the alert for danger. *Damn it, Sarah used to be like this. Always cool and on top of things when underneath she was scared shitless.*

'I'm sorry, but I still think you know something about this guy. I'd like you to tell me.'

'I don't understand.'

The hell you don't. 'OK, OK, forget it. Let's get him in before we all freeze to death. I could use my jacket back right now.'

The door opened into a tunnel-like passage with a cobbled courtyard beyond. It was surrounded on all four sides by a range of limewashed single-storey buildings roofed with heavy thatch. The thatch surprised him, especially in the middle of a modern city suburb. The range to the left rose a little higher than the others; in front of it, a stone stairway flanked with elaborate wrought-iron railings led up to a green double door. Distracted, Brockman stumbled on the cobbles.

'*Gud!*'

'Sorry. What kind of place *is* this?'

'It used to be a – a *gård*. A farm. My family's.'

'Weird place for a farm.'

'It was all open land here – *åh Gud!*'

'OK, I'm not going to drop him.'

What is this guy to her? Black sheep of the family? Alcoholic father come home to roost?

The crash as the double doors swung open startled him out of his thoughts. The girl had been wrestling with the door-handle, and in the process she had almost lost her grip on the old man. She swore under her breath and threw him a look of pure venom as she struggled with her burden.

'*Anja, hvad er der i vejen?*' The voice came from inside the house. It sounded old, and a little tetchy. '*Hvad laver du?*'

'So you're Anja. Pleasure to meet you, Anja. Who's that?'

'She is my grandmother, Mr –?'

'Brockman – Peter Brockman. And you're right, it's none of my business. But I would like to put down our friend. I'm not complaining, but he's no lightweight and he doesn't exactly smell of roses.'

She made a pretence at a smile. He wished she hadn't.

'*Anja?*'

13

'Ja, ja. Vent lige lidt, Mormor. In here, Mr Brockman –'

'Peter. This is some room.'

He had never seen anything quite like it. At first it seemed opulent, a mass of carved and painted wood. A bed with decorated side panels filled an alcove in the far wall. A glorious wooden chest stood in one corner, and next to it a tall chest of drawers painted, like everything else, in red, green, black and white. On the opposite wall was an iron stove that Noah might have used on the ark, polished to a silky shine. Yet the room itself was simple – bare, polished wood on the floor, scatter rugs, and whitewashed walls. It took him long moments to realise that almost everything he was looking at was original. In this room, time had stood still for a hundred and fifty years ...

'I would like to put him down also,' said the girl.

'What? Sorry. Yeah. Hey, the bed's kind of short, isn't it?'

'He is a tall man, and my – how do you call it? – great grandfather was not.'

'This is your family's house?'

'Since four hundred years, ja.'

He whistled. 'They live here now?'

'Just me and Mormor.'

Christ, she did it. Sounds like we're old friends. And I trust her about as far as I can throw him.

'Look – er – shouldn't you call a doctor? I mean, the way they beat up on him ...'

She looked startled, then angry. 'That is not necessary.'

'You have to be kidding. Exposure, assault – this guy could keep a sharp medic in martinis for life.'

'I don't think so.'

'I do. You want to tell me what's going on?'

'What do you mean?'

'I mean something stinks around here.'

'I don't understand.'

'Oh sure. Let's try some basic English, Anja. What's

14

the game? What the hell are you trying to do?'

'I am trying to look after this man, Mr Brockman. There is no game. If you want to help me, OK. Else you can go.'

'He needs a doctor.'

'I *am* a doctor.'

Brockman's mouth opened and stayed open.

'I must get my bag and some hot water. Call me if he wakes up.'

Well I'll be damned. He squatted down by the bed, tucking his jacket around the old man. *What do you reckon, chum? And why did you want to get in here so badly?* He rubbed his aching wrist. The old man had bruised it – and there had been no doubting the intensity in his eyes. He had known exactly where he was, and exactly what to do. If there were only two people in the house, then Anja had to know the old man. *So the lady is a doctor. And the doctor is a liar.*

For a moment the old man's eyelids flickered. Brockman leaned forward expectantly, but there was no further sign of life.

Dreaming, maybe. If it's about whoever or whatever did this to him, I wouldn't like to be inside his head . . .

* * *

For a moment – just a moment – there were voices, and a room that was familiar, though Erik Larssen did not know why it should be or what he was doing there. There was something he had to remember – something important, a journey he had made, something he had found. Perhaps that drive back to Oxford, so many years before. There was cool air on his face, like the first breeze of autumn. It had been autumn then.

Remember. I must remember, or it will all be for nothing . . .

September – he had always loved September without knowing why. Only now, with thirty years of life behind him, did he begin to remember the vividness of those autumns, long ago, when his mother had taken him to see

15

her family in Denmark: hot afternoons in Uncle Henrik's garden, scrambling up the trees to pick apples, pears and plums, and eating more than went into the baskets; endless drives across an open landscape, so different from the narrow Oxfordshire lanes that crept between the hills behind hedgerow veils as if they were ashamed to be seen. And the light: that was different, too. In Denmark it was clear, clean. Sometimes, as a child, he had known that if he could only find a hill to climb he would be able to see for ever. Oxfordshire had hills, but no light. The world was bounded with walls of cloud, mist and haze. Eternity was never more than a dream – or a memory.

When he saw the burning car his mind was twenty-five years and hundreds of miles away. For a moment he did not understand why his foot was jammed down on the brake pedal. The tyres screeched and slithered on the mist-dampened road as he banged the car clumsily into reverse and stabbed down on the accelerator.

The white sports car was nose down in the ditch on the left side of the road. In the tricky evening light the driver had missed an unsignposted bend – he could see the twisted flame of her red-gold hair spilling out of the window. At the same time, with a sudden, appalling clarity, he saw the answering flame creeping along the bonnet of the car.

Then there was no more time to think. His body was an automaton, detached from his mind. He saw his hand open the door and felt himself half fall, half jump out onto the road, striking it with an impact that tore the skin from both his knees. The pain was happening to someone else, but the sports car lurched towards him as he floundered clumsily to his feet and flung himself forward. He flinched at the chill of the metal on his fingers and the trickle of condensation as his hand slid towards the open window. With a thrill of horror he saw the two flames touch, and caught the momentary stench of burning hair. There was music blaring out of the open window – a rock band, all guitars and drums, with a bass line that hammered senseless lyrics through his head. Somehow there was time to see the long, white curve of the woman's arm draped over the steering wheel, the smear of red on the windscreen, the slow, dark trickle of blood on her forehead, even the intricate paisley pattern of her short cotton dress as he tugged uselessly at the door-handle. Before he understood that the buckled door was immovable he was already reaching in to pull her bodily through the open window. He toppled under her weight, rolling down the damp bank into the crumbling mass of dead leaves and vegetation at the bottom of the ditch, slapping at her dress to kill the hungry flames already feeding there, throwing himself across her with an unthinking desire to protect . . .

The explosion was like nothing he had ever imagined – a flat, almost muffled crack, then a giant's punch that hurled him aside, deafened him, and left his head ringing with aftershock. He heard pieces of metal and glass from the wrecked car whine over his head and pepper the bushes on the other side of the ditch. Fragments of glass quivered in the tree-trunk above his head. A fine rain of debris continued to fall until it seemed impossible that there should be any more. Shaking his head, he crawled back to look at the woman.

Her face was pale and still, smeared with the blood that flowed from her forehead. It was a beautiful face, but in no ordinary way – broad, triangular, with slitted, almost oriental eyes. The flickering light from the burning car was splashing her dress with livid patches of red, like blood from a dozen hidden injuries, yet he felt an almost irresistible impulse to reach out and touch her. In throwing himself across her he had pulled open the front of her dress, ripping off the top two buttons to reveal a silver pendant on a chain around her neck – a curious design of three interlinked triangles . . .

* * *

'We had better remove his clothes. I wish to see from where that blood is coming.'

17

'And if it's not his you'll call the cops?'

'If he is hurt I must treat him, Mr Brockman.'

'Peter. Call me Peter.'

'You may call me Doctor Kristiansson. Lift him here, please.'

Brockman gave her a twisted smile. 'Something I said?'

'I don't think you like me, Mr Brockman. I don't think I like you either. Just cut away these rags now, *ja* – oh, *Herre Gud*!'

The man's chest was a mass of raking criss-cross wounds, like the clawmarks of a giant's hand. As Anja Kristiansson sponged away the dirt Brockman realised that the wounds were old, already half-healed. Parchment-coloured bruises covered a body stretched taut over gnarled, heavy bones.

'Looks like he lost an argument with a grizzly. Why the frown, An – sorry, *Doctor* Kristiansson?'

'Someone has treated him. Look here, these stitches.'

'Mm. Nice bit of embroidery. Recognise the style? I mean, is it cross stitch or hem stitch for a six-inch gash?' She threw him a withering glance. 'OK, OK, just making conversation. You don't seem too talkative yourself.'

For a moment he felt a brief pang of guilt. Everything he said to her seemed to have barbs in it. For some reason he felt furiously angry with her; yet nothing she had done could really justify it. Nothing could justify his curiosity, either, but the feeling he had had in the church, as he copied the frescoes, was still with him – that he *belonged* here, that the farm and its occupants were somehow a part of his life.

'He should rest now,' said Anja.

'What is that stuff? Morphine?'

'Just a sedative. The blood is old. He is just very weak and a little cold.'

'A little cold? He must've been out there all night ...'

'I don't think so, Mr Brockman.'

'OK, so he was taking a nap on his way to breakfast. What about those "old wounds"? Any ideas?'

'None at all. A dog, perhaps.'

'More like a wolf. I still think you know more than you're telling.'

'I cannot help what you think.'

'Fine. Then why did he use all the strength he had to get himself in here?'

'That you can ask him when he wakes – and after he has rested. I think you should go now.'

'Shall I tell the cops about him on my way home?'

'Cops?'

'OK, you don't understand "cops". *Skal jeg fortælle hele historien til politiet?*'

'You – you speak Danish?'

Got you. I hear the sound of cool breaking. Or ice, maybe.

'Mother tongue. Mother's tongue, anyway. But you speak English a whole lot better – when you're not playing dumb, that is. You haven't answered my question.'

'It deserves no answer. You are curious, Mr Brockman. You wish to stay, so you threaten me. I find that ill-mannered.'

'I find that I don't trust liars, as a general rule. Let's just say I'd like our friend to be as safe as he thinks he is.'

'So you are staying. Coffee?'

'I could use a straight answer.'

'I have only the coffee.'

'Anja?'

The voice startled them both. The face it belonged to startled Brockman. Square, slightly jowly, grey-haired, bright-eyed – he had seen it in sepia in his own family album.

'Mormor, må jeg præsentere Hr Peter Brockman.' Her words were formal, mocking. 'Mr Brockman, my mother's mother, Mrs Hansen.'

'Fru Hansen?' The courtesy was automatic. He was watching the old lady's eyes as they fell on the man in the bed. Her face did not seem to change – it was as though she were looking at a stranger. But something in her eyes, some faint gleam of recognition, suggested his suspicions might be right.

'You speak English, Fru Hansen?'

'A little. You are a friend of Anja's?'

'Not quite. She's a very – unusual – woman. Good looking, too.'

Anja snorted and Fru Hansen forced a smile. 'When I was a girl people said that our family took their looks from the *alvar*.'

'I'm sorry?'

Anja was embarrassed. 'You would call them elves, I think.'

'Elves?' *Is this supposed to distract me from that poor bastard on the bed?*

'Oh, there are many old stories about the farm. They say the mound in the churchyard is an – an elf-hill. On – how do you call it – *Juleaften*?'

'Christmas Eve.'

'On Christmas Eve you can see the elves inside eating their dinner. It is a silly story.'

'I've heard worse.' He glanced significantly at Anja, and then at the old man. Now the dirt had been washed away he looked younger – and there was something peculiar about him. Outside, he had been lying on his back near the stone, with his arm outstretched towards it, and ... 'Just a minute. His hand. Did you see his hand?'

'What do you mean?' said Anja.

'When I first saw him his right hand was clenched.' He pulled back the covers. 'It still is. It's like he's holding something he doesn't dare to let go.'

'Please don't touch him.'

'I need some answers.'

'You will hurt him.'

'I'll be as gentle as a lamb. God, it's like his fingers are locked around it ...'

'You will break them!'

'No chance. There. Mean anything to you?'

20

It did. He could see it did. But neither of the women said a word.

In the palm of the unconscious man's hand, its points piercing his flesh, lay a silver pendant in the shape of three interwoven triangles.

CHAPTER
2

If thou beest born to strange sights,
    Things invisible to see
Ride ten thousand days and nights
    Till Age snow white hairs on thee;
Thou, when thou return'st, wilt tell me
All strange wonders that befell thee,
    And swear
    No where
Lives a woman true and fair ...

John Donne

A motionless silver mask, eyes closed, beard sculpted in fine wire, lips black and slightly parted, lay bathed in the moonlight that streamed through the uncurtained window. Only the slight rise and fall of the old man's chest betrayed that this was a living face. Brockman watched patiently, fingering the pendant. There was nothing else he could do.

Who are you, old man? And what are you to her?

Her. It always came back to Anja Kristiansson. A liar, but a bad liar, more used to telling the truth. Independent, self-possessed, yet curiously vulnerable. Beautiful, but in her own extraordinary way. Watching her as she tended the old man he had seen undercurrents of emotion break through the professional mask of the doctor – a tear concealed beneath lowered lids, a grimace like a moment of shared pain, a touch just a little too much like a caress. Was she daughter? Niece? Or something else, something less obvious? The more he saw, the more he wanted to stay – and the less excuse he had for staying. Anja had seemed strangely unconcerned about Brockman's threat, and he had felt strangely unwilling to implement it; yet somehow his feeble blackmail had made him an unwelcome passenger on an uncertain voyage of discovery. The delicate balance of deception had survived a largely silent supper; but now the sun was down, and he was caught in the spell of the old farmhouse.

Inside, the bustle of Egerød was reduced to a distant murmur, a wind in the ghost of some primeval forest. A long-case Bornholm clock meted out time in slow, heavy pendulum strokes, its waterfall chimes echoing the hours and quarters across the cobbled yard outside. The windows opened on a lost world: a kitchen garden crammed with herbs and vegetables; a little orchard; a screen of conifers; a gravel drive up to tall wooden gates; and the churchyard, with its neat rows of monuments aping the stern simplicity of the ancient burial at its heart.

The atmosphere of the house struck distant chords in his mind, like some half-remembered moment of childhood. As an archaeologist in the jungles of South America his imagination had reached across hundreds, even thousands of years to lost civilisations remote from his own. Here the feeling was different: it was a more intimate past, as close and personal as the paintings in the church. Nothing lacked the human touch – timbers, skilfully shaped by the tools of craftsmen; whitewashed walls, the plaster rippled with age; carved and turned furniture, perfumed with generations of careful waxing; embroidered cushions and cloths, their motifs handed down from mother to daughter in unbroken succession. Even the simple things – kettles, jugs, saucepans – belonged to a time gone, but hardly forgotten. Everything spoke to him, and he was a part of everything, the last in an unbroken line of makers and farmers that stretched back beyond the dawn of history to a moment when the first stone axe cut into the timber of a primeval forest. And he knew the pendant belonged to that succession. He could feel it . . .

He smiled faintly. There was nothing rational about his feelings; they were like the last dim memory of a dream, the same dream that had made him an archaeologist. It was self-indulgent and a little crazy to remember the dream and forget the science it had become. But in the last light of a clear evening, in an old house lit by oil lamps and candles, it was, perhaps, forgivable – and there was truth in the dream. The church outside was nine centuries old, but the mound was far older. The farm might be older still. His ancestors could have settled this land hundreds of years before Christ. No wonder it felt like home – or that he could reach back across the centuries and sense the presence of a fellow spirit.

'Mr Brockman?'

A silverpoint Leonardo angel smiled at him from the doorway, veiling her face in the shining silk of her own hair. For a moment he thought she was naked: her robe covered her from neck to ankle, but moonlight cut through the veil. The half-concealed silhouette was a dancer's shadow, slim, narrow-hipped and small-breasted.

'Don't you go to bed, Mr Brockman? It's a cold night.'

The smile fell from grace. It was provocative, knowing, and mocking, its magic borrowed from the moon. He looked away, trying to pretend that his surge of desire was meaningless. 'No. No thanks.'

'I have set a bed for you in the kitchen. Near the stove. In case you are cold. We do not have – central warming.'

'I can manage without.'

'How is he?' she asked.

'Huh?'

'The man who so concerns you.'

One up to you, Ms Kristiansson. 'He's OK. Nothing new.'

'Let me see.' She came purposefully forward and knelt by the old man's bed, feeling for his pulse. In the shadow

24

her nightgown was as modest as a nun's. Perhaps he had only imagined that fall from grace; or wanted to imagine it.

'He will sleep for many hours,' she said. 'You should sleep, too – if you can.'

He ignored the barb, turning the triangle pendant over and over in his hands. 'Something weird about this.'

Her head jerked up, as though he had touched a raw nerve. 'Weird?'

'Yeah. No hallmark – and I'd lay odds it's solid silver. Take a craftsman to make something like this. Should be hallmarked.'

'Perhaps it is very old.' She sounded defensive.

'*That* old, it should be in a museum. You think our friend knocked over a museum?'

'Knocked over?'

'Robbed. You reckon he's a thief?'

There was a kind of panic in her eyes. 'No. No, I don't think so.'

'How would you know?'

'I – I don't. I am tired. I am going to bed.'

Nothing provocative now. She was frightened.

'OK. Pleasant dreams.'

I'm close. Close enough to rattle her. And this damn pendant is the key . . .

* * *

'Always you look at this. Why?'

Reluctantly, Erik let go of the pendant. Eleanor never took it off – even in bed, when she wore nothing else. 'Because it came from the same place as you. Because it's part of your mystery.'

'You find it strange?' She snuggled closer into his arms, her fingers stroking his beard, the warmth of her breath on his cheek. His life as a lonely bachelor don in draughty halls and smoky common rooms was already a dream. They had always shared his shabby flat and his rickety bed; her brightly-coloured dresses and scarves had always hung with his tweeds and his battered duffel

25

coat in the corner cupboard; the side table had always been littered with tubes and bottles and crumpled tissues. He could hardly remember living alone, and yet . . .

'Isn't it strange for you,' he said, 'remembering nothing?'

Her eyelashes fluttered against his shoulder.

'What matters, I remember. That you found me; saved me.' Her hand moved down onto his chest – her fingers, with a maddening lightness, circled his nipples.

'Nothing else? Parents? Family? Someone you loved? I don't even know your name –'

'Eleanor!'

'No, I mean your *real* name.'

She smiled, mockingly. 'Names! I am not one of your words. I am the shadow behind these eyes that sees the shadow behind yours.' Her lips brushed his skin, making each word a caress.

He stroked her hair, feeling the softness of it between his fingers. 'Sometimes you frighten me. The things you say –'

She laughed. 'You? Frightened of words? Are you not their master, with all your books?'

'Eleanor, every word has a – a life-story. You under-stand? It was born somewhere: a forest, maybe, or a plain, or some frozen night in the ice age. Then it grew, changed, learned new meanings. We try to tie it down with dictionaries, but words are like people: tie them down and they die. They need to change, marry up with other words, make new words. Like – like a family. When I hear you talk – it's as though you're *thinking* with words from another family, and *saying* words from mine instead.'

She smiled, archly. 'I am not one of your students.' Her straying fingers had found a nerve centre; each touch was a sharp stab of pleasure. He held her hand, struggling for a moment against the inevitable.

'Don't you see? When you talk, I can hear the words that answer to yours in a hundred other languages, but there's no pattern, no match. Where did you come from?'

She laughed, hugging him tightly. 'Out of the fire – I was born in your arms.' She moved against him slowly and sinuously, her lips busy with butterfly caresses.

'It's like hearing half a story. I want to understand you.'

'What is so hard? I am like you; I am the desire you cannot fulfil, the longing you cannot reach. Through me you fulfil, you reach, you find.'

He hesitated. 'You know I love you?'

Her lips curved upwards into something like a smile, but her eyes were fixed on his, clear, merciless. 'You should learn what is said without words.'

She rolled across him, clamping his hips between slim, muscular calves, kneeling upright and astride him, pushing the covers behind her with her arms, a predator with claws outstretched to tear him. Her lightest touch was an agony, inflaming almost beyond endurance. When she leaned forward on her elbows, burying his face in her hair, he was drowning in perfume. When she kissed him, the sharp little tongue invaded his mouth till he could barely breathe. He felt his arms gripped and held by hers. The pendant touched his chest, an icy finger between the warm, rolling caresses of her breasts. Body and soul, he was her prisoner. As she busied her tongue about his face, he could feel her hardened nipples brushing against him with a maddening, insistent rhythm. Tenderly he traced the outline of her shoulder-blades with his fingers, then moved his hands slowly down her spine to cup her buttocks and search out the warm crevice between them. She smiled, baring small, sharp teeth, and bit his neck. Her tongue caressed his throat and left a damp line along his breastbone and on, down . . .

Who taught her that? And how could she forget him? My God, she's got me doing things I never dreamed of . . .

The first time he had been shocked, even repelled, a fastidious bachelor suddenly confronted with the animal reality of sex. In a single night she had swept him into a new world of sensuality – and now that same uncontrollable passion was rising inside him, wild music summoned by the breath and the touch of a master player, driving out thought and reason in the sheer joy of fulfilment. For a moment, even now, the musky scent of her arousal repelled him, but in that moment he was lost. With a slow sureness that left him gasping she impaled herself on him, bending back impossibly far until her hair swept his calves in a cascade of moonlit silver. It went on almost longer than he could endure it, hovering on the tingling border between pleasure and pain, held this side of agony only by her low, sensuous laughter. The pendant drew his eyes, glittering hypnotically in the moonlight, trapped between her breasts, quivering with the bowstring tension of her body. Her sharp cry of triumph came a moment before his own – but as she laid her head beside his on the pillow and huddled her small body into his arms, her face was as strange and empty as it had always been.

Like a lost child – no. Like an animal at bay. As though I frightened her. The joke is that I'm the one who's frightened.

'Erik?'

'Mm?'

'I want to see the stars.'

He smiled. She had asked the same thing the very first time they had made love, and he would never forget that first night of his new life – a life where the darkness was no longer a place of fear, where the end of the day brought warmth, love, and a beautiful woman in his arms. Now, still trembling from the violence of their loveplay, he sat up, drew her towards him, and carried her to the window. Outside, a steely mist transformed the river into cloud castles and the trees into skeletal sentinels. Above it the sky was clear and hard, an iron casket studded with diamonds.

'Look at the moon,' he said, aching with the beauty of its light on her pale skin.

She screwed up her eyes. 'It's so bright.' In his arms

she felt frail, feather-light. It seemed impossible for this delicate shell to contain the violent passion they had just shared.

'Cold?'

'A little.' She tightened her arms around him, drawing warmth from his body. She did not see his smile; she was staring out towards the fading stars, her ice-blue eyes fixed on infinity. Just four weeks ago, in the hospital, he had seen them open for the first time. For the longest moment of his life he had thought that intelligence and perception would never brighten them again. He had shuddered and drawn back from the vacancy, not daring to hope, yet already half in love with what he saw. In a dream at the edge of nightmare the pale, white hand had reached out to him, and the vacuous mask had melted into that mixture of fear and hope, fragility and power that was Eleanor.

'Erik ...'

'Mm?'

'It's done.' She turned her head. For a moment – only a moment – a trick of the moonlight changed her lazy smile to something strangely triumphant.

'Done?' What d'you mean?'

'I feel him. The child. Our child.'

* * *

The boy was an imp with a shock of red-gold hair, chasing a dog across the cobblestones of the farmyard outside. Brockman found himself smiling. The whole wall was filled with family pictures, the older ones in heavy, gilt frames. In the wavering light of the oil lamp they seemed curiously alive, with the strange vitality of those early photographs that somehow captured the soul as well as the features of the sitter. But there were no pictures of the old man, or of anyone who might have been his younger self.

Brockman shivered. Anja had fuelled up the stove in the injured man's room before she went to bed, but the stove here in the parlour had been allowed to burn low.

29

Unthinkingly he huddled close to the pool of light from the oil lamp: it left more than half the long, low-ceilinged room in semi-darkness. The clutter of heavy Victorian furniture and panelled cupboards had become a patchwork of shadows, half-hinting at another world and another time. Sitting at the massive oak table, on a long bench topped with embroidered cushions, he was keenly aware of the windows – and the darkness – at his back. His bed in the kitchen had been comfortable but draughty – Anja, with ingenuous malice, had placed it just below the window he had smashed. In any case, sleep had refused to come. Images and questions had turned over ceaselessly in his mind, driving him to seek some distraction from the well-stocked bookcase.

He had found a medley of Norwegian, Swedish and Danish publications. Some of the paperbacks still had uncut pages. Others had been cut by someone who cared more about their contents than their appearance. There were dozens of novels, many in English; an encyclopaedia, long out of date; some picture magazines from the thirties, extravagantly bound in leather and gilt; and a curious assortment of reference books. He'd picked one at random, a Danish book called *Legends of the North*, hoping that a struggle with the half-familiar language would crowd out other, more disturbing thoughts. The book was well-thumbed, and several slips of paper had been left to mark particular passages. It fell open towards the end, at a section describing the mythical history of Denmark's first kings. One section was marked in pencil.

... and after that King Helgi slept always in the outhouse. One night, soon after the Yule feast, he had returned there as was his custom and gone to his bed. But that night sleep was slow in coming; it seemed to the king that some woodland creature was scratching at the lintel, and as the wind rose he could hear it moaning piteously outside the door. At last he could bear it no longer: he rose from his bed and threw open

the door. There, crouching in the snow, was a withered, grey-haired hag, dressed in filthy rags. She
darted inside and knelt at the hearth, scrabbling in the
ashes to find what warmth she could.

Seeing her plight, the king was moved to pity. 'You
shall sleep here,' he said. 'I shall bring fresh straw
from the stable, and you shall be covered with skins
from my own bed.' He had expected grovelling grati-
tude, but the eyes that met his were bright and sharp,
burning with a strange inner light.

'My lord,' said the woman, 'it is not enough. The
chill has struck too deep. I will die this very night –
unless I lie beside the king.'

Helgi hesitated. Age and disease had left little of the
woman in the creature who knelt at his feet, and her
clothes carried the stink of ordure. But the burning
eyes compelled him in ways he could not understand.

'Come, then,' he said, 'and lie by my side if you
must.' Eagerly she accepted, her long, wrinkled fingers
clawing at the skins to draw them aside, and the king
turned away, unwilling to look on such ugliness. As
the creature from the woods pressed against his back
he felt a burning pain, as though a knife of ice had
been drawn down his spine – and then a slow,
comforting warmth.

'You are a true king,' said a voice in the darkness –
a thrilling voice. 'This night you have saved me, and
placed me eternally in your debt. But now I must leave
you –'

Helgi reached out to grasp his bedfellow, but
instead of rags and wrinkled flesh, he felt the caress of
silk over firm, young flesh. As he turned, he saw the
eyes of the hag reflecting the fire – but they were
framed in a face of such beauty that he could not turn
away.

'You cannot leave,' he said. 'The night is chill as
death – and your debt is easily paid.'

She nodded, her eyes never leaving his. 'As you

wish, my lord.' Easily, mockingly, she drew his hands towards her body – and Helgi remembered nothing more until the chill half-light of the false dawn showed at the lintel of the door. Then, in his waking dream, he heard a laugh that was not of human making.

'It is done, my lord. I feel it. I feel your child.'

He turned restlessly, but the woman was no longer by his side. Dimly he heard her voice, bidding him return to this place in a year's time – for then he must fetch the child of his desire, as he valued his very soul . . .

A raucous, mewling cry cut through the dark silence at his back, and Brockman jumped despite himself. A cat, hunting by moonlight – but in this strange house it was easy to imagine a world of magical visitations, where elven creatures scratched at the door, waiting for the fatal invitation to cross the threshold. What was it the old woman had told him? 'When I was a girl people said that our family took their looks from the *alvar*.' He smiled at the stolid farmers in their frames of tarnished gilt. It was hard to imagine them having much truck with elves and fairies – but he was thinking like a Californian. If he had grown up close to the earth, when Copenhagen was a day's journey away and all the land around was open fields; if he had learned the old stories at his mother's knee; if he had practised, unthinkingly, the little rituals and superstitions of his parents and his grandparents; then, perhaps, there would be nothing strange about an elf-hill outside his window, a gateway to another world . . .

There was one face in the little picture gallery that he seemed to recognise, a lovely young girl on the brink of maturity, with a river of golden hair like a fairy-tale princess.

Anja.

He picked up the lamp and walked across to the bookcase. The photograph had faded over the years, and its colours had lost their edge. He was reminded of an old hand-tinted postcard: the schoolgirl face had a disturbing depth beneath its mask of innocence ...

Photographs. He cursed himself for a fool. All day he had been letting his imagination get the better of his reason, missing the obvious as he searched for the obscure. If Anja had been lying about the old man, then the answer would be here, right under his nose. Every Danish household had its photo album, and the bookcase was the only logical place to keep it. It took him less than five minutes to find a massive untitled volume bound in leather and gilt. He carried it back to the table and eased it open.

The album was old – far older than he had expected. Each picture had been meticulously labelled in a fine, delicate hand. The flourishes and curls were attractive but functional – he seemed to see the handiwork of a disciplined mind. Only the fading ink and sepia-toned photographs suggested that the writer might well be lying in the churchyard outside.

At first the pictures were like the oldest of the photos on the wall – formal studies of square-jawed, square-faced farmers taken in the local photographer's studio. There were one or two faces like Anja's, as though an older thread of the family's ancestry was reasserting itself; her triangular face and broad cheekbones looked no less exotic beneath the formal hairstyles of the nineteenth century. Other pictures showed the house itself, long exposures with the blurred smears left as farm-workers went about their business. One, dated 1892, showed a matronly woman filling a bucket from a hand pump while three children in smocks encouraged a huge horse to drive a mechanical turntable at the centre of the yard.

He swore under his breath, cursing his own lack of concentration. *I'm letting this damn house get to me. Time was I could go a couple of nights without sleeping and still think straight. Must be getting old.*

He moved on rapidly, turning over a dozen pages at a

time with quick, angry motions. In his irritation he skipped through sixty years before he realised that the writing was now the methodical copybook hand of a serious-minded child. The turntable had gone, but children still played in the cobbled court and the building itself had hardly changed. One family group – a man, his wife, and a small boy – seemed to return every summer. Then, quite suddenly, the woman was gone. The boy was shown pushing a little girl in her pram, climbing trees with her in the orchard, building sandcastles with her on the beach. Skimming the next few pages he saw the girl changing, maturing, the face quite unmistakable as she grew from precocious child to elfin teenager. And every summer the boy was there, his eyes shadowed with a premature sadness. Their love for each other showed in every picture – a closeness, a trust, that could only exist between people who had known each other all their lives. Brockman felt a pang of jealousy.

Hey, who's this?

The handwritten caption – *Anja med Erik og Elennor* – was unhelpful. The spelling of the other girl's name puzzled him, but her arrival had changed everything. Anja was shut out. The physical closeness of Erik and 'Elennor' was blindingly obvious, but in every picture her face was slightly blurred, as though the camera made her nervous. The next page carried a small clipping from an English newspaper pasted in next to an invitation and a couple of amateur snapshots.

> *Erik Larssen and Eleanor Rigg*
> *warmly invite you to share the*
> *celebration of their marriage*
> *on Saturday, 28 July 1978.*
>
> *Lunch will be at 12.30*
> *for 1.00pm at the Eastgate Hotel,*
> *Oxford ...*

Not a church marriage; maybe religion didn't run in the

family. 'Eleanor Rigg' as a name was barely believable. As for the new husband . . .

Fat kid becomes college nerd. The beard is a plus. Something different about the face – seen it before somewhere . . .

'Holy Christ!'

Brockman scrambled to his feet with the album in his hands, tripped over the leg of the refectory table, and stumbled against a chair. The scrape of its legs along the wooden floor was like a pistol-shot in the cramped room, but he barely noticed it as he half-ran through the dining-room, past his bed in the kitchen, and into the old man's bedroom. The moon had risen higher, and the enclosed bed was shrouded in shadow. Brockman lit a candle, put it on top of the chest of drawers, and knelt down by the bed. In that flickering, other-worldly light it was hard to be certain, but the old man looked very much like Erik Larssen.

So I was right. She knows him, and she's covering up. There is something going on . . .

'Good morning, Mr Brockman. I am so glad you sleep well.'

'Well . . . The good Doctor Kristiansson. You're a damn liar, Doctor.'

She was furious – so angry that for a moment she choked on her words. '*And what are you?* Who allowed that you take our food, and stay here in our house, and search in our things? You – you –'

Her voice failed her. Angry tears threw back tiny candle flames at the corners of her eyes. For a moment he was ashamed of his brutality – but then the strange, sourceless anger he had felt before resurfaced.

'The tears don't help, Doc. Why don't you tell me what's going on?'

She brushed the back of her hand across her eyes with a gesture of fury and frustration. 'You don't see? You have the photo and you don't see?'

He shrugged, and laid the album on the pillow next to Larssen's face. The old man's breathing was noisy, but

35

steadier than it had been for a while. He did look very like the photograph, but time had cut deep into his forehead, trapping his eyes in a web of wrinkles.

If that's what marriage has done to him, he won't collect on his pension.

'You see it now, Mr Brockman?'

'Sure. No wonder the poor bastard ran away.'

'You fool! Look at him! Erik was twenty-six years old when he married that – that girl! *Look at him!*'

For a moment he saw only what he had seen before – the proof he needed that Anja had been lying to him. Then he swore fluently, took down the candle, and held it closer to Larssen's face. The sleeping man, lost in some private nightmare, moaned and turned away from the light. His hair and beard were a grizzled grey. His skin was dry and wrinkled.

'You trying to tell me he's thirty-six? Jesus Christ, what happened to him?'

She laughed – a hideous laugh, distorted with the anger and grief she had suppressed until this moment. 'You go to your police, Mr Brockman – go now! Tell them my cousin is dying because they don't find his wife and his son –'

'His *son* –?'

'– and if you are so clever, Mr Brockman, *you* find them!'

'Hey, slow down –'

'Get out! Do as you wish, but get out!'

'Listen, Anja, I just want –'

'To spy on us and threaten us! Oh yes, you want –'

'*To help you!* But I don't like being lied to! Can you understand that?'

He put the candle back on the chest of drawers, throwing its wavering light onto her face. Without make-up she looked younger, more vulnerable; her cheeks were streaked with angry tears. Despite himself, he could feel his annoyance and suspicion slipping away.

It's what Sarah used to do. Hold herself in, never let me

36

know how much I'd hurt her . . .

'Look, I'm sorry I gave you a hard time, but you could've told me this right away.'

'And of course you would believe all I told you.'

'Yes. No – I guess not. But what are you hiding? OK, he's lost his wife and kid, hit the bottle, bummed around for a while –'

'That is what you think?'

'How else . . .?'

'I don't know. But he has lost everything, Mr Brockman – everything he cared about. His job, his home, Eleanor, the boy . . .'

. * * *

'He is calling for you.'

Erik looked up from a wretched student essay, glad of the interruption. 'Me? When he can have a sweet thing like you?' He had hoped for a smile, but Eleanor's face barely moved. 'Sorry you married me?' Again no smile. She looked at him curiously, like a scientist examining a specimen.

'Don't be so afraid,' she said. 'All is – what it should be.'

It was not the answer he wanted, but nothing she said was ever predictable.

'Come here.'

Obediently, she sat in his lap. He tried to remember where he had seen an expression like hers before, and couldn't.

'Closer, love. Even if Bjørn doesn't want you, I do.'

Still obedient, she put her arms round his neck, laid her head on his shoulder. Suddenly he found the image he had been searching for – the empty face of a mentally handicapped child, clutching at some absurd soft toy. 'Eleanor . . .' What was it she had said? *You should learn what is said without words.* He held her close, tilted her face towards him, and kissed her, parting her lips with his tongue. She sighed and held him tighter, responding with a warmth that swept away his fears. Now she smiled,

37

now that they were touching, now her body could speak for her, now she knew he wanted her. He felt a fool for ever doubting her.

'Wait!' she laughed, brushing away an exploring hand. 'Bjørn would like that you tuck him in.'

'Have you told him a story?'

'Yes, but he wants the dragon story.'

'We did that last night.'

'He likes it. Tell him again the dragon story. Then you can tuck *me* in.'

He grinned, drunk with relief, and reached for her again. She slipped out of his arms with a low, mocking laugh. 'Later, evil man. Go see your son.'

Erik shrugged, knocked out his pipe, and bounded out of the armchair. He took the stairs up to Bjørn's room two at a time, bursting through the door just in time to see a flurry of bedclothes.

'Right, young man. You don't stay in bed, you don't get a story.'

A tousled mass of red-gold hair peered out from under the blanket. The face behind it looked at him accusingly.

'You promised!'

'Wrong. Mummy promised, if you were good. And you're not good, are you, Biarki?'

'What's "Biarki"?'

'You are, you little monster. Bjørn means "bear". Biarki means "little bear". Got your sword, little bear?'

'Yes.' He held up the toy sword they had given him on his fifth birthday.

'And your shield?'

He nodded, eyes wide.

'Remember, the dragon breathes out fire and poison. Don't let it catch you in the open.'

'Will you help me?'

'Me? I'm just the shield-bearer. You'll have to do the fighting. We're getting close now. Can you smell it? Can you hear it?'

'I can hear it breathing. It's asleep, isn't it?'

'Yes. Inside the mound. No – it's waking up. It's heard us. Its claws are scraping on the stones inside the passage. It's coming, Biarki!'

'Can you see it?'

'I can see its shadow. It's taller than the cherry-tree! The light's glinting from it – it's all covered with golden scales.'

'Is there a weak place?'

'I think so ... Yes, under the leg – but you'll have to get it just right. It's seen us! It's coming!'

He pulled the covers up over Bjørn's head, and the boy squealed with delight, stabbing at the air with his plastic sword.

'Did I get him, daddy?'

'Not quite. He's coming again. Careful! There! That's it!'

'I'm wounded, I'm wounded! He breathed on my arm!'

'Then you'd better lie down while I tend to it. Here, give me the sword. You won't be able to hold it if your arm's hurt.'

'Will I get better?'

'Yes, but only if you go to sleep straight away.'

'Am I the best hero?'

'The best hero was a Biarki – Battle-Biarki they called him.'

'Did he kill dragons?'

'Uh-huh – just like you.'

'Was he wounded, too?'

'I expect so.'

'Who was Battle-Biarki?'

'Oh, he lived a long time ago, when there were elves in the woods and dwarves in the caves and giants in the mountains.'

'Are there still elves and things?'

'Perhaps. They hide with the shadows now, so people don't see them any more.'

'Daddy ...'

'Mm?'

39

'Daddy, where do shadows go at night?'

Erik smiled. 'Where do you think they go?'

'Sometimes they hide. In my picture.'

'You mean the one *Bedstemor* gave you?' He always called Kristine 'Bedstemor' – grandmother – to encourage Bjørn to use his Danish. The wall hanging that the boy called 'his picture' had been her christening present for him, even when Eleanor had stood out against christening the boy at all. It was beautiful hand embroidery, Kristine's own work, illustrating a Danish nursery rhyme. 'Do the shadows go to the party?' said Erik.

'What party?' Bjørn looked puzzled.

'The eagle's party – in the forest. You remember the rhyme, don't you?'

'*I skoven skulde være gilde . . .*' the boy recited in a sing-song voice. 'Not like that, daddy. I see them sometimes at night, hiding there when you and mummy go to bed. I like to talk to them.'

'Talk to them? What do you say?'

'Well, they say how it's lonely and dark and they don't like it. And I say the stars will come soon and then they'll be all right.'

'Does that make them feel better?'

'I think so. It's sort of hard to tell with shadows.'

'And it's sort of hard to get you to sleep, young man. Shall I leave the light on?'

'No, daddy. I want it dark.'

Erik shook his head and turned out the lamp over Bjørn's headboard. He remembered his own childhood fear of darkness, the way he had clung to the security of a night light even when other children were reading and enjoying horror stories. Bjørn was so much more like Eleanor – Eleanor who loved twilight and starlight, and shrank from the sun.

He waited till the boy's breathing was soft and even, then bent over and kissed his cheek, wrapping the blanket close around him. A faint smell of toothpaste was mingled with the fresh, innocent scent of a young child.

Glancing up, Erik saw the wall hanging caught in the oblique light from the landing. It was transformed. The embroidered shapes of birds and trees and animals had gone – instead there was a world of shadows, moving gently in the breeze from the window. He shivered. Even now, shadows frightened him. Childhood nightmares of invisible creatures hidden in dark places still haunted him – he could measure the intensity of a fear against those unforgettable moments when he had woken screaming for his mother and realised she would never come again . . .

* * *

'Erik is my cousin. We were – we have always been very close. Since his mother died.'

Brockman caught her momentary hesitation. They *had* been close – before Eleanor arrived.

'And what about the boy – Bjørn, you called him? Strange kind of name, isn't it?'

'To you, perhaps. Not in Denmark. Eleanor, she chose it from a story . . . In Danish it's *Ringenes Herre*. A man called Tolkien –'

'And a book called *The Hobbit*. Same author. You're right, though. There was a character called Beorn.'

'Erik used to read it to her, that book. She liked to hear him read, especially at night. Sometimes, when they were here, they went out for long walks at night.'

'Moonlight walks? Sounds romantic.'

'No, it was not that. She said that sunlight hurt her.'

'What, she was an albino or something?'

'No. I – inspected her, and there was nothing in the way with her.'

'Nothing wrong, you mean. Your English is slipping.'

'I am tired,' she said, sounding it. 'The next visit, it was the Christmas time. That was better, that time: they were married then, and she was . . . *gravid*.'

'Pregnant. I hate to say it, but a doctor's supposed to know words like that.'

'I said I am tired,' she snapped. 'Bjørn was born in this room. He was – early.'

Brockman nodded vaguely, trying to remember the date on the wedding invitation. July? Summer, certainly. A baby at Christmas wasn't just early, it was downright embarrassing. Maybe another reason why Anja should resent the girl, for tricking her favourite cousin into marriage. 'And after that? They visited again?'

'Always in the summer. Eleanor was not happy, but she came because Erik wanted it. He is a professor. It was the only time he could have a vacation.'

'Every year?'

'*Ja*. It was so Bjørn could see his family.'

'How about *her* family?'

'She had no family.' Anja looked uncomfortable. So the big secret was something about Eleanor. Maybe she thought it would sound like jealousy. He was faintly amused. Anja reminded him of a small-town girl trying to make a good impression, when a touch of jealousy would have made her a human being – and a much more interesting one, at that.

'So they were all here, and the woman and the boy vanished?'

'No. This time Erik did not come. It was the spring, he was working. Just Eleanor and Bjørn.'

'OK, how did it happen? You woke up and they were gone, right?'

Anja nodded.

'Just like that?'

Her brows knitted. 'I do not have to make you believe it.'

'How can I? You're not *telling* me anything.'

'There is nothing to tell.' He had annoyed her, and meant to, but there was more than annoyance in her voice. 'She took Bjørn to the zoo. She came back for the evening meal. We went to bed. The next morning she and Bjørn, both were gone.'

'No note? No sign of a struggle?'

'No. Most of their things were still here – they had taken just the outdoor clothes.'

'And the night before? Anything happen then?'

'No.' She hesitated. 'No, nothing . . .'

'Will you stop holding out on me? What was it? *What happened?*'

She glared at him. 'I said nothing! I did nothing!'

'But?'

She shook her head miserably, but her eyes were on the young-old man in the bed.

'I get it. Whatever it was, you couldn't tell *him*. But I'm not him. What was it? What was so bad, huh?'

Anja made no reply. For a long moment she seemed to see nothing but her cousin's face. When she looked up, her hesitation had gone. 'Next door, in my room. I have it there.'

Best offer I've had all night. 'OK. Lead on.'

The room surprised him. He had expected something more feminine. It was neat and functional, and there were none of the frills and fripperies that often made him detest women's bedrooms. The nearest she came to cute was a family of cuddly dinosaurs in coloured felt, but they did not seem out of keeping with the simple painted wood of the old house, or the traditional pattern of the comforter on the bed. Anja took a robe from the back of the door and slipped it on. She was shivering. Now he had seen her cry she seemed much more vulnerable, and he could almost believe the seductively fallen angel in Larssen's bedroom had been nothing more than a trick of the light. Anja searched for a few moments in a drawer and came out with a yellowing scrap of paper. She passed it to him without a word, turning up the lamp on the bedside table so he could read it.

For a moment he was nonplussed. It was a clipping from the local newspaper about a woman who had run away from a mental hospital. Some of the words defeated his limited Danish, but the description was as vague and useless as most descriptions, and the out-of-date photograph was little better.

'I don't get it.'

'The date, Mr Brockman. Look at the date.'

'The ninth of September 1977. So?'

'Again you don't see, Mr Brockman.'

'So *show* me.'

'Look at the album.'

He sighed noisily and did as she asked. Many of the pictures were dated, but there was nothing between August '77 and the wedding invitation, except those few shots of the camera-shy Eleanor ...

'Oh, for God's sake. You *can't* believe that ...'

'Now you see?'

'Sure, I see that the picture in this clipping looks like Eleanor. So you're saying that she does the Great Escape, follows your cousin to England, convinces him she's sane, and then marries him? Come *on*! OK, you didn't like her, she wasn't good enough for him –'

'You think that is why –?'

'Damn right. That's why you haven't married?'

The slap was harder than he'd expected, but he managed a laugh all the same. 'You know, for a doctor you pack a mean punch.' He laughed again at her evident embarrassment. 'OK – tell me how wrong I am.'

There was no answering smile, and no more tears. Instead he saw a calm determination so shockingly familiar that for a moment he was back in Israel, in the light of a sickle moon ...

'You *are* wrong, Mr Brockman, I cannot expect you to believe me, but there is so much you don't know –'

'Try me. *Tell* me what I don't know.'

Briefly, she told the strange story of Larssen and Eleanor. How he rescued her from the burning car. How he spent hours watching by her bedside, only to learn that she had lost all memory of the time before her accident. How he created a new life to replace the one she had lost. How they married – and how the boy had been born, here, in the family farmhouse. And how she had found the clipping, the morning after Eleanor and Bjørn had vanished ...

'You're saying someone *left* it here?'

'I don't know – but we don't use that newspaper. I had never seen this piece before.'

'And you found it in the kitchen?'

'Yes. Eleanor, she cooked the meal that night – they were late home. It was in the waste-bucket next morning. I was making the coffee, I was curious. And when I went to her room she and the boy, they were already gone.'

'So let me get this straight. Someone left this where Eleanor could see it. She read it, she realised that someone knew the whole sordid story, and she ran for it.'

'I know what you think. To me, too, it seemed crazy. But the date, that is right – the same month Erik found her. The picture is right. And Eleanor, she was always so strange. Erik did not realise. He had no women friends, he never really knew how a woman should be.'

Brockman was barely listening. Anja's story was ridiculous. Besides, her guilt was out of all proportion to anything she had told him about, and there was a simpler, more obvious explanation. He took the clipping and held it up like a piece of evidence.

'You ever show him this?'

'Erik? Never. He loved her so much ...'

'Yeah, but you didn't. She was doing things you just dreamed about: making love with him, having his child. *You* got her out, didn't you? God knows how, but I reckon you could do it. No wonder you're so damned guilty.' He paused for her next outburst, but it never came. She just stared at him coldly, silently, daring him to finish. 'Then you found the clipping, when he was crazy enough to believe just about anything. It was beautiful. You could pick your time, show it to him, *prove* she was no good for him. Only it didn't work out, did it? After all those years he still doesn't know you're alive. All those years, knowing that you could never replace her, watching him rot because of what *you'd* done –'

'I did nothing, Mr Brockman.' Her voice was ice-brittle.

'And it has been just six months. *Six months . . .*'

He wanted to laugh. Shock and bereavement could age people, even in six months, but they couldn't turn a man in his mid-thirties into the silver-haired wreck in that bed. 'Oh Doc, this time you've *really* done it. Six months? OK, he's had a bad time, but –'

'You fool! You understand *nothing*!'

'Now listen –'

'No! You listen! This is not your world, Mr Brockman – it is ours. We know it, a little; you do not. Yesterday Erik was a man like you, young, strong, and oh, so very sure of himself. Today he is what you see – what you found.'

'You're saying that happened in *one night*?'

'That is the truth. You can believe it or not. I don't care what you believe.'

'And those wounds? Those "old wounds"? I guess he picked those up on a trip to the drugstore.'

'He did not have them yesterday.'

'Look, either you're crazy or you think I am.' He was no longer amused. Anja's story was an insult to his intelligence – and here was a girl from a dead-end suburb in a backwater country telling *him* he'd led a sheltered life! He grabbed at the lamp, ignoring her protests, and pushed past her through the door and back into Larssen's room.

'No! Leave him *alone*!'

Shadows fled from the lamplight, and so did the mystery and strangeness of the old bedroom. He cursed himself for a credulous idiot. By candlelight the illusion had been complete – and because the girl had wanted to believe it, he'd believed it himself. The man on the bed was no more and no less than he seemed to be: an old tramp, the veteran of a dozen drunken fights. The rest was all in Anja's hyperactive imagination – and he had given in without a struggle, surrendered reason and common sense to a beautiful woman, a trick of memory, and the imagined spell of an ancient farmhouse. 'Look. Erik's gone, you think something's happened to him, so the first old bum that looks like him has to be Erik –'

Her eyes blazed. 'I grew up with him! I *loved* him! You think I wouldn't know him? You think –?'

'Quiet!'

'I will not be quiet! I –'

To her amazement he clamped a hand tightly over her mouth. She struggled fiercely, kicking out at his shins, but her soft-soled mules cushioned the blow. He was less lucky with her elbows.

'Whoof! Hold still, damn it! *Listen!*'

Desperately he grabbed for her arms, drawing them tightly together behind her back as he strained once again to catch the faint noise he had just heard. For a long moment there was nothing – and then, distinctly, came the rustle of gravel shifting under a cautious tread.

'Wait here,' he breathed.

'But –'

'And keep quiet.'

Pushing the startled girl gently aside, Brockman turned down the lamp and moved silently towards the window. The flood of moonlight had gone, cut off by a stand of conifers, but the scene outside was a black and silver tapestry of swaying shadows. Brockman twitched aside the blind, keeping his head well down.

Yes. There. A shadow out of step with the rest – out of step with the wind. And something strange about it, a curiously ill-defined border, as if – no. That, at least, must be an illusion. But the pattern of movement was human, and that meant an intruder who had already climbed one wall. It would be a hell of a lot safer to call the police – except that Anja did not want them. Besides, it would probably scare off their visitor. That would leave another unanswered question; which was exactly one too many ...

Slowly, with infinite care, Brockman unlatched the window and eased it open. Even a careful watcher would barely have noticed its motion. It was hardly an ideal exit, but all the house doors faced inward, towards the courtyard, and the main doors out to the drive were too big to open quietly.

Joe Slow's on the move. Casing the joint. He's good, too – just unlucky with that gravel. Now . . .

Carefully, quietly, Brockman slipped out of the open window, checking the ground at each step, pushing his body close against the wall so the overhanging eaves concealed his shadow, struggling to remember the combat skills he had started to learn after Sarah's death. Their visitor seemed unpleasantly professional . . .

The wall turned round and hit him.

For a moment Brockman was half-stunned, unable to defend himself against a hail of punches and kicks that seemed to come from every direction at once. Half-remembering his training, he dropped into a crouch under his opponent's guard and rammed the man full in the chest. He saw a tall silhouette stumble backward, a blacker shadow against the darkness of the surrounding trees; and then he saw a flashing, metallic gleam.

Knife. Oh, shit . . .

Half-closing his eyes, he struck out with his left fist, aiming deliberately wide, and saw his enemy's head turn to follow the motion. At the same time he kicked out with his right leg. His trail boot connected with the man's wrist, there was a snapping sound, and a glittering, tumbling shape arced away towards the churchyard wall. But the move had left Brockman off-balance. He staggered backwards against the wall with bruising force, swearing obscenely – and froze.

Light glowed around his opponent's head like the mockery of a halo. It was the pallid, flickering blue of burning swamp-gas, yet somehow it seemed to darken the shadows around it, concealing rather than revealing the face it framed. And now, for the first time, Brockman saw the eyes – eyes that burned with the same icy fire.

It's a trick of the moonlight – it has to be . . .

With a yell of defiance he threw himself forward, but his opponent seemed to melt into the shadows. Brockman turned clumsily, trying to regain the initiative, as a chill, unyielding grip closed on his throat. Desperately he chopped at the unseen arm with the edge of his hand, feeling bone jar against bone and iron-hard nails rip along his neck. As he turned once more to face his enemy there was a flash like summer lightning and a paralysing pain at the side of his head. The stars turned a cartwheel, and his skull struck the ground with numbing force. Dizzy and disoriented, he saw a running shadow, backlit by the moon, jump for the churchyard wall and scramble over the top. He struggled upright, but his legs buckled and he sprawled headlong in the frosty grass.

For a few minutes he lay frozen between times in a world of silver and starlight where each twig, each leaf, each spider's web, was etched in white on a ground of dark velvet. The sparkling thatch of the house was as old as the first farmer, and as young as the new harvest. The church beyond was a deeper darkness framed in trees, as much a sacred grove as a Christian watchtower. This place had always been, would always be ...

A shadow passed between him and the moon – a human shadow. Something warm and soft dabbed at the back of his head, and a stinging pain brought him sharply back to reality.

'*Stille.*' Anja's voice. 'Lie still, Mr Brockman. A nasty knock, that is all.'

'Will I ever play the violin?'

'Is everything a joke with you, Mr Brockman?'

'My friends call me Peter.'

'I am only your doctor.' There was the faintest trace of amusement in her voice. 'Get up now. I will help you.'

He shrugged. A few hours ago he had fantasised about something like this. Now it meant nothing at all. He let her half-carry him around the corner of the house towards the double doors that opened into the main courtyard. No more climbing through windows – and no more fantasies. After all, he'd spent most of the night accusing her. Of lying, of cheating, of jealousy, of ruining her cousin's life – and all on the pretext of helping her. The truth was that he was curious. 'In fact,' he murmured, 'full of satiable curiosity.'

'*Hvad siger du?*'

'Kipling,' he grunted. Anja looked vaguely alarmed, and he laughed despite himself. 'I'm only half mad, Doc. Kids' story by Rudyard Kipling. *The Elephant's Child*. A tidy pachyderm, but too curious by half. Got itself spanked.'

'I think you are punch drunk, Mr Brockman.'

'I think you are right. I'm seeing bi-coloured python rock snakes.'

'*Hvad for noget?*'

He pointed a shaky finger at the double door. The paint spattered across it was still wet, glittering with reflected moonlight. But the symbol was familiar, even to Brockman's muddled mind. He had seen it himself, clenched in the old man's hand.

Three triangles. Three interlinked triangles.

CHAPTER
3

And see not ye that bonny road
That winds about the fernie brae?
That is the road to fair Elfland
Where thou and I this night maun gae.

Thomas the Rhymer

The voice was singing words that he knew, in the half-remembered language of his great-grandparents – and in his waking dream he was a child again, safe and warm in his bed, lulled to sleep by his mother's music.

Hr Oluf han rider så vide om Land ...

She had told him the story many times – the knight riding to his wedding, caught up in the magic of the deep woods, who stumbled on an elven dance ...

Der dansede fire, der dansede fem,
den Elvermø rækker Hånden frem!

Even now he could see it so clearly – the flickering, windblown light of an unearthly fire, throwing the spidery shadows of the dancers high among the circling pines until the trees themselves were a part of the dance. The half-seen figures of the elves, their dark limbs whirling in furious motion, their eyes glinting with reflected flame. The single outstretched hand, slim and

51

shapely, beckoning that lone traveller to join them, to become immortal like them – or to refuse and die. The face, broad, high-cheekboned, slant-eyed, framed in shimmering silver hair. The golden eyes, bright and shining. The lips, full and sensuous, calling, calling . . .

'Sarah!'

His own cry broke the dream – and his eyes opened on semi-darkness, a simple sparsely-furnished room, and a single patch of dim light that might be a window with the blind drawn down. The voice had stopped, but he could still hear the keening of a distant wind, and the crackling of the elven fire . . .

No. It was water, the sound of rain beating against glass.

The door opened a crack, half-blinding him with light. He covered his face instinctively.

'Åh, Hr Brockman! Takket være Gud du er vågen!'

Unthinkingly, he replied in his stumbling Danish.

'Yes. Yes, I'm awake. I was dreaming . . .'

For one crazy moment it was his mother by the window, drawing up the blind. But the young-old face was Kristine Hansen's, flecked with the shadows of raindrops, and the sky was the pallid grey of a Danish autumn shower, a world apart from the electric blue of his California childhood – or the merciless, unendurable heat of Israel . . .

'I am sorry, Hr Brockman. I had no wish to wake you with my singing, but you have slept almost the whole day – and I heard you cry out. Sarah, that is your wife?'

Sarah.

He found that he could say nothing. The simple mention of her name had conjured up the merciless dream that had haunted him every night for fifteen years.

'No. Sarah is – was . . .' There were no words that would answer. Sarah was a set of memories that should have been shared, an unfulfilled promise, and a single image, cruelly detailed, that made all others as grey as the daylight spilling into this tiny bedroom.

'Then she is someone you love?'

'No – I mean, I did. She's dead. Years ago.'

'And you do not love her still?'

'Yes ... No. I don't know ...' A familiar fury roared into life. How dare she ask about Sarah? How dare she smile like that, as if she could understand, as if she knew his thoughts, as if she were a mother indulging a wilful child? As if she were *his* mother?

'Hr Brockman, I am a very old lady. All the ones I love are gone – out there, in the churchyard. So I am like you, with your Sarah. There is so little love: we must keep what we have, I think. But anger, hatred – why do you keep those, too?'

'I don't want to talk about it.'

'But I do, Hr Brockman. I wish to understand you.'

'It's none of your damn business!'

'I care about Anja, Hr Brockman. I think that you begin to care for her also. Perhaps she reminds you of your Sarah. And so from the very beginning you are angry.'

'You seem to know a lot about me.'

'I know myself, Hr Brockman.' She turned away, looking out towards the churchyard through the drifting veils of rain. 'When he died – my husband – I could not forgive him.'

'Sarah was murdered,' said Brockman coldly. 'A Syrian fighter out for a day's fun. The bullets damn near cut her in half.' Despite himself, his voice shook. Only anger or despair could make him talk about Sarah's death, because every time he did he seemed to kill her again. He had expected to see the old woman surprised, embarrassed, perhaps shocked, but when at last she turned her head he saw nothing he had imagined. There was anger, regret, and guilt – the mirror-image of his own feelings – and something else as well, something he could not understand. 'For Johan,' she said, 'it was a German firing squad.'

For a moment he was appalled. Her tragedy dwarfed his own. He had read about Denmark in the Second World War: occupied, subjugated, her men of courage reduced to sabotage and guerrilla warfare, risking imprisonment, torture, or death. Till now it had been no more than words in a book and hazy, comfortably remote, black-and-white photographs. Now, seeing her face, the story touched his heart.

'He was a good man, my Johan – always laughing, always joking. It was New Year's Eve, when we have the fireworks – like your Fourth of July. Johan and his group, they had been told of a factory that was making weapons for the Germans. The owner himself gave them the keys. He could not bear that his machines should make things to murder our friends. People saw them from the houses, and they laughed, and raised their glasses, and said *skol* to Johan and the others. When all was ready, Johan rang up Gestapo headquarters on the telephone.'

'He did *what*?'

'He said "Good evening, Hr Gestapo Chief, this is the Danish Resistance. Happy New Year!" And then he pushed the button! Oh, such fireworks!'

'What happened?'

'In one house there was a quisling. The others escaped, but Johan . . .'

'I'm . . . sorry.'

'No, Hr Brockman, you are angry. With yourself, with the world. And now you will be angry with me. What was it you saw last night?'

Blue light, shadow – a trick of the moon. Must have been.
'Don't you mean "who"?'

She did not seem to hear him. Her eyes were fixed on the churchyard, and now, for the first time, he was aware of her age; that and a haunting sense of oppression, as though outside, beyond the windows, she saw a tireless and implacable enemy. 'Once there was a young girl in this village, Hr Brockman. One who saw what others would not see. There – there, on that mound – they burned her as a witch.'

'Nowadays they'd make her an analyst. What's your point?'

She ignored both the jibe and the question. 'Hr Brockman, I cannot imagine a more terrible death. For me the churchyard still stinks of burning flesh, of an innocent young life destroyed for the sake of blindness like yours. You have seen a thing you choose not to understand. Anja and I, we do not have that choice.'

'What are you saying?'

'For better or worse, Hr Brockman, you are part of this. Your fear, your anger, they are no longer enough. If you care for Anja as I think you do, then you must *act*: or she will be lost more terribly, more completely, than Erik.'

'OK, you know so much, you tell me! What was it? What *did* I see?'

'What did you think it was?' said Anja from the doorway. She looked pale and tired, but her cotton check shirt and denim overalls gave her the appearance of a moody teenager. 'Oh, Mr Brockman, you are so clever when you ask your questions – but can you answer them?' As she moved to join her grandmother her face vanished into shadow, and the light from the window behind them touched her hair with silver. Unbidden, the image of his assailant howled up from memory like a malignant ghost – the circling nimbus of blue-silver light, the tangible darkness around the face, the sense of a creature infinitely more powerful than it appeared to be . . .

'Well, Mr Brockman?' Her voice was sharp, almost accusing.

'I don't know. It was dark –'

'It was the clear moonlight. You saw him just like you see me. Better, perhaps.'

'Damnation, I was *fighting* it –'

'It? Not human, then?'

'Of *course* he was human! What else –?'

'Stop it! How can you *be* so blind –!'

'*Så, så pigebarn.*' Kristine half-smiled. 'You are angry because he is too much like you.'

'*Mormor*, will you please –?'

55

'Hr Brockman, yesterday you were foolish because you knew nothing. Now I think you are foolish from choice. I have already told you there is more about this place than folk wish to believe. Must I help you any more?'

'OK. I'd like to believe that what I saw was human. You'd like to believe it wasn't. So convince me.'

Anja moved away from the window. 'Then look at this place – really *look*. Come to the window; I will help you.'

'Damn it, I don't *need* your help!' He scrambled clumsily out of the bed and took three long strides before his legs buckled and he collapsed into Anja's arms with a vitriolic curse. She said nothing, and her face betrayed no emotion at all – she simply supported him till he recovered his balance, and then helped him to a seat next to her grandmother.

Kristine smiled. 'What do you see, Hr Brockman?'

'What am I supposed to see?'

'Do as Anja has asked. Just look.'

The colours had washed out of the little world beyond the window, and the church was blurred into a shapeless grey mass by drifting curtains of rain. The ordered ranks of headstones had lost their individuality. Like some neolithic monument, they had become anonymous markers for a spiralling set of circles focused on the ancient burial mound, the silent sentinels of a besieging army. Farm and church faced each other across the disputed ground like opposing generals. Once he had seen nothing here but harmony, peace, a fragment of the past preserved in amber. Now he could almost feel the conflicting energies, a precarious balance of forces with its centre in the single upright stone near the crest of the mound.

'It's the mound,' he said. 'There's something about it ...'

Kristine nodded. 'A place to burn witches, Hr Brockman. Once it was a pagan shrine. Oh, not a clean place. Not a place to pray for fine weather, or a good harvest. A dark place, full of dark stories – stories a sensible young man should not believe.'

He waved a hand impatiently. 'And these – these stories, they have something to do with ...'

'With what you saw. Yes. They say the mound is haunted, that evil things live there. It was never holy, Hr Brockman. More like the mouth of hell.'

'Yes ...' He was remembering the judgement fresco in the church. The time-worn painting was burned into his mind as clearly as that other image it had recalled. For the unknown medieval artist, Hell was a symmetrical hill raised on pillars like those of the church itself – like the veranda of the beach hotel at Haifa where he first met Sarah –

Damn it, this is crazy. Any minute now they'll have me believing in fairies!

Kristine was still talking, her voice level and emotionless. 'There is a legend that on one night in the year the mound opens, and the creatures that live there come out to do mischief. But the grave of a good Christian, that is something they cannot cross. Sometimes, if the night is very dark and long, they reach beyond the wall. Then terrible things happen in the village. But mostly the sun comes before they can leave the churchyard, and withers them away. You are smiling, Hr Brockman. I think that I waste my breath.'

'I'm sorry,' he said, without sincerity. Something was nagging at his memory, something to do with the fresco, but he couldn't pin it down. *No. No, it isn't possible ...*

Anja sensed his change of mood.

'What is it? What have you remembered?'

'I'm not sure I believe this myself, but – that thing. Last night.'

'Yes?'

'I've seen – it – before. In the church. Those demons with the personal bonfires –'

'The Judgement,' said Anja. 'It is a famous piece.'

Kristine nodded. 'You were fortunate. The *alvar* are terrible enemies.'

'Excuse me – *alvar*?'

'The Germans killed my husband – but the *alvar* have taken souls and bodies since first there was a house in Egerød. And now, today, their strength is greater still, because people like you will not believe they exist.'

Brockman felt his jaw drop. Once again Kristine had him at a loss for words. He struggled to translate his thoughts into Danish, and for the first time realised how much pressure he had put on Anja by forcing her to argue in a foreign language. It seemed incredible that the old lady could discuss her dead husband and a creature out of legend as if they both belonged on the same plane of reality – yet he himself had grappled with something that was both more and less than human ...

My God. They've done it. They've got me believing in fairies.

'All right. Say you're not crazy. Say I'm not crazy. Say that thing *was* – what you said. How does Erik fit into this? I mean, what happened to him?'

'Hr Brockman,' said Kristine, 'I know you do not believe our stories. I know you smile at our foolishness.'

He tried to deny it, but this time the words would not come. He looked to Anja, but she would not meet his eyes. She sat with her elbows on the window-ledge and her head cradled in her hands, staring steadfastly into the middle distance.

'Anja?'

'Yesterday I thought that you understood. But you choose differently, don't you?'

'Look – what do you *want* from me?'

'She wants you to trust your own senses,' said the old lady. 'You have met one of the *alvar*, you have fought with it, you have found its mark, and still you cannot believe that here is something real. You have seen the mound, you have seen the paintings in our church, but for you it is easier if these things are a children's tale. Perhaps that is true – but children have a wisdom of their own.'

'That's a nice thought, Fru Hansen, but –'

'You are an archaeologist, Hr Brockman. Is there no child in you that says "Dig here and you might find buried treasure, or a hidden city, or the image of a lost princess"?'

Brockman smiled despite himself. 'I can't argue with that.'

'I think all people like you have such a child in them. Surely it was the child in Heinrich Schliemann that led him to Troy? He remembered something every child knows – that the oldest stories, the stories told not once but a thousand times, they have a heart of truth. It may be hidden – but we always hide what we cannot bear to see.'

'So I have to believe in – what do you call them – *alvar*?'

Her grin disconcerted him. The face was old, and marked by the years, but the eyes were a young girl's, bright and full of mischief. 'Have you truly forgotten the terror of darkness? Oh yes, your parents told you there was nothing to fear, but you *knew*! We teach children to be like us – to forget the fears they cannot deny, to belittle and mock them because they dare not face them, to turn mighty *alvar* into foolish little sprites. But once you – even you – knew that other world, that world of shadows. And you knew there were creatures in it beyond all our understanding.'

'I'm listening, but . . .'

'My little granddaughter, who sits there with such a long face, she once spoke just as you do. Now she chooses not to remember, because she wishes to be angry with you.'

Anja crimsoned. '*Åh, Mormor* –!'

'She, too, is a scientist. She, too, thinks me a foolish old woman –'

'Fru Hansen, I never –'

'But I, even before I saw it I believed in the shadow-world. Because my mother did, and her mother, and her mother before her.'

'I don't understand! What is this – this shadow-world of yours?'

'It is a dream. It is immortality. But not for us. Not for creatures with souls.'

'Excuse me?'

'The stories tell it, Hr Brockman – so many stories, and not just here in Egerød. The men and the women who went into the mound for an hour, or a day, while a hundred years passed under the sun. Or those who came back crippled with age after a single day had passed in this world.'

He stared at her – at this ageless woman who could accept as fact what he could only see as myth – and understood why that serene face troubled him. Once before he had seen a face like that, in Arizona: an Indian *shaman* recounting the legends of his tribe. But for that man, and for Kristine, there was no boundary between legend and reality. The myth was life itself; and by accepting it, becoming part of it, and passing it on to her children and grandchildren, she had come to terms with her existence. Seeing her inner peace, her confidence, her total lack of fear, he felt a surge of jealousy. For years he had travelled the world, angry and rootless, in a futile search for contentment – and here was a woman who had spent her whole life in a single village, a woman with nothing but her home, her family, and her legacy of dreams, who had everything he lacked. Once he might have thought her mad. Now, remembering the *shaman*, he finally understood that the madness was in him, in all who cut themselves off from the world of legend and myth that was their true inheritance. In that world there was nothing strange in the idea of a man who entered the shadows – and returned with their mark on his mind and his body ...

'I know the folklore, Fru Hansen. It's part of my job. But you're not saying that Erik ... I mean, do you seriously think –?'

'I do not think, Hr Brockman. I *know*. Come, I will

show you. You, too, *pigebarn*. Enough of your sulking.'

Anja glared at him. 'You can stand now?' Her voice sounded petulant.

'Probably, but don't go away. My legs feel like wet noodles.' This time he moved more cautiously. The little room swam for a few moments, then drifted back into focus. Gently but firmly he pushed aside Anja's half-offered hand. 'OK. Now where?'

For an answer she opened the door. After the cold, grey bedroom the kitchen was warmth, light and humanity. He could smell bread straight from the oven, and the sweet scent of newly-washed fruit mixed with the burnt-toast aroma of dark coffee. As the women shepherded him to the kitchen table it seemed impossible that the farmhouse could belong to the same universe as the dark mound outside. Yet this, the very heart of the farm, was the only important room with a direct view of the church. For the first time he remembered that out there, in that defensive ring of graves, he had found his own ancestors. He was as much a part of this as Anja and her grandmother.

'Coffee, Hr Brockman?' asked Kristine. 'You must be hungry, too. Help yourself to *rundestykker*.'

'Ah – thanks.' Automatically he reached for one of the crisp, seeded white rolls, breaking it clumsily over his plate. 'About – about Erik . . .' Anja glanced up. He found it hard to meet her eyes. 'Look, I don't know how to say this, but I still have trouble believing the man in that room *is* Erik.'

She laughed. 'You think I do not know my own grandson? Really, Hr Brockman, do I seem to be senile?'

'Hardly. But you must admit –'

'No, Hr Brockman. *You* must admit that here is something you do not properly understand. But we shall help you, because Anja and I, we *know* that Erik crossed into the shadow-world. And we know why.' Again his eyes met Anja's – and this time he saw the traces of a sadness that echoed his own. 'We know,' said Kristine, 'because we

61

saw all the things that Erik saw. Some we do not understand, others meant more to him than to us, but we can show you all the signs –'

'Whoa, hold on. What signs?'

'Anja. I think the Bible now.'

'*Mormor* –!'

'Come along, Anja, you must get it down for me. I can't reach so high, Hr Brockman: my arms, they were born a little sooner than I. They have not worn quite so well.'

'Fru Hansen, you are quite a lady. How does someone as down-to-earth as you get to believe in – in *alvar*?'

'Young man, how does someone as clever as you fight one and *not* believe in it?'

'*Mormor*, I –'

'The Bible, child! *Du godeste*, when I was a girl I was taught to obey my elders!'

Brockman laughed, despite himself and despite a withering glare from Anja. Her footsteps on the tiled kitchen floor echoed through the house as she stamped towards the living room to do her errand.

'Take this piece with the ham, Hr Brockman. It was fresh today from the *mejeri*, better than that dreadful supermarket.'

'Fru Hansen, there's something I need to ask you – something about Anja.' Kristine inclined her head, like a patient mother listening to a very young child. Brockman tried to ignore the gesture. 'That story she tells about – what's her name? – Eleanor. That's for real? I mean –'

'You think, perhaps, that she was jealous? And so she was, Hr Brockman. She is human, after all, like you or I – and yet she wished to love the girl for Erik's sake.'

'But she couldn't, right?'

'Nor could I, Hr Brockman. When first I saw Eleanor I knew her to be fey.'

'Fey? How do you mean?'

'There is a look about the eyes that cannot be hidden. Oh, you would say "mad", Hr Brockman, but there are many kinds of madness. Erik was more her slave than her husband. His love, that was real enough – but the girl, she had no love to give. She had no soul. Anja knew it, and for that she hated her.'

'It sounds like she was – well, "obsessed" is a word that springs to mind.'

'I don't think so. My granddaughter is not a fool. She has strength, and courage, and love, and she asks nothing in return. If you care about her, you should know that. Even now, she would do anything for Erik – anything at all.' She put her fingers to her lips with a conspiratorial smile. 'And here is Anja with the Bible. Come and eat, *pigebarn*!'

Anja all but slammed the battered, leather-bound Bible onto the kitchen table. 'There, Mr Brockman. This was the first. Erik found it open, like this, just where I have put it.'

'In the wrong place, you mean?'

'*Ja, præcis.* And marked here with a pen – look.'

'OK – but this ink's faded – brown. Whoever made that mark did it a long time ago. Centuries, maybe.'

'Read the verse.'

'I wish I could. This old print is rough on the eyes. What's it say?'

'*Men sidst af Alle har han viist sig for mig som for det utidige Foster.*'

'Which means?'

'"And last of all he showed himself to me as to one born out of his proper time." It is a letter of St Paul.'

'I'm not too much wiser –'

'There was another book next to it. This one.'

He started momentarily. It was *Legends of the North*, the book he had opened the evening before. This time the passage was clearly marked with a black ballpoint pen.

Some scholars believe the Old English poem *Beowulf* is an Anglo-Saxon retelling of a far older Danish legend: the curious story of Bodvar- or 'Battle-' Biarki, heroic leader of King Rolf Kraki's band of warriors. Both men fought a dragon, and this in itself is distinctive – Sigurd is the only other dragonslayer in northern mythology. Both were foreigners who delivered a king of Denmark, throned at the old capital of Lejre, from a great evil. Even their names are similar. 'Beowulf' probably means 'bear-wolf', while 'Biarki' simply means 'little bear'. But Biarki is the more mysterious of the pair, and his birth is the greatest mystery of all.

'All right, I give up. What's the connection?'

'Very simple,' said Anja. 'Erik's nickname for his son was Biarki.'

Brockman frowned. 'I hope you don't mean what I think you mean –'

'Let me say it for you,' said Anja. 'Erik was crazy with grief and worry. He made the marks himself – or at least the second one. And the rest, that was his own imagination.'

'Thanks. Couldn't put it better myself.'

She laughed, with an edge of spite. 'Good. Because the night it happened I was outside his room all night. I was worried for him – for what he might do. He never opened the door – but in the morning I found the books here, just as you see them.'

'Oh, come *on*! You could have dozed off, you could –'

'I don't think so, Mr Brockman. I drank coffee instead, and I feared for him, because it seemed to me that he might try to end his life.'

Brockman met Kristine's unblinking grey eyes. 'And you?'

'I? I think you should know the rest before you judge. Show him the chest, *pigebarn*. It is in Erik's bedroom, Hr Brockman – I believe you know the way.'

The remark irritated him, as it was probably meant to. Anja had already got up, leaving her sandwich untouched on the plate. Her rising anger was infectious – he could feel his own self-control beginning to slip as he followed her into the old man's bedroom.

The window was a shimmering curtain of water fed by scattered fusillades of raindrops. Its cold light drained the colour from the room, muting and aging the greens and reds to shades of grey. The place seemed cramped, almost stifling, and the pious texts and pictures were oppressive rather than quaint. Erik's breathing was shallow and his face, like everything around him, was colourless. Anja knelt by the bed, taking his pulse. Her other hand rested lightly on his forehead, as though she were trying to smooth out the tracks that time and loss had left there. There was an echo of that loss in her own face. Brockman had always felt like an intruder in the house but now, for the first time, it mattered.

'How is he?' She did not seem to hear the question. 'Doc –?'

'In the corner.'

'What?'

'The chest. It is sixteenth century.'

'I don't –'

'Just look at it. Pull it out into the room – that was how we found it.'

It was a massive linen chest, its wooden panelling decorated in the same greens, reds, blacks and whites as everything else. Each of its sides was blazoned with a short biblical text, worked in circles around a simple design of flowers – pious, pretty, and unremarkable. The thing was the size of a large packing-crate, and it had been pushed firmly into the corner of the room. Moving it by himself would be something of a challenge.

'You going to help me?' He spoke in English, half-aware of the annoyance it would cause her.

'You can manage.' Her voice was still infuriatingly flat, but he made the effort to check his anger. Even so, he found himself wrenching and tugging at the massive chest, pulling it along the wall with a strength born of pure rage.

65

'For the record, this thing weighs half a ton.'

'Yes. Too heavy for me. Too heavy for Kristine –'

'OK, you've made your point. But – also for the record – not too heavy for Erik. Now, let's take a look at the body.'

The paintwork on the shorter of the two hidden sides was damaged, but the design was clear – and totally unlike the others. Instead of flowers, the central motif showed two stylised figures locked together in combat. The words were written in a crabbed, Gothic-style script that defied his attempts to read it. To make things worse, some of the letters had been painted in green or red. Now they were almost invisible.

'I'm sorry, Doc, my Danish isn't up to this.'

She did not even look up. 'It says *Og Dragen vrededes paa Kvinden, og gik bort for at kæmpe med de Øvrige af hendes Afkom.*'

'Meaning exactly what?'

'"And the dragon was angry with the woman, and went to make war on the remnant of her seed." Before you go look it up, it is –'

'Revelation of St John the Divine. One hell of a text for a linen chest. You knew about this?'

'No. Nor Kristine. One morning she comes here to tidy the bed, and the chest is dragged out from the corner –'

'By person or persons unknown?'

'Yes.'

'This doesn't make much sense.'

'Look at the back also.'

With a final heave that set his joints cracking, Brockman dragged the back of the chest out into the room and the light from the window. The last of the four panels was in a parlous state, faded and battered, and the paint had peeled away in long, crumbling strips. Even so, most of the text was readable, but the central design was badly damaged. It seemed to show a stone-framed gate set at the crest of a hill, though the architrave and one doorpost had flaked away. He made a valiant attempt to read the inscription.

'*"Hvor snever er porten, og trang veien"* – Wait up, that has to be the "strait and narrow path". Right?'

'Almost. "How strait the gate, and narrow the path, that leads to salvation – and how few they are who find it." A good text. You should have more faith, Mr Brockman.'

His patience snapped. 'God damn it, woman! You're not *telling* me anything! What the hell am I supposed to have faith *in* –?'

'Be still, *for Satan*! Erik is sick – or had you forgotten?'

'No,' said Brockman, struggling to lower his voice. 'No, I hadn't. But you show me a couple of books that add up to exactly nothing, and a chest that's been sitting here minding its own business for the last four hundred years. Then you act like an ice maiden when I want to know more. You have to *give* a little. Right?'

For a moment her mask crumbled, and behind it he saw a confused and frightened woman on the verge of tears. Instinctively he reached out his hand, but she turned away.

'Doc – look, I'm *trying* to understand –'

'I, too, Mr Brockman. I try to understand *you* – why you concern yourself with us. Why it should matter to you.'

'Because . . .' He hesitated. 'You really want to know?'

'Is the truth so bad?'

The truth is everything you are reminds me of her. The truth is . . .

'Because of you. The way you talk. Things you do. Even your clothes. You're very like someone I – care about.'

Anja's smile was bitter. 'It is strange, this caring of yours. Does she enjoy it, do you think?'

'Damn you, woman, she's –!'

'Mr Brockman, *I* am not the one who died.'

There was a kind of sympathy in her voice, but her face was strangely empty, giving no clue to the feeling behind her words. Her eyes were looking towards him, but they were focused on the window behind him, staring into the grey heart of the rain as though the world outside were occupied territory, bristling with hidden enemies. It was the same look he had seen in her grandmother's face.

'So you heard us,' he said. 'You know about Sarah.'

'There was no need to hear. Grief, death, they are things a doctor learns to understand. I have known almost since we met.'

He tried to smile, and failed. 'Didn't know I was that obvious.'

'First I thought that finding Erik had shocked you so. But you would not go away. And they were so foolish, your excuses ...'

This time he managed the smile. 'You *are* like – her. Prickly as a *sabra*.'

'Sabra? What is that?'

'Desert cactus. Stubborn, too, but I like that. I'm stubborn myself. Look, if you want me to say that I've been seven kinds of idiot up till now, I'll say it. I'll even say I'm sorry if you think it'd help. Now tell me about the chest, Doc.'

She grinned faintly – a lop-sided, urchin grin that reminded him irresistibly of her grandmother. 'My name is Anja, Mr Brockman. And it is better that Erik tells.'

'We can't wait that long –'

'His notes. *Mormor* will have them ready by now.'

'I'm beginning to feel manipulated – Anja.'

'Good. And you will please speak Danish to my grandmother.'

In the kitchen a pile of papers had joined the two books on the table, crowding out the rolls, rye bread and cold cuts of their abandoned meal. Kristine held up a single sheet covered with crossings-out and cryptic comments – but in the midst of the chaos Brockman could just make out the two biblical quotations from the chest. 'It is a code,' she said, 'but a very simple one. The green letters only – the red and the black, they do not matter.

68

See here – Erik has marked them.'

Brockman nodded vaguely and took the sheet. The green letters were marked with neat underscores.

OG DRAGEN VREDEDES PAA KVINDEN, OG GIK
BORT FOR AT KÆMPE MED DE
ØVRIGE AF HENDES AFKOM
HVOR SNEVER ER PORTEN, OG TRANG VEIEN,
SOM FØRER TIL FRELSEN!
OG DE ERE FAA, SOM FINDE DEN.

Underneath, Erik had written three simple words:

GANG A STEININOM

'That isn't Danish,' said Brockman. 'Looks Scandinavian, but –'

'*Oldnordisk,*' said Kristine. 'What the Vikings spoke in the old time.'

'Old Norse? But that's crazy! Why bury an Old Norse inscription in a sixteenth century Danish text – and so obviously that a child could break the code?'

'Perhaps a child was meant to. It means "Go to the stone."'

'Fine. What stone? No, wait, let me guess – the stone in the churchyard, right?'

The old woman's eyes twinkled mischievously. 'There are stories about that, too, Hr Brockman –'

'Yes, don't tell me. Stories a sensible young man shouldn't believe.'

She nodded with a wry smile. 'Once they called it *den gangende sten* – the walking stone. They said that as the years went by it moved around the mound. Anti-clockwise, like a witch at the sabbath. The old people in my childhood, they had a different name for the stone. They called it *Helvedsmund* –'

'I know. The mouth of hell. Like the painting in the church. And that means Erik missed something. Those biblical quotations – they aren't just a way of hiding the code. They *mean* something, too. "The strait gate, and the narrow path, that lead to *salvation*" – maybe the stone isn't so bad after all. And that stuff about the dragon – there's a message in that, too.'

'You are right,' said Anja. 'But to find it you must come outside.'

'Whatever you say.'

Outside, the yard was a grey and silver patchwork of puddles that glittered and rippled in the fading light as drips from the darkened thatch stirred them into life. The air was sharp and clean, intoxicatingly fresh, as though time had slipped, and the sprawling suburbs of Copenhagen had vanished into the cornfields and open grassland of another century.

'Look here – look closely.'

Kristine was pointing at a massive stone block that formed a single step up to the kitchen door. For a long moment he stared at it without understanding – and then, like an Escher print, the perspective shifted and the meaningless marks on the stone became a coherent pattern. It had been meant to stand upright, but now it was lying on its side – and its carved inscription had looked like nothing more than abstract decoration. Twisting his head he recognised the awkward, branching shapes of pre-Christian runic letters, though he lacked the knowledge to translate them or even identify them.

'So it's a runestone. Interesting, but what's so special?'

'Hr Brockman, my family have been here since four hundred years, and we did not know of it. Yet one morning Erik found it, just like you see it now.'

ᛘᚱᛁᚲ · ᛒᚡᚱ · ᚱᚾᛁᛦ · ᚡᚱᛁᚻᛁᛘᛦ ·
· ᛘᛒᛏᛁᚱ · ᛒᛁᚠᚱᚲᛁ ·
ᚻᚡᛏ · ᛏᚱᛦᚻᚱ · ᚻᚱᛘᚲᛁᚠᛊᛏᛁᚲᛁᚻ ·

He knelt down carefully, feeling along the edge of the stone. A band of dark colour showed where soil had accumulated, burying the inscription – and fresh scratches suggested that some sharp-edged tool had scraped it away.

'I don't see the mystery. Someone cleaned off the dirt – could've been anyone.'

'Not anyone, Hr Brockman. Anja, Erik and I, we were alone here. He had just come to look for Eleanor and Bjørn. I could only think they were kidnapped – so I locked the doors and set the bolts on them. But when Erik came out in the morning, the stone was – like this.'

'Maybe you took a while to notice it. I mean, how often d'you even *look* at this step? It's just another bit of the farm, you've seen it a million times before . . .'

'I thought you had opened your mind!' said Anja, with more than a touch of anger.

'*Men dog, Anja*! Hr Brockman says these things because he wishes to think me a crazy old woman.'

He smiled, despite himself. 'You have a transcription of these runes?'

'Yes, of course,' said Kristine. 'I have it here.'

He took the sheet she offered, but even the transcription meant very little to him.

Eirk þar runo faihiðo eptir Biarki.
Han troðr drekijastigin.

'Old Norse again?'

Kristine nodded. 'From the very earliest times – fifth, maybe sixth century.'

'What does it mean?'

'The words are simple,' said Anja, 'but we do not understand them.'

'But if they're simple . . .?'

'It means,' said Kristine, '"Erik made these runes to honour Biarki. He walks the path of the dragon."'

'Wait a minute. You're trying to tell me that Erik's son –?

But that would mean – No. That's *crazy!*'

Kristine pointed a tremulous hand towards the house. 'You have perhaps a better explanation?'

He shook his head unwillingly. *Only a total fruitcake would swallow the idea of a child being taken back in time. And if Erik cut the runes – Jesus, I don't even want to think about it* ... 'So what about this "path of the dragon"?'

'The hero Boðvar Biarki was a dragonslayer,' said Anja. 'That was in the book that Erik found. Perhaps the "path of the dragon" is death. And the St Paul letter –'

'Yeah, all that stuff about people out of their time. But there's something we're missing – something obvious.'

He saw the two women glance at each other in surprise.

'We have shown you everything,' said Anja.

'Yes – except the stone in the churchyard.'

'The stone?' Kristine frowned. 'But how –?'

'Isn't there an inscription? More of these runes? What do they say?'

Anja shook her head. '*Mormor*, we have been foolish. Because the stone has always been there –'

'You took it for granted. Wait up – I think there's a piece on it in my guidebook.'

'Come inside,' said Kristine. 'I shall make some more coffee.'

'Eleventh century,' muttered Brockman. 'Funny about the gaps – sixth century runestone, eleventh-century inscription, sixteenth-century chest.'

'But look here, what it says!' Anja was sitting at his side, leaning over the book, and the natural perfume of her hair made it hard for him to concentrate. 'The runes, they are a verse from the poem *Völuspá* –'

'Hold on, don't tell me – that's *The Prophecy of the Seeress*, right? Kind of a Viking version of Revelation?'

'Yes!' She nodded vigorously, catching the wavering light of the oil lamp in the glittering highlights of her hair. She looked younger and more vulnerable than ever, and he was half-ashamed of the way such a simple gesture could arouse him. 'You might say it was the Viking Armageddon.' She read it aloud in a sing-song voice, like a child reciting something half-understood.

> *Kialar ferr austan, koma muno Muspellz*
> *Stynja dvergar fyr steindurom, veggbergs visir*
> *Dreka hann drepa, en draugar risar*

For the tenth time he stared at the translation. It was all but meaningless.

> *Kialar drives eastwards, Muspell's time has come*
> *The dwarves groan before the stone door, the captain of*
> *wedge-stones*
> *He slays the dragon, and the dead arise . . .*

'Kialar – what *is* that?'

Anja frowned. 'The book says it is a name of Odin.'

'Not a great guy, as gods go.'

'He was a warrior –'

'And a black magician. And tricky. Typical father-figure.'

She pretended to frown. 'So you hated your father?'

'Enough with the analysis. What about "Muspell"?'

'Here it says – wait – "day of judgement".'

'Then all this garbage with dwarves and doors.' He rubbed his chin. 'Could mean the stone itself. *Your* stone, the one on the mound.'

Anja shook her head dismissively. 'Those words are in the poem – much older than the stone.'

'Whoa. You mean much older than the *runes*. There's no law against carving new runes on an old stone – and maybe the *poet* was talking about your stone.'

'But why should he?'

'Because all these clues, all the things you've shown me, have been trying to tell us there's something special about it. In which case I want to see it for myself.'

'But Peter, it is almost dark!'

'So we'll take a torch. Unless you don't go out with strange men after dark.'

'Not if they are as strange as you.'

'I hate it when your English is that good. Coming?'

'Yes. Yes, I suppose so.'

A copper moon on a bed of streaming cloud rode the last, lingering light of day, tinting the thatch of the old farm with a lurid orange light. Beyond, the stepped gable of the church tower was blackness cut from a turquoise sky. The rain-swept cobbles glittered with the flickering light of the oil lamps in the main house, and dark shapes stretched across the courtyard. Anja kept herself at a discreet distance from Brockman, moving with a natural ease and grace that accentuated her slim, lithe body. He found his eyes continually drawn to her by some new and momentous detail: the shadow of her underlip in the moonlight, the slight motion of her breasts under the thin raincoat, the swing of her hair as she tossed her head. From the orchard came the lucid song of a bird.

She smiled. 'We call it *rødhals* – red-throat. You know that bird?'

'In California you mostly hear crickets. Or owls.'

'Peter ...'

'Yes?'

'Did you love her very much?'

For a moment his old anger flared up, but now he fought it back, struggled to confront the feelings it disguised. He had clung to the memory of Sarah's death, as if that alone were important. Now memory betrayed him. Somehow everything that mattered – the living, breathing Sarah who had teased him, kissed him, and talked with him – was gone. He could not remember the real woman, only the image he had created for his own private shrine. 'I don't know if I loved her. I guess I would have done, but – well. Never had the chance to find out. Maybe like you and Erik.'

He heard the hiss of her indrawn breath. 'I am sorry,' she said. 'It was wrong of me to ask.'

'I didn't mean it that way. Oh come on, I can see how you feel about him. I'm not blind. And I can guess what happened when Eleanor came.'

'He – he was older. To him I was always a little girl.'

'But you must have had boyfriends!'

'No one special. I was studying. There was too much work.'

'And now?'

'Now – now I must care for Kristine.' She moved away, her heels clicking on the cobblestones of the courtyard as she fumbled in her pocket for a key.

'What about your parents?'

'They are too far away to help. My father is with the – how do you call it? – the oil riggings. They have a house in Esbjerg. On the west coast, where the ferries from England come.'

'Couldn't Kristine move there?'

'She will not leave the farm.'

'So you have to stay?'

She hesitated at the shadowed entrance to the passageway between the house and the stable. At the far end he could just see the heavy door, round-headed like the doors of the church. On this side it was fixed with massive wrought-iron hinges curled and hammered into claws and dragons' heads. It was so much older than the farm that it looked like the door to another world.

'This is my home, also. I have patients here in the town – people who need me.'

He touched her shoulder, drawing her round to face him. 'Like Erik needs you?'

She frowned slightly, searching his face for the mockery she had come to expect from him. She did not find it.

'What do you want with him, Anja?'

Her eyes dropped. 'I – I don't know any more. I feel – I feel there should be someone who still cares. He has nothing left now ...'

'You're still hoping. Aren't you?'

'No.' She met his eyes, and he saw her uncertainty. 'No. I don't know.'

'I know. I've watched it tear you apart, this dream of yours. I see it every time you look at him, and every time you talk about him. And because of that you've cut yourself off from anyone else who might –'

'What right do you have to –?'

'No right at all. Just like I've no right to be falling in love with you. But I am, Anja, and there's nothing you can do about it. There isn't too damn much *I* can do about it.'

She pulled away from him into the passage, her voice echoing between its timber-framed walls. 'It isn't possible, Peter. I am sorry.'

'So don't be. Try being happy.'

'Please – leave me alone.'

'On a cold night, with Christ knows what waiting in the shadows? I don't think you mean that.'

'Then we should go to the stone, or go back inside. But please – please don't . . .'

'OK, OK. Let's do what we came to do.'

Anja was already working a large key in the old lock. It yielded with an audible click, and the big door drifted silently open on well-oiled hinges.

And beyond it there *was* another world.

Above the churchyard a rising wave of clouds was blotting out the moon, and the doorway framed a silent shadow-landscape traced out in mist and starlight. The clock-tower was lost in a crouching darkness of huddled trees, and the mound was a deeper blackness against it – but something at its crest seemed to catch and hold the last, flickering silver of the vanishing moon.

'The stone!' he whispered. 'Look at it!'

'I see it! That light!'

'Come *on*!' He was already running, convinced that what he had seen would be gone in a few seconds. But far from fading, the light was growing more intense, a

76

numinous haze without source or direction that rose like an exhalation from the earth itself. Among the serried tombstones shadows moved and stretched in response, as though his need were a call to arms that had summoned the guardian spirits of his ancestors. His rational mind saw only the mist, and the stones, and the dying moonlight – but something within him that was primal and instinctive felt rather than saw the deeper shadows around him, and one shadow, deeper yet, that seemed a part of the runestone itself.

'You! Who are you? What do you want with us?'

His voice shattered the spell. As the last of the moonlight flickered and died, the tenuous images died with it. The shadow behind the stone seemed to vanish as his fingers touched granite scorched by ancient fires, spider-webbed with the intricate carving of a half-forgotten past. Yet at its heart he felt a familiar shape cut deep into the stone.

Three triangles. Three interlinked triangles. The shape of the pendant that Erik had gripped till the points pierced his flesh. The sign Brockman's attacker had sprayed on the doors of the farm ...

In that moment he knew he had found a link between the stone, Erik, and his own heightened perceptions – and with that knowledge came an inescapable sense of strangeness, of something utterly remote from the ordered, bloodless world he had always thought of as reality.

'Peter? You – you saw it?'

'Yeah. Thought it was next to the stone –'

'It is still here. I feel it. I – think it means no harm.'

'I'm not so sure. So *stay here*!'

He grasped her hand, drawing her with him towards the stone. He could feel each of her long, slim fingers, cool against his palm, and the flutter of the pulse in her wrist. He could hear the faint whisper of leaves in the ghostly breeze that carried the maddening perfume of her hair mixed with the rich scent of damp earth and seeding grasses. And as he gripped the stone, he felt the tremor of an inner power as real as the fire-blackened granite and the deeply-incised signature of the forgotten runesmith. He had never felt more alive – because he knew that he stood at the very brink of death.

'You – whatever you are – if you've got a message then *talk* to me!'

For a moment something moved among the graves, and in that moment he saw the image of a terrible beauty: the shadowy mask of a face, broad, high-cheekboned, slant-eyed, framed in shimmering silver like the mist; the golden glint of eyes, bright and shining; the full, sensuous lips; the outstretched hand, inhumanly slim and shapely, beckoning its invitation. Then there was nothing. He felt a tingle of returning circulation as Anja loosened her death-grip on his hand. He had scarcely noticed the pressure. 'Uh – did you ...?'

'It was there, Peter! *It was there!*'

He nodded slowly. 'I thought you were crazy. I thought I was *going* crazy ...'

'Can you believe us now, Peter? Can you understand?'

'Believe, yes. Understand, no. This doesn't feel like any world I know.'

'I told you, Peter. It is our world, not yours. You should go – *now!*'

He shook his head. 'I can't. Not now. Maybe not ever. There's something about this place, and something about you. I belong here, Anja – and you belong with me.'

'You *must* go!'

He took her hand, drawing her towards him. 'What are you afraid of? Betraying him? So what are you betraying? A dream you had when you were kids together? You can't live on dreams, Anja – not even in your world.'

'Why do you say these things?'

'Because I just found out they're true. Because I've been like you – living on dreams and memories about Sarah because I couldn't face being ripped apart again. I've been travelling for fifteen years, and all that time I've been running away, trying to believe that somehow – in my mind, maybe – she was still alive.' All those years he had courted death, like the dancers in the fresco – and here, for a moment, he had seen its face... 'She's dead, Anja. She's been dead a long time. And I can't follow her.'

'Peter ...' She hesitated a moment, staring back towards the mound. 'If that was where Erik went, I can't follow him, either. But I am not sure how I feel about you. Not yet.'

'Then we'll find out.'

'I don't know if ...'

'Neither do I. But right now I think we need each other.'

She reached out to him blindly, desperately, as an island of reality in a world changed beyond reason, burying herself in the shelter of his arms – and he held her close, drinking in her warmth, her sweetness, the life that pulsed through her body.

'Come on,' he said. 'We're going back inside.'

Later, in the stillness of her moonlit bedroom, he lay in a dazed half-dream where faces and hands reached towards him out of darkness, and all were Sarah's.

I hear you. I know I have to follow you. But not yet. Not yet.

Even in his dream, he clung to the reality in his arms: the slim, slight body still trembling in the vibrant after-math of passion, the slow heartbeat echoing his own, the warm breath against his cheek. But outside, beyond the open window, lay a haunted shadow-world of black and silver.

'Peter?'

'Mm?' For a moment, between dream and waking, he saw a flickering ghost-face at the window – then nothing but the image of the moon, trapped in glass. 'What's the matter?'

'What was it, Peter? What did we see?'

Death. I saw death. 'I don't know. Trick of the light. Imagination –'

'You know better than that, Peter –'

'Look, whatever the hell it was there's nothing we can do about it.' *Except that there is. The sign on the stone. It has to be the key.*

'It was warning us, Peter. It was trying to tell us something –'

He pressed a hand gently over her mouth, drew her closer, half-closing his eyes to shut out the mocking image of the moon. She trembled in his arms, responsive to his slightest caress, caught, like him, between her fear and her hunger. He felt her cool fingers trace a line of fire down his chest, catch and hold the core of his desire, felt her hair tumble round his face in a fragrant veil, and her tiny, little-girl nipples brushed against his chest, urging him to another passionate outpouring of desire. But now, though his hunger for her was no less, he could control himself, allow his strangely heightened senses to record every last detail – the touch of her in a hundred places, the darting motions of her tongue flicking between his teeth like a tiny animal, the glittering sheen of her salt-tasting skin, beaded with the sweat of their loveplay, the delicate scent of her arousal – and her eyes, clear and shining like a girl on the brink of womanhood.

Like her grandmother. As though she's too young to know anything, and so old she knows it all.

His desire peaked for a second time, and he grasped her arms, lifting her bodily into the union she longed for, gasping at the strength of her response as she met his passion with a vibrant energy of her own. They slid together so easily he scarcely knew it had happened. He felt unbelievably young, supernaturally alive – every caress, every slightest touch, was driving out the lingering image of death. Her face was a study in passion, eyes narrowed, full lips parted above small, perfect teeth. The fluid motion of her breasts answered the rhythm of their lovemaking like a silversmith's masterwork brought to strange and passionate life in the mad light of an autumn moon. He drew himself upright, clasped her tightly against him, and felt her legs lock around his hips as he half-turned, sliding sideways off the bed and onto his feet. She gasped in amazement and passion, and as she clung to him with a desperation that was half fear and half renewed desire, he felt the fulfilment shudder through her body to meet its answer in his.

'Cold?'

'A little.' She tightened her arms around him, drawing warmth from his body.

'Back to bed, then.' She held him close, her head cushioned on his shoulder, her legs still clamped around his hips, until he kissed her and laid her gently by his side. She said nothing, asked for nothing, and her stillness was a part of this place, a part of the strange shadow-world that had swallowed up the meaningless clamour of his past life. He had come here lost, rootless and alone – and found, beyond hope and beyond reason, something he had never known he lacked. The city around them had vanished: there was nothing left but the creaking of ancient timbers, grumbling with age and the weight of years. Outside, the trees whispered forgotten secrets in the rising wind, and a solitary creature cried its defiance to the moon. It was a strange sound, more than animal yet less than human, filled with a desperate intensity yet somehow soulless, unfeeling.

A fox, maybe. Heard that in England once, scared me half to death. Like a lost child.

'Peter . . .?'

'Yeah, I heard.'

'I did not mean that. There is someone in Erik's room.'

'What! How d'you know?'

'The floorboard there, it creaks a little. What are you doing?'

'Get my jeans, will you? I'll go take a look.'

'No, wait –'

'Won't be more than a minute. You stay here, shut the door.'

'But Kristine –'

'You take care of her. And yourself.' He grabbed his battered leather jacket from the back of the chair. It was cold against his bare skin, and in the moonlight from the window it gleamed with a faint metallic sheen like ancient armour.

The kitchen was impenetrably dark after the brightness of Anja's bedroom, and for precious moments he was blind, reduced to hearing and touch to find his way. The muted sounds of the house no longer reassured him: each seemed to presage some sudden attack from a hidden enemy. Erik's door was open, but he could see nothing beyond it save a deeper darkness. As he hesitated on the threshold another bitter cry rose from the churchyard, but this time there was an answer: a human cry, a passionate cry of anger and hatred and despair. A strange, pallid light flared beyond the kitchen window, throwing watery shadows across the bed in the alcove.

It was empty. Erik had gone.

CHAPTER
4

Hnigin es helgrind, haugar opnask,
allr es í eldi eybarmr at sjá;
atalt es úti um at litask . . .

Hell's gate gapes, and graves are opening,
All the isle's ablaze with flame;
Savage sights surround the watcher. . .

The Waking of Angantyr

Running as if in slow motion, his feet slipping and
twisting in the treacherous sand . . .

A fallen parasol, twisted ribs tearing through stained
and faded fabric . . .

A crushed can, at the tip of a comet's tail of darkened
sand . . .

A radio, half-buried, its whining, rhythmic complaint
all but muffled into silence . . .

A babble of voices – men, women and children
screaming, shouting, crying and praying in a meaningless
welter of noise . . .

A single voice, calling his name . . .

A rising, high-pitched whine with a rhythmic, clock-
work counterpoint . . .

A figure, struggling towards him, arms outstretched,
mouth gaping and ugly . . .

Sand exploding into twin lines of fury . . .

'Sarah!'

* * *

'Peter, what is it? Where is Erik?'

For a moment he was bewildered. The cry from the churchyard had touched the very heart of his endless nightmare, and Anja's face seemed to merge with Sarah's death-mask and that other, inhuman face he had glimpsed by the runestone. In her thin robe and her absurd mules she looked utterly defenceless, and her vulnerability terrified him. 'Jesus Christ, woman, *stay in your room*! You *saw* what happened last night!'

'So perhaps you need help.' Her voice was suddenly very cold.

'For a smart woman you can be so damn *stupid*!'

She drew her robe defensively around her. 'I make my own choices. Where is Erik?'

'If he's crazy like you, my guess is the churchyard.'

'Then we shall follow him.'

'*I'll* follow him. You do like you're damned well told!'

'I said –'

'Yeah, I heard!' He grabbed her shoulders to shake her like a doll, and found himself embracing her like a lost child. 'For Christ's sake, can't you understand I *care* about you?'

Her face softened. 'Yes. Yes, I can. But I am *me*, Peter. Not Sarah. Not anyone else. And I can mind myself.'

'Your English is slipping again. And I'm the one with the armour-plated skull. Didn't I just prove it?'

She half-smiled, and kissed him with a passion that startled him. 'Just remember that I also, I care about you.'

'Don't fuss about me. Just look after Kristine.'

'She will look after me, I think. Well – go if you must.'

The words seemed to echo maddeningly in his head. *Damn it, even the voice. It could be Sarah talking.*

'Peter –'

He barely heard her. He was already running, driven by the bitterness of a hatred that had never really died.

Not again. Not this time. This time you don't get the chance!

The front door was open, just as Larssen had left it, and beyond it the roofs around the courtyard were etched

84

in moonlight. Below, a rolling, waist-deep bank of mist was burying the world he knew in glittering filigree. It was a landscape of black, white and silver, a child's nightmare where shadows hid what imagination dared not conceive. Yesterday, a lifetime ago, he had believed in a predictable and logical universe. Now it was lost for ever. Somewhere out here was the enemy he had fought before, a creature both more and less than human. Somewhere at the edge of vision was the death-pale face that had summoned him at the runestone. And somewhere in the shadows was Erik Larssen.

At the end of its passageway the churchyard door gaped open. Beyond it each cross, each gravestone, was the shadowy heart of a rising spire of mist touched by the magic of the setting moon. Between farm and church was a sea of pallid smoke. The mound had all but vanished. In its place stood a flickering column of white and silver, ringed by sentinel shadows. For one terrible moment he remembered the evil of the witch-burnings, and seemed to see a devouring flame that masked the obscenity of death by fire. But there was no sound, no colour, no warmth – and no victim. What he saw was as old as the mound itself: a shadowy hill raised on pillars of darkness to reveal the pale, cheerless light of another world . . .

But the pillars were alive.

The demons. Oh Christ, the demons at the mouth of hell . . .

Each pillar, each flickering shadow, was a living creature shrouded in mist and balefire, burning with icy flame. And there were others, dozens of them, all around him.

Alvar . . . !

He had expected human shapes; he saw shapeless shadows cloaked in silver. He had expected an enemy he could fight with his bare hands, but these creatures seemed to belong to another dimension. He had expected a focus for his anger – and found the terror of the unknown.

'*Du! Løb nu, eller dø!*' A single, implacable figure stood

silhouetted between him and the mound, half-crouched, clutching a crude weapon in both hands – and all around it swarmed the alvar.

'I came to help, you asshole!' His own voice sounded cracked.

'I said *run*! Run or die! There's nothing you can do!' Roaring his defiance, Erik Larssen struck out at his opponents – and Brockman saw that his weapon was a heavy iron crucifix wrenched from one of the graves. But the old man was alone, and the shadow-creatures were surrounding him. It seemed impossible that he could hold them off by himself, unless ...

Iron. That's it! They can't bear the touch of iron!

Understanding came too late. On every side the living corpse-candles that were the alvar moved silently towards him.

Nothing to be scared of. How the hell can they hurt me? They're not even real ...

He stumbled at the edge of a grave-plot. Sharp pain lanced up his left arm. As he staggered to his feet he realised it was numb, useless, hanging at his side like so much dead meat.

Must've caught it on something. Terrific timing, Brockman.

Light arced across the nearby gravestones, and he stumbled again as his right ankle twisted awkwardly on the gravel. He could walk, but only just: his leg felt as if it ended at the knee. And the alvar were still advancing.

That light – like a flash of lightning. But all I did was twist my ankle. It couldn't be ...

To his left, at the edge of vision, the ghostly shadow of an arm shimmered like a rippling reflection in a clear pool. He whirled to face it, but his leg crumpled beneath him and he fell headlong, grabbing at a tombstone to save himself. In the same instant an after-image of silver fire seemed to cut across the stone. It cracked with a sound like breaking timber.

'Jesus!'

Larssen's battle was all too real. The alvar were deadly

adversaries – and Brockman was surrounded. Pale fila-
ments of light flickered around the advancing shadow-
creatures, casting a shimmering network of blue-edged
shadows. The air crackled with power – and he was
helpless, defenceless. All about him were visions out of
nightmare: the spectral figures of approaching alvar, the
other-worldly light from the mound, and the memory of a
medieval fresco where pygmies ran in aimless panic,
naked, powerless, searching for somewhere to hide ...

The light changed.

Silver became copper, the supernatural glow of the
new moon in the old moon's arms. Blue-silver fire flared
in response, and he rolled behind a tombstone as it
scorched the grass where he had stood. A tawny column
of red-gold flame soared up from the mound, flooding the
churchyard with light and throwing deep, rich shadows
all around. It was the warm, familiar light of smithy and
forge, hearth and homestead, but amidst the silver and
shadow of the churchyard it was dazzling. In its light the
quivering flames of the attacking alvar seemed to shrink,
half uncloaking the shadow-creatures they concealed. He
glimpsed ruddy highlights on inhuman limbs. He met the
hooded glimmer of golden eyes – demons' eyes – and in
that frozen moment saw the distorted mirror-image of his
own fear. Whatever this was, the alvar were afraid of it ...

At the crest of the mound, the fire roared outward in a
widening circle that centred on the runestone – but there
were gaps in the circle, and now he could see that the
red-gold flames concealed dark, shadowy figures ...

A twisting jet of fire lashed out into the churchyard,
flaring into yellow-green as it struck the flickering blue-
silver nimbus of a fleeing alv. For a moment the form it
veiled was laid bare, and Brockman felt his eyes widen
with shock. What he had seen was more like the embodiment of an ancestral nightmare than anything real –
a sculpted tomb-guardian or a Harpy transmuted from
stone to moving, half-decaying flesh – but it was already
gone. With a thin, eerie wail the shadow melted into

coppery flame like a candle in a furnace. Then it vanished, as a network of blue light and red fire spread a crackling spider's web of power all across the churchyard.

Mist and bale-fire vanished like gossamer, lost in a silent, dazzling tumult of fire and shadow that baffled the eye. It was a new battle: a battle between equals, a battle where he and Larssen had no place. But there was no way they could escape from it. They were trapped in a labyrinth of flame. He saw Larssen raise the iron crucifix like a battle-scarred banner – saw it catch and seemingly hold a deadly blast of raw energy till it glowed with a pallid light of its own. Larssen staggered and fell to his knees in the shelter of another stone as a tongue of red fire arced across his head and found its mark among the alvar ranks. Beyond him, as if in a dream, Brockman saw the ancient runestone writhing with light, as if it alone were the source of the savage energies all around them. But now the circle was closing, contracting inwards, as though the mound were calling back its own. The battle was no less furious than before, but its fires looked insubstantial and other-worldly, a vision half-glimpsed through a distorting mirror. The stone flared again, and for an instant there seemed to be a hideous, misshapen figure at its very heart. Then the world exploded in a silent cataclysm of light.

When he could see again, all that remained of the supernatural battle was a dazzling series of after-images – and the shadowy figure of the man he had come to rescue, still holding his makeshift weapon at the guard.

'Larssen?'

'Who the hell are you?' Larssen showed no sign of lowering the crucifix, and his voice was still sharp with a hatred that Brockman understood all too well. Once he had found it in himself. Now, trembling with reaction, he could see its futility. He staggered to his feet, his arm and leg still numb. 'Name's Brockman. Peter Brockman. Occupation seems to be saving your life.'

'Don't bother.'

'Damn right. You have a talent for killing yourself.'

'What the hell is that supposed to mean?'

'We met yesterday morning – right here. At the time you seemed to be rather more dead than alive.'

'*You*! You took me into the house?'

'Got it in one.'

'You shouldn't get involved. You don't know what's happening –'

'Correction. I know *most* of what's happening. You've been out of it a long time.'

Larssen hesitated. 'But Anja, Kristine – they'd never –'

'They had to. You and I should compare notes. Unless those dime-store demons are coming back.'

'Not yet. They've already risked too much.'

'Fine. What the hell are they? What do they want?'

'*Svartalvar* – the ones who attacked us. The others, the *liosalvar* – I'm not sure. I suppose they were trying to help.'

'Hurray for our side. Can we get indoors now? Not that I feel the cold, but I like the idea of a nice solid wall between me and your friends.'

Larssen grimaced. 'It won't help. They – What's that?'

'Huh?'

'There. By the gate.' He gestured with the incongruous crucifix. For a moment Brockman saw the unmistakable silhouette of an alv framed in the dark gateway between churchyard and farm – the slender limbs, the glimmer of golden eyes . . .

'Erik?' The voice was Anja's, and he felt a pang of jealousy that Larssen's name had been first on her lips. 'Peter, are you all right?'

'We're alive,' said Brockman, 'more or less. What the hell are you doing here?'

'I brought this.' A thin shaft of moonlight flashed across her body and upwards into a formal salute.

A fencing foil? She must be out of her head . . .

'You little fool!' roared Larssen. 'This isn't a game!'

'And this, Erik, this is not a toy – I know how to use it.

Don't you understand? We want to help you!'

'So who's *he*?' The edge in Larssen's voice was all too obvious.

'Peter is –'

'Your lover? I should have guessed. After all, I've been away a long time.'

Pity choked Brockman's rising anger. *My God. He doesn't know. He doesn't know that for her it's been just one night . . .*

Anja stepped hesitantly into the light, reaching out a hand to her cousin. She looked younger than ever, her face full of the open, utterly vulnerable love that belonged to Erik Larssen, and to him alone. Larssen took one step towards her, then froze.

'Your face. You look . . .'

'Erik, don't. Please don't . . .'

He seemed to be looking through her, beyond her, to some distant horizon. When he moved again he was walking like an old man, stumbling towards the house as if she were no longer there. As he reached the gate he hesitated, staring at the broken-off crucifix as though he had never seen it before. Then, with something approaching reverence, he propped it carefully against the wall.

In the moonlight, Anja's face was glistening with tears, and when Brockman slipped an arm around her shoulders she scarcely noticed. 'Come on,' he murmured, 'we'd best follow him.'

She nodded vaguely, sliding the untipped foil into a loop in her belt with unnecessary concentration.

'Anja, what the hell else could you do? He had to know some time.'

She glanced up with an expression that mingled horror and pity. 'You did not see his face. Never shall I forget it. As if all that mattered was gone.'

And you're still in love with him. He managed not to say it, but his jealousy was harder to control. *Damnation, I'm no better. Kristine was right – every time I look at her I think of Sarah.* 'Where's Kristine?'

'She is – indoors. She told me that iron can drive the alvar away, and I thought . . .'

'You thought. Me, I just reacted. And I called *you* stupid.'

'It is not important.' She paused by the gate, turning into his arms as she linked her hands behind his head. 'But I wish you to promise me something.'

'Whatever you say.'

'That next time you will not leave me behind.'

He laughed, despite himself. 'I wouldn't dare.'

Her smile was brave rather than joyful as she drew him down into a lingering kiss that filled his mouth with warmth and the salt of her tears. But as her head sank onto his shoulder he saw Kristine standing in the doorway to the kitchen – and Larssen slumped in her arms, his head pressed against her chest like a frightened child while she ran trembling fingers through his lank, grizzled hair. Her face was in shadow, but her voice carried a gentle strength that made a nonsense of age and time alike.

'*Velkommen hjem, min dreng.* Welcome home, Erik.'

'He has changed,' said Kristine, 'but that I expected. He has spent too long in the other world.'

The oil lamp shone from the kitchen window like a beacon, defying the darkness of the churchyard beyond. More than ever the farm felt like a strongpoint awaiting the attack of besieging forces. Inside, Kristine was the only one who seemed calm. Brockman's arm and leg were burning with slow fire, and Anja's embrace was more like a plea for reassurance.

'But *Mormor*, he is like a stranger! I don't know him any more!'

Kristine nodded slowly. 'In a little while, perhaps, he will again learn to be among men and women. But he will need all the love, all the care, we can give him.'

'He makes me feel so helpless, *Mormor*. I can dress his wounds, but when I speak to him I think he doesn't hear me.'

91

'Listening is better, *pigebarn*. When he is ready, Erik will talk to us – and when he talks, that will heal the wounds you cannot see.'

Brockman frowned. 'And that's it? End of story?'

'So impatient, Hr Brockman!' The old woman smiled with gentle mockery. 'If there is more, we shall know soon enough.'

'You can just bet there is,' said Brockman. 'He told me so himself.'

Kristine nodded slowly. '*Så*. Again five hundred years have passed, and again come the alvar to make their evil in the world. *Du godeste*, that it should happen in our lifetime!'

'You know something about this?'

'Of course she does,' said Anja sharply.

'*Rolig*, Anja. A little I know, Hr Brockman, but not all. Always there have been times when human power was not enough to stop the alvar – times when the demons walked abroad for their harvest of souls. I think such a time is coming, and we must make ourselves ready for it.'

'You're right,' said a voice from the doorway.

Anja paled. 'Erik! Sit down! You shouldn't be out of bed!'

'I don't have the time, Anja. I need to talk to Kristine.' He stared hard at Brockman. 'As for you, you'd better leave. Quickly. And if you really love Anja, take her with you.'

Brockman shook his head. 'I'm in too deep.'

'Then you're a bloody fool, but that's your business. Anja is mine. You should go, Anja. Go now.'

'No. Erik. I stay with Peter. And – with you.'

He laughed. There was a world of bitterness in the sound. 'Well, maybe it's best. You'll die a little sooner.'

Brockman felt her flinch back into his arms, and for a moment he hated Larssen. 'You bastard! What is it with you? You *like* hurting her?'

'That will do, Hr Brockman,' said Kristine firmly. 'Erik, we know the stone is a gateway to the twilight – and that the alvar use it also. But why do they hunt you? And what has become of Eleanor and little Bjørn?'

Brockman saw naked pain in the older man's face. 'I saw them. Talked with them. And now they're lost – lost for ever.'

Brockman frowned. 'You mean the alvar have them?'

'No. They're dead. They've been dead a long time.'

'But hell's teeth, Larssen, if you *talked* to them –'

'Hr Brockman,' said Kristine with the slightest hint of reproach, 'we have little time. Erik, you shall tell me all that happened when you went to the stone. The alvar are not all-powerful, but I need to understand *everything*. Else they will destroy us, and waste all that you have done.'

Larssen sighed and nodded slowly. For a moment Brockman saw a glimmer of courage in the ruined face – courage, or that same fanatical hatred that had almost driven the man to his death ...

'All right. It happened after we found the second stone – the buried one. Remember how I locked myself in my room? I had everything there – everything we'd found. I spent most of the night thinking about it, and got nowhere. Funny thing – the moon came up, and caught Eleanor's pendant; I'd left it by the bed. And I *knew*. It was so simple! The stone was the gate – and the pendant was the key. I just had to do what I'd been told to do. I just had to go to the stone ...'

* * *

Hesitantly, almost reverently, Erik Larssen reached out to touch the ancient runestone.

Its granite surface was cool and grainy beneath his hand, and he imagined a faint, throbbing surge of power that was surely no more than his own pulse. In the darkness of the churchyard he could hardly see anything, but his fingers sensed every slightest mark, every dint of the maker's chisel. On this side, where witch-fires had ravaged and blackened the stone, there was no other way to rediscover the forgotten craftsman's work. Closing his eyes, he tried to piece together the image that was taking shape beneath his hands.

Here a spreading web of lines, opening like a flower – or a tree. Below it, unmistakably, a human figure. He could pick out head, arms, and legs, but the face was curious. He found a mouth, twisted into a grinning rictus, but there was another line as well, curved like a protruding tongue. The nose was a crude gash. On one side, but not the other, he found an eye.

I should have guessed. Odin – Odin on the tree.

He had known the legend as long as he could remember: how Odin, the one-eyed lord of the Aesir, had suffered ritual sacrifice, hung and speared on the ash Yggdrasil, to master the magic that would open the gates of death. But here, below the image, someone had carved a runic inscription. With trembling fingers he traced it out, sensing a power that even its maker might never have guessed.

Með. With.

Run. The rune.

Hangins. Of the hanged one.

Opnask. Is opened.

Dyrrinn. The door.

Til. To.

Lifs. Life.

Uendeligs. Eternal.

With the rune of the hanged one is opened the door to life eternal.

He almost smiled. The Vikings had never really lost their faith in the old gods: this was a typically ambiguous inscription. Both meanings were clear to anyone with the necessary knowledge, but no Christian could possibly object – 'the hanged one' might be Christ or Odin. But what was 'the rune of the hanged one' if it was not the sign of the cross?

The answer lay under his fingers. There was no denying the familiar shape.

Three triangles. Three intertwined triangles, the

endless knot that was the sign of Odin and of eternity. The same sign that he held in his hand, the last precious relic of Eleanor. Breathing a silent prayer, he pressed the pendant into the faint impression on the stone.

There was no response. The stone was inert, as it had always been. Once again he had given rein to his hope, and once again he felt the bitterness of failure . . .

Something snapped at his fingers like static discharge from a steel guardrail. Instinctively he snatched away his hand. The even, granular surface of the stone was flickering, as if it were beaded with a thousand tiny points of light. A pale, luminous mist clouded his vision, throwing faint shadows all around the churchyard – and within it narrow lines of blue fire seemed to flow out and upwards from the stone like the branches of a clambering vine. It was almost as though the solid granite were melting away from a tree-like core of shimmering energy, energy that snaked gently outwards towards the silver pendant in his hand . . .

Power exploded through his body, power beyond imagining. For a long count of seconds he was blind, dazzled by coruscating after-images. The shock had thrown him flat on his face, and even when his eyes cleared he lay still, trembling with reaction, too shaken to understand what had happened or why. His fingers touched frost-brittle grass. His cheek was moist with dew. It seemed, for a moment, that nothing had changed, that he lay on the mound in the churchyard with the old farm just out of sight over the crest – but he could hear nothing at all except the quick, uneven rhythm of his own breathing.

What happened to me?

He tried to get up, but it was hard to catch his breath, and his arms and legs would not respond properly. He rolled helplessly onto his side.

Lightning. Must have been. But where did it come from . . .?

He glanced up. Tendrils of cloud half-obscured the stars – cloud where there had been none before – and something was wrong with the sky.

Maybe I passed out – lost track of time.

It was a faint hope, and he clung to it despite a growing sense of strangeness and unease, battling the cold fear that kept his eyes locked on the stone. Slowly, reluctantly, he allowed himself to see what he could not yet believe or understand.

Beyond the dark spiral of the clouds, ribbons of brilliance spread across the heavens: stars by the thousand, by the myriad, spiralling to infinity. And beneath them, bathed in a strange, steely twilight, lay a silent, alien world of barren hills marching endlessly towards a dark horizon, half-hidden from his view by the tangled shadows of a wood that stretched as far as he could see.

His hand was bleeding. The fall had driven one spiked tip of the pendant deep into his flesh. Till now he had barely noticed the wound, but somehow it was reassuring: wherever he was, this was still a world where he could bleed, feel pain, perceive cause and effect. He stared at the red-stained metal – the key to infinity, in the palm of his hand. But where did it lead? Where should he go?

Go to the stone . . .

It was there, still, the only familiar object in a nightmare landscape – but the terrible light of this other world had robbed the ancient stone of its age. Hard-edged, sharp-shadowed, it seemed a thing newly made. And beyond it lay an almost tangible darkness, as if the stone itself marked the border of twilight.

His legs refused to carry him. He crawled on his hands and knees, lowering his eyes from the alien sky, and sprawled against the base of the stone with the pendant still clasped in his bloodied hand. For time without measure he lay numbed and helpless, staring at the three silver triangles in their endless, eternal knot. He was no stranger to loneliness, but this was something more – he had stumbled into a world that did not know him and had no place for him, a lifeless, silent dimension which his mind could not yet encompass. Yet somewhere, some-where *here*, he had to believe that he would find his wife and his son.

'Can't just sit here ...' Talking to himself, now, like a child – like the lonely, childless man he had once been. His voice sounded strangely flat in the dead air.

How strait the gate ...

The stone was the gate – a single stone, like the battered image on the chest in his bedroom. The thought gave him new strength, and he scrambled to his feet, supporting himself against the stone. Its shape was comfortingly familiar, but there was something wrong about it, something different ...

Sudden terror filled him as he ran his hands over the rugged granite, searching every ridge and hollow. There were no carvings – no runes, no figures, no symbols, and nothing to show they had ever existed. He was trapped – lost forever in a place beyond life, beyond hope, beyond understanding ...

There was a darker shadow against the darkness. And then another. And another. The stone – his stone – was only one of many. He stood at the edge of a vast circle.

Ship burials ...

The image was unforgettable: evening sunshine in northern Jutland, a salt-tasting sea breeze, and an endless vista of ancient burial places scattered down a long slope to the glittering waters of the Limfjord. Around each shallow mound a long, narrow oval of stones, like the outline of a Viking ship. Bjørn, five years old, playing among the stones. Eleanor in his arms, warm, alive, passionate ...

But now he stood alone – and if this were a ship burial, then the mound itself must be vast beyond imagining. What had Kristine called the runestone? *Den gangende sten* – the walking stone. She had told him how the stone moved with the passing centuries in an endless circle around the mound. To see it like this he had to be standing outside time itself. It was like stories he had read

97

long ago, as a student – stories of the Tuatha Dé Danann, the Celtic gods, of entire worlds contained within ancient mounds and tumuli, of a place where time had no meaning . . .

Avalon. Valhalla. Where the heroes go – where no one ever dies . . .

That was what his ancestors had believed. Those stones by the Limfjord had been built as gateways to an eternal world of twilight.

Then this is the twilight world – the place of the alvar, Alvheim itself. Outside time, beyond the fields we know. 'As to one born out of his proper time.' Was that what you meant, damn you? Did you mean me to find this place? So what about the rest? What else were you trying to tell me? Each clue, each phrase, was burned into his mind. To remember them was easy – but to understand them, even here, even now, that was something else.

How strait the gate, and narrow the path . . .

The stone was the gate, but where was the path? In the darkness beyond the stone it was impossible to see anything at all – but there, surely, lay his answer. Outside the circle was nothing but thorn, thicket and trackless wilderness, an abomination of desolation. His path must lie within, inside the ring of stones, onward towards the mystery at the heart of the mound.

He climbed ever more steeply, till the stone and the encircling wood vanished in the gathering gloom. The silence was complete: all sight and sound of life was lost, except the ragged rhythm of his own breath and the distant, echoing drumbeat of his labouring heart. On either side, dimly, he could see what might be the outlines of other paths, parallel with this one yet never meeting it.

How strait the gate, and narrow the path . . .

The sense was clear: to leave the path, even for a moment, might bring eternal loss. But already he had climbed so long that time itself was meaningless. The mound he had known was a shallow tumulus, beaten and weathered by countless winters, yet the trackway seemed unending, a ribbon spiralling towards infinity. His world had become an endless struggle with aching and protesting limbs, an endless effort to discern the narrow limits of the path, and an endless battle with his own imagination.

As a child he had lived in fear of the dark. As an adult he had buried those childhood nightmares almost, but not quite, beyond recall. Now, in the silence and the darkness, they were returning. There, just at the edge of vision, was the shadow-creature of his first remembered dream, a shapeless emanation concealed in every doorway, every cupboard, every hidden place of the sprawling house where his mother had died. Slowly, almost imperceptibly, it was sucking out his life: paralysing tired limbs, darkening his failing sight, silencing the tumult of his thoughts. Soon his last resistance would die – and then, finally, he would see the true shape of his own destruction . . .

No. It's not real. It's not real!

In growing desperation he rallied other, kinder memories to battle his fear: Bjørn in the sunlit garden at Egerød, scrambling in the old cherry tree while he and Eleanor sheltered in its shade. Imagination brought the touch of long, slim fingers twined in his hair, warm breath against his cheek, a cool hand drawing him gently into a passionate embrace. But here, in the twilight world, sunshine had no reality: it was a child's distortion of the starlight beyond the circle of time, and starlight itself was a half-forgotten dream.

As memory failed, so did his senses. Faintly, like the whispering of a sea breeze, came the distant echoes of his own gasping breath – yet somewhere, somewhere close by, was the ghost of another sound like the panting of a horse at the end of its strength, or a wolf weary from the hunt. Dimly, at the edge of vision, the outline of another path compelled his attention, and a shadow that might or might not be his own. And then, without warning, a figure blocked his way. It seemed human, but the cloaking darkness masked its true shape – he saw only hooded, golden eyes that glittered with unnatural radiance . . .

'Far have you come, Erik son of Lars.'

The voice was very nearly human; the language was a guttural Danish. For a moment Erik struggled for words. Somehow the habit of speech had deserted him.

'What – are you?'

'What is it that I seem to be?'

'This – this is *your* place?'

The creature made a sound that was close to laughter.

'This place belongs to none, son of Lars, and to me least of all. You went to the stone, as you were bidden. You found the gateway and the path, as you were bidden. And now, at last, I show myself to you – as to one born out of his proper time.'

'*You . . .!*'

'A thousand years have passed in your world, son of Lars. Many times we have crossed the borders of twilight. Many times we have moved the minds and the hands of men to make the signs and the symbols that brought you here. But now, at last, you come.'

Suddenly Erik was too weak to stand. His legs gave way beneath his weight, and he sank down onto the path. 'Where are they? Where are my wife and my son?'

'They are safe, and waiting for you. Your journey is almost over.'

'But *why*? I *must* understand –!'

'There is no time. Already you are dying.'

'No! I must keep to the path!'

'It has brought you to me, as was meant. Now you must follow me or perish. Will you lose everything at the final throw?'

'I *have* to go on –',

'You fool! The years, it is they you have climbed with each step of the path! Such stairs were never meant for creatures that bow before Time's sceptre. Come with me and climb no further – or crawl onward into your grave!'

For a moment Erik glimpsed the embodiment of nightmare – the shape of a destroyer framed in silver and shadow, its long, fine-clawed fingers reaching hungrily to suck out his soul. Then it turned away into the darkness. He hesitated – and then followed, blindly, no longer certain where he was, or where he was going, stumbling exhaustedly downwards in the wake of a half-seen silhouette, listening to words that drifted out of the twilight like memories of a dream.

'In the beginning, son of Lars, light and dark were created from the void. In the skies the starlight battles everlasting night – and beyond the circle of time and the Ironwood that guards it, light and dark battle everlastingly throughout the nine realms. There is one called Kialar. He would bring darkness to the circle, and make your world his plaything. He it was who stole your wife and your child.'

'Why?'

'He sought a joining of the world outside the circle and the world within it – your world. He hoped for the birth of one who might be like his kind and yours – together, in a single flesh.'

'But where are Eleanor and Bjørn? What's happened to them?'

'They are where they have always been.'

'What the hell are you saying?'

The shadow-creature turned, and for a moment he saw the glimmer of its eyes in the darkness – that, and a trembling, pallid nimbus ...

'Look within yourself, son of Lars. Look into your thinking!'

He frowned helplessly. 'I – I don't understand.'

'They are *here*, son of Lars! They are with you now! They live in your memories and your thoughts and your dreams – and I have brought you to that place where only dreams have substance, and all else is the shadow of a shadow!'

The inhuman eyes seemed to shimmer with a deeper, paler light, like beacons on a distant hilltop.

'Dream, son of Lars – dream, and remember!'

Somewhere deep in his mind a doorway opened – a doorway into the past. Images flickered into life, disjointed at first, then increasingly vivid: images of Eleanor, of Bjørn, of places they had been, of things they had done; images of love and pain and longing; images of joy and mystery; images of the son who had loved darkness and shadows; images of the farm at Egerød where he had brought Eleanor in the first happiness of their love. Here Bjørn had come into the world – and here they had returned, again and again, like faithful pilgrims marking the passage of another year . . .

'Your eyes, son of Lars. Open them.'

'I – don't see –'

'*Think!* You are master here! All depends on you!'

Again the images flashed through his mind – and now he saw a deeper shadow against the darkness. Shapes emerged – familiar shapes, seen in a light like the first sunrise of a new-made world. The gate stone – eternal, changeless – cut the horizon in two; and beyond it the frost-whitened thatch of the farmhouse glittered like a precious casket. Above it the sky was clear and hard, an iron helmet studded with myriads of diamonds.

'They are waiting, son of Lars. You have only to go to them.'

Erik hesitated, new hope battling with tiredness and fear.

'Go *now*! The gate you have opened is already closing!'

'It isn't real. It *can't* be –'

'Would you lose them for ever! *Run*, or they are lost beyond all hope!'

'Eleanor? Bjørn?'

'They cannot hear you, son of Lars! You must *go*!'

Suddenly he was running, his legs buckling beneath him as he stumbled down the last, grassy slope, between the shadows of the stones, towards the open door of the farmyard. Inside, dark shapes on icy cobblestones made a ghostly and distorted shadow-play – a young child clinging to the skirts of a slim, slight woman . . .

'Eleanor?' His voice was no more than a whisper. Surely this was another dream, an image that would vanish like all the rest . . .

'Erik? It is . . . you?'

Her voice. Her words . . .

His mouth was dry. He could no longer speak. He dared not move – he felt that if he did, everything around him would fade back into the darkness that had given it birth.

'Erik? Don't be afraid. All is what it should be.'

She stood silhouetted in the doorway, just beyond the rune-carved step into the kitchen. And behind her the boy clung to his mother's hand, staring out into the courtyard, saying nothing.

'Erik, have you no word for your own son?'

'Bjørn?' he croaked. 'It's really you?'

'Come and see,' she said. 'Come in and see.'

For a moment he could not believe; but his need was too great. It had to be true. He could feel the cobbles beneath his feet, chill with frost. He could see the faint mist of his own breath. The farm was just as it had always been, would always be . . .

He stepped across the threshold into the warmth and the light of his dreams.

'Where is this place?'

'It is the place that always you have sought,' she murmured. She snuggled closer into his arms, her fingers stroking his beard, the warmth of her breath on his cheek. 'Always you have asked where I came from. Now I have brought you here, to me, for ever.'

'For ever? You – you *mean* that?'

'Before you were born, I loved you. Now you shall never die.'

'I – don't understand.'

'You have entered the stone, as I never dared to hope that you would. Time has no hold on you any more. Here there is no time. There is only life, and love, and twilight.'

'Who – *are* you?'

She laughed softly. 'I am what I have always been. I am the shadow behind these eyes that sees the shadow behind yours. But twilight is the birthplace of shadows.'

'This place ... It's the farm, but there's something –'

'It is the farm as you have made it. As you will it to be, so it is. You have great power here, Erik.'

'And – outside?'

'Outside is the Watcher.'

'The Watcher?'

'It guards all paths, all gateways into time. It is more terrible than you can imagine.'

'But how did you –?'

'I found you at peril of my very life – and you have risked the same. Would you have come, if you had known?'

'You know I would. Don't you realise how much I love you?'

She smiled with a joyous warmth that bubbled into laughter. 'Erik, shall you never learn that there are better things than words?'

He laughed in turn, grappling with her in a mock-battle that slipped inexorably into loveplay. He could barely control his passion – he had never known her so responsive, so aware of his needs and his secret desires – and when she laid her head beside his on the pillow and huddled her small body into his arms, her face was full of love.

There's something about her – something different. As if she finally understands me, and I understand her. As though I never really loved her till now ...

There was no evening, and no morning. When he opened his eyes, nothing had changed: the window was filled with the myriad stars of the twilight world. Yet this was home, as no place in the world of time had ever been. Only its perfection troubled him. The roofs were thick with new thatch, and the smell of it was heavy in the air. Every stone, every gable-end and window-frame, every door and window-sill looked clean and freshly made, glistening like cobblestones after a spring shower ...

Except that here there were no rainstorms, no seasons, no nights, and no days – only the endless, drifting wheel of cloud over the mound.

Yet it was enough. If the churchyard door was closed, then that was as it should be – and if the double doors out to the drive were also barred, he was content to walk within the courtyard. Sometimes there were hints of a world beyond the farm. Looking from the windows into the darkness of the shadowlands he would see huddled shapes moving just beyond the reach of his light. Sometimes he would hear the distant cries of unknown creatures in the vast and mysterious Ironwood, but his curiosity never lasted more than a moment. The farm gave him everything he needed – a home he had known since his earliest childhood, and the company of the two people he loved best in the world, for all eternity.

But for all his contentment, there were shadows in his mind: thoughts of Anja and Kristine, aging and dying in a world beyond his reach; and thoughts of the Watcher, fearful thoughts like the memory of childhood nightmares ...

'Daddy ...'

'Mm?'

'Daddy, where do shadows go when you take the light away?'

Erik smiled. 'Where do you think they go?'

'Sometimes they hide. In my picture.'

'You mean the one that mummy made you?' It was beautiful hand embroidery, Eleanor's own work, showing a ring of tiny elves circling a bewildered-looking caterpillar. 'Maybe the shadows go dancing. With the elves.'

'It isn't like that, daddy. When you turn the light out,

the elves go away. Then the shadows come. I can see them moving. I don't like it.'

'You needn't be frightened, Biarki. You've got your candle here if you want it. They can't hurt you.'

'Please don't leave me, daddy! Please don't ever leave me!'

Remembering the remorseless terrors of his own childhood, his heart went out to the boy.

'Of course I won't leave you. I'll be right next door. If anything happens. I'll be with you before you know it. And here's your sword. Keep that by your bedside and *nothing* can hurt you ...'

He could not remember finding the halberd – could only remember hanging it above his bed as if it had always belonged there. Once, in the half-forgotten worlds of time, Kristine had told him that an ancient weapon lay hidden in the house. She had never told him where, but he knew its legend. Long ago, or so the story went, it had been the sword of a great champion who died in battle. His mother kept the sword, vowing vengeance on the enemies who had killed him, but the hilts were twisted and broken beyond hope of repair. And so, at her bidding, the blade was fashioned into a new weapon – a long, razor-edged spearhead mounted on a rune-carved staff. It was said that the halberd had passed from mother to daughter all down the generations, and with it another story – a story that only women might know ...

Sometimes, when he needed to be alone, he would take the halberd out to the old barn. There, in darkness and solitude, he would strike at mounds of straw or balks of timber, battling with the strange sense of frustration and hopelessness that still haunted him. When the dark mood took him the perfection around him palled, and he longed for the busy noises of the city, for the company of other human beings, for the things of time that had no place in twilight. Yet every thought of them seemed like a betrayal ...

He no longer needed sleep, but when he made love with Eleanor it came without his bidding. Despite his growing unease, she seemed softer, even more loving than at first. Her little quirks of speech remained, but the emptiness had gone from her eyes. Bjørn was changing, too. More and more the boy began to seem like Erik's younger self, troubled by the dark world beyond the farm, happy to remain within its walls, bookish and serious as Erik himself had been. There were many books: Erik was constantly finding something he had read long before, in the old world, and all but forgotten. If reading tired him, he would talk with Eleanor. But she never spoke of what lay beyond the farmhouse, and he was increasingly aware of the shadowlands and the nameless creatures that lived there. Once he heard a hideous snarling in the outer darkness, and the cry of some being in mortal terror. When he found Eleanor she was crouched in a corner with Bjørn in her arms.

'What was that? Why are you frightened?'

'It was the Watcher! Just outside! If it finds us . . .!'

'Why should it trouble us?'

'You don't understand!'

'Then *help* me. Why are you so afraid of it? As long as we stay here . . .'

'Yes,' she said. 'You're right. It cannot harm us here . . .'

But the fear and uncertainty had not left her face. For some reason, a reason she would not share with him, she was terrified of the Watcher . . .

In the barn, he made bales of straw into horrors out of shadow, striking at them, scattering them, imagining the shock of steel cutting into flesh, imagining the dying screams of the creature that Eleanor feared. He had found a book of sixteenth-century prints that showed the proper use of his weapon, and now he set about mastering his skills, conscious of a growing fear that he might be called upon to use them. Increasingly he was troubled by cries and whispers from the shadowlands. He lived in a world without time, yet it seemed that time was passing in a slow, returning cycle – and each cycle brought the threat of the Watcher a little closer ...

'Don't you know how much I love you?'

'Erik, shall you never learn that there are better things than words ...?'

'Please don't leave me, daddy! Please don't ever leave me!'

'Of course I won't leave you. I'll be right next door. If anything happens, I'll be with you before you know it. And here's your sword. Keep that by your bedside and *nothing* can hurt you ...'

Thrust. Parry. Strike – on guard. That's it. And that's one for the Watcher ...

A voice woke him – a guttural voice that he half-recognised. He often heard voices out in the shadowlands, but there was something different about this one.

It was calling his name.

Eleanor lay fast asleep at his side, and he could see the light from Bjørn's candle throwing long, flickering shadows across the kitchen.

'Erik! Erik Larssen!'

Slowly, carefully, he slipped out of the bed, taking the halberd down from the wall. No need to disturb Eleanor or Bjørn – but if someone out there knew his name, he needed to talk to them ...

'Erik Larssen!'

At first he thought there was someone in the courtyard – someone lost on the maze of paths around the mound who had stumbled, like him, on this secret enclave. But there was no new shadow on the frost-rimed cobbles outside. The voice was coming from beyond the wall – but close by, closer than anyone or anything had ever come before.

He dressed hastily, wrapped himself in the coat that hung by the door, and strode out into the courtyard.

'*Erik!*'

The churchyard door. The voice was just beyond it. All he had to do was walk down the passage, open the door . . .

Perhaps it was the Watcher. Perhaps it had found them at last. Perhaps, like other supernatural creatures, it had to be invited across the threshold . . .

He walked slowly, uncertainly. He could not remember the last time he had been in the passage. His footsteps seemed to echo strangely.

'*Erik. Open the door.*'

He hesitated, his fingers poised on the heavy iron handle.

'Daddy?'

'Bjørn! What are you doing here! You should be asleep!'

'I heard something outside. I'm frightened.'

'*Erik!*'

'Daddy, *please*! I need you!'

'Yes. Yes, of course. But first I must . . . I must –'

Without understanding why, he wrenched open the door.

A rising wave of clouds was blotting out the sky, and the doorway framed a silent shadow-world traced out in mist and starlight. The mound was a vast, crouching darkness – but something at its crest seemed to catch and hold a flickering gleam of gold.

'Please shut the door, daddy! I don't like it here!'

'*Erik! You must not do as he asks! This is not your son – it is only a dream of your son . . .*'

'Please, daddy!'

Trembling, Erik shut the door.

Oh God, if there is a God, tell me it isn't true – this can't be true . . .

'Come with me, Bjørn. Come on. There's nothing to be scared of.'

He left the halberd propped at the entrance to the passageway and carried the boy in his arms, wrapping his own jacket close around him as they passed the kitchen window. For a moment – just a moment – he saw a man's face in the glass, caught in the merciless glare of a dream-light that showed every crease, every wrinkle, every furrow of flesh. It was an old face, hair streaked with grey, eyes and mouth marked with the pain and dis-appointment of a wasted life.

He knew the face. It was his own.

'Erik! If you cling to shadows, you are lost for ever!'

The child moved in his arms, and unthinkingly he reached down to stroke back straying hair. His fingers touched bare, corpse-chill flesh.

'Bjørn ...?'

In the darkness beneath his hands, two glimmers of bronze unfolded into bright, piercing eyes.

'Father ...'

Lustrous, death-cold fingers grasped at his wrist. Long, narrow nails drew tiny beads of blood. The face that stared up at him was emotionless, inhuman – and beyond it, in the doorway, another dark face was watching.

'Did you think me barren, son of Lars? Behold the beauty of your true child!'

'What – are you?'

'I am all you hold dearest, all you most long for. I am yours for ever.'

Briefly, the alien face flickered and was gone. Briefly, the starlit mist around it was a tumble of copper curls framing the elfin face he loved – then darkness returned, and pale flesh became ebony touched with silver, hooding glittering eyes of gold.

'Eleanor!'

'She never loved you as I have done. She never gave you your dreams.'

His dreams ...

How often had he longed for Eleanor to return his

love? How often had he dreamed that the pallid, haunted face was laughing with him in the sunlight of an endless summer? How often had he met the strange, invisible barrier that always lay between them? And now his dreams had betrayed him.

'No!'

Anger and hatred flared within him – hatred of himself, of the creatures who had robbed his dreams, of whatever vile purpose had conceived such deception. The changeling squirmed in his arms, clawing at his chest, and with a groan of revulsion he hurled it towards its mother. For an instant she bared a glistening row of needle-fine teeth, snarling in frustrated fury, and raised her arms as if to strike – then her eyes widened, and she turned and ran as the courtyard, the farm buildings, and all that they contained melted away like summer haze. All around was the tangled wilderness of the Ironwood; and beyond it were other things that blindness or deception had masked from his sight – massive structures silhouetted against the stars, drifting smoke from half-seen encampments, the trailing plumes of starlit banners. To his left, the mound was wreathed in mist and cloud like the dark heart of an eternal storm, with the pale tracks of a hundred paths vanishing into the veiling depths. And behind him . . .

'Erik. Erik Larssen. Look at me!'

Slowly, fearfully, he turned. If this was the Watcher . . .

'You strayed from the path, Erik Larssen.' The figure seemed human, but the cloaking darkness masked its true shape – he saw only hooded, golden eyes that glittered with unnatural radiance.

'Who – are you . . .?'

'This world is not yours. It has left its mark on you.'

'What do you mean?'

'You are older than I had hoped.'

'Older? But . . .'

Once, in another world, his fingers had traced the forgotten handiwork of an ancient craftsman, the runesmith of the gate stone. Now they traced the handiwork of time – a network of wrinkles around narrowed, harsh-set eyes; deep lines of pain across his forehead; furrows that twisted his mouth downwards into a bitter scowl. And suddenly he knew that he was old.

But it isn't possible . . .

In his dream there had been no time, and nothing that could mark its passing. He had thought himself in eternity. At each waking he had looked out on the same dark landscape, felt the same flesh huddled in his arms, heard the small noises of a child at play in the next room. Now, too late, he understood the truth. Gently, imperceptibly, his own dreams had trapped him in an illusion of eternity while each passing year chiselled its own indelible mark on his face and his body. How easily his longing and hope had seduced him from the path! He had left his own world behind him to find the wife he loved – but now, after all his sacrifice, all his pain, he had nothing . . .

'It is not too late, Erik Larssen.'

And now he knew the voice. Once, long years ago, he had heard it on the path, followed it to this very spot . . .

'You!'

'You do not know me –'

'Like hell I don't! You're the one who brought me here – trapped me here!'

Instinctively he reached for the halberd, then cursed his own folly. His weapon was a dream – like the farm, like the images of Eleanor and Bjørn . . .

'I have searched for you, Erik. It is my enemy and yours who has done this –'

He felt a violent surge of anger. 'Oh, no! You don't fool me again. Somewhere out there is my *real* wife – and my real son! Not dreams, not shadows – human beings! I'll find the path again! I'll go back! But there's one thing I need to do first –'

'There is danger, Erik Larssen – the mound has many paths, and the Watcher –'

'The Watcher? Now I *know* you're lying. There *is* no Watcher – that was just a story to keep me here!'

'You have heard many falsehoods, Erik Larssen. That is not one of them.'

'I don't believe you. Why the hell should I? You're going to pay for what you've done – right now!'

His anger surged, out of control. For the first time in his life he felt the burning need to kill, without thought, without mercy. He could imagine the feel of the great halberd in his hands, the impact of its blade on alien flesh – but his hands would be enough. He hurled himself at the shadowy shape of his enemy – only to see it melt away into darkness. His fists struck empty air.

'More illusions? Still afraid to face me?' He narrowed his eyes, straining to see where the shadow-creature had gone – and saw a faint gleam near one of the stones.

The gleam of starlight in alien eyes . . .

So it's heading back to the mound. But this time it won't get away from me . . .

Already he, too, was running, fixing his attention on the stone, knowing he must find the precise path that his enemy had taken. The anger within him burned with unquenchable fury, filling him with a sense of raw power. Before, he had started his climb tired, frightened, and uncertain. Now he believed he could follow the alv to the very crest of the mound, and beyond. But when he passed the stone he was astonished to see the crouching shadow of his enemy barely twenty paces away, half-cloaked in drifting mist.

'Waiting to die?'

'I have told you I am not your enemy, Erik Larssen.'

'The hell you're not! You won't escape me here!'

The golden eyes glittered. 'Then follow – if you can!'

With a breathtaking leap, the alv vanished into the mist, and the sound of its laughter echoed among the stones. Erik swore obscenely and launched himself in pursuit, but the path was harder than he remembered. The first time, darkness had concealed the climb, and fear

113

had worn him down – yet now, already, he could feel the strength trickling from his limbs.

No – not this time. This time I'll have you ...

Mist swirled around him, tumbling in eddying torrents from the distant heights. Ahead, where the path climbed steeply between tumbled heaps of stone, skittering pebbles betrayed his enemy. Erik hurled himself forward with a desperate effort, pain lancing his side – and once again he saw the dark shape of the alv just at the edge of vision. He stopped, half-doubled up, panting for breath.

'Kialar! That your name?'

The alv did not move. 'You are deceived.' The alien voice was faint, mist-muffled. 'I am Niord of the liosalvar. I roused you from the dream-spell. The creature who seduced you from the path, that one is Kialar.'

Erik laughed mirthlessly. 'Try again. I *saw* you. Know you – what you did. If you can die, you're going to.'

The shadowy arm seemed to wave aside Erik's words. 'Kill me, and your lover and your child are lost for ever. Kialar it was who stole them, not I.'

'One reason. Give me one reason to believe that.'

'Kialar is the anarch. He is master of svartalvar, lord of trickery, ruler of dreams and shadows. My shape, that is known to you; but you have never seen me till now. Kialar, I think, took my form in order to lead you aside from the true path, which path we follow now. I tell you, to find woman and boy you must pass the gate a second time. There only I can lead you. So follow if you dare – or die, and with nothing accomplished.'

'Not so bloody fast ...' He felt his anger surge again, bringing new energy to aching and exhausted limbs. The alv was already half-lost in the mist, but he staggered after it, brushing away the moisture that dripped from his hair. His breath was noisy in the blanketing fog but distantly, like the muttering of a ghost, he could still hear the voice of his enemy.

'For all eternity, Erik, dark has warred with light. When my people found the gate, we hoped that here at

114

last was escape and the end of conflict. But in your world, Erik, we are shadows without power or substance.' For the first time he detected an edge of fear in the half-familiar voice. 'Beasts of the field we can master, or minds that are lost in sleep or in darkness – but the realms of time we cannot touch in our proper bodies. It was we, not Kialar, who left the signs that brought you here – and the price was a score of my own folk lost to the Watcher.'

You're lying. Damn you, you're lying!

'Understand this, Erik. Kialar's folk lie all around, in perpetual siege. My people hold the circle, but we are dying. Time kills us as it kills you, and the Watcher brings true death to all that it finds in the circle. Yet only so can we ward your world.'

'Then you've failed,' he croaked. 'Besides. You, Kialar, you're the same . . .' He tripped and fell, bruising his shin on the stony ground, but his hatred drove him on.

'No!' The voice seemed even more distant now. 'But there are many paths; we are too few to watch them all. The dark court are numberless as the stars! We do not know what evil they make in your world – only that they prey on weak and broken minds. They ring this place as the ocean rings the land, ever watchful, ever striving to win the gate, and the mastery of time.'

Erik stumbled again, but now, strangely, he could feel new energy flowing into his limbs. The ground was covered in fist-sized chunks of fallen rock, and he snatched at them, imagining splinters of shattered bone tearing through Kialar's face.

'I'm coming! You hear? Turn and face me!'

He was running now, revelling in his new-found strength, jagged rocks clenched in either hand. His enemy was an outline in the mist, unmoving, seemingly unafraid.

'First you must listen, Erik! Understand what Kialar desires of your son! Then do as you will!'

A gust of wind from the heights blew back the cloaking mist. The creature stood unprotected and alone, a hunched black shadow staring out towards the stars.

Loose stones scattered under Erik's pounding feet.

'Too late –'

Starlight touched the shadow, and it changed before his eyes, dwarfing him as it reached to its full height, arms outstretched to meet him, skin gleaming with an almost metallic lustre, mouth agape, eyes burning with green fire. From somewhere just behind him he heard the alv's last desperate cry.

'The Watcher! Beware the Watcher!'

CHAPTER
5

Hete was onhrered, hordweard oncniow
mannes reorde; naes ðær mara fyrst
freode to friclan. From ærest cwom
oruð aglæcean ut of stane,
hat hildeswat; hruse dynede . . .

Then battle began: the Watcher recognised
the speech of men, nor was more time granted
to ask for friendship. First came
the smoke of the dragon in the stone,
its burning breath; the barrow resounded . . .

Beowulf

'Erik! Run! It will destroy us both!'

The words meant nothing. Facing the Watcher, he was
trapped in the mirrors of its eyes. His limbs no longer
obeyed him. His legs were too long, too slender, too
lacking in power. His arms hung feeble and useless by his
side. His shoulders sloped downwards, leaving his head
unsupported. Around and beyond the ensnaring eyes was
mystery, a baffling mosaic of shadows and starlight. But
within was the light of understanding, even of reason, a
mind like his own, suffering pain like his own . . .

'Follow the path, Erik! *Run,* or all is lost!'

The head turned. He saw, or dreamed that he saw,
curved, dagger-sharp teeth glistening in a lipless grin,
and wide-set nostrils that flared with the scent of living

prey, a monstrous, distorted shape at the same time familiar and totally alien – then the mist rolled down like a smoking exhalation and he ran from his own shadow, ran with the sound of his own heartbeat hammering in his ears, pursued by the echoes of his own gasping breath. Rocks and pebbles scattered and fell before and behind him, and he could not know whether he or his hunter had disturbed them. There was no turning back, yet he dared not leave the path. Blindly, instinctively, he followed its spiralling course downward, ever downward, towards the stones that made up the circle of time, stumbling headlong into the gathering mirk with terror at his heels. Darkness and mist overtook him, veiling the light of the stars till even the ghosts of the distant hills were lost. His world was a haunted circle of mist, plumed with the vapour of his breath. He was running through a labyrinth older than time, pursued by a nightmare older than man.

Shapes loomed out of the darkness – threatening shapes like the frozen outline of the horror that pursued him, shapes that resolved into jagged outcrops of rock or stunted, leafless trees that clawed him with skeletal fingers. Chill droplets of mist ran down his cheeks like forgotten tears. The path itself lay clear before him, though it turned and twisted with a wilful unpredictability. Streams spilled across it, splashing downwards into darkness, but the mist muffled their sound. There was another sound, too – a sound like distant singing, as though far away, just beyond the boundaries of reality, people were dancing out the line of a parallel path. With a shock he remembered the fresco in the church – the dance of death – and the horrific figure that led it.

Then, quite clearly, he heard his pursuer's footfall splashing through a stream. In the mist it was impossible to judge distance or direction – every sound seemed close, and he could see nothing at all. For a moment he hesitated. A mistake could send him straight into the jaws of a nightmare – but he dared not stay where he was. In growing desperation he threw himself forward into the mist at a staggering run.

For a moment the mist-veils parted. In that moment he saw the starlit cliff edge that dropped into darkness inches from his feet – and heard a hideous, deep-throated roar from behind him.

Scylla and Charybdis. Oh Christ . . .

Again he ran, struggling to keep his footing on the treacherous rocks along the cliff-edge, heart pounding, each pluming gasp of his breath seeming to foreshadow that of his pursuer. Mocking veils of mist drifted across his path, concealing and then revealing the dark chasm to his right. Each new step was a gamble – a single mistake would cost him his footing, and probably his life, but he dared not stop. The vile taste of fatigue poisons filled his mouth, and he knew they must be pumping through his overstrained muscles. His legs were already aching, and his lungs were straining against his ribs. Yet fear and need drove him on, slithering across glistening outcrops of smooth rock, splashing across grassy marshland that caught at his feet like clutching hands, stumbling and sliding down treacherous screes. Yet always it seemed that the breath of the Watcher was pursuing him, surrounding him, masking everything that he saw in chill, drifting vapour . . .

A black shape reared out of the mist, and his heart lurched as he saw the squat, muscular legs of the Watcher coiled beneath its body, ready to leap . . .

No. It's a stone. Part of the circle.

He sagged to his knees, gasping to fill his lungs with the air they needed, staring at the stone. His pursuit of the alv and his wild flight from the Watcher had taken him clear across the mound, from one side of the stone circle to the other. There was a kind of comfort in the familiar shape: here was something he had known from his earliest childhood, something that had been a part of his life for as long as he could remember, even though it had kept its greatest secret to the very last. Beyond it lay the thorn-toothed fastnesses of the Ironwood, daring him to enter them, to exchange the known danger at his back for a hundred imagined perils in the deep, entangling darkness ahead. But he could not stay here – and there was only one other option.

He went to the stone.

Beneath his hands the ancient granite was damp and slippery with condensation. He pressed himself against it as though it could somehow shelter him from his terrible pursuer, running his fingers across its surface – and this time felt the unmistakable channels and indentations of the runic inscription, and the familiar sign of the three intertwined triangles.

So it's a gate. And probably one I can use. Except that I don't know where it'll take me.

He opened his shirt and took out the pendant, lifting its chain over his head. He had hung it there long ago – perhaps years ago. He had never imagined that he might need it again . . .

A breeze from the mound touched his hair, and he turned to see the path he had travelled –

Claws like stained ivory ripped across his chest, scattering a fine spray of blood. He was looking straight into the gaping, snarling jaws of the Watcher. His sudden movement had saved his life, but the next blow would kill him – and now there was no time to run and no time to think. His hand seemed to move of its own accord, sliding the pendant into the carved symbol on the stone, holding it there as he pressed himself against the unyielding rock . . .

The power struck his body like a hammerblow and threw him aside. The pendant was flung from his grasp, and as it whirled through the air he saw, for one frozen moment, that it was pulsing with energy. He hurled himself after it, straining desperately to grasp it, knowing that without it the gate stone would be closed to him for ever . . .

There was a roar that might have been the Watcher –

but the sound was muffled, almost unreal. A shimmering net of raw energy was blazing out from the stone, and with it a pallid blue haze that seemed to sweep away the twilight landscape of the circle. It was as though a new landscape was forcing its way through a veil of darkness, tearing it aside to reveal the colours and textures of another dimension.

His fingers touched the pendant. It seared his skin, but he held it tightly, closed his hand over it, knowing how near he had come to losing it for ever.

The Watcher had gone, and with it the black and silver world that had held him captive so long. At first he could see nothing, understand nothing. Light and colour blinded him, a tapestry of vivid green, red, gold and brown beneath bands of crimson and vermilion that slowly darkened to a rich, midnight blue. Once, very long ago, he had dreamed a world where such colours might be possible, a world where twilight was a passing moment – but this was too vivid and too bright to be a dream. Though he closed his eyes tightly, Erik could not shut out the reality of what he saw. Everything he heard, everything he touched, brought back the world of his birth, and piece by piece all that he had lost under the spell of twilight was returned to him. Memories flooded into his mind, memories of sunlight and seasons, of changing times and changing places, of love that was earthly and imperfect. After the hollow silence of the twilight world every sound was new. Each birdsong was startling, a musical cadence bubbling with vitality. The whisper of leaves was an orchestra. And the cry of a hunting animal was the sound of life itself – life he could understand, life that grew old and died ...

He had come home – but not unscathed. Blood still flowed from the deep, parallel cuts across his chest. There was little pain, but he felt dizzy and nauseous. When Erik opened his eyes the colours still dazzled him, but he could see trees all around and a clear, cloudless sky overhead. The first stars were already shining. They

121

looked small and scattered, as if a million suns had grown old and the Watcher had harvested the heavens. He tried to pick out constellations, but the familiar groups of his childhood seemed distorted and hard to recognise. As an adult he had spent his time in libraries, studies and common rooms, and the stars above Oxford had always been dimmed by the lights of the city. Erik struggled to remember the last time he had seen them as clearly as this – and suddenly understood his growing sense of unease.

There were no lights. There were no buildings. The church and the farm were nowhere to be seen. He stood beside the stone in a broad clearing; and beyond it stood an encircling wall of trees. The sounds he had heard were natural enough, but they did not belong to a city suburb. Some were the everyday sounds of the country, reassuring and familiar. Others he had never heard before.

No. I don't believe it. I won't believe it . . .

Erik began to walk, as if moving away from the stone would somehow bring back his old, familiar world, but even the gathering dark could not conceal the strangeness of his surroundings. The path he followed was rough, more like a hunting trail or an animal track. The trees on either side were wild oaks, matured to incredible size. In their deep shade it was already night. He made little noise, yet something large stirred at his approach, crashing away through the undergrowth and startling flights of birds from the branches above. Everything around him seemed real, real with an intensity he could hardly bear; but this was primeval forest, untouched by man, a wildwood where each shadow was an enigma and each ancient, immemorial tree enshrined an eternity of mystery. Erik had stepped out of one legend and into another: into the great forest, the heart of darkness that had given birth to all mysteries, to all races, to all creatures of nightmare. There was a whispering all about him in the warm, breathing, all-enfolding darkness of the trees, a whispering like the stealthy movements of an army out of folklore. He could imagine speartips and mail glinting in the moonlight, harness creaking, faces lost behind masking helmets, flesh enfolded in steel. There was something inhuman about his vision, something that reminded Erik of his own reflection ensnared in alien eyes, something that belonged in the world he had left on the other side of the stone . . .

It's like those dreams I had when I was a kid; the ones that wouldn't let me wake up. I'd think I was OK, I was back in my room and everything was fine; and then that – that thing would come round the door . . . No. I'm not thinking straight. Losing blood . . .

He struggled to shut out the fears that beset him – that everything around him was another illusion, another trick of his own imagination; or, worse yet, that it was real, but not *his* world, his time . . .

Path's getting wider. As if people used it. Still feel like the first man who's ever seen it. Got to shake this off. Maybe part of me is back there, in the twilight . . .

Erik tried to think of Eleanor and Bjørn but that, too, led him back to memories of twilight. How many years had passed in the terrifying comfort of that empty dream? How many years had the same, longed-for images and thoughts and feelings circled in his mind? How many years had Kialar the trickster imprisoned him with his own desires? Even now he could not escape them. Each shadow was a hiding-place – and each clearing was an imminence, the half-expected hope that now, suddenly, he would see the familiar shape of the farm loom out of darkness, catch the flickering light from the windows, see the image of his wife and his child painted in shadow . . .

There was a shadow on the path ahead of him, a huddled shadow that did not belong in this primeval landscape. Erik had seen a shape like that once before: in Oxford, at the busy junction of Holywell Street and the High. The memories it stirred had no place here: the rhythmic ticking of a bicycle wheel, slowing by imperceptible degrees, a trickle of blood along the stone-lined gutter, and the crumpled shape slumped against the kerb ...

No. It couldn't be. How ... ?

He knelt down stiffly, reluctantly, and his hand was trembling as he reached out to touch ice-cold flesh.

Erik snatched his fingers away too quickly, striking the upraised shoulder. The dead man seemed to roll towards him, eyes wide and staring, pallid blue lips parted and dribbling blood over blackened teeth, throat opened into a second gaping mouth. For a moment Erik could see nothing but that ragged gash and the lolling head above it, fixed in a ludicrous expression of bewildered outrage. Then terror filled him, a blinding, irrational fear that whoever had done this must be hiding just a few feet away, waiting for a second victim.

Why kill him? What was the point? For God's sake, the man's dressed in rags ... !

He looked again. The clothes were strange, but they were not rags. In the failing light it was hard to see details, but there was something familiar about them: worn, curiously-cut shoes of soft leather; coarse, baggy trousers fitting tightly at the ankles; a loose tunic with a broad leather belt and a knife in the hanging scabbard; a broken thong around the neck ...

No. No, that's crazy ...

Another thought had struck him, another incongruous memory sharp with remembered detail: a display case, all polished wood and glass, shimmering with the muted glare of striplights that half-concealed the reflected faces of a dozen Danish schoolchildren. And inside – serene, almost noble, yet seemingly moulded in leather – the face of a man who had died by ritual violence centuries before Christ, his flesh and his clothes perfectly preserved by the marsh that had been his grave ...

No. These clothes are different. Later. But who the hell would wear them now ... ?

Reason tried to rescue him. There was a place not far from the farm, a centre for experimental archaeology. Tourists, archaeologists, and a hard core of play-actors gathered there every summer to live as their ancestors had done: to wear their clothes, eat their food, and sleep in draughty, smoke-filled huts that might or might not be accurate replicas of their Iron Age counterparts. In Denmark it was just possible that a man in Iron Age clothes could be lying a few yards from a busy main road. But this man had been murdered. There was no road, or anything like one. And the Denmark Erik knew, even the Denmark of his childhood, had no forests like this one ...

He forced himself to look at the dead man, to look hard and searchingly. The cloth of his tunic was finely woven and well cut, though now its embroidered edging was stained with blood. The outstretched hand was pale and soft, with the faintest of calluses along the fingertips – except where one finger was missing, half-cut, half-torn away from the jagged, bony stump. He retched drily, turning aside; and turned back despite himself to stare at the face. Something about it was badly wrong. It looked old, yet everything else pointed to a younger man, certainly no more than thirty.

The teeth. That was it. Most of them had gone, and the few that remained were all but rotting in the gums.

A man who's never seen a dentist, wearing Iron Age clothes, robbed and murdered in a forest that was cut down for farmland so long ago that no one can even remember it ...

Erik could see the dried blood, touch the chill flesh and the coarse-fibred fabric of the clothes, smell the lingering odour of woodsmoke and sweat mingled with the sickly-sweet scent of decay – yet still he could not accept what they meant. He had faced the unknown, he had faced his own dreams, and he had faced the terrors of twilight. It was enough.

This can't be real. Even this corpse isn't real. If I take these clothes, it'll vanish. Just part of Kialar's game – making me believe I'm in the past, have to change my clothes. But I'll play along, pretend I've been taken in. Then all I have to do is go on – go on and believe nothing that I see. He can't fool me for ever.

He dared not admit what he feared – that he was

125

alone, at the edge of night, and lost.

Lost in time.

At the borders of the forest, dressed in the borrowed clothes of a past age, Erik Larssen stopped to confront a new world.

For a moment he seemed to see moonrise spilling its trail of silver over an endless ocean; moonrise in that magical moment when land and sea are one, and mist unites with water in a single, numinous element. But within that element dark shapes rose and fell – vast shapes like the topmost ridges of submerged mountains, whale-backs returning to a world they had half forgotten.

He drew in his breath, sharply, feeling the chill bite of the mist at the back of his throat. In the light of the rising moon Erik could see the round-edged wooden roof-tiles, mist-wet and glittering like serried ranks of shields. He could see the dragon-finialled gables and the hart's horns at their crest, clear against the scudding clouds. It was a place built to command awe and respect, just as it commanded the mist-veiled marshland at the edge of the forest. And beyond the upturned hull of that great and kingly hall rose other darknesses and other, lesser halls: barns, stables, storehouses, and all the panoply of power.

The wind rose, and the mist parted like a curtain. In the distance low hills rolled down to the still waters of a wide inlet. Below him, on its nearer shore, was a shallow, swampy bay. All around its edge the old trees had been ruthlessly cleared, making an open space to prevent any surprise attack from the forest. The hall and its attendant buildings lay on a palisaded island linked to the shore by a long, narrow causeway. On the far side, beyond the encircling stockade, a low jetty cut into the glittering waters of the fjord like a drawn sword. Either side of it ships rode at anchor. One was long, lean and deadly, a war-canoe grown into a fully-fledged warship. The other was broad and full-bellied, built to carry trade goods: horses and cattle, woven cloth and furs. The shapes were almost familiar, but somehow smaller and less graceful than Erik expected. A drifting scent of woodsmoke filled the air, and the low murmur of human voices. There was song, even laughter, but after the silence and the solitude of twilight they seemed almost frightening.

He glanced back towards the warmth and darkness of the wood, but there could be no return. Since finding the dead man he had been constantly aware of the slightest sound, the slightest movement, and Erik had felt rather than known that something was pursuing him. For a while he had tried to dismiss his fear, to believe that what he heard was a wanderer like himself, at worst some wild animal hoping for an easy kill. Later he had thought of the dead man's murderer, and imagined a half-mad outlaw stalking him in hopes of a few coins, or even a ring; the jagged stump of that severed finger still haunted him. After that had come stranger, darker thoughts, images out of twilight, as though his death were seeking him out from beyond the stone . . .

No. Got to stop thinking like this. Just the wound. Loss of blood. Like being drunk . . .

Erik tried to walk, but he felt weak and unsteady – his legs would barely obey him. In the forest, fear and need had driven him; now, in sight of an end to his journey, a terrible doubt held him back. He could not know what lay within the stockade. It seemed a place of men, true enough, but he had no way of knowing for certain. And if they *were* men like himself, how would they receive a stranger? What language would they speak? And what could he say to them?

Slowly, reluctantly, Erik walked out of the trees and down the long slope to the causeway. In the bright moonlight the damp cobblestones along its surface glittered like jewels . . .

What was that line in Beowulf?' 'Stræt wæs stanfah' – 'the causeway was bright with stones'. But that led to Heorot – to the great hall of the Danish kings.

Now I know I'm dreaming.

127

All along the causeway torch-flames bobbed and flickered in the gentle wind blowing off the fjord. The view from the edge of the wood had given him a false perspective – from here the stockaded settlement was almost lost against the dark silhouette of the further shore. All around him the marsh glittered in the moonlight beneath a vast and empty sky; its turbid waters were troubled, restless, as though great forces moved just out of sight beneath its surface. The causeway was an endless torchlit procession into darkness.

Erik walked slowly and stiffly, staggering a little. His chest tingled faintly, but there was no pain – it was his legs that pained him, still stiff and aching after his desperate flight to the gate stone. The Watcher already seemed like a half-forgotten nightmare – but like a nightmare, it lurked in the shadows of his mind, waiting to strike again. The forest, the causeway, and the fortified island beyond it matched the distant memories of his own world. For a little while he had been ready to accept their reality – except that now he seemed to be walking into a legend.

'And it came to his mind to command a hall-building, call on his craftsmen to lift up a meadloft mightier than any that the children of men had yet seen on earth ...'

From the causeway, the palisades and watch-towers that girded the island all but shut out Erik's view of the main hall – but he could still see the horns and carvings on the gables. As his vision blurred the dragons seemed to move, gape their jaws ...

'For heroes under heaven that was the brightest of buildings – its light shone out over many lands ...'

Nightmare stirred in the shadows of his mind. This was a haunted place.

'Eternal night cloaks the misty moors, and none can tell where the demon walks abroad.'

Erik smiled weakly. His imagination was a little too good – once already Kialar had turned it against him. It must not happen again. And there were other matters to occupy his mind.

From the edge of the wood the stockade had seemed a small barrier; now, as he came to the end of the causeway, it loomed against the night like a giant's fortress. As he hesitated, caught between opposing fears, an owl swooped low above his head to settle on the palisade in a shiver of wings. There was something at its feet – a rounded shape, barely visible in the moonlight. There were others on either side, cresting the sharpened stakes of the palisade like ornaments on the baluster of some baronial mansion.

The bird cried out sharply and leaned down to peck between its splayed claws. Erik heard a soft tearing sound, saw the strip of flesh hanging in its beak, and understood.

The parapet was lined with severed human heads.

But at least they are *human. And human beings can be fooled. I should know.*

The dead man had been robbed and murdered in the midst of his journey. Erik could take his place, and his own wounds would explain the blood on his tunic ...

'Hei! þu! Hvat í Helju viltu hér?'

The voice came from somewhere above, but his sight was draining away into a pool of blackness. He struggled to interpret the string of sounds, twisting them by all the rules he knew to make them intelligible. The language seemed to be Norse, but an accent or a dialect that wrenched every vowel out of shape, slurred consonants, and added an unmusical growl to mask whatever sense was left. It was useless. The universe became a dark torrent sweeping Erik into nothingness.

A rhythmic motion brought him slowly back to consciousness. He was being half-helped, half-carried along a network of cobbled paths that glinted with new frost in the moonlight. He dreamed figures that scurried in and out of the great hall, animals everywhere, and a lingering smell that mingled offal and excrement with woodsmoke and the salt tang of the sea. Then there was darkness. It seemed that hands touched him – a woman's hands. Her body scent brought memories of another life and another world. A voice murmured words Erik could almost, but not quite, understand, bandaging his wound with rough efficiency. Arms supported him along a path and into a dark entrance rich with the smell of charcoal and roasting meat, guiding him to a bench set against a narrow trestle table. An earthenware beaker was thrust into his hand. He drank mechanically, half-choking on the sour, watery ale. As he threw back his head, coughing helplessly, he saw the great hall for the first time.

For a moment it overwhelmed him. After the chill desolation of twilight, this was warmth and shelter and firelight, a dazzling tapestry of red and gold and orange that flickered up the walls to be lost in the blue and smoky shadows of the rafters. Woven into that tapestry, and taking its colours, a hundred faces slipped in and out of shadow like demons at the mouth of hell. Some were human – stern, bearded men; pallid women with their hair tied up in linen kerchiefs. Others were inhuman. In the ever-shifting shadows the pillars and rafters seemed alive with crawling animals that clutched and clawed their way upwards into darkness, while grotesque masks with bared teeth and staring eyes peered out from crudely-carved foliage like spirits of the ancestral forest.

In Erik's dream of pain and fever the hall and everything in it seemed veiled in mist and darkness, as though the breath of the Watcher pursued him even here – but he knew this world as well as he knew the poems and legends that had given it birth. He had sought it, studied it and dreamed of it since his earliest childhood, but only now did he begin to understand the squalor and despair that lay just beneath the dream. This was a world so grim that even its gods must die in the final battle with darkness; so savage that a man's fame as a warrior was his single hope of immortality. In the shadows beneath the rafters, chain mail, swords, axes and halberds glittered like an icy ocean rippling in sunlight, as though the hidden army of the forests had followed him here.

Weapons in the hall? Something strange about that ...

Again his vision blurred. He was losing control of his own thoughts, playing into Kialar's hands. What he saw could not possibly be real. Once before his own imagination had woven a world from what he knew – now it was at work again, building halls out of poetry, snatching faces from the depths of his memory, clothing and weapons from half-remembered museum exhibits, and a language from the fragments of his own knowledge. The men around him were shadowy spear-carriers, burly and incurious, but their faces troubled him. They seemed older than their years, and the woman who served him was a grey-haired crone with the eyes of a sad young girl. The food he ate and the beer he drank were the savourless stuff of a dream, yet higher up the table Erik seemed to see the scattered remnants of an older, richer dream where gold gleamed amid fur and leather, and firelight flickered on clasps and brooches crusted with jewels and enamelling. There was wealth here, and feasting, and celebration; yet the voices and the faces were joyless.

Even so, he saw the things he had always imagined – the two lines of trestle-mounted boards either side of the long, blazing firepit, flickering light on the faces of long-dead men and women, and all around him the roar of a forgotten language spoken in a hundred conflicting voices – voices slurred with drink, raised in anger or drowned in laughter. Gradually words and phrases seemed to take on meaning. Erik heard a man ask for more ale, and add some sidelong comment to the woman who brought it. He heard a child crying repeatedly for its mother. And there was a name – a name he knew, repeated again and again, clear and unmistakable among all the other words that still tantalised his understanding.

Rolf konung ... Rolf Kraki ...

He smiled – secretly, mocking himself. In England he might have dreamed of King Arthur's round table – here in Denmark, what dream more likely than the court of

Rolf Kraki, the fountainhead of Norse legend? To his court had come the great heroes, each with his own story and his own destiny, to share the doom of their king. Because the great hall at Lejre, and Rolf himself, lay under an irredeemable curse . . .

He studied the proud faces at the centre of the table. There was no doubt which was the king – he had to be the dark-haired, scowling patriarch in the place of honour at the centre of the table. In the stories Rolf had been a great and powerful ruler, the greatest in all Denmark. His henchmen were lords of broad farms, captains of dragon-prowed warships, masters of sword and ringmail, helmet and shield. But there was little happiness in the face. Pride he saw, and strength, and the confidence befitting a leader; but the eyes were slitted, hedged about with tight lines of suspicion and hidden fear. And even when he drank, the king's gaze was fixed on the high-seat opposite, just out of Erik's sight. This was no hero of myth. This was a merciless warrior who had carved out a kingdom with his sword – and a gang of bullies to help him.

The champions. Who would be here? There'd be Svipdag. And Hialti. And there'd be Biarki – Battle-Biarki himself, the one who killed the dragon . . .

Again, there could be no doubt. The broad-shouldered, square-faced warrior with the long, triple-plaited red beard had to be Rolf's chief henchman. He was young – surely no more than eighteen – yet his bearing and his manner carried an unmistakable air of authority second only to the king's . . .

A voice was whispering in his ear. The speaker was a white-bearded man in a richly dyed tunic edged with fine braid.

'I am Hallgrim. You are the stranger who came to the gate?'

Danish. Twentieth century Danish, at that. Now he knew that he was dreaming. He wanted to laugh, but the hall seemed to be dancing in the flames from the fire.

'Yes,' he mumbled. 'But I don't belong here. I'm just dreaming this –'

'*Enough*! In Tyr's name be quiet, as you value your life! This is no dream! We have prayed that you would find us since first Kialar drew you from the path – but now you are here we are all in peril. Your coming may be all that he needs to drag this world of yours into twilight and chaos.'

'Who –?'

'Listen! This place swarms with the *fylgjar* of Kialar's vile followers! There are three of us, and three alone, who can speak with human lips as I do, and Niord has commanded us to –'

'*Hallgrim!*' The voice was the king's. '*Hallgrim, ek kalla á þér at halda upp svörum fyrir oss. Þat muntú segja, sem segja skal.*'

'You – you Erik – *keep silence* till my return, or you are a dead man!'

The hubbub in the hall was dying down, but the tension Erik had sensed before was stronger than ever. This moment seemed to be the nub of the matter, but Erik was too confused to concentrate on what was happening. What had Hallgrim said? *Your coming may be all that he needs to drag this world of yours into twilight and chaos.* But if this was real ...

It's not possible! How could I be sitting in the hall of Rolf Kraki? How could I share a bench with people from a storybook?

If it was true, then his first impression had been right: he had returned to his own world, but not to his own time. And somehow, out of all the stones in the circle, he had picked the one that would bring him to this precise place, this precise time.

But he had not chosen the stone. He had been driven to it, and beyond it, by a merciless pursuer. As though the Watcher itself had *meant* him to be here ...

Erik made these runes to honour Biarki. He walks the path of the dragon.

Now he himself had walked the dragon's path, and lived. Was his Bjørn, his Biarki, somewhere in this hall, now? Or was everything he saw and heard just another temptation from Kialar? He squeezed his eyes shut, struggling to break through the entangling net of fear and suspicion, struggling to find just one fixed point, one reality that was undeniable, pressing his hands against the rough wood of the board –

Something sharp bit deep into the flesh of his hand. He could have screamed aloud with the shock and the pain of it, but in the strange and threatening silence all around him he choked back the cry. A splinter of wood some three inches long was buried in his palm; blood oozed from the wound, and suddenly he remembered his first moment in twilight, when the pendant had pierced his hand. As he drew out the splinter he saw the white line of the old scar.

It's real! My God, it's all real! It's as though I'd come full circle – as though I was meant to be here. But why? And why now?

All eyes were on Hallgrim, even the king's, but the old man was waiting for absolute silence. There was something about his eyes – almost a flash of gold beneath the brow. It was difficult to look away from them. His voice, when he finally began to speak, was vibrant and powerful, as though the aging body masked the mind and spirit of a younger man, seasoned and experienced without the reserve and inflexibility of age. Hallgrim spoke clearly and precisely, and Erik found he could follow almost every word.

'My lord Rolf; my lord Jorvard. This gathering of the great in the land brings honour to the hall. But to you, my lord Jorvard, goes the glory of the day, for you carry away the greatest prize we have to offer – nothing less than the king's own sister.'

There was a low murmur of voices all around the hall. Rolf's face showed little gladness at the match: Erik saw only fear, hidden under a mask of anger and resentment. He racked his brains to remember who Rolf's sister might be – and who Jorvard was . . .

Rolf's under-king! There was a story about him – some trick Rolf used to make Jorvard his vassal ... And then – damn it, what happened then? Why can't I remember?

In his confusion he missed the end of Hallgrim's speech – but suddenly, all around him, men were rising to their feet with drinking horns in their hands, cheering heartily and gulping back their ale with noisy appreciation. He stood up himself, though the hall seemed to spin around his head as he did so, and drank with the rest. The ale was watery, but he was weak from the wound, and his head was buzzing with conflicting ideas. For now there was nothing he could do – he was bound to silence by the only person who seemed to share his language. He drank because his neighbours drank, and because he dared not talk to them. He drank until the men around him were snoring under the benches, and the leaping flames of the hearth-fire had become flickering orange-red tongues among the black and white and grey of the wood that fed them. For a long time Erik could not sleep, but the lack did not trouble him. He had learned to fear what dreams could bring. The smoky, ember-glowing half-darkness was full of human sounds, almost familiar now, yet somehow strange as well. All around him slow breathing mingled with drunken mumblings in a language he was never born to hear. A man turned in the straw, and metal rang dully against wood as his knife struck the floor. Three or four times he heard couples making love – but soundlessly, obeying social customs he could barely begin to understand.

As if they were afraid of something. But what could frighten them in a place like this?

The thought pursued him through restless dreams that hovered at the edge of sleep. Once again he walked in the ancient forest, but now, all around, the mail and weapons of a phantom army chinked and rustled in the darkness, and the footfall of a terror older than time echoed faintly among the trees, answering the thudding rhythm of his own heart. Erik's fear was instinctive, like an animal's, and lingered even when he woke to the smoky darkness of the hall. It was almost as though these strangers shared his nightmare; as if the severed heads on the battlements were much more than a warning to outlaws . . .

More like an offering. Or a propitiation . . .

He dreamed a hall like Rolf's beneath the myriad stars of the twilight world, compassed about with armies and engines of war culled from the imagination of some old Flemish painter. All along the battlements warriors stood their ground, glittering in chainmail, faces hidden under bronzed and enamelled masking helmets, spears at the ready. From out of the darkness came a single cry, more than animal yet less than human, filled with a desperate intensity. The sound was impossible to place. It seemed to come from everywhere, echoing back from star-studded sky and twilit hills alike. It was a hunting howl that filled the universe with fear, and with it came the sound of a creature that did not belong to the human world, sniffing out its chosen prey. Now Erik could hear the soft sigh of the earth as it parted beneath the feet of a being as powerful as time itself . . .

His own cry woke him – that, and a distant sound like a tree falling to the woodsman's axe. There were voices outside, raised voices shouting in anger or in panic. Others were stirring around him, bleary-eyed with drink and sleep . . .

The end wall burst open. Timbers bent and shattered, splintering like breaking bones. An angry, orange moon peered through the gap, washing the hall in pallid light as it rippled across the chainmail and weaponry behind the benches. Mist rolled through the broken wall in a silent flood, and a frosty cold sucked away the heat of the dying fire. Beyond lay a world drenched in blood and cloaked in mist – and a shadow that blotted out the stars. Erik saw the outline of a bestial head, and long, snaking arms tipped with dripping, scythe-like claws. It was the Watcher.

It's another dream. It must be. In a minute I'll wake up . . .

There was panic in the hall. All around him men were crying to their gods, groping for weapons left just out of reach, struggling with their armour.

It isn't real. It can't *be real.*

The shadow moved. An arm lashed out like a striking serpent, and dark stains spattered across the silver-lit hangings at the gaping new mouth of the hall. Something arced through the air like a bale of hay flung from a pitchfork, and fell in a tangle of limbs not two yards from Erik. A moving, growling darkness strode into the hall, smashing benches and tables in its path, striking randomly with great sweeps of its arm. In the dying firelight the Watcher's eyes were twin flames, beacons turning this way and that to search out its prey. Another man, mad with fear, ran naked at the Watcher with a drawn sword in his hand – and was impaled on its outstretched claws. With a dreamy langour it lifted its threshing victim clear off the floor. Its jaws parted in a gaping, lipless grin and closed like a trap on his head, cutting short his scream with a crunch of splintering bone. The body fell in a heap across the broken benches, blood still spouting from severed arteries. It was impossible that the man could still be alive, yet somehow he was. The ruined head moved with a semblance of purpose. The arm groped helplessly for a weapon. The legs drummed against the ground, struggling to lift the shattered body, and then froze in spasm as an eddying column of mist rose from the gaping mouth. There was a faint, mewling cry, like a child's shriek of frustrated malice – and then the dead man slumped back, motionless, among the wreckage of the hall.

This can't be happening!

It was a fever dream, or worse – but nothing he did could banish it. He could feel the biting cold of the breeze from the fjord, smell the stench from bodies torn open by the Watcher's claws, see the blood and brains spattered across the smoke-darkened tapestries, hear the frantic shouts and screams of the men around him. Weapons

137

were striking at the Watcher now – gold-hilted swords, ash-shafted spears, bearded sea-axes, whining arrows from hastily-strung bows – yet nothing seemed able to touch it. He found himself staring into its burning eyes. They were the eyes of an impartial executioner, dispensing death without malice, without guilt, without emotion – and within them was the same calm, cool intelligence he had seen before.

It's come for me. It was hunting me in the forest, and now it's come for me. If it kills me, then no one else will have to die. And why not? I must be crazy anyway.

He climbed shakily to his feet. This, in truth, had to be a nightmare – but it was the worst kind of nightmare, where the only solution was to kill yourself. This was not courage, or foolhardiness; it was the inevitable logic of a dream. But as he stepped forward a strong hand gripped his arm and thrust him to one side. It was Battle-Biarki, unarmed and unarmoured.

'þu. Eigi lengri. Gestr okkar skal á mer velkominn vera.'

His words were boast and threat, the easy bravado of a warrior: 'No further – I shall welcome our guest.' He seized a glowing brand from the fire-trough, raised it high above his head and swung it around his head in a flailing circle, fanning it into flame. The sudden fire shone back from the creature's eyes. For a moment it hesitated, claws half-sheathed, hands half-clenched, head turning this way and that as it studied this new challenger. Slime and mud mingled with the blood and offal that dripped from every part of its body.

Biarki took a single step forward, crouching like a wrestler, the torch held out at arm's length. Sea-wind fanned the smoke into a spreading blue plume that brushed for a moment against the creature's nostrils. Its eyes widened. It shook its head – and stepped backwards.

As Biarki followed it, pressing his advantage, the flickering light of the firebrand uncovered the devastation of the hall – tables and benches overturned, planking and carvings smashed, tapestries torn down and trailing in pools of blood along the floor. And everywhere the living flinched away from the light, cowering in terror among the shattered bodies of the dead.

Step by step, the young warrior forced the creature back down the hall. It seemed paralysed, unable to strike, its eyes locked on Biarki. They were no longer the eyes of an executioner.

That look. I've seen it before, but I can't remember where . . .

Biarki had reached the broken end wall – but now the creature held its ground, claws open, arms raised to strike. The man made no further move. He simply stood at the threshold, legs slightly apart, his left hand on his hip and the torch raised in his right hand, pointing outwards into the night. Once again the Watcher shook its head. Then, almost like a human being suing for peace, it stretched out an arm. The limb was curiously articulated, rising to a strange peaked shoulder almost higher than the head. Biarki seized it at wrist and elbow and twisted it sideways in a single, fluid motion, kicking aside his abandoned torch and bracing his feet against the broken timbers of the wall.

The creature turned away, not even trying to strike with its free hand, head swaying from side to side as if fighting intolerable pain. The man was less than half its height, yet somehow his strength seemed to overmatch the strength of his opponent, and its efforts to escape served only to increase the pressure on joints and sinews. Dark blood burst from under the frantically working claws. Bones and joints creaked under the force of Biarki's grip. And then came a sound such as Erik had never heard. It was a scream – the scream of a creature whose voice was slow and deep as a river that flows in the roots of mountains. It was a scream without sound that shook the earth beneath his feet and pounded like slow hammer-blows into his brain. Hangings and weapons tumbled to the floor, benches and tables shook and fell, and the walls themselves trembled. With an echoing clatter something dark, trailing dark liquor, fell to the floor – the Watcher's arm, torn off at the shoulder-joint, writhing and twisting with an obscene life of its own, the dagger-like claws opening and retracting in their sheaths, still, even in death, grasping for their prey.

Something gripped Erik's ankle. He felt the sharp pinprick of claws against his flesh, popping one by one through the skin, as he struggled to wrench his leg free, stumbling and half-falling across the shattered bench.

'Erik ... !' The voice at his feet was an agonised whisper, trembling at the edge of extinction. In the half-light from the shattered end wall Erik could barely make out the face of Hallgrim, the herald, yet the old man's eyes seemed already glazed in death. The lips moved like a mockery of the living, sucking the last breath from lungs that would never move again. '*They – are – here!*'

'What – what do you mean? Who –?'

He never finished his question. The herald's corpse was moving, just as that other corpse had done – as though a different life were trapped in its flesh and struggling to break free. Its hands clenched and then opened. Its legs kicked in the last, meaningless action of a hanged man. Its back arched in some hideous final agony, jerking its head from side to side. Its eyes bulged, its mouth gaped in a silent scream – and a thin column of mist, for all the world like a distorted human figure, rose from it like smoke from a dying fire. The herald's body sprawled sideways, lolling against the full, rich skirts of a silent and motionless woman.

Erik looked up into a face he knew as well as his own.

* * *

'I should have known – even then, I should have realised.'

Anja's face was full of apprehension. 'What do you mean?'

'She hadn't changed – a little older, hardly enough to notice. But that place was a hell on earth, and she looked as though – as though it didn't matter. As though it had nothing to do with her at all. She didn't look – well, human.'

'But she knew you?'

'Yes – but she didn't seem surprised. As though she *expected* me. She said ... she said: "Not here. We must be alone. Meet me in the boat shed." And then she was gone.' He rubbed his beard with his hand, biting at his knuckles.

'And you did as she asked?'

'Oh, yes!' His voice was savage with bitterness. 'Because I was stupid. Because I couldn't – I wouldn't see what Kialar had done to her!'

Anja shuddered. 'What do you mean?'

'I *knew* how I had once imagined her. For years I had lived with that – thing – that wore her shape, that took my dreams and made them seem real. And now, at last, I was looking at my wife – the woman I loved, the woman I trusted more than anyone else in the world. If she seemed strange, it must be *my* fault – because I was expecting something different, more like what I'd imagined. God, I made it so *easy* for her ...'

'To do what?' said Brockman.

'To betray me. It was dark in that boathouse. Probably saved my life. When she came in, all I could see was her face. She looked – she looked *pitying*. You understand, Anja? You understand how that felt? At first I didn't even see the others. But when I did, I *knew* that she wasn't mine. Not any more. That after all I'd been through, everything I'd done – after all that –'

'The alvar had taken her.' Anja's voice was little more than a whisper.

'I'll get you a drink,' said Brockman. 'Beer OK?'

Erik nodded vaguely. 'There was something about her – almost like a light around her head, a halo ...'

'I've seen it,' said Brockman, pulling off the cap with unnecessary force.

'And the others – all of them the same ... As if it was some kind of game. They drew their swords, and they came at me.'

He took the glass that Brockman gave him and held it

in both hands, staring through it towards the bright flame of the oil lamp.

'I couldn't believe it. I felt the way I had when the Watcher came – that this was a nightmare, that I'd wake up and find her in bed beside me.' He took a long draught of beer, and set the glass on the table in front of him, cradling it in his hands. 'But it had to be part of the same dream, because everything fitted. Now I'd seen the alvar, I knew why the Watcher had come.'

Brockman frowned. 'Meaning exactly what?'

'The Watcher was searching out the alvar – sending them back into twilight. Until it saw Biarki. I *still* can't understand ...'

'Why it spared him?'

Erik nodded slowly. 'Or her. I might never have known ...' His voice trailed off. He was looking at Anja with a strange, tortured expression. 'But you – how did *you* know?'

She flushed. 'What do you mean?'

'You said "The alvar had taken her." As if you *knew.*'

'How could I? You had not told us – I mean ...'

'Anja, *min pige*,' said Kristine gently. 'It is better that you speak the truth.'

She nodded slowly, and sighed. 'I am sorry, Erik. There is something I must fetch from my room – and I must fetch your tablets also, *Mormor.*'

Kristine shook her head, struggling to her feet. 'No, *pigebarn*, I think that I shall fetch them myself. There is another thing I must also do.'

Brockman turned away. A few hours before he had accused Anja of driving Eleanor from the house, of inventing the very story that was now unfolding as the truth. He saw his own face reflected in the window – a hard face, cut with sharp lines of grief, thin-lipped, narrow-eyed, but softening, changing, at the edge of a new beginning. For Erik, everything he had loved and valued was already lost. In a few moments Anja would bring the telltale newspaper article, and he would finally learn the truth about Eleanor – that he, like the legendary Helgi, had been duped from the beginning by an alv wearing stolen human flesh ...

Yes, but why? What the hell was it all about? What do the alvar want?

'Erik?' Anja's voice – he had not even heard the women come back. 'I found this – after they had gone. As though someone had given it to her.'

'I don't ... Wait. That's *her*! That's Eleanor! But ...'

Brockman scowled at his own reflection. He could almost remember how the article had put it. '*Doctor Fabrin said that the woman, Katja Laufssen, suffers almost total memory dysfunction. "She is quite harmless, like a little child, but she cannot look after herself." Anyone finding the woman should take her at once to the nearest police station ...*'

'All those years ... I loved her. You *know* how I loved her –'

'Erik, *min dreng* –'

'Don't say *anything*, Kristine. I've seen things you'll never see, things even you couldn't understand! I saw this madness called love twisted and turned against me like a weapon, and *still* I believed in it. And now this!'

'Erik, it changes nothing at all.'

'It changes *everything*, Kristine! From the very beginning I've been *nothing* – nothing but a pawn in Kialar's game. And this woman, this woman I thought I cared about! She –'

Brockman had expected grief, even despair. Instead he saw an anger he knew all too well – a burning, destructive anger tearing at the older man's soul. He found himself almost shouting. 'So why, Larssen? What the hell was she after? I mean, you're an OK guy but you'd hardly bring an immortal to the wrong side of eternity.'

'I don't know you, Brockman, and I don't want to know you. Stay out of this!'

'Peter, I –'

'Anja, honey, I want to *help*. We need to know what's going on – what Kialar *wants*.'

'He is like all the alvar,' said Kristine. 'He plays games with human lives.'

Brockman banged his fist on the table. '*Yes!* But what *is* the game, Larssen? Do you know? Does anyone know?'

'*I* know,' said Erik, in a voice that was suddenly and icily calm. 'Niord tried to tell me – I didn't give him the chance. Kialar wants ... he wants my son.'

Anja's eyes widened. 'Bjørn? Why? What could he *possibly* –'

Erik ignored her. 'Why else did he hide them like that? Why else take such trouble, run such terrible risks, to trap me in twilight? Why else follow me, try to kill me – even here, even now? He's *afraid* – afraid of what might happen if I talk to my son, remind him of the world where he grew up!'

Brockman shook his head. 'For God's sake, you don't even know where he is!'

'Oh, I know,' said Erik. 'I know because I saw him myself. I was as close to him as I am to you. Closer, perhaps.' There was a wild, mad look in his eyes. Anja reached out a trembling hand to comfort him, but he thrust it aside, picked up the newspaper cutting, and slowly, deliberately, ripped it to shreds.

'Erik,' said Kristine, 'you must tell us what happened. All of us now, we are a part of this story. We must know as much of it as we can.'

Anja's voice was quiet, pleading. 'Please, Erik – we want to understand.'

'Understand? How can you? Can you understand a son who would try to kill his own father – without even a word?'

'Bjørn? But he's only a –'

'A child? Only a child? Oh yes, once he was a child! Once he was a child I loved, a child I fed and comforted and coaxed to sleep! But now ... Oh yes, now –'

'For God's sake,' said Brockman, 'tell us the whole story, will you? I'm damned if I can understand a word you're saying.'

'And what do *you* know, Brockman? What can you possibly –?'

'Erik ...' Kristine's voice was slightly sharp, like a mother gently but firmly correcting her child. 'We must know, Erik. What happened in the boathouse? How did you see Bjørn? And how did you come back to us?'

The older man shuddered, as if even the memory of what had happened was more than he could bear. He stared at the floor, twisting the torn strips of newspaper around his fingers. 'I was wounded – weak, and sick, and dizzy. They hunted me – like an animal! Can you imagine it, Brockman? Can you imagine being hunted through a thick, dark forest, where anything at all might be waiting to pounce from the shadows? Can you imagine twisting, turning, trying to escape, and finding every path blocked? Every time I doubled back, they were waiting – waiting to kill me, smiling that same damned smile, forcing me back to the gate stone!'

Anja frowned. 'But – you saw Bjørn?'

Erik laughed. It was an ugly, empty sound. 'No. I saw a man – a man called Biarki. Not like the others, Brockman – no halo. But he stood with *them*, and he drew his sword with the rest. And his eyes ...'

'What're you saying, Larssen?'

'I *knew* them. I'd seen them before. Not in the hall, not there – *here.*'

Kristine reached out a trembling hand. 'So you found your son.'

'I found a man who didn't know me. Who would have killed me. Without a second thought ...'

'So what happened?' said Brockman.

Erik buried his head in his hands. 'I don't *know*! They were moving in on me. I had my back to the stone – only way I could defend myself. Something hit me – maybe something they'd thrown. And when I came round I was here, in the churchyard.'

Brockman pulled the cap of another beer bottle and took a long draught, wiping his lips with the back of his hand. 'So what are you saying? Why should Kialar want your son?'

'You still don't see? It's the Watcher. It has to be the Watcher. My son – if that killing machine *is* my son – came close to destroying it right there in the hall. And if the legends about him are true, he *will* kill it.'

Anja stood up and walked to the window, staring out into the dark as though it might never end. '*Herre Gud*, Erik, if you should be right ...'

'I *am* right. With the Watcher dead, there's nothing standing in Kialar's way. Nothing but Niord and the liosalvar – and there aren't enough of them to stop him. He'll have another world for his plaything. A world of time. *Our* world.'

Anja did not seem to hear him. 'Peter?' Her voice was strained. 'Peter, please come here.'

'What's up, honey?'

'I think that something is happening – something in the mound.'

Erik laughed again, the same ugly, mocking laugh that had grated on Brockman's nerves before. 'Then it's starting. He's won. And he's coming to take his own.'

CHAPTER
6

Seven hundred elves from out the wood
Foul and grim they were
Down to the farmer's house they went
His meat and drink to share ...

Traditional ballad

'What is it?' said Brockman. 'What did you see?'

She did not answer. Her eyes seemed to be locked on the churchyard.

'Anja ...?'

As Brockman stumbled to his feet, he knew a moment of premonition that seemed to lock all his previous life behind an immovable door. Beyond the window, where the mound should have been, was an emptiness – a blackness so absolute that it seemed to deny life itself. He felt dizzy and disoriented, as though he were staring down into the void of Ginnungagap. There was nothing to focus on, nothing to see – except that far away, unimaginably far, a pinprick of light was swirling, growing, spiralling upwards.

With a curse he wrenched his eyes away from the window. The lamp still burned on the kitchen table, but its light seemed ineffectual, a pale and struggling imitation of what real light ought to be. The darkness and the silence outside were invading the house, stealing colour and life from all that they found there. Erik's face was milk-pale. Only Kristine seemed untouched, as if the light in her eyes could somehow banish all darkness, all evil.

'What is it?'

Kristine half-smiled. 'A storm is rising, Hr Brockman – the storm that brings the Great Hunt.'

'You know what's happening?'

'I think so. I think that once before the Hunt has come to Egerød. Once – or maybe twice. Perhaps he saw it also, the one who painted the church.'

'You *expected* this?'

She shook her head. 'Hr Brockman,' she said ruefully, 'there are some things even I have no wish to believe.'

He laughed, despite himself. He knew the story of the Wild Hunt – how the lord of the otherworld would ride the storm wind with a savage rout of supernatural beasts, pursuing his chosen quarry over field and fen, mountain and moor. It had survived in a hundred different folk-tales – yet each had taken it a little farther from the original, changing it in subtle ways, disguising the core of truth that was here, now, in this very room. For Kristine there was no distance at all between the modern city all around them and the village world of an unknown eleventh-century painter – and now Brockman, too, felt a curious affinity with that world, as he watched the ancient churchyard opening into the pit of hell, and darkness falling all around.

'So Kialar's won,' said Erik. 'He's taken the gate.'

Kristine shook her head. 'We cannot be sure of that.'

'I'm as sure as I need to be.' There was a passionate energy in his voice that Brockman recognised – the consuming energy of a despairing man hell-bent on revenge. 'And this time – *this* time I'll find him!'

Kristine laid a cool, frail hand on Erik's wrist. 'You should stay here, *min dreng*. You have no power to stop him.'

'Then I'll die trying! That's better than –!'

His fists clenched. In the depths of the vortex, energy flared like distant lightning. Its reflections glittered in the calm, grey depths of Kristine's eyes.

'Hr Brockman, there is a tale I left half-told, because I am sometimes as foolish as first you thought me.'

He forced a smile. 'Meaning you didn't believe it?'

'Not till this moment.' Her eyes were fixed on the rising heart of the vortex, unflinching and unafraid. 'The girl who burned as a witch there, on the mound – she was a child of our family. Her mother told the story, who stood at this window and watched her die. One night, long ago, there was a fearful storm –'

'Like this one?' said Brockman.

'Exactly like this one.'

Brockman saw Erik's shoulders hunch. 'So what happened?'

'The people of the village, they were terrified. They ran to the church, and they said to the priest that demons were abroad. He took his Bible in his hand, and out he went into the wind and the darkness. Next day they found him stark dead on the mound.'

Brockman nodded slowly, remembering the battle in the churchyard. 'Burned?'

'As if by a great fire – he, and every house in the village but this one. So they, too, they must burn something – a girl, an innocent girl.'

'Why the hell – ?'

'Because, Hr Brockman, she told them the truth. Things they did not wish to hear.'

'What things?'

'They said she was an alv-child. They said the alvar had come for their own, and now they would send her back to them.'

'And that storm was the Hunt?'

'Once I doubted it. Now I am certain.'

Beyond the window darkness had a shape, a rising whirlwind surging out of eternity. Anja turned away from it, her face as pale as Erik's, and sat down by her grandmother's side, reaching out to touch her yellowed, wrinkled hand.

'*Mormor* – we should leave while there is still time.'

Kristine shook her head. 'For the moment we are safest here. This house is well and cunningly built.'

'I don't understand, *Mormor*.'

'In the open we have no protection, *pigebarn*. We should be at their mercy. Here ...' She raised and opened her hands in an eloquent gesture.

Anja shivered. 'What will happen?'

'I cannot be sure. But I think for a little while we shall stand at the very borders of twilight. We shall see what Erik saw – things we were never born to see. And afterwards ...'

Anja's eyes widened, and Brockman seemed to see the livid light of a bale-fire reflected there.

'Will you pray with me?' said Kristine. 'All of you?'

Anja hesitated, then mumbled a 'Yes'. Erik shook his head.

'Will you, Hr Brockman?'

'I – can't.' He frowned and turned back towards the window, but Erik gripped his arm.

'Better not to look.'

'I'll take my chances. If a truck's going to run me over I want its number first.'

'Your choice,' muttered Erik. 'Your mistake.'

'*Fader vor*,' said Kristine. '*Du, som er i himlen.*' Anja whispered the words like a small child – a child battling the all-embracing terror that only children can know. Despite himself Brockman found his lips moving, joining with Kristine's prayer.

Thy kingdom come. Thy will be done, on earth as it is in heaven ...

Deep in the vortex, volleys of lightning made glittering spiderwebs of light, powerful beyond belief, yet unimaginably distant.

Give us this day our daily bread ...

Now there were shadow-shapes, too, like distant birds tossed on a storm-wind from the sea.

And forgive us our trespasses .... ·

Erik's face hardened, and his clenched knuckles were

ivory. 'It's true,' he said. 'The gate has fallen. Only Kialar would come like this.'

As we forgive those who trespass against us . . .

'I can't just wait here! I *have* to face him!'

'What are you going to do?' said Brockman. 'Take him on bare-knuckled?'

'It doesn't *matter!*'

And lead us not into temptation . . .

Erik dived for the door, throwing back the bolt in one quick, easy motion. Brockman reached after him, stumbled, and half-fell against the table, knocking the spirit lamp to the floor. Its glass chimney shattered on the tiles, plunging the room into darkness as Brockman grabbed Erik's shoulders and all but hurled him back into the kitchen.

But deliver us from evil . . .

'You damn fool! What in hell are you doing!'

Erik's face was hard. 'It's me they want, Brockman – just me. Now *let me go!*'

Brockman shook his head in reluctant admiration. 'You've got courage, Larssen, I'll give you that – but the alvar won't stop to count heads. And if Fru Hansen's right, the only chance you've got is right here in the house.'

'They are coming,' said Anja. Her voice trembled with the fear she was struggling to control as she stared out into the darkness. To Brockman it seemed as though the vortex was dragging him and everything near him downward, ever downward, into an unknown abyss. The trees around the churchyard bent and swayed to a wind he could neither hear nor feel, and the outlines of the church and the city beyond seemed to blend with the lowering sky to form a single tapestry of darkness with its heart in the mound. Then, somewhere far away, a thin cry of torment cut across the rising dark. Another came, and another still, bloodless and remote, a wailing chorus of despair beyond all knowledge of salvation – and with it a deep, booming counterpoint that rose from a distant rumble to a roar like a breached dam.

A blinding triple flash of lightning shattered the darkness. In its blue-white glare Brockman seemed to see a tree – a tree that moved like a man, enclosed in a living carapace, face helmeted with bark, head crowned with two living branches. It sat astride a shapeless, armoured hulk that bucked and heaved with a motion and intelligence of its own. Behind it, rising out of infinite darkness, a myriad twisted, half-animal shapes rode the wind like leaves on a gale, an uncountable host soaring out of twilight. Lightning flashed again, and for a second that chilled his blood the golden eyes beneath those horns were locked on his. Then darkness fell like a curtain, and a savage, roaring wind battered against the side of the house, whistling through the broken kitchen window. Pots and pans rattled in their racks. A plate tipped sideways, fell, and shattered on the floor. Cupboard doors swung open, groaning back and forth on their hinges and battering against their frames. Spice jars tumbled from a rack, spilling their contents as they smashed on the tiled floor. All around them the house itself seemed to tremble under the onslaught. Yet Kristine sat calm and still, the same half-smile seemingly frozen on her face.

As suddenly as it had begun, the wind dropped away to nothing.

'What was that?' yelled Brockman. 'What the hell *was* that?'

'The horned god,' said Kristine, in the same measured voice as before. 'Or perhaps you would call him the devil. But the Hunt has passed – or I do not think, Hr Brockman, that we would still be alive.'

'Everything's dark,' said Erik.

Brockman shook his head in disbelief. The sky was utterly black. It was as though the city and all its people had been swept from the face of the earth. Copenhagen had become a necropolis; even the ancient church was a blank-faced mausoleum. But there were outlines in the darkness, shapes he recognised – and somehow this was a landscape he knew. Long ago, in San Francisco, he had walked through tall canyons he could barely recognise as streets ...

'It's a brownout. Don't you see? It's just a goddamned brownout!'

'It is darkness,' said Kristine, 'no matter how it began.'

'So maybe the alvar took out the power plant. Either way, let's call up some help.'

Erik smiled grimly. 'Any particular kind?'

'You *could* pick up the phone.'

'And say what?' hissed Erik. 'That the Wild Hunt just passed our window? Who d'you think they'd take away?'

Anja picked up the receiver, grimaced, and slammed it down again. 'No use to argue,' she said. 'It is not working.'

Brockman shrugged, 'Someone'll come. The whole neighbourhood must have heard *that* little party.'

'No,' said Kristine. 'No one will come. She had found another lamp, and was lighting it with methodical care.

'Fru Hansen, we're in the middle of a city!'

The lamp-flame soared into life, and for a moment Kristine seemed like some ancient wise-woman, the lines of pain and experience on her face overlaid with the peaceful acceptance of old age. 'No one lives here,' she said. 'The shops, the supermarket, the offices, they are empty. Later – six, seven o'clock – people will come. But now, now there is no one.'

'So what do we do? Sit here and wait for them?'

'The Hunt has begun,' said Kristine. Her eyes were clear and calm. 'If the stories are true, it will end with a death.'

For a moment, inexplicably, Brockman seemed to see another scene outside the window – a spark that grew slowly into a roaring column of fire; a struggling figure, little more than a girl, dragged to the gallows by strong, brutal hands; and a cry of horror and despair that ended with the sickening stench of burning flesh and a writhing black bundle that had once been a living human being ...

'No, *Mormor*! 'Anja's face was white, as if she had seen the same vision, but her eyes were fixed on her cousin. 'There must be another way!'

'Don't waste your sympathy,' said Erik. 'Kialar's come this far – the least I can do is go out and meet him. All I'm asking for is a fair chance.'

Brockman scowled. 'Reckon you'll get it?'

'You are right, Hr Brockman,' said Kristine. 'And you, Erik, you must stay with us. For the alvar, all that they do to us is a kind of game. They will not understand.'

'They'll understand cold iron.'

'Don't be a jerk,' said Brockman. 'You were plain lucky in the churchyard. Those friends of yours came just in time – and right now I don't see them.'

'I don't *care*, Brockman! It doesn't matter what happens to me!'

'To me it matters,' said Anja. 'To *Mormor* also.'

'And to me,' said Brockman. 'I was like you, Larssen. Wasted half my life waiting to get even – '

'I don't have time for this, Brockman. Kristine, there's something I need. You've kept it well, and you've hidden it even better – but I need the halberd. Right now.'

The old woman sighed. 'I know it, *min dreng* – but I had hoped never to see it again.'

Anja's eyes widened. 'The halberd?'

'You must help me a little, *min pige*. I have grown stiff from sitting too long.'

'Wherever it is, *Mormor*, I can fetch it.'

'You would not know where to look.'

'I'll come with you,' said Erik.

'You will stay here,' said the old woman firmly, as she opened the door. 'Remember, Erik – it is a man's weapon, and a woman's secret.'

For a little while after they had left there was silence in the old house. In the darkness it seemed the whole world was holding its breath, waiting for some unimaginable apocalypse. Erik stood by the window, hands pressed against the sill, staring out into the night as if he were willing his enemy to return. Beyond him, the silhouette of the ancient church was a crouching, threatening darkness. Brockman could no longer see it as a sanctuary – it shared the corruption of the mound, the guilt of a long-dead community who had sacrificed an innocent life to their ignorance and their fear.

And nothing's changed. We keep doing it, over and over again.

The door opened on blinding light. Anja held the lamp high in her right hand while her left supported Kristine. And cradled in the old woman's arms, like an offering to a pagan shrine, was a long, tightly-wrapped bundle of cloth. As Anja set the lamp on the table, her grandmother laid the bundle next to it with something approaching reverence.

'Open it, Erik.'

He hesitated briefly, then stepped across to the table and tugged at the cloth. The outer layers crumbled like parchment in his hands – but within the remaining folds a shifting, flickering reflection answered the quivering flame of the lamp.

'Take it,' said Kristine. 'It is older than even you can imagine.'

Erik was not listening. The fabric clung to its secret like bandages on an old wound, and he was struggling with it, tearing it free piece by piece.

'There,' said Kristine. 'Now it is yours. Use it wisely.'

It was a halberd like none Brockman had ever seen. The blade was long and straight, twin-edged and pointed like a sword, with a curious, irregular sheen under its thin layer of oil. A wooden shaft was packed by its side. Erik picked up the blade and wiped it with a brittle piece of cloth. It caught the light; and a metallic serpent snaked down its length and vanished into the shadows.

'Christ,' said Brockman, 'its pattern-welded!'

Anja glanced up. 'What is that – "pattern-welded"?'

Erik locked the shaft into its housing at the base of the blade. 'It's a way to make good weapons from bad metal,' he said, studying the light-play up and down the steel. 'Weld a bundle of rods together and shape the blade out of that. Leaves a pattern on it – see?'

She nodded. 'When . . .?'

'It is very old,' said Kristine. 'Not the shaft; that has been made over many times. But the blade is sharpened only when it must be used. My mother showed me this, and what must be done to preserve it, and her mother before her. But I, Hr Brockman, I was foolish. I kept it hidden from my own daughter – so Anja knew nothing until now. But its time has come. Look at the runes on the shaft.'

Erik nodded. 'They say "*Dreka hann drepa, en draugar risar*".'

'That's a little close to home,' said Brockman. '"He kills the dragon, and the dead arise."'

'Very good. Where d'you learn Old Norse, Brockman?'

'I didn't. It's on the gate stone. The lines from *Völuspá* –'

'Yes. But *that* line was never written down. Except on the stone – and here.'

'Fine. What's it mean – to us?'

'It means, perhaps, that Bjørn has killed the dragon,' said Kristine. 'If he has, Hr Brockman, it is time for the last great battle.'

'How long've we got?'

She shook her head. 'Perhaps the rest of the night. Perhaps a few moments. But the alvar must return before sunrise. They will – what is it?'

Brockman had put his finger to his lips. 'Could be they already did. Hush up a minute, all of you.'

Quietly, he eased open the connecting door to Erik's bedroom and tiptoed across to the window. For perhaps twenty heartbeats he stood there, straining to hear. Then he came back, looking sheepish. 'Just a couple of kids. Heading for the churchyard.'

Erik frowned. 'I'd better check.'

'We'll *all* check,' said Brockman. 'But stay inside the house. And no lights.'

Kristine stepped quickly across to the dining room door. For the first time that evening she looked pale and nervous. 'I shall see after my own room, Hr Brockman.'

He could not hide his surprise. 'Yes. OK. Whatever you want. Something wrong?'

'No. Nothing. I am a little nervous, that is all.'

'I don't blame you. I am *very* nervous.'

'You and I shall look in the big room,' said Anja, 'the – the parlour, you would call it.'

'In a second,' said Brockman. 'Come here, by the window. Not too close. See them? There, by the big stone.'

Anja shielded her eyes. In the darkness of the church-yard, two shadows were moving.

'What do they do there?'

'I'm not sure – yet.'

He watched intently for a few moments, then let out his breath with a sigh.

'Know something? Nine months after the New York brownout, the birth rate went crazy. In the dark we're all just little kids looking for comfort.'

She moved closer to him, nestling her head against his shoulder. Her body was trembling, just as it had a few hours earlier, and the perfume of her hair was touched with the richer, mustier scent of their lovemaking.

'Was that what happened to us, Peter? Just two children frightened of the dark?'

'You know it was more than that.'

She reached up to clasp his neck. 'For me also. I was wrong, Peter.'

'Wrong? About what?'

'About you. How I feel about you. Perhaps I am beginning to understand you – what you do, things that you say. Perhaps I am beginning to love you.'

'Can't imagine why.'

'Nor can I.'

He grinned, and kissed her. 'Your place or mine?'

'Neither. We must look in the parlour.'

He sighed, and let her go. 'Lead on. I'm liable to kick over the coal-bucket.'

In the darkness, the little dining-room beyond the door seemed oppressive and claustrophobic. The rhythmic ticking of the big Bornholm clock measured out his heartbeat with mechanical indifference, but now there was another sound as well. All around him, the old house was moving.

The night before he had woken from uneasy sleep to hear the creaking music of the old timbers shuddering and groaning in the chill of an autumn night. This was a different, sharper sound, as though the beams were being buffeted and tormented by a force almost greater than they could bear. At the same moment every window in the house began to rattle wildly, and a deep sigh, like the exhalation of a sad giant, swept through the roof space over their heads. Anja's grip tightened on his hand. With an effort, he smiled. 'Has this place got a storm shelter?'

'Come *on*!'

In the big parlour the window-blinds were flapping wildly. Two or three had already rolled up. Outside, the shadows of the trees bent and sighed in the rising gale, but there was another movement, too – one that did not answer the furious keening of the wind.

'There is light,' said Anja. 'Over there.'

'Where?'

'In among the trees.'

'I see it. What the hell –?'

A green glow lit up the lower branches of a massive oak, shifting gradually to blood red. Tossing leaves and branches broke it into scattered fans of light, growing stronger and brighter with every passing moment.

'What is it, Peter?'

'Christ knows. There's another one over there. See it?'

'No – yes. Oh God, let it not be the alvar!'

'Amen.'

'We should tell the others.'

'You're right, but – hold it. Hold everything.'

158

'You have seen something else?'

'Yes, I sure as hell have.' Suddenly he laughed, louder than the rising roar of the storm wind. 'Those are torches – coloured torches! We're being invaded by a bunch of kids!'

She smiled uncertainly. 'I should have known. Sometimes they come here, the young people – for a dare, or a bet, perhaps.'

'Hell of a night for it.'

'Hell of a night for necking in a graveyard,' said Erik's voice behind them, 'but there's two of them at it right outside the kitchen. Saw the lights – thought something was up on this side.'

'Just more of the same,' said Brockman. 'Where's Fru Hansen?'

'Here, Hr Brockman. There are two boys outside my window, also with torches.'

Erik frowned. 'What the blazes do they want?'

'Right now,' said Brockman, 'I don't give a damn. If they're human, they're welcome.'

'Are you sure, Hr Brockman?' There was a strange edge to Kristine's voice. 'Are you *sure* they are human?'

'Fru Hansen, I've *seen* alvar, and they don't –' He hesitated. 'Damn it. I'm sorry.'

'What is it, Hr Brockman?'

'What do you know that I don't?'

'The truth, Hr Brockman. The truth a young girl died for. That those who burned her, it was they themselves who killed the priest.'

For a moment Brockman was struck dumb. Once again there was an image in his mind, an image of startling clarity, as though somewhere just beyond remembrance he had *seen* what Kristine described. 'What are you saying – that those kids are the alvar?'

'Remember what Erik has told us – that the alvar can master weaker minds and turn them to darkness.'

There were four torches now, three of them with the coloured filters that had seemed so alarming at first. They

159

moved erratically, changing colour from red to green and from green to yellow or a livid blue. Although Brockman could see shadowy shapes behind them, the torches seemed almost to have a life of their own. He scowled. 'I wish you didn't make so much sense. Sounds like Kialar's way – using humans for his dirty work.'

Erik's face twisted, and Brockman felt a surge of pity for the man.

'*Mormor* may be wrong,' said Anja. 'It might be nothing – just children playing foolish games.'

'If it's nothing,' said Brockman, 'then Kialar's given it one hell of a buildup. Either way, we'd best talk to them. Can you open one of these windows, Anja?'

'I think so.' She reached for the catch, but Kristine caught her hand. '*Nej, pigebarn* – we must keep it closed. The catch is of iron – it is part of what protects us.'

Anja shook her head. 'I – I don't understand.'

'It is more important that you believe me, Anja.'

The children were closer now. All were dressed in voluminous anoraks and Arab scarves, like every other Danish teenager, but there was something odd about their faces.

'What is this?' muttered Brockman. 'Some kind of game?'

'It's not a game,' said Erik tonelessly. 'Look away.'

Anja frowned. 'I don't understand –'

'*Do it*,' said Brockman. 'Do whatever he –'

His sentence tailed away into silence. For a moment a ghost of his former vision had come back to haunt him; as though somewhere, just at the edge of perception, the horrors out of twilight still encircled the house.

'You see them, Brockman? You see the alvar?'

'I'm not sure . I see *something* . . .'

'I see them, Erik,' said Kristine. 'What can we do?'

'There's one way –' He hesitated. 'I think you know.'

Brockman nodded slowly. 'Sure. You saw how to deal with alvar. How the Watcher did it, anyhow. But we can't just –'

'What choice do we have?'

'*No!*' shouted Anja.'They are children, Erik – and most are my patients. We have no right to harm them.'

Brockman slammed his fist on the table. 'Which is just how Kialar planned it! He uses our weaknesses – love, pity, caring about kids. And while we argue, they'll kill us.'

'So what's *your* idea?' said Erik.

'Go out and kick their asses home to bed. Coming?'

'That would be foolish,' said Kristine. 'It is true they have the bodies of children, but they will surely have the minds and powers of the alvar who control them. You cannot face them.'

Erik shook his head. 'You gave me the blade, Kristine. And I've got *nothing* to lose.'

'We need you alive, Larssen –'

'Which doesn't change the situation.'

'OK, then we'll *all* go – except Fru Hansen.'

The old woman gripped his wrist. 'Hr Brockman, you should not do this – you must not leave the house!'

'We'll be protected, Fru Hansen; we'll all carry iron. Anja, what have you got?'

'There are two of the – the swords –'

'The foils?'

'Yes, the foils. And an axe – we use it to cut wood for the stoves.'

Kristine shook her head firmly. 'It is not enough. Even Erik's blade cannot guard you against Kialar himself. You *must* not go.'

'Kristine,' said Erik, 'you can't stop me. And I won't let you stop the others. Not this time.'

The old lady pushed herself to her feet. 'Then I shall come also,' she said, 'and give what help I can. But this is sheerest folly, Erik.'

'A car would be handy,' said Brockman. 'I don't suppose you have one hidden away?'

'The garage,' said Anja.

'You're kidding.'

'*Gud i himmel*, Peter, I am a doctor! Of *course* I have a car!'

'So where's the garage?'

'In the old barn. There is a door to the courtyard, and another out to the drive – next to the house.'

'Then we'll try it. You and Fru Hansen get in the car, get ready to –'

'No, Peter. You must drive – or Erik.'

'What d'you mean?'

'I *know* these children, Peter. I must talk to them.'

'But –'

'I am their doctor. I am responsible.'

'And I have the blade,' said Erik. 'Which means you drive, Brockman.'

'I guess it does.' He looked unhappy. 'Hope to Christ it doesn't have stick shift.'

'Stick shift,' growled Brockman. 'I knew it.'

'Something is wrong, Hr Brockman?'

'No, Fru Hansen.' He struggled for a moment with his Danish. 'Nothing important. Just wish Anja would hurry it.' He was itching to test the Volvo's motor, but starting it now would betray exactly what they were doing. Meanwhile something was nagging at him – an idea, or a memory, that remained tantalisingly elusive.

Something Erik told us – or something about Erik. Damn it, I should have been taking notes . . .

For a moment he was hardly aware that the double doors out to the driveway were opening; Anja and Erik were moving them slowly and quietly, hoping to surprise any watchers outside. Brockman held his breath, willing the drive to be clear – then let it out in a long sigh.

Damn. Why couldn't it be easy, just this once?

The two children stood directly in the path of the car, holding hands like innocents in a fairy tale. Even so, he tightened his grip on the key. If Anja and Erik could distract them, just for a moment, he might have a chance . . .

'*Hej*, Søren, Margrethe,' Anja's voice was clear and

firm, without a hint of fear. 'What are you doing? It's late. Your parents will be worried.'

'Please help us, Doctor Kristiansson – we don't feel well ...' The boy's voice was strained, yet strangely unexpressive, as though acting a part he could not quite understand.

'What's the matter, Søren?'

'There's something in my head. It *hurts*.'

'Come here. Let me see.'

For God's sake! She must be crazy!

Glancing in the mirror, Brockman saw Kristine frown – and half-saw two ghostly armoured figures, part human and part beast, raising their hands in a gesture he remembered.

He yelled desperately to Anja and Erik, but it was already too late. As Anja staggered and fell the whole courtyard flared into a savage radiance. He could see the faces of the children contorted with a hatred and fear that had no place there, arms outstretched – then Erik stepped across Anja's prostrate body, whirling the shaft of his halberd in a windmilling circle. Again the old courtyard shimmered with pale light, like the dim reflection of a summer storm – and Erik staggered with the impact as sizzling arcs of light rebounded from his blade, fountaining across the drive in a flurry of sparks.

With a desperate yell Brockman turned the key in the ignition. The motor coughed once and died, but the Volvo's quartz halogen headlamps flared into life, flooding the drive with light. The glare half-blinded him, but he seemed to see dazzling bolts of light to left and right of the opening that were nothing to do with the car. The children were covering their eyes, cowering away from the headlamps ...

Light! That's it! Eleanor couldn't stand bright light!

The double doors slammed shut. There was another crackling discharge of energy that made itself heard even above the noise of the storm – and a voice like the wind itself.

'There is no sanctuary, son of Lars!'

Brockman tried the motor again. It gave no response at all.

'She is not badly hurt, Hr Brockman; it is only that she struck her head as she fell.'

He nodded, watching silently as Kristine sponged the ugly cut on the younger woman's forehead. Together, he and Erik had carried Anja into her bedroom. Now Erik sat by the window, staring moodily out into the encircling darkness, hunching himself against the shaft of the halberd. 'If it weren't for me she wouldn't be hurt at all. Does he know us that well, Brockman? Does he *know* what we'll do?'

'Call it a lucky guess.' He grimaced. 'A damned lucky guess. Now he's got us penned in – right the way he wants us.'

Kristine smiled. 'You think so? Perhaps he is not so well content.'

'How's that?'

'Already I have told you, this place is protected from Kialar and his kind. It is true we cannot leave – but neither can he enter, unless first he is invited.'

'That sounds just a touch too good to be true.'

'Nonetheless it *is* true, Hr Brockman.'

Erik moved uneasily in his chair, shifting the halberd from hand to hand. 'So we just wait, is that it?'

'Wait, and pray for the sunrise, *min dreng*.'

Brockman forced a grin. 'This gets more like a vampire movie every minute. What happens at sunrise?'

'They lose the darkness, Hr Brockman – and the greater part of their power. These children, they are not foolish or mad – they have been taken in their sleep, while their minds are locked in dreams. In the morning they will waken, and the alvar will have no grip upon them.'

'So we're OK once the sun is up?'

'*Ja præcis*, Hr Brockman. And then, Erik, you can take

the battle to your enemy if you wish.'

Erik grunted non-committally. 'He's killed the Watcher and destroyed the liosalvar. He won't be stopped by an old farmhouse.'

'You sure of that?' said Brockman. 'If he's really won, why take this much trouble? He has to be afraid of something – something right here. What do you reckon, Fru Hansen?'

'I cannot tell, Hr Brockman – but I think you were right, Erik. I think it is you that he fears. The father of such a one as Biarki must surely have great power.'

Erik laughed dismissively. 'Oh, yes. And a remarkable ability to make an ass of himself.'

'Can it, will you?' Brockman growled. 'I'm up to here with your self-pity. There's four of us here, and right now Anja's a hell of a lot worse off than you.'

'Can we do without the sermon, Brockman? I don't –'

He stopped in mid-sentence, transfixed by something outside the window.

'What's up, Larssen? What do you see?'

'There's something happening,' said Erik. 'Someone out there –'

'I hear it,' said Brockman. 'It's on the gravel.'

Kristine pushed herself painfully to her feet. 'It is a sending, Erik.'

The older man ignored her. 'I can hear something like – like whimpering.'

'It's a child!' said Brockman.

'*Daddy? Please let me in, daddy. I'm cold . . .*'

Erik's face was a rigid mask, as if he were deliberately suppressing all emotion. 'You hear it, Brockman?'

'I hear *something*.'

'You, Kristine?'

The old woman made no reply. Instead she took down the crucifix above Anja's bed, picked up the lamp, and walked awkwardly to the window.

'It looks like Bjørn,' said Erik. There was the slightest tremor in his voice.

'Daddy? Where do shadows go at night, daddy?'

In the window, the lamp's reflection held the night at bay. Kristine clasped the crucifix close to her chest, peering over Erik's shoulder. 'This is what you saw in the twilight?'

'Yes. He's mocking me.'

'Please don't leave me, daddy! Please don't ever leave me!'

Kristine turned to place the lamp on the oak dresser by the window, and for a moment Brockman glimpsed a creature with the face of Erik's son, clutching at the window ledge. It was whimpering like a human child – but its flesh was polished ebony, it had claws like curved needles, and its burning eyes gleamed like brass. There was something sickening about it, something so hideously unnatural that Brockman turned away.

And then, with a cry of rage and horror and grief, Erik flung open the window, grasped the halberd with both hands, and thrust it twice into the body of the creature outside. It screamed, but the sound was like nothing Brockman had ever heard – a drawn-out, ululating wail that might have been pain, or laughter, or a cry of triumph. The wind rose to a deafening roar, hammering against the side of the house like a battering ram. It threw back the open window and shattered it against the wall, driving Erik and Kristine back from the aperture. Hands clawed out of the shadows, reaching for the window, slithering, grasping – and then Brockman lashed out with the axe. He felt it bite against bone before it crashed into the window ledge, and something dropped to the floor at his feet with a soft thump – something that writhed and wriggled and then lay still.

'Help me with the shutters,' said Kristine, as if nothing had happened. Mechanically, he did as she asked, struggling to close the heavy shutters against the force of the wind, and holding them as still as he could while she wrestled the bolts into place. The axe was still buried in the sill, and dark liquid trickled down the wall.

'What – *was* that?' he said at last.

Kristine pointed to the floor. 'See for yourself.'

He hesitated, but the serenity in her face reassured him.

At his feet lay the withered tip of a tree-branch.

'Illusions, Hr Brockman. Illusions and trickery. Kialar wished merely to drive you from the window – but your iron barred his entry.'

'I'm sorry,' said Erik. 'He knows my weaknesses, and he's playing on them. I won't be drawn again.'

Anja stirred uneasily on the bed. Kristine sat down by her side, sponging her brow. 'You are better now, *pigebarn*?'

Anja nodded. 'It is cold in here.'

Kristine handed the lamp to Brockman. 'We shall go back to the kitchen, *pigebarn*. There is warmth there, and good iron – we shall be safe enough. No, Hr Brockman, leave the axe where it is. It has another purpose now, and we have weapons enough. Pray God we shall not –'

She was interrupted by a dreadful cry from the churchyard – the cry of a human being in unbelievable pain. As Brockman flung open the kitchen door a red, flickering light flooded into the bedroom. He ran to the churchyard window – and saw the mound engulfed in flame. The stone had vanished, lost beneath the pile of kindling and fallen branches heaped around it, feeding the furnace above. And at its heart, arms raised in a last, desperate plea, was Anja. In the few heartbeats it took him to reach the window he saw her hair swirl up in the flames to become a soaring column of orange-yellow fire, saw the flesh of her face break, blacken, and fall away from the bones, heard the skull crack open as the brains boiled inside it ...

'*Anja!*'

'I'm here, Peter! I'm all right! Come away, *please* come away!'

Brockman rubbed his eyes, as if he were trying to drive out the memory of what he had seen. Anja laid a hand on his shoulder. 'What happened – there on the mound? It

167

was me. Wasn't it, Peter? You saw me die!'

'Anja, I –'

'Hr Brockman,' said Kristine, 'mine is a very old family, and our features are very strong. There have been faces like Anja's in every generation.'

'I don't want to talk about it.'

'Because it seemed real? Perhaps it was. Something from long ago – from the last great storm.'

The girl they burned. Oh, God, her face! But why show me that? What was he trying to do? 'That's *it*! He's afraid of death! It terrifies him, so he thinks it'll terrify us!'

Kristine shook her head. 'I do not think the alvar know death as we do – but Kialar plays a subtler game. He shows us the death of those we care for – those we are responsible for.'

'The fire's real enough,' said Erik. 'Think he's going to burn us out?'

Kristine shook her head. 'It would be the coward's way – a humiliation in the eyes of his followers. And until now we have been lucky.'

Brockman grinned. 'That's an interesting definition of luck, Fru Hansen.'

'Hr Brockman, I –'

'*Son of Lars, I weary of waiting!*'

It was the same voice they had heard in the courtyard. It seemed to come from every side of the house at once, and Erik's face twisted into a mask of hatred at the sound of it.

'*You hear me, son of Lars?*'

'Yes,' he shouted, 'I hear you. What do you want?'

'*You shall not escape – you, or the others.*'

'You didn't take this house last time, Kialar – you won't take it now.'

'*Do not be so sure. The Watcher cannot help you – your son has done well.*'

'You don't belong here, Kialar. There are things in our world you could never understand – things that can destroy you as easily as you crush a butterfly.'

'*There is nothing in your world that can harm me, son of Lars –*'

'Iron harms you, Kialar – and I'll be glad to prove it.'

'No!' said Anja. 'You must not listen to him, Erik! He wishes only to make you angry!'

'*– but there are creatures from my world that can destroy you! Farewell, father of warriors – and a long farewell to all you hold most dear!*'

'This time he means it, Anja. Listen.'

For a few heartbeats there was silence in the old kitchen – then distantly, half-drowned by the keening wind, came a faint but strangely familiar cry. Anja shuddered, and her eyes met Brockman's. 'The cry that woke us – you remember?'

He nodded. 'You were out there, Larssen. What was it?'

Erik shook his head. 'I never saw it. Never wanted to. It sounded like – like . . .'

Kristine shielded her eyes, straining to make out what was happening. 'What do you see, Hr Brockman?'

'Mist's rising again. Tricky to see anything.'

'Look at the mound,' said Anja, in a voice near a whisper. 'The mist – it moves so strangely . . .'

'That isn't mist,' said Erik. 'Not on a night like this. It looks – it looks as though the *mound* is moving . . .'

The cry came again – but closer, louder, with an eerie, almost human quality that set Brockman's teeth on edge. Beneath the fire, deep within the shadow of the mound, a deeper shadow answered its summons with the whisper of dead leaves on a winter wind. He seemed to know it as well as he knew himself in this place that was at once familiar and utterly beyond his understanding – because now, at the borders of time and twilight, there was nothing left but a shuffling, dragging darkness that belonging to both worlds and to neither. Its footfall on the frost-hardened ground was iron on iron, dried bones rattling on stone, leather flapping in a wind from the sea . . .

Something struck the side of the house, something

vast and moving and alive. For a moment, no more, Brockman seemed to see a single eye, bloodshot and wide with madness – and then the next blow fell, and he heard the crash of breaking glass from the room where he had slept.

'Quickly!' cried Kristine. 'The shutters!'

Brockman raced for the door and flung it open. In the dim light from the kitchen he could see the window-blind flapping like a tattered banner in the wind from the mound, and beneath it a dark shape like the arm of a giant fumbling around the opening. Erik pushed past him, striking out with the halberd. For a moment the older man was off balance, and in that moment his weapon was wrenched from his hand. Brockman dived forward, grabbed at the shaft, and rolled sideways to twist the halberd out of the creature's grip. There was a roar from outside that chilled his blood – and the blade dropped to the floor. It was stained with a dark, sticky liquid. Before he could recover, Erik had seized the shutters and slammed them shut.

'Nice work, Brockman. Give me a hand, will you?'

For a few feverish minutes they struggled to close and bolt the shutters all around the outer wall. Outside, the crack of breaking stone and the crash of shattered timber rose even above the keening howl of the wind. It seemed futile to set wooden shutters against the demonic powers of Kialar's sending, but when Anja and Brockman reached the parlour they found Kristine already there, just setting the last bolt.

'These shutters can't stop it for long,' said Brockman. 'Better get more wood – build a barricade.'

Kristine smiled. 'The bolts will stop it – and the blacksmith's work.'

'Excuse me?'

'The hinges are of iron, Hr Brockman – and *very* long. And there are iron crosses all around the wall.'

'That'll keep it out?'

'If the stories are true.'

'You know what the hell it is?'

'It *is* hell, Hr Brockman – the hell-horse that was born to destroy all living things. There is a painting in the church – I think perhaps you have seen it.'

Anja stared for a moment at her grandmother, then ran from the room. Brockman barely noticed. 'Yes,' he said, 'I've seen it. Something like a black horse with a naked rider, battering at the tree of life. You're saying that ...?'

The old women nodded. 'Old stories, Hr Brockman. Old wives' tales. But there is always truth in them. Kialar did not lie; he calls on forces we cannot understand.'

Brockman nodded vaguely. 'That painting. Something else about it. Yes ... There was a man there – a man and a woman – and *he* had –'

'A bow,' said Anja. 'Like this one.'

The weapon she carried was a composite bow with a grip that seemed to be sculpted to her hand. A large and well-stocked quiver hung at her waist. Brockman swore feelingly. 'You can *use* that?'

'I was last year's champion in the – how do you say? – community.'

'No kidding.' He had learned to use a bow himself, in South America, and he knew for himself the strength and dedication needed to make a good archer. Anja continued to surprise him.

'We must go to the roof,' she said. 'There is a stair by the room where you slept.'

'Sleep? I remember sleep. You should try it some time. I'll get a lamp.'

'I'll stay here with Kristine,' said Erik, hefting the halberd in both hands. 'Could be the ironwork's not enough.'

'One thing, Larssen,' said Brockman.

'What?'

'I've called you a few lousy names tonight. But then I've spent most of my life being a son of a bitch, with a lot less reason than you. If we get out of this –'

Erik grinned mirthlessly. 'If we do, we'll be the luckiest people on God's earth. If it's still His.'

The roof space was taller than the downstairs rooms, but thick with dust. it was clear that no one had been here for many years, and the darkness was almost impenetrable. The space was continuous round all four sides of the house, but there were only three or four windows on each side, and all were set close to the floor.

'What do you reckon?'

Anja strung her bow with a practised movement that almost took his breath away. 'From here I can shoot, yes – but we cannot cover every part of the house. The gap is too great between the windows.'

'Sounds like you've tried it.'

'When I was little we used to play here – Erik and I.'

'Doctors and nurses?'

She laughed, without conviction. 'Cowboys and Indians. I think perhaps nothing has changed.'

'Except the noise. Hell's *teeth*, listen to that wind.'

At first there was little else to hear. In the enclosed attic it sounded even louder; timber groaned and re-verberated all around them, with a whistling counterpoint from the chimneys and a deeper, sighing note from the trees around the house. As they moved back towards the main part of the house they might have been inside some forgotten sailing ship weathering out a gale in a sheltered anchorage. But from the churchyard came a sound like a distant battering ram. Plumes of dust fell from the joists, answering the rhythmic hammer-blows from outside. The old farmhouse was under siege.

Brockman tried to smile. 'Story of my life. I get to the best thing I ever found, and some bastard shows up with a bulldozer. What *is* that, anyway?'

Anja grimaced. 'We shall see soon enough.'

'If we can trust our eyes. We already know a few of the tricks Kialar can play.'

'Here. From this window I should –' Her voice trailed off.

'What is it? What's out there?'

She shook her head, gesturing to another window as she eased her own quietly open and nocked a shaft onto her bowstring. In the flickering light from the fire he could just make out the tip; it was an unbarbed target arrow. No matter: at this range its impact would be just as damaging as its penetration. He knelt down by the next window, but from this angle the darkness by the wall was absolute; shadow moved within shadow, and only the sound of its fury revealed their attacker.

'How 'bout some light?' he asked.

Anja made no reply. She was staring steadily into the night, the bow poised in her hand. She had drawn and released the arrow in a single, fluid motion before he even realised she had taken aim.

'Damn it, you're *good*! How the hell can you see without your eyeglasses?'

'Eyeglasses?'

'I've seen you squinting. Don't tell me you don't need them.'

'I don't. My night vision is good, but I am like Eleanor – it makes pain in my eyes when there is bright sunlight. Now please be quiet, Peter. I must concentrate.'

Again she drew and released, but this time there was a response – a deafening, animal roar that rocked the floor beneath Brockman's feet. At the same moment a shape staggered back into the flickering firelight, and for one terrible instant he saw what Kialar had sent against them.

The face that stared up into his was filled with pain and hatred. Once it might have been human – once very long ago. Now it was nothing but a network of sinews and black, pulsing veins. Ropes of muscle clenched around burning, yellow eyes, as it raised a flayed and twisted hand clenched into a raw-fleshed fist. Anja's arrow stood clean out of its shoulder, and a dark, oily liquid trickled from the wound. Below, he could half-see a trunk sheathed in cable-like muscles that vanished into shadow . . .

Brockman found himself gasping for breath, struggling

to deny the evidence of his own eyes. Such a thing could not be real in any sense that he understood – but he had seen it, watched it move ... 'You saw that, Anja?'

She nodded, her face betraying no emotion. 'I saw it to loose at it.'

He whistled softly.

'Remember I am a doctor, Peter. I have seen many terrible things.' The hammering began again, with re-doubled force, but she seemed unmoved.

'You believe what your grandmother said?'

'Yes. It cannot get in – and we can hurt it. And the longer we can hold it off, the less time Kialar will have.' She drew and loosed again, to be answered by another angry roar from below. Brockman peered through the narrow window.

'Sky's lightening already. If Kristine was right, that means Kialar's going to have to – oh, Christ, Anja –'

'I see it. I think he plays his last card.'

One by one, the children were leaving their stations around the house and gathering by the fire on the mound. Brockman clenched his fists in helpless frustration. 'I don't believe it. We can face off a thing from the pit of hell, but we can't stop a few kids burning us to death.'

She nodded. 'He believes we will not harm them.'

'Is he right?'

Anja looked him squarely in the face. 'They are children, Peter – and they are my responsibility. If I hurt them now I am no better than Kialar. I would deserve all he plans for us.'

He sighed. 'I can't argue with that –'

'But you wish that you could.'

'No. How'd I explain it to *our* kids?'

She flushed. 'What are you saying?'

'I'm saying I want a daughter like you. Damn it, I'd settle for a *son* like you.'

Her eyes glistened. 'I wanted ... It doesn't matter. Hold me, Peter.'

He took her in his arms, feeling the perfumed silk of

her hair against his cheek, the warmth of her body against his. 'I know what you want. I've been like you; taking second best because it was all I could handle. Tonight we found something else – and I won't give it up. Not yet.'

'How can we stop them? Look – they are bringing torches already. We have only a little more time.'

Brockman swore softly. 'You're right. But that's all we need – a little time. We'll want water, and plenty of it – can you and Kristine see to that?'

'What will you do?'

'*Hurry!* Follow me!' Brockman ran to the narrow staircase and thundered down it, all but colliding with Erik at the door into the bedroom.

'What the hell – ?'

'Kialar's having a barbecue. Us. Anja, get that water. Erik, I need you upstairs.'

The older man smiled faintly. 'Erik?'

'So I need friends. Come *on*!'

Erik's halberd was difficult to manoeuvre in the confines of the staircase. By the time they reached the roof space, the flickering firelight from the mound revealed a red haze of smoke under the eaves.

'What's the idea, Brockman?'

'Peter. We can't stop them torching the roof – but we *can* stop it spreading. Give me that thing, will you?'

'What –?'

Erik had no chance to protest. Brockman snatched the halberd out of his hands and slashed at the thatch immediately above their heads.

'What the hell are you doing, Brockman?'

'Firebreak! Keep the fire – in one place!'

'Give me the halberd. I can handle that!'

'*No!* Help – others!'

Erik hesitated for a moment, then ran back to the staircase as he saw Anja bringing up the first of the water. Flames were already glowing at the far end of the roof space, and a rivulet of smoke crawled towards them along the eaves. Desperately Brockman hacked and slashed at the growing hole in the thatch, gasping with the effort, coughing helplessly as the smoke caught the back of his throat, trying not to watch the slow, inevitable victory of the flames. He knew they had no chance of stopping the fire – but if they could control it, even for an hour, the new dawn would bring an end to Kialar's power. Soon both his arms were an agony of tense, twisted muscle, but the ancient roof had been well and soundly laid: the network of connecting beams made his task all but impossible. He imagined firebrands falling on every side, flame spreading from each of them like an opening flower. With every passing minute the fire grew stronger, hissing and popping in the damp thatch, roaring as the wind fed its hunger and fanned it towards them.

He felt a cool touch at his lips – Anja, sponging down his blackened face, trickling water into his throat. 'Save it!' he croaked. 'Gonna need every drop!'

'It's no good, Peter! There is no time!'

His answer was drowned by a splintering crash as the far end of the roof collapsed in a tumbling ruin of flaming, fire-blackened timber. A second, answering crash reverberated through the house as the ceiling gave way and blazing wreckage thundered down into the parlour. As the wind fed the new fire, a column of flame roared up to lick at the skeletal frames that now stood clear against the cloud-wracked sky like the gallows at a witch-burning. Brockman saw rather than heard Anja's cry of horror as Kialar's hellish sending roared its answer from below.

'*Mormor!*'

'Kristine! She was down there?'

'Yes – I must go to her!'

He grabbed at her wrist. 'There's nothing you can do!'

She pulled away from him with a sob and ran towards the stairhead. Brockman ran after her. Erik hesitated, snatched up her fallen bow and quiver, and sprinted after them. Seconds later the floor where they had been standing fell away into the house below, and a massive tongue of flame twisted upwards towards the rafters. Anja was already halfway down the staircase, but flames were licking at the woodwork near the bottom and smoke funnelled upwards all around them.

'Anja!' roared Brockman, 'if she was anywhere near that she's dead already!'

'I have to look!' she shouted. 'I must be sure!'

'*Wait!*'

Anja never even heard him – and as she flung open the door he saw her framed, just for a moment, in the livid light of the fire beyond it.

'*Anja!*'

As he rushed after her down the stairs he felt the timber giving way beneath his feet. Tiny flames stabbed at his ankles and the soles of his shoes as he hurled himself into the inferno that had once been the guest bedroom.

Anja was nowhere to be seen.

CHAPTER
7

Austr sat in aldna í Iárnviði
oc fœddi þar Fenris kindir;
verðr af þeim öllom einna nøkkorr
tungls tiúgari í trollz hami . . .

In the east dwells a hag, in Ironwood
Suckling there the sons of Fenris.
One of all that bastard brood
Shall savage the everlasting sun . . .

Völuspá – The Prophecy of the Seeress

'Anja! For God's sake! Anja!'

'She's gone, Brockman! There's nothing you can do!
Come *on*!'

A roof timber cracked and fell in a flaring surge of fire,
crashing to the floor in a flurry of sparks. Brockman stood
transfixed, seemingly unable to move, staring wide-eyed
into the rising flames. Erik snatched the halberd from the
American's nerveless hands and thrust him towards the
door.

The kitchen was dense with smoke, and Erik forced
Brockman to the floor as they battled towards the
courtyard. All around them the house was dying. The
door to the dining room had fallen inwards, and beyond it
the old Bornholm clock was wreathed in fire. Flames
licked about its face, and the ornate metal hands were
melting in the heat. From the parlour beyond came the

178

thunderous crack of breaking timbers as the rest of the roof collapsed into the roaring inferno below – and beneath the choking cloud of smoke, the air was filled with the sickly-sweet smell of dry timber burning with a fierce, inextinguishable flame.

The kitchen door was jammed in its frame. Erik had to batter the lock with the butt of his halberd until it tore away from the wood, and they staggered into the courtyard in a thick miasma of smoke, coughing helplessly.

They stood at the heart of a raging circle of fire that flailed from side to side in the grip of an unrelenting wind. All around them the ancient roof-timbers stood bare to the heavens in a corona of flame that sent black curtains of smoke into the pre-dawn sky. As the last of its ceilings fell the house began to collapse into its own ruins, the brick and plaster infill of its walls crumbling and falling away from the smouldering frames. The Volvo still stood in the middle of the courtyard, doors agape, facing a smoking heap of ruined timber that blocked the gates out to the driveway. Beyond it the old stable block gushed fire and smoke from every window, but by some miracle the roof still held. Erik thrust Anja's bow and quiver into Brockman's hands. 'Churchyard door!' he shouted. 'Only way out – fight for it!'

Brockman stared vaguely around him, eyes still wide with shock. Erik had to drag him to the door, steering him past blazing balks of timber and scattered heaps of burning thatch. The roof over the passageway was untouched, though fires raged on either side. Kialar had left a single avenue of escape – but the door at the far end was moving with a regular, insistent rhythm. Something was pounding against it with force enough to shake it in its frame. The long, iron hinges were tearing slowly away from the wood, buckling inwards under the strain.

Brockman rubbed his eyes. Then he strapped the quiver to his belt, picked out a target arrow, and nocked it on the string.

'Welcome back,' said Erik. 'Any good with that?'

'Does it matter?'

'Probably not.'

'Anja – she's gone?'

'I'm sorry, Brockman. Be lucky if *we* get out.'

'Erik – just one thing.'

'What?'

'Anja could've stopped those kids. She wouldn't do it. She wouldn't hurt them –'

'All right, I hear you. Now cover me – and get ready to run.' Erik pressed himself against the side of the passageway, and tugged at the upper bolt of the church-yard door. It was an awkward angle, and the battering from outside had all but jammed the bolt in its stays. He had to hammer at it with the butt of the halberd to move it at all. The sound brought another frenzied attack from the far side of the door. Erik smiled grimly. 'Weak in the brains department – thank God.'

'Can you get the other bolt?'

'I'm not sure. The stays are bent right out of shape.'

Again he hammered at the bolt with his halberd – then stumbled backwards into the courtyard as the door flew open and crashed against the wall of the passage. For a few seconds he blocked the line of fire, and Brockman saw the silhouette of the hell-horse, black against the bale-fire on the mound. Almost instinctively he drew the bowstring back to his ear, sighted along the shaft, and released.

From the corner of his eye he saw Erik recover himself with the shaft of the halberd as the creature in the doorway reared up and sideways – then he had another arrow on the string, and another, drawing and releasing like a deadly machine. The thump of target heads against alien flesh was drowned by the roar of the fire all around them, but the half-animal, half-human cry of the wounded hell-horse cut across all other sounds. Brockman nocked another shaft, but their attacker was hesitating, drawing back . . .

'*Now!*' roared Erik, and threw himself into the

passageway, swinging the halberd two-handed in a looping figure-of-eight. Brockman plunged after him into a firelit arena.

All around the churchyard wall stood the blank-faced children of Egerød, stripped of their humanity, the torches still in their hands. In the light from the flames they seemed to stare with the eyes of alvar, alien and uncaring. On the mound itself the fire still burned like a breath from the pit; the gate stone was lost in its glare. and before it crouched the hell-horse.

Brockman froze.

Once – just once – he had glimpsed it in the full light of the fire, and wiped the memory from his mind. Now its reality could not be denied. The forelegs were sleek and black, without the slightest trace of white around the fetlocks. The head was proud and erect, with burning golden eyes that glimmered with sparkles and flashes of blue. The dark, tangled mane streamed in the wind, half-shielding the rider Brockman had seen from the window. He saw arms like ropes of fleshless muscle, and hands like bundles of sinew clutching at one of his arrows. He saw a lipless, skinless face twisted with a terrible anger.

Like he'd been flayed alive ...

But where he had thought to see legs clenched against the horse's flanks there was nothing but a network of tendons, pulsing arteries and squirming muscles merging with the dark flesh below. And the hindquarters were an oozing, pulsating mass of corruption ...

'Brockman! For Christ's sake!'

Erik's shout jolted him back to full awareness. He nocked another shaft against his bowstring, drawing it with the fluid motion that had taken so long to achieve. The creature hesitated, horse-nostrils flaring, the lipless face behind it open-mouthed and snarling with fear or hatred. Then, with terrifying speed, it reared up to strike. He loosed his shaft full into its belly, and heard the thump as his arrow went home, but there was no time to escape the deadly hooves. He felt a snap of breaking bone as he was hurled against a marble gravestone, but in the heat of battle he barely noticed the pain. He rolled sideways to avoid the next strike, nocked his next arrow, rose to his knees with the bow held sideways, drew and released.

'*That's* for Anja, damn you!'

The creature's lipless mouth gaped open in a ragged, ear-splitting shriek, and the hideous hands clutched at the eye transfixed by Brockman's shaft. The horse-eyes filmed over; the forelimbs flailed blindly, stumbling backwards towards the mound, and the deafening, inhuman cry was repeated as the creature's trailing hindquarters touched the column of living fire that burned before the gate stone. A stench of corruption blew across the churchyard and vanished on the wind, but Brockman had no chance to savour his triumph. Agonising pain lanced up his side – and before he could draw breath the air crackled with alvar fire, and the gravestone shattered into fragments.

The children were moving forward, arms raised and shimmering with the raw power of the alvar. The raging fires beyond the wall threw a flickering tapestry of light and shadow over faces contorted with fear and hatred. Beyond and behind the children nightmares flickered in and out of vision, miscegenations as vile as the hell-horse, decked in armour or encased in their own hard-plated shells and hides. From every side came the flaring light of elf-shot. Erik was fighting for his life. The halberd moved in a dizzying, twisted spiral, fencing him in behind a web of moving steel – but his movements had lost their precision, and with every twist and turn of the heavy shaft he winced with pain. In the light from the fire Brockman could see the scorching burn along Erik's right arm, the cloth of his jacket still smoking from a chance hit. Now a single moment of respite, a single mistake, might spell the end; but Brockman himself had no defence, and others were turning towards him, hands raised to strike . . .

Suddenly he knew what to do.

'Erik! Follow me!'

Elf-shot flickered all around him, and he heard the splintering crack as a granite cross shattered and fell. Behind him the hell-horse flailed and struggled in its death-agonies, hindquarters threshing in the fire, scattering brands and embers far and wide. A gust of wind caught the funeral pyre that had been the farmhouse, drawing livid flame and black, sooty smoke upwards and outwards in a ragged, twisting column. Brockman felt the long grass of the mound brushing against his legs as he ducked and weaved backwards, moving as unpredictably as he could towards the undefended gate stone.

'Erik! To me! Now!'

For a moment, as Erik manoeuvred purposefully towards him, Brockman seemed to stand in two worlds. In one he saw the ruin of the farmhouse and the chill, windswept horror of the churchyard under a sky banded with midnight blue, vermilion and turquoise. The other was a silent, twilit world of drifting mists, where hills marched endlessly towards a darkling horizon. At the outer rim of his universe the hell-horse thrashed and screamed in the dying fire, and the grim-faced children, trapped in their waking nightmare, closed in on him step by relentless step. Then he was shoulder to shoulder with Erik.

The older man grinned savagely. 'I could – uh! – get to like you, Brockman.'

'Peter – and keep that halberd moving. Where the hell d'you learn that?'

'In twilight. Kialar's mistake. Lots of time to learn – how to kill him. Now *run* – as you value your soul!'

He grasped Brockman's wrist with brutal force, thrusting the younger man forward towards the face of the stone. For a moment Brockman felt its texture against his hand – coarse, still warm from the fire – and then a jolting shock hammered through his body. He saw Erik stiffen with the same shock. For one terrible moment the older man's face was ringed with blue fire, and flickering lines of energy wove a blinding network of light around his limbs – then darkness fell all around. The grotesque silhouettes of the alvar, the blank-faced, staring children, the funeral pyre that was the farm – all had vanished, and with them the terrible sounds of the burning, the dying screams of the hell-horse, and the crackling discharge of elf-shot. He was blind and deaf, and his ribs were a jagged island of pain . . .

'Peter? *Peter! Come on!*'

'What the hell . . .?'

'No time! I told you, *run!*'

He moved without understanding, without conscious thought, following the older man's path, steeling himself against the pain of each footfall, and barely aware of his surroundings. As his eyes adjusted to it, the half-darkness seemed little different from the pre-dawn light of Egerød – but now mist coiled about his ankles, and the ground sloped sharply upward ahead of them.

We're inside the gate. But I still don't believe it. Any minute now we'll see the farm again, and the kids . . .

Fragments of colour and light floated in front of his eyes, and his limbs ached with the strains and exertions of the night. But their flight was real enough: he could feel the ground changing beneath his feet from marshy, sodden grass to bare, stony rock. He could feel the droplets of mist gathering in his hair and dripping onto his face. He could see his own breath carried away behind him as they ran, feel the stab of pain in his side as each foot touched the ground – and it was easier to look down and seek his footing than to look around and accept the reality of what he had done. When Erik stopped, without warning, Brockman barely avoided running into him.

'What the –?'

'We have company, Peter.'

Brockman brushed a hand over his face, as though he were trying to wipe away the ghostly after-images of the burning farm and its fearsome besiegers. They stood on the rising slope of a dark mountainside. Above was an impossible sky roofed with stars as thick as beech leaves in October, shining with a light half as bright as the sun – and half-obscured by a whirlpool of cloud and darkness that had its centre behind them, at the crest of the mound. Below was a landscape in which nothing seemed familiar and nothing tangible, a surrealist fantasy without scale or proportion, beautiful as only mystery can be. Around the mountain – all around it – was the great stone circle that formed the gate. Beyond the stones was a flickering, broken ring of green-blue fire. Beyond the fire was an endless armed encampment that stretched from the shadows at the base of the mountain to the distant hills that marched along the midnight blue horizon.

And before them, out of the rising mist, the forces of twilight marched in ghostly procession.

The cold light of a million stars glittered on dew-spangled metal and enamel – on fluted armour, engraved with symbols and images of power; on helmets like the metal masks of Japanese samurai, bedecked with horns, caprices and grotesques; on glittering nets of link-mail blending with mist and darkness; and on weapons as alien as the hooded, golden eyes of those who bore them. In the half-light and the mist it was hard to judge distances or sizes, but in their unearthly armour the alvar seemed taller and more powerful than any man – and their leader sat astride a creature out of nightmare decked, like its rider, in a fantastic carapace of scaled and jointed metal and gleaming ring-mail. Brockman grunted in amazement.

St George in person. Just like the painting – and none too saintly . . .

The alv wore a great helm, cast in the shape of a hideous gape-jawed beast, and crowned with razor-edged horns. His visor was framed by the open mouth and snarling tusks. His cloak hung from two curving bars of metal that rose from his shoulders like demonic wings. He carried a bloodstained trident.

Wearily, Brockman nocked the last of his arrows to the string.

Good run, I guess. Pity it had to end like this.

'*Velkommen*, Erik Larssen,' said the *alv*. '*Velkommen, og godt gjort.*'

The words were Danish, spoken with a curious and all but impenetrable accent, but the voice was like Kialar's – harsh, emotionless and inhuman. Brockman raised his bow; Erik pushed it gently aside, but charged his own halberd ready to strike. 'Don't do *anything*. Not yet.'

'You crazy, Larssen?'

'Not quite. Oh, they're alvar all right – but not like Kialar. They're liosalvar the ones who helped us.'

Brockman felt an old fury surging up inside him. 'Where were they? Where the hell *were* they?'

'That's what I want to know.'

As if in answer, the alvar leader pointed silently towards the armed encampment beyond the stone circle. It had a savage beauty of its own, but no place at all in this landscape of stars and wilderness. It was like fire devouring a painter's masterpiece, or floods rushing down a fertile valley – wild, lovely, and deadly. Everywhere was a maze of structures that seemed half artificial and half organic. Some were machines, engines of creation or destruction. Others were buildings. Some were both, or neither – and all swarmed with movement like a conglomeration of gigantic hives.

'*Svartalvar,*' said the grating voice behind the mask. '*Der er for mange af dem.*'

'Too many of them.' said Erik.

Brockman nodded. 'Don't worry. I'm starting to catch his drift.'

Now, finally, he understood what he was seeing. Each tiny figure was an enemy, waiting to prey on the worlds of time. Each was a threat as potent as those few that had destroyed the farm and condemned Anja to death by fire. Each, like Kialar, was an inhuman shadow whose only thought was power. And here, drawn to this place of power like pilgrims to a miracle, they waited for the single moment of earthly time that would give them the gate stone. But between the mound and the alvar encampment was the ring of light he had seen before – a cold, flickering light that seemed to be filtered through a dark network, like a barrier ...

'They set their fires in the Ironwood,' said the alv, 'but the burning goes badly – many passed from the flesh before they could come at us. Even so, they drove us deep into the maze. We could not follow you – nor could we warn you. What has happened?'

Erik made no move to lower his halberd. 'Kialar burned the farm. This man fought at my side.' He paused for a moment and added, bitterly, 'My family are dead.'

'May they find life.' The alv made a curious sign with his hand. 'But you, you are in danger here. Kialar's forces follow close behind – his creatures befoul every path. Soon he will destroy us – all of us.'

Erik gestured to the silent circle of alvar. 'You have other forces?'

'None. Soon we, too, will be driven from the flesh. Kialar will hold the gate. The eternal battle will end at last, and your world will know us no longer.'

Erik narrowed his eyes, as if he were trying to see behind the grotesque mask of the tall alv's helmet. 'Your voice – I *know* you ...'

'I am Niord. I command the liosalvar. I it was who released you from Kialar's dream-spell – I who spoke to you here in the maze. And once, long before, I it was who entered your mind, Erik Larssen – entered it as you slept, and wrote the signs I found there in your hand. It was all I could do – my kind have little power beyond the gate.'

Brockman and Erik exchanged glances.

'Often I came to that place, but for fear of the Watcher I sought many paths. And so I left signs for you in many places, Erik – the signs of all your kind, but meant for you only. Always I had hope of finding you, to speak of your son within your mind. Always I had hope in you, his father, that you might bring him back to your own place. And then at last you came – but Kialar led you aside and destroyed my purpose. Once I had many hopes.'

Erik frowned. 'There's nothing you can do?'

'A single thing,' said Niord.

'What is it?'

'That you will see,' said the alv, and lifted the helm from his head.

His face was like the mocking mask of a human being. The slanted, golden eyes looked out of narrow, high-cheekboned features that seemed almost skeletal, hung with flesh darker than ebony. His expression was set in what seemed a mask of determination, centring on the piercing eyes, and within them Brockman seemed to see a great weariness – the weariness of immortality wasted in an endless, meaningless struggle for power. But the alv was already turning away; Niord was urging his mount sideways to face the silent ranks of his own followers, unbuckling the carapace of mail and metal that sheathed his body. Again Brockman saw dark skin stretched tight over a curiously distorted ribcage as the wing-like cloak and the dark-scaled armour were cast aside. The alv raised his arms high in a gesture that might have been salute or submission. He spoke a single, sharp word of command – and then the mist flared red as mount and rider alike vanished in a tumult of destructive fire that consumed flesh and bone in a blinding instant.

It was finished almost before it had begun. The thin grass was burned black, scattered with grey ash; and beyond it the ranks of the liosalvar stood silent and unmoving.

Brockman gaped. 'I don't believe it. They *killed* him!'

Erik ignored him. He was staring at a flickering flame that still burned amidst the ashes – staring with a furious concentration.

'Did they, Peter? *Did they?*'

'What you saying, he's gonna – Jesus H Christ!'

The tiny flame was growing, though nothing seemed

to be feeding it. Before Brockman could draw breath it had become a drifting, flailing column of red-gold fire.

'What *is* that?' said Brockman. 'What the hell *is* that?'

'I've seen it before,' said Erik. 'In the hall – at Lejre. But there's something different about this ...' He backed slowly away, and Brockman felt himself gripped by an unreasoning terror. He, too, had seen something like this – in the churchyard, in their first battle with the svartalvar ...

The flame was moving, as if it had a will of its own. Erik was still retreating, uncertain what to do, but the fiery column was advancing on him, gaining ground second by second. Brockman opened his mouth to shout a warning, but all that came out was a cry of horror as Erik was engulfed in living fire. The older man's hands beat at his face as though it were burning, and he opened his mouth to scream – but no sound came. For a moment he was transfigured: an intense light shone out from his face and his hands, as though his flesh had become no more than the pallid, translucent shell of something infinitely powerful. Then his head drooped, and he fell forward with a shuddering sigh. When, at last, he looked up, the inner light had gone. Brockman saw the cold eyes of the alvar set in a face that was no longer entirely human. It was an expression he had seen just once before – on the faces of the children around the farmhouse at Egerød.

Erik was lost.

He levelled the bow, half drawing it, and felt an answering stab of pain in his side. 'Keep back! Keep back, you hear?'

'What troubles you?' said Erik's voice soothingly. 'Do you fear me now, when once you trusted me so completely?'

'You must think I'm crazy.'

'So? Your friend is with me, Peter Brockman. I did only what had to be done for our sake and yours. Listen, and you will understand.'

The body of Erik Larssen was moving slowly towards him, arms outstretched in a kind of supplic

Brockman stepped carefully backwards, keeping the arrow firmly on its target. 'I'm listening, but don't count on convincing me.'

'There is no time for that, Peter Brockman. Matters move too quickly. Is it not enough for you that Erik trusted me?'

'I've just seen where it got him. Try again.'

'Already we have waited too long. Look!'

Unthinkingly Brockman glanced down the mountainside in the direction Erik's arm was pointing – and gasped. Little points of light were threading inwards from every stone in the circle; step by step, a thousand torches were revealing the slow inward spiral of the maze.

'*Svartalvar!*' he breathed.

'No less,' said Erik's voice. 'They seek the final victory. Soon they will find us and take our flesh – unless another takes it first.'

'Another? What the hell do you mean?'

His question was answered by a terrible screaming cry from higher up the path.

'The Watcher,' said the creature with Erik's face.

'It can't be! You saw – it's dead! It has to be!'

'Your friend was mistaken, Peter Brockman. The Watcher comes as it has always done, to defend the gate – and destroy all that it finds. None can stand against it and live.'

'If it's not dead, how the hell did the svartalvar get through?'

'Over the burned and broken flesh of my people! Now *come* – or die where you stand!'

Erik shouted a single word of command to the alvar troops on the path. For a moment they hesitated, as if they, too, doubted the reality of what had happened to him – then a phalanx of pikes turned to the rear, and the whole force began a slow retreat along the path. Brockman had no choice but to move with them.

'I don't get it. You're taking us right towards the svartalvar.'

'Yes,' said the Erik-creature, 'that is so; but only to bring the true death down upon their heads.'

'Where I come from,' said Brockman, 'we'd call that playing with fire.'

'You're telling me.' For a moment he saw the old Erik in the half-alien face, and the ghost of a weary smile. Then the mist seemed to surge and rise all about them, and the earth-shaking cry they had heard once before was repeated – closer, louder, and more insistent. For a moment the alvar force was hidden from Brockman's sight; but when the veils of mist parted, a grim battle had already begun. Their attacker was hard to see in the half-light of the stars, but it stood taller even than the alvar who confronted it. Remembering Erik's description, Brockman could just make out the high-peaked shoulders, the long-jawed head, and the narrow eyes protected by thick ridges of bone – but one of the creature's arms ened at the shoulder in a dangling remnant of torn ligaments, tendons and muscles. Even so, its power was horrifying. Its remaining arm swept aside the line of pikes like so many matchsticks, picked out a victim seemingly at random, and crushed the fully-armoured alv against its chest, buckling metal plate like parchment. Dark liquid oozed from the crushed and twisted metal shell, but the only sound Brockman could hear was the furious roaring of the Watcher itself as it cast aside the broken husk of its first victim and searched for another. In the red-gold light of flaring elf-shot Brockman saw the battle in vivid flashes; the terrible jaws closing on a beast-mask helmet; the single arm striking out like a trident to impale another of the alvar; the narrow, reptilian eye meeting his own in an instant of time that froze into eternity.

He seemed to sense an intelligence older than life, trapped in an aging, failing body whose power was already dying. He sensed a mind that might once have been human, weakened by time and the inescapable demands of a dreadful duty till it was little more than an unthinking force of destruction ...

The spell of terror was broken as Erik roared another command. The whole alvar force broke into a loping run, forcing Brockman on ahead of them into mist and darkness. He weaved desperately between the stones and fallen rocks that littered the treacherous path, stumbling and cursing, leaping from one rocky shelf to another and splashing through mud-filmed pools. His side was an agony – with each step the broken rib seemed to scrape against his flesh, and he was soon giddy and confused. As he passed through the wreaths of mist that drifted across the mountainside he entered a silent, claustro-phobic world where time and space obeyed other rules. Each time he emerged into the alien light of the maze the stars had moved in their courses, as though every step carried him farther into the womb of time. And the pursuing footfalls of the Watcher drummed insistently, unfalteringly, to the rhythms of his heartbeats.

Glancing back, he could see the Watcher's silhouette like a dark, haunting shadow behind the fleeing ranks of the alvar – but it, too, was changing. For a few seconds he glimpsed it clearly as one alv, in desperation, loosed a red-gold bolt of elf-shot. To his amazement the flaring light seemed to show a human face, half-hidden by a bestial alvar helmet – then he stumbled and fell headlong into a darkness lined with rocks and stones that battered his body and tore Anja's bow from his grasp. Alien hands seized him and dragged him onward, their armoured gauntlets bruising him, their needle-claws puncturing his skin – and when he glanced back again, head swimming with pain, the Watcher was nowhere to be seen.

But there were other hunters in the maze.

The second battle had begun before Brockman could gather his wits from the fall. He saw it first as a blur of light – the ice-blue of svartalvar fire touched with green and yellow as it met the red-gold of elf-shot from the liosalvar around and behind him. In the deadly light of their combat he saw the half-familiar shapes that had beset the farm – an ordered, impenetrable array of figures out of nightmare, mixing beauty and strangeness with decay and corruption.

Like fallen angels . . .

And now, for the first time, he was truly afraid. Kristine, for all her wisdom, had died in the flames of the farm. Anja, for all her courage, had perished with her. Erik, for all his knowledge, was gone – an empty husk in the lingering shape of a man. Brockman was alone, in a place no human being had ever been meant to see, in the midst of a clash of powers beyond his understanding. Anja's bow was lost somewhere on the terrible slopes of the mound, and all he had to defend himself were his wits and his bare hands. For the moment he was shielded by the armoured forms of a dozen liosalvar, but already their strident battlecries were lost in the crackling crepitation of elf-shot, and the agonised, inhuman howls of casualties on both sides. It was hell and judgement together – but Niord and his people were hopelessly, impossibly outnumberd. Unless . . .

Unless the alv's desperate gamble was successful. Unless he could bring the mindless, destructive horror of the Watcher down on a preoccupied and unsuspecting foe.

The trick is surviving till then. If I could just –

Lightning blinded him. For a moment he saw the alv in front of him transfigured, as Erik had been – shot through with a coruscating blue-silver light that burst through black flesh with a blinding, golden-brown radiance. Clinging spider-webs of energy flickered around the creature's armour like a hundred fiery hands, reshaping, sculpting, destroying. Metal sagged, buckled and dropped away like wax from a candle. Flesh, bone and sinew became a single glory of light – and then they were gone. All that remained was a glowing puddle of molten slag, and a twisting column of golden mist that whirled up into the darkness that cloaked the mound, and vanished like the breath of the Watcher.

It was hopeless. He would die here, with the liosalvar –

And then a voice was shouting in an unknown, incomprehensible tongue, a voice that carried even above the roar of the battle – a voice that Brockman knew. The creature that had once been Erik burst through the line of liosalvar into the chaos of conflicting energies at the heart of the battle. He was unarmoured, unprotected, utterly alone – but his face was an angry mask, and a pallid golden light flickered along the blade of his halberd as he lowered it to charge the ranks of his enemies. For an instant the svartalvar hesitated, and in that instant Erik had closed the gap between the two forces. The ancient weapon flickered with red-gold flame, spitting tongues of fire as its bearer swung it in a flashing figure-of-eight. His nearest opponent thrust a claw-like billhook into its path. The pattern-welded blade sliced clean through the weapon and into the winglike shoulderpiece of its bearer's armour. Pale fluids oozed from the cut as Erik's return thrust pierced the svartalv's cage-like breastplate. As the metal was ripped apart Brockman glimpsed something inside – something like a distorted face, its mouth gaping in agony. Then the creature was gone, trampled beneath Erik's boots, and the whole svartalv line was bending inwards. Against cold iron the powers of twilight had no defence – the blade glistened and ran with their lifeblood, and their ranks parted before it like flesh before the surgeon's knife.

With cries of triumph, the liosalvar surged forward, dragging Brockman with them, and suddenly he was in the thick of the fight, throwing himself aside as a curving, saw-toothed blade slashed across his path. He was vaguely aware of a lipless mouth like an open wound, lined with slim, needle-sharp teeth – and of the snapping, tusk-like fangs beyond them, framed in a second, inner pair of mucilaginous jaws. As he fell, his outthrust hands touched worked timber. Instinctively he grabbed the alvar pike and lunged upwards, striking deep into the belly of his opponent. He heard it squeal with pain and outrage, felt its claws sink into his arm – and then Erik thrust him aside, striking out with the halberd, and his attacker vanished in a crimson aureole of flame. Beyond it Brockman caught a brief glimpse of the fires he had seen from the mountainside – blue-green svartalvar fires burning in the midst of a bizarre, twisted forest, hung with strange fruit. There was a dark shape silhouetted against them, a shape that was somehow familiar ...

Then, from behind, came the unmistakable hunting cry of the Watcher.

He's done it!

'Come *on!*' roared the Erik-creature, seizing his arm. 'We cannot remain here!'

'Know anywhere else to go?'

'*Come!* It is our last chance!'

For a moment Brockman struggled, but the strength that drew him on was far more than human, and he could not resist for long. Behind them the sounds of battle were changing as the broken ranks of the svartalvar found themselves pinned between their enemies and the destroying fury of the Watcher. Before them, lit by the dwindling flames within the Ironwood, hung the torn and tormented bodies of the svartalvar who had died to force open a path to the mound. The thorny branches that enmeshed them seemed to move with a will of their own, twisting around armoured limbs, tearing at ebony flesh till bone glinted blue-green in the firelight ...

'To the stone!' roared Erik.

The stone? What ...?

Mesmerised by the crawling terror of the Ironwood, he had scarcely noticed the dark outline of the stone silhouetted against it. Around him, Erik's piteous handful of surviving followers were forming a ring to encircle the stone, shields out, weapons spitting flame, driving their enemies back into the jaws of the Watcher. Glancing towards Erik, Brockman saw the red-blue flash of the silver pendant as it caught the battle-light around them, saw him thrust it into the faint lines of the carving ...

And then, for the first time, he saw the true power of the stone.

It began with a deep, penetrating vibration that shook the ground beneath his feet till the clustered stars of twilight seemed to tremble in the heavens. The surface of the stone glittered like a gem-encrusted sceptre – and flowered. Shimmering arcs of energy spread outwards and upwards, throwing a brilliant silver light over the tumult below. He saw startled svartalvar faces glance up and cringe away. Higher and wider it spread, till the mound itself lay naked beneath it, its shape mapped out in silver and shadow, each path, each track, each twist and turn echoed by the spreading trails of light overhead . . .

It isn't just here. It's the other stones . . .!

As silver banished twilight he could see the same blinding discharge from the other stones in the circle, wreathing the mound in light, striking down at it, forging, reshaping –

As though it were making *the paths . . .*

And then there was no more time to think. He saw a human hand transfigured with power, and felt a sharp grip on his wrist. Then he was hurled bodily into another place and another time.

The tumult of battle faltered and died away to nothing. The silver-shot skies of twilight dimmed to the grey-blue glimmer of a winter morning. The hellish wood beyond the stone was gone – in its place stood a ring of giant oaks whose few remaining leaves rustled in a gentle earthly breeze. But at their feet a pool of mist lay thick upon the forest floor, drifting out from the stone like water from a fountain-head.

Erik stumbled and fell to his knees – in thick, crisp snow. Emotion flickered in the unmoving face.

'I had not known – your weakness . . .'

Brockman hesitated, then reached out a hand. 'Join the human race.'

'We must – bar way – to Kialar . . .'

'For Christ's sake *how?* You've opened the gate! You

think the svartalvar won't follow with *that* thing on their tail?'

'My followers – will hold – stone. Stop them – coming through. Even if – they too must die . . .' He stumbled again, clutching at the trunk of an oak for support. 'Only my chosen ones – my *einheriar* – followed me here.'

Brockman frowned. 'I don't see them.'

'Look – again . . .'

The floor of the glade was cloaked in mist – but now he could see a dozen slow, ghostly spirals rising from it, drifting like the vapour of his own breath on the morning breeze. Niord had not lied to Erik – it was true that he and his liosalvar had little power beyond the gate. As the terror of immediate pursuit began to fade, Brockman felt a surge of pity for the creature that Erik had become. In the battle by the stone it had saved his life – but here it was as frightened and helpless as he had been in twilight. 'You think the Watcher will stop them?'

'For a little while – yes. But in this place it is weak. It is touched by the – passing of your world. There comes a –' He struggled with an unfamiliar concept. 'A – *time* – when it must renew itself. That is when Kialar strikes. And now – now he has his – weapon. My son.'

'You're not making sense.'

'My son belongs to twilight and to – time. In this he is – like the Watcher. Only – such a one – can be Watcher's bane. And I, too – I am becoming – such a weapon – as Kialar has forged.'

'A weapon?'

Alv and human. Time and eternity. Twilight and sunlight – together. One being. Kialar has power. I have – humanity.'

'Can't say I'd noticed. You talk like an alv.'

'Not the – man – you knew. Nor alvar. I remember – Erik. I remember Niord. But I am – neither. I do not know – what I am . . .'

'So what do I call you?'

'Call me – what you wish. Do – as you wish. I seek the

– the hall of Rolf Kraki. I seek – the son of this flesh.' For a moment, the pain of loss transformed Erik's face. 'I – begin to understand – the hatred ...'

Brockman nodded. 'It was just about the only thing Erik had left. But at least he was human.'

The young-old eyes stared into his. 'I too – Peter Brockman. I am becoming – what you call "human".'

'I'll believe it when I see it.'

'You – will come?'

Brockman managed a grimace that was less than half a smile. 'I've got damn all else to do.'

For Brockman, their slow and dangerous journey through the snowbound forest was like a walk with a precocious child. They dared not speak when any shadow, any tree, any tiny creature might be the eyes and ears of Kialar – yet to Erik, drawing on the understanding and the memories of his mortal half, everything they saw was a revelation, and with each new miracle his response became more human. Brockman, despite the pain of his wound, found his own sense of wonder renewed. It seemed incredible that he could be walking through the heart of a living forest as old as the land itself, seeing creatures that had left the world hundreds of years before his own birth, in a time and a place that had long since passed into legend. He had visited Europe, but the forests he had seen were tiny patches of woodland that gave no hint of their ancestry. This was the great wood that once stretched unbroken from Scandinavia to the heartlands of France and Germany, and even into Italy. This was the dark birthplace of legend, as savage and unbridled as the creatures that slipped in and out of its shadows. Long after sunrise, it sheltered the drifting mists of morning; skeletal trees speared their way into the upper air, their snow-crusted branches like the pikes of the army of time. In some places the oldest had fallen to wind or lightning, and the forest floor lay open to the sky. Here thorn bushes, creepers and brambles sprawled in a tangled, impenetrable web, turned to fantastic arabesques by the snow, and silent movement was impossible. In one such clearing a dozen fallen trees had collapsed into a great mound of rotting timber, ripe with fungus and overgrown with climbing plants. The snow had made it an ice-palace, half veiled in mist, half glittering in the light of the new sun –

An enormous weight slammed against Brockman's shoulders, hurling him face-forward into the snow. Pain from his broken rib stabbed through his side as something ripped at the fabric of his jeans, scraping along his thigh. He struck out blindly, wildly, and found his fingers grasping at warm flesh through chill, wet fur. He tried to roll sideways, but the weight on his back was too great. There was nothing he could do. In a moment teeth would tear at his neck, or claws would rip out his throat ...

Needles punched through the leather of his jacket into his back. Something heavy rammed the side of his head, leaving him momentarily stunned. Something warm and wet trickled across his face. Then the weight was gone, and he rolled desperately aside, tensing for the next attack.

It never came.

Four dark grey shapes lay strewn across the snow, dark blood oozing through thick pelts and spattered in arcing trails of crimson across the snow. The last wolf was still impaled on Erik's halberd. Its claws had burst through Brockman's jacket in the very throes of death. Its glazed eyes stared up at him, empty and unseeing, jaws agape and dripping. For a moment he seemed to see a curious, misty shape around the head, as though even now there was breath in the ruined body. Then it was gone, and he was staggering shakily to his feet.

'Thanks. I –'

'Be silent!'

'What –'

With a raucous cry, two black birds flew up from a tree at the edge of the clearing. Brockman, still trembling from the fury of the attack, never even saw his new assailant leaping down from the cover of a fallen tree. Unarmed and unarmoured, he would have had no chance at all – but Erik reacted with unbelievable speed. The deadly halberd lashed out before the outthrust sword could reach its target, striking the hilt clean out of the man's hand. Brockman dived to one side, groping for the fallen weapon as Erik's halberd flashed again, slicing through their attacker's neck. The American staggered to his feet with barely enough time to parry a slashing blow from a faceless, mask-helmeted warrior in a ringmail byrnie; then he was fighting for his life. At his back he could hear the ring of metal against metal as Erik fought off other ambushers, but he dared not look to see how many there were. The man he faced was a powerful and experienced fighter in full armour – and he had nothing but his leather jacket and his own reflexes to protect him. Again and again he parried, ducked and sidestepped as his opponent's short sword cut a blinding network of light in the misty morning air. There was no time to think, and no time to be afraid – all his attention, all his effort, was concentrated in his eyes and his hand, as his own sword responded to the effortless swings and thrusts of his enemy. And then, suddenly, the man was clutching at his throat, gasping, falling, as Erik's halberd swung clear and splashed his lifeblood across the snow. The last man tried for a low upward stab, but Erik caught his arm with the backswing, cutting the tendons. The weapon dropped from his nerveless hand, and Erik's final stroke lunged up and under the man's breastbone. He coughed bloodily and died, eyes still wide with shock and disbelief.

'That's another one I owe you,' said Brockman. His voice was shaking.

Erik was already stripping the corpses. 'Perhaps it will bring trust between us. Tyr knows we have need of it.' He handed Brockman a baggy pair of breeks, splashed with fresh blood. 'Wear these. And take this sword.'

Brockman nodded vaguely, testing the balance of the

iron weapon in his hand. It was better made than the one he had been using, but its smithcraft could not match that of the halberd blade – and fencing had never been his best sport. 'Who were they? Who the hell *were* they?'

'Svartalvar. The animals, and the creatures they led here.' Erik pointed with the bloodstained blade of his halberd. All four men were dead – yet their bodies still writhed with the alien life that had stolen their minds, churning the snow into a pink froth. Brockman stepped back in horror as he saw his opponent's features distorted by the same savage hatred he had seen in the children's faces at the farm – then the blood around the man's mouth foamed and bubbled, and his last breath rose like a misty exhalation into the morning air. For a moment Brockman saw the spectral face of an alv, twisted with fury. Then the ghost melted into nothingness, and the twitching corpse was still.

'Kialar's people,' said Erik dispassionately. 'Thus they use the power they have gained, that power we will not seek – to search out spirits like their own, creatures that love secret murder and the ways of darkness. Such offal has no right to life – may their *fylgjar* be houseless till the stars fall.'

'I – don't understand.'

'Our life is not like yours, Peter Brockman. Alvar do not die: it is only that the *fylgja* leaves the flesh to find another home. The *fylgjar* of the First Made have great power; they can drive another from its fleshly shell, and leave it houseless for all eternity. In your world they can unhinge a human mind, or transform it. But these were *niðingar* – cowards, as you would say, with spirits of less worth than the merest beast.'

'So these were once – human beings? Ordinary human beings?'

'Yes, this carrion was once of your kind – but the most brutal of your kind, such as delight in preying on the weak and helpless. Spare no pity for them. And keep your eyes open, in Tyr's name. I cannot always be your guardian.'

When they reached the edge of the forest the sun was high in the heavens. In its clear light the ice floes far out on the fjord glittered like burnished silver, and the great hall was a dark silhouette against the sky.

I know this place. It's the Roskilde Fjord. And the island – the island has to be Lejre. The real Lejre . . .

Brockman gaped. Nothing had prepared him for the size of Rolf's hall. Despite Erik's description he had imagined a glorified turf hut, but what he saw was unmistakably the palace of a great king.

I don't believe it. This is the sixth century! Damn it, it's not possible . . .

'There is truth in legends,' said Erik. 'The stories say that Rolf was a king among kings, rich in gold, and open-handed. But they say also that he was accursed of the gods.' The strange, half-human eyes glittered. 'In this time and this place the Watcher is weak, Peter Brockman. For long years the svartalvar have crept out of twilight, and into the minds and the hearts of men. There is darkness here, and corruption.'

Brockman was barely listening. He was staring at the scene spread out below them, matching the knowledge gleaned from a dozen excavations and a hundred reports to the island fortress that was Rolf's stronghold. He had read of Iron Age causeways, and studied their remains, but this was a giant by any standards – half a mile long, supported by heavy oak piles sunk deep into the marsh, and paved with frosty cobbles that shimmered in the sunlight. Broad enough for two good-sized waggons to pass each other, it cut like a sword across the glittering wetlands on either side.

No wonder there were stories. Rolf chained the marsh – and the marsh took its revenge . . .

The island, too, had caught him unprepared. In his own mind he had dismissed Erik's description, replacing it with drawings and photographs from archaeological journals. What he saw now dwarfed anything he could ever have imagined.

The roof-ridge of the main hall was cut from a single, gigantic oak, and the building itself was like a monstrous galleon, stripped of its masts and rigging and turned belly-up on the rising ground at the centre of the island. There was nothing crude or unfinished about it – no archaeologist would have dared to imagine the skill and craftsmanship that showed in every detail of the hall, from the perfect joinery of the gables to the interlacing tracery of the dragons' heads that crowned them.

Even the outer defences were more than the crude palisade his imagination had furnished. There was worked timber here, and the watchtowers scattered around the perimeter carried pitched roofs to shield the garrison from foul weather and enemy fire. The gate-house was protected by taller, flanking turrets. Beneath the grisly, snow-encrusted heads impaled on the palisade the gates stood wide open. Slow ox-carts lumbered in and out along the cobbled road from the forest, bringing fresh supplies from the outlying farms – huge carts, like longboats mounted on trolleys and fitted with thick-rimmed wheels six foot or more across.

In the cleared area between the forest and the shore nothing but grass was allowed to grow – there were no bushes, shrubs or trees to give cover to an advancing enemy. Beyond them, to the right, a stream plashed down towards the distant waters of the fjord in a glittering cascade of icicles, and a snowbound path ran back from it to meet the main forest road into Lejre. There were figures on the path – distant figures, down by the stream. He narrowed his eyes, trying to see their clothes. Each new detail was a revelation, giving meaning and depth to a dozen half-remembered observations and records, clothing the excavated bones of the distant past in living, breathing flesh. Unthinkingly he groped for a sketchpad, desperate to make some record of what he saw – and touched the long, parallel scratches that the wolf's claws had left along his thigh.

'Peter Brockman!'

'Huh?'

'Best we conceal ourselves here. News of our coming has gone before, if those carrion in the forest had word of it. Come.'

He dragged a fallen branch across to a group of low shrubs to form a natural-looking hide. Brockman studied it critically. 'What exactly do you have in mind – or is that a human question?'

Erik ignored the barb. 'You know what I seek, Peter Brockman: the son of this flesh.'

'He's coming to *you*?'

'Kialar's puppets will say that enemies stalk the forest – and Biarki is the king's champion. He will seek us out himself, just as he will seek out the Watcher.'

'Wish I had your confidence.'

'Wait. There is nothing else we can do – unless you would find your death within the walls of Lejre.'

'Well, if you put it *that* way . . .' Brockman crouched down next to Erik, and stretched himself full length in the snow, favouring his broken rib. The place was well chosen – it gave a clear view of all the approaches to Lejre – and for a while both men were silent. Brockman found himself listening intently to the strange world all around him. From the forest came echoing birdsong, and the distant cries of animals. From the marshes below came the shrill music of wading birds. From the fjord beyond them came the screaming of seabirds, and the slow lapping of water against the shore. And from the island came the muted sounds of man – voices raised in greeting or in anger, the haunting lament of a wooden pipe, the lowing of animals, the clatter of hooves and cartwheels on cobbled roads and paths.

'What does he want?' murmured Brockman. 'Kialar, I mean.'

Erik's attention was firmly fixed on Lejre. For a

moment it seemed he had not heard the question.

'He seeks what he has always sought – power, and the winning of *fimbul-spillinn.*'

'What?'

Erik half-smiled. 'You, I think, might call it the great game.'

'Game? This is some kind of game?'

Again there was a long silence.

'I begin to understand,' said Erik. 'This is strange to your kind – your lives are bounded. But in our world – in the place you call "twilight" – there is nothing but *fimbul-spillinn.* Even the *fylgjar* of the First Made cannot recall its beginning, but they weary of it. They long to see something they have never known, to be housed in flesh that is not of the twilight. Of those *fylgjar,* Kialar is the chief – and when first he discovered the gate, it seemed to promise a new world of infinite possibilities.'

'So what makes the liosalvar different?'

'We fear the destruction of our world. Kialar meddles with things beyond his understanding. And there is the matter of the Watcher . . .'

Brockman shivered. He had barely glimpsed the Watcher, but its strength and power had terrified him. Remembering Erik's story, he could almost imagine it following their trail through the wintry darkness of the great forest . . .

'None knows how it came to birth,' said Erik. 'None knows how it lives, or why it should seek the true death of all who enter the gate. Its powers are beyond our understanding, but they are not without limit. Like the alvar, it does not die – but like your kind it is subject to time. It changes, even within the maze: in one place older and weaker, in another young and strong. It has been seen in other guises and other forms. Again and again Kialar's followers have entered the maze, seeking those places where its powers were weakest. Again and again they have died the true death. And then he sent the child of his own flesh – that one you know as Eleanor.'

'Eleanor?'

'She was the first to pass through the maze and live. She discovered the secret of the gate: that each path touches a different part of your world, a different – *time*. And here, in this palace, she bore the first of her children.'

'You mean – there was more than one?'

The other man nodded. 'Erik knew nothing of this. Bjørn's sister is here also. She is the daughter of King Helgi, and half-sister to Rolf Kraki himself. Her name is Skuld – and it was her wedding-feast that Erik saw when first he passed the gate.'

'So what's Kialar's plan? What will he do?'

'He seeks the true death of the Watcher – and if there is truth in your legends, he will achieve it. With the Watcher gone, and my forces scattered, the gate will lie unguarded. Kialar will have his dream – a new world of infinite mutability that he can turn and change at a whim. But for you, and your kind – chaos. Chaos without end. And now be silent.'

'What –?'

'*Silent!*'

Erik was staring intently towards the stream, along the path that passed their hiding place on its way back to Lejre. The group of women Brockman had seen before was returning to the island, carrying linen and washing in great wicker baskets. Most were young, and they giggled and chattered amongst themselves – but one, an older woman with a stern, lined face, walked apart and in silence. Two armed warriors escorted her.

'We are honoured,' muttered Erik, rising to his feet. 'The lady Eleanor and her maidens have come to greet us in person, with her *hirðmenn* to attend us. Now, Peter Brockman, let us see your skill with the sword.'

Brockman had no chance to refuse – the battle had begun before he could open his mouth. As soon as Erik stepped out of the trees the guards rushed at him, the first swinging a heavy single-bladed sea-axe. Erik side-

206

stepped, swinging the halberd low to catch the man's unprotected legs. He leapt to avoid it, toppling off balance, and the axe veered off its true line. As he twisted clumsily to recover, the halberd struck again, this time at his neck.

The blow never connected. At the last moment, the other *hirðmann* thrust his spear in the path of the falling blade. The shaft splintered, but Erik's halberd rebounded over the first man's bowed head. Now he had two opponents – but the first was still down. The second man cast aside his useless spear and reached for a sword. He had a helmet and shield, but no mailshirt. Erik moved back, drawing his attacker on and away from his companion, then dropped his halberd suddenly to the horizontal and lunged forward. The man's mouth opened to scream as he ran his own body onto the blade, and the shaft rammed into the ground as Erik gave it a savage twist. The corpse swung into the air, scattering blood on the snow as it hurtled over his head, tumbled grotesquely head over heels, and struck the ground in a tangle of nerveless limbs.

The first man lunged once again with his axe, but Erik's halberd was already moving to intercept it. The *hirðmann* was a fraction too slow, and the pattern-welded blade hammered into the axe-shaft, cleaving it in two. The heavy blade spiralled slowly through the air as the axeman staggered, unbalanced by the blow. Then the halberd whistled in a full circle, and struck again.

The man's head leapt from his shoulders. His body tottered, as though it kept some independent life of its own – then fell, slowly and clumsily, like mown hay. Above it the head turned over and over through the air, trailing a curling banner of crimson, and fell into a snowdrift with a soft, meaty thump.

Brockman lowered his sword and stared at Eleanor. Her women had run away as soon as Erik stepped onto the path, but she stood her ground, unafraid and unmoving. He had pictured her as a young woman, younger even than Anja, but the face he saw was middle-aged, ravaged by years of pain and hardship, and the hair beneath her kerchief was streaked with grey and white. Only the eyes betrayed a curious, restless energy, as though a younger and more vital spirit were trapped in the aging body. Her expression was unreadable.

Erik hesitated, his knuckles whitening around the shaft of the halberd, but the cold alvar mask did not change.

'You – must die,' he said at last. 'You are the daughter of my sworn enemy, and you betrayed me to my everlasting death.'

CHAPTER
8

Ic hit ðe gehate: no he on helm losað,
ne on foldan fæ þ'm, ne on fyrgenholt,
ne on gyfenes grund, ga ðær he wille!

Hear now my promise: night's helm shall not hide her,
earth's womb shall not cover, not forest conceal her,
nor ocean enfold her, wherever she flies.

Beowulf

'Do you hear me, woman?'

She nodded slowly. 'You have the right to unflesh me
here. But what is your right to the flesh *you* have taken –
the flesh that was my husband's?'

Erik was already raising the halberd to strike, but now
he hesitated.

'The flesh I took was empty,' she went on, 'without
purpose or will of its own. Those I gave, freely – and
there is a price that I alone have paid.'

Erik frowned – then reached out, gripped her arm, and
dragged her into the shelter of the skeletal trees, forcing
her back against the massive trunk of an ancient oak.
Above her head, the timeworn scar of a lightning strike
leered down like an avenging demon. 'What are you
saying?'

'I have waited for my husband's coming – waited all
those years that his own folly held him in twilight. But I
think that only his body is here – and if that is true, then I

shall not be sorry if you kill me where I stand.'

'Have you not deserved death?'

'Richly. But what says the man who was my husband?'

Erik laughed, bitterly, 'His love for you died long ago. What little was left you betrayed.'

The woman held his eyes. 'Not by my own wish. It was Kialar, not I, who commanded his murder. When I came to the boat-shed, I came alone – to speak of a thing that I had learned.'

'What *thing*?'

'A small matter, of little concern to our kind. A human matter . . .'

'Human?'

'To you it will mean nothing, as once it meant nothing to me. But now – now I understand it, as I have come to understand time. I yearned for my husband's return, with that yearning that comes only to the children of time; but first my father, and now you, have taken him from me.'

Brockman's eyes widened. 'You're saying you *loved* him? You loved Erik?'

As she met his eyes he saw no trace of fear – only an enduring pain and a helpless, hopeless longing. 'My husband was a good man, but I knew nothing of men. Now, too late, I know; and now I understand what a treasure I cast aside.'

Erik scowled. 'You are your father's daughter, Sigrun. Your words are ever sweetest when your heart is darkest. Do you hope for rescue even now?'

'No. You have destroyed my last hope.' She looked at him steadily, and Brockman saw the tears that stood in her eyes. 'I know you, Niord. You have taken the husband I learned to love and made him in your own image.' The shadows of the old forest stripped the years from her face and hair. Brockman saw the ghost of that strange, childlike beauty that had once entranced and entrapped a human being like himself. For a moment Erik hesitated; then he raised the halberd a second time.

Brockman gripped his wrist. 'Strike her now and I'll

know there's nothing left of Erik. He *dreamed* of this –'

'Be silent!' growled Erik. 'This is not your affair!'

'It's not that easy! If you *are* the man I knew, you have to listen to her!'

Erik shuddered, clutching at the halberd. 'No! She is my deadly enemy!'

Brockman tightened his restraining grip, staring at the woman that Eleanor had become. In her eyes he saw the knowledge and understanding of death – and now, for the first time, he felt the reality of Anja's death.

'I ask no mercy,' she said. 'I deserve none. Too late I learned what Erik offered – too late I offer it in return. Better that I die. But first take pity on my son.'

Erik paled. 'What of him?'

'Kialar would use him as he uses all about him – even his daughters. He would sacrifice Bjørn to the game. To *fimbul-spillinn.*'

'What are you saying? Without Bjørn all that we have done – all that Kialar has done – is meaningless!'

She shook her head. 'Once the Watcher is dead, Kialar has no need of Bjørn. He dares not let him live.'

'Dares not?'

She half-smiled. 'You have stolen a mortal body, Niord. Bjørn was *born* mortal, with the heart and *fylgja* of an alv. He is a creature of both worlds – as I am, now. That is a power beyond Kialar's understanding, and he fears it. Punish me as you will; I ask nothing for myself. But Bjørn is innocent of all harm.'

'He hunted me, Sigrun – hunted me like a dog!'

'Do you think he *knew* you? He remembers only this place, this time. To him, your world is nothing but a dream. And, gods, how you have changed! I barely knew you myself.'

Erik's face darkened. 'Your father has many wiles, Sigrun – and the man I once was understood none of them. Kialar trapped him in twilight with a deluding dream – the dream that you loved him as he had always desired. Do you truly think that dream still lives?'

She looked at him bitterly. 'Erik's dreams are no concern of yours. You have destroyed them for ever, just as you destroyed him.'

He shook his head. 'No. I share his dreams. I know them all. He is a part of me, as I am part of him. He is a good man; better than he ever imagined –'

'And yet you would kill me for my father's sake. Is that what a good man does, Niord? Is that what my husband would wish?'

'She's right,' said Brockman. Erik's self-righteousness was beginning to irritate him. He could not see Eleanor as the cold, scheming creature the older man had described. There was something about her that reminded him painfully of Anja; not only the face, marked by long years that Anja would never see, but the longing and the clear-sighted intelligence in her eyes.

'I told you, Brockman. This is not your affair.'

'No? What you do now could save or destroy everything I care about. That *makes* it my affair.'

The woman's eyes narrowed. 'And what of Bjørn? What of my son?'

'*Your* son?' There was mockery in Erik's voice.

'Yes. Oh, yes. I was a part of the body that gave him life. I felt his weight growing in this belly. I felt his heartbeat within this womb, his feet kicking against these ribs. He is my son, Niord. Where is his father?'

For the first time, Brockman saw the beginnings of human emotion flickering beneath Erik's uncaring mask: love for her that had never truly died, pity for the loss of her vigour and her beauty. But there was anger, too – anger and doubt.

'You bore another child, Sigrun, in another stolen body. The Helbitch Skuld –'

'Do you reproach me with *that*? I was an innocent then, playing with human lives as I might play with *skak*-pieces upon the little board in my father's hall. I did his bidding without question, because that was my destiny and my duty. But now –'

'What has changed?' snarled Erik. 'Still you are the daughter of Kialar, and a child of the First Made! Still you hold all the powers of the Aesir, and still you use them to spoil and destroy the lives of others!'

Again he raised the halberd to strike, and again Brockman grabbed his wrist. It was like holding a tensioned steel cable. 'Wait! For God's sake, why not *listen* to her first? Erik loved her enough to give up his whole world! All she's asking is a few moments!'

'You do not understand, Peter Brockman. She is a word-weaver like her father, and each word draws you deeper into the weft. You plead for her because you are already trapped in the tapestry of her lies –'

'Am I? Look at her! *Look*, you soulless bastard!'

'He will not,' said the woman. 'He fears a power I no longer have. He will never understand.' Erik swore under his breath, but the halberd did not move. Brockman could feel the tendons flex and turn as Erik's fingers twitched along the shaft. Sigrun smiled faintly. 'If you dare not meet my eyes, then look inside yourself, Niord. *Find* whatever remains of my husband. Touch him with your thoughts, as I have touched him with my flesh.'

Erik's eyes fell, half-closing. A tremor passed through his body, and his hands clenched. When he spoke again, it was in a different voice – hesitant, troubled, and almost human.

'I cannot understand. He would *die* for this. For nothing. For a dream, a *trick* . . .'

'You *will* understand,' said Sigrun. 'And when you do, his dream will change you as it changed me. My father – all of us – we were wrong. They are not pawns, these humans. They are not tools lying ready to our hand. They can wound us, and break us, and destroy us, in ways we can barely understand. And they can change us, as I have changed. No longer am I Sigrun the daughter of Kialar.'

Erik laughed bitterly. 'So now you are human? Like them? Like this Peter Brockman, who is caught in your words just as Erik was?'

She looked at him unflinchingly. 'You do well to rebuke me. It is true that I trapped my husband with my words and my body, but now I am trapped in my turn. Once I conceived a child, and laughed, and left her to fare as she would. Kill me for that, if you will – for creating a thing of darkness and hatred. But first remember Bjørn. Remember that child whose life I have shared from the very beginning, who taught me the meaning of love.'

'You hypocrite! You care *nothing* for Bjørn, nothing at all! If you –'

'I could have left this body, and gone back to my father's hall. My father commanded it, but I would not leave the child. And now I cannot.'

'Cannot? What do you mean?'

'I have stayed too long among humans. I am bound to this flesh for ever. And when this body dies, then I, too, must suffer the true death.'

For a moment Erik was aghast. 'You – will – truly *die*?'

'I can see it,' said Brockman quietly. 'She's not like you. She *knows* about death – you just talk about it. And there's been enough killing already.'

Erik made no reply. Once again, Brockman could see him struggling with the human feelings and motivations of the man whose shape he wore.

'This – love ... It is a hard thing to understand ...'

'First, my lord, you must understand time; and it passes with each word that we speak. Soon my son – Erik's son – will be drawn to his death. Do not listen to me; look within yourself, and see what my husband would do.'

This time Erik did not hesitate. 'Very well. For the sake of what I once was and you now are, I will do what I can for Bjørn – but I promise nothing. Now tell me – tell me all you know.'

On the last day of the world, they came to the great hall of Lejre.

The low afternoon sun was hidden behind streamers of

cloud piled above the rim of the forest. Its light brought answering flashes of iridescence from the stones along the causeway, polished by the passage of countless lumbering ox-carts. Beyond it lay the murky flatness of the marshes, their waters still moving beneath slowly thickening plates of green-grey ice. Ahead, sunlight caught the ice-decked dragon-carvings on the gables of the hall, and snow glittered on the wooden shingles like a field of gems. Out of the fjord the mist was rising, and the air was chill with the promise of new frost.

Brockman stared up at the palisade. The sentries, wrapped in heavy cloaks of dark wool, blew on their hands to keep warm, staring out towards the sprawling shadow of the wood with superstitious fear. He could see the fresh timbers around the gate where the havoc wrought by the Watcher had been repaired, seemingly months before. Now that he was here, watching reality slide into the stuff of legend, he understood what Erik had felt. He, too, seemed to be walking in a dream – but he already knew that this dream was dangerous.

'This is purest folly,' muttered Erik, his voice muffled by the full mask of his helmet. 'We shall be cut down as soon as we pass the gate.'

'Why?' said Brockman. 'The sentries think we're Eleanor's – I mean Sigrun's escort.'

'Her women must have told them what happened.'

Sigrun's mouth curved into a faint smile. 'No one will listen to them – not when they see me safe and well. I shall say we were beset by thieves, and my escort earned their mead.'

Erik scowled. 'I shall be listening, Sigrun. Remember that.'

One of the sentries shouted a challenge. Sigrun's reply meant nothing to Brockman, but he saw Erik give a small nod of approval.

If I'm wrong about her . . .

The severed heads on the parapet were shrivelled and white-haired with frost – icicles hung from their draggled beards. He eyed them uncomfortably as the gates swung open.

Jesus, just staying alive in this place is a full-time job.

Sigrun walked through the gates as though she were in a procession, head held high, ignoring both Brockman and Erik. In the courtyard outside the main hall a buzzing hive of servants and slaves was unloading an ox-cart with massive wooden wheels, and carrying barrels and sacks of grain to the storehouses. The lean, muscular flanks of the oxen steamed gently in the cooling air, and the cobbles at their feet were already rimed with frost.

Sigrun walked past them towards the main entrance of the great hall. From below it looked even more like an upturned ship. The roof ridge, some thirty feet above, was its keel – from there, massive ribs curved down under the wooden shingles to emerge again some ten feet above the ground. The space between the ribs and the inner wall was a sheltered gallery where women might sit in summer. Today the empty benches were dusted with windblown snow, and the overhanging shingles were decked with icy stalactites. As they came to the main door Brockman saw, to his utter amazement, that every piece of exposed timber was elaborately carved with twisting knotwork, fantastic beasts, and leering, sculpted heads.

Near the door stood a heavily armed warrior with a ringmail byrnie under his cloak and a helmet of embossed plates bound together with chased, etched and gilded metal bands. His face was dark, lined with old wounds, and as he turned to meet them Brockman saw that one eye was covered by a patch of worn leather. It only half-concealed a long weal running straight down from his brow to the corner of his mouth. The man's throat, beneath the gold ring that circled it, was a twisted mass of scar tissue. Sigrun greeted him as 'Svipdag'.

Svipdag. I know that name. One of Rolf's heroes – came to Lejre from Sweden, with his two brothers –

The thought was driven from his mind as Erik moved to follow Sigrun and the big man barred his way,

216

growling something in thickly-accented Old Norse. The scars along his throat made a drawling mockery of his speech – and Erik's answer was charged with angry resentment. Brockman cursed silently.

Christ, this is no time to pick a fight – we have *to get inside. What the hell is Erik playing at?*

He thought quickly, struggling with elusive memories of Anglo-Saxon and Norse texts. It was years since he had read about anything to do with the sixth century. What had happened when Beowulf came to Lejre ...?

That's it!

'He wants our weapons,' he muttered. 'It isn't an insult, it's their normal custom. They think they're safe from the Watcher – so no weapons in the hall.'

Erik nodded angrily, giving his halberd to the man with obvious reluctance. Svipdag paused, looking sideways with his single, narrowed eye from Erik to the halberd and back again, then placed it carefully in a rack next to the door. He stared at Brockman's sword suspiciously before he hung it in a lower rack on the other side.

If he recognises that, we've all had it ...

The doorkeeper mumbled a few unintelligible words and gestured towards the inner hall with his spear. Inside smoke hazed the air, stinging Brockman's eyes as they slowly adjusted to the light. Along the centre of the hall, flames danced the span of the log-trough, questing towards the trestles of well-laden tables. Ale-reddened faces glanced at them incuriously, half-masked in leaping shadows, half-highlighted from below by the crests of the flames. Heavy-pelted wolfhounds snuffled under the tables, searching for scraps among the dry rushes.

The reality of the scene was overwhelming. Once before, in Denmark, he had stepped into a reconstructed Iron Age house and felt the past strike him in the face, but that had been a carefully fostered illusion. There was no illusion here. All around him was the roar of a language long lost, its memory preserved only in a few half-intelligible lines scratched on wood and bone, or hammered into stone. The faces were just as Erik had described them – like parchment dried and cracked by the wind and the weather, marked by each year of pain and deprivation, lined by each grim winter on the edge of starvation. A bird swept through the rafters overhead and fluttered out through the smokehole under the farther gable, and Brockman remembered an ancient poet's image of the life all around him – like a bird, flying out of storm and darkness into the light and noise of a meadhall, and back into darkness again. But there was something else here, something Erik had failed to see. The men had a hardened vitality, and their eyes burned with an inextinguishable lust for life. In this place, where death stood close by every man's shoulder, life was a treasure to be savoured to the last drop. The women were old before their time, but their faces held a wisdom and a warmth that reminded him of Kristine.

They're like her – a part of their world. They belong here because they believe they do ...

But one thing did not match his idea of a world long lost.

At the centre of the hall, above the high-seat, a dark shape hung from the rafters. At first Brockman could barely make it out in the flickering firelight. Then a single flame flared high, and he saw the pallid green gleam of unsheathed claws, a curled, inhuman hand, and the smoke-blackened flesh of a massive, misproportioned arm. At its far end, bone glistened amid a grisly tangle of ruptured tendons and torn muscle.

'Hví glottir þu við tönn, piss-höfuð?'

The voice was close to Brockman's ear, and it did not sound friendly. The smell that came with it was a heady mixture of sweat, dirt and stale beer.

'Ertu deyft, þin hestsfreti?'

Brockman turned to face a man who stood naked but for a thick pelt of hair and a filthy pair of leather breeks. A wood axe was thrust casually into his belt, as another

218

man might carry a knife or a dagger. His eyes were slightly dilated, and he was chewing something that dribbled darkly into his matted beard, foaming with his spittle. He was at least eighteen inches taller than Brockman, with shoulders to match.

'*Sa? Hvat seistu, niðing?*'

Brockman's grasp of the language was too slight to allow an answer, but he knew that here, within the hall, he was under the king's protection. Anyone might insult him, but no one would actually attack him. He grinned, and raised his finger in what he hoped was an unmistakable gesture.

It was. The man gave an animal roar. The axe was out and moving before Brockman could react, and he felt the wind of it as he threw himself aside, grabbing an earthenware goblet from the trestled board at his right hand and hurling its contents full into his attacker's face. Again the man seemed to move faster than thought, avoiding the blinding spray as his next stroke shaved the side of Brockman's head. The American stepped back, stumbled, and fell flat on his back. He saw the axe rise above him and then, slowly, begin to fall ...

A hand reached out and gripped the big man's arm, halting the axe in mid-flight. On either side of the grasping fingers Brockman could see the flesh puffing out, darkening, till his attacker gave another, even louder howl and the weapon dropped from his quivering fingers. Brockman rolled aside as the axe clattered along the earth floor of the hall. The haft carried some twenty notches, and it was blackly stained with what looked like old blood.

'Back to your kennel, berserk!'

To his surprise, Brockman could understand the newcomer. He spoke slowly, with a different accent from those around him, and the slight cast to his features suggested a Lappish ancestor. His hair was dark and straight, his face open and straightforward. As Brockman stumbled to his feet he saw that his rescuer was little more than five feet tall, but muscled like a wrestler. He still held the big man's arm, twisting it slowly back till Brockman's attacker was forced to his knees in the rushes.

'Better, Ketil. Much better. Ketil begs your pardon, stranger. He knows that he belongs here among the scraps and the bones, like our lord's other housepets. Do not judge our welcome by such offal as this.'

So much for the cover story. I guess everyone knows everyone else in a place like this.

'I am called Hialti,' said the small man. 'Once, when I was called Hott, I suffered such insults – until Biarki showed me how to behave like a man. I will not allow that one who defies the king's animals should die for his courage. Now go. Sit over there – it is a good place, not so high that you will be overly noticed. And keep your counsel.'

Hialti winked and was gone, and Brockman found Erik tugging urgently at his sleeve. He nodded vaguely, following the older man to the place that Hialti had indicated. He had expected filth, but the rushes were clean, and the only smell was the clear, sharp tang of woodsmoke. He had expected darkness, but the firelight was almost too bright to bear. Back down the hall a group of burly warriors stared at them, muttering among themselves in low voices.

The king's animals ... Berserkers, I guess. Not exactly God's gift to a civilised society, but they're probably useful in a fight ...

'*Must* you stare?' whispered the older man. 'Thanks to you our lives are already in peril!'

Brockman shivered. Again, he was beginning to understand how Erik had felt. It was almost impossible to believe that the hall and the people who lived in it were real, and his lack of belief had nearly killed him. Yet everything around him was strange – and strangest of all was knowing, or seeming to know, exactly what would happen next.

220

The reign of King Rolf Kraki was almost at an end.

Once, long ago, Peter Brockman had read the myths and legends of ancient Scandinavia with avid hunger, using his knowledge of Danish to battle through Norwegian, Swedish and even Icelandic books from his mother's collection. As a boy he had known the names of Rolf's champions, the king's heroic deeds, and the manner of his death. Now, piece by piece, he struggled to remember what had once come so easily.

There had been a king of the Danes named Helgi, a man cursed by fate. Helgi had been tricked into a marriage with his own daughter – and the child of that horrific incest was Rolf Kraki. But Helgi had fathered another child, born of the strange and magical creature who had come to his threshold on the dark of a winter night . . .

The elf-woman. Brockman had reread the story in another world – long ago, in the farmhouse at Egerød. Now he knew more. The elf-woman had been Sigrun, daughter of Kialar. And her child had been the strangely-named Skuld – a girl-child, unfitted to take up arms against the Watcher.

Helgi had died in Sweden, at the hands of the sorcerer-king Adhils. For a little while his brother ruled, and then his nephew. Finally Rolf, last of the Skioldung dynasty, was proclaimed king of a weak and divided nation.

Then came a time of legends.

Rolf gave out his father's treasures with a lavish hand, and heroes gathered in his hall: Svipdag, the strong-thewed thane from Sweden; Biarki, whom legend said was the son of a bear; Hialti, raised out of cowardice to the king's right hand. In his power, Rolf fared against Sweden, and avenged his father on the body of Adhils.

But there was darkness beneath the gold.

For years the island of Fyn had resisted Skioldung rule, until its king, Jorvard, was enslaved by the beauty of Skuld. Some said he had given his fealty to Rolf for the sake of her hand. Others said that Rolf had tricked him.

Nonetheless, Skuld and Jorvard were married in the great hall of Lejre.

It was not a happy match.

Skuld grew restless and resentful, envying her brother's power and reputation, keenly aware that next to Rolf her husband was less than half a man. She was said to vanish from the court of Odin's Isle for days at a time. Travellers spoke of a vision in the dark woods – of a woman, pale and terrible, surrounded by whispering ghosts . . .

At night, Skuld whispered in Jorvard's ear, filling his mind with thoughts of power and riches, feeding his sullen resentment of Rolf, tempting him with the prospect of supreme kingship . . .

Brockman's head was spinning. The stuff of legend was all about him – but nothing was quite as it should be.

At the centre of the hall, seated in a great carved chair set about with dragons, Rolk Kraki brooded over his kingdom. Brockman had expected a confident warrior, secure in the power and wealth his courage and ability had won for him. Instead, he saw a dark and moody man, his skin tight against his skull, his eyes glittering with reflected firelight. At his right hand sat Battle-Biarki, his hair and triple-plaited beard flaming like the fire itself. Brockman had expected maturity – instead he saw a boy with a man's face. Next to them sat Hialti, whom legend set among the most courageous of Rolf's followers. Brockman had expected a tall, lean warrior – but Hialti was more like an over-muscled dwarf, with keen, hooded eyes that constantly surveyed the hall. At Rolf's left hand sat Svipdag – but there was nothing of the hero about him. He sat like a brooding shadow, his single eye glittering in the firelight. The hall rang with shouts and boasting – but there was no music, and no laughter. This was a royal feast – but the food was thinner than the ale. And outside, in the gloom of the ancient forest, death stalked among the trees.

If Sigrun told the truth, that is. And if she didn't, we won't

222

*be around long enough to cuss ourselves out. What was it she
said . . . ?'*

'Jorvard and my daughter are coming, with a great army.
They will wait for a signal. Then they will fall upon Lejre,
and destroy all they find there.'

'Will they come alone?' Erik's gaze burned deep into
the gold-flecked eyes of his wife.

'I think not.'

Erik nodded grimly. 'A faring from twilight, then. But
why? What does Kialar have to fear from Rolf?'

'Rolf is a strong man,' said Sigrun, 'and strong men
follow him. Kialar will never control them. Jorvard is a
weak man – already he is Kialar's puppet, and when he is
no longer useful, Kialar will strike him down.'

'What about the Watcher?' said Brockman. 'We know
it's not dead. How does Kialar expect to win through?'

The strange eyes seemed to look right through him.

'My father's folk are all around you, even now. The
Watcher is weaker since Biarki grappled with it; my
people slip through the stone by ones and twos, eluding
its watch. And they have learned what the liosalvar never
knew – how to master and direct a weaker will than their
own.'

'That won't help them against the Watcher.'

'They have my son. He is proud, and courageous, but
he is young, and easily swayed. They will drive him to
seek the Watcher a second time. They will escort him, to
be sure that he finds it. Then, surely, the Watcher will die
– and the gate stone will stand open for ever.'

In the great hall of Lejre, the tapestries behind the
benches trembled in the updraught from the fire.
Brockman watched the embroidered figures of women
and warriors weave in and out of shadow. He imagined a
being without scruples, without imagination, tugging at
the threads one by one, drawing them slowly apart,
studying their intricate interplay – while inch by inch the

223

images they formed were whittled away. How long would it take? And what would happen to the threads – to the individual human lives that made up all recorded history?

He'll change a few, perhaps – cut some short to start with, save others, play god for a while. But how long before the picture itself has gone? How long before there's nothing left to change?

He looked around him. A skald was singing, matching complex patterns of verse to a repeating series of chords on a beautifully carved wooden harp. By now Brockman could follow much of the chatter around him, but the poetry was too intricate to be easily understood. Even so, he could hear that Biarki's name was repeated many times – and so was another name.

Greniandi. Sounds familiar, somehow.

He leaned closer to Erik. 'What's going on?'

'They taunt him,' muttered Erik. 'But they do it cunningly. The skald sings of his prowess against the Watcher – but the story is not finished. He says that Greniandi, the Bellower, wanders the hidden places of the world, thirsting for revenge. If it is not destroyed, others will die.'

Biarki moved uneasily in his seat, taking long draughts from a massive drinking-horn that the women of Lejre were constantly refilling. It was clear the song troubled him – but there was something about the singer that troubled Brockman . . .

The outer door opened for a moment, and a blast of cold air flattened the flames in the fire-pit. In the half-darkness Brockman could just see the pale nimbus around the singer's head. There were others – many others.

My father's folk are all around you . . .

'Don't look now,' murmured Brockman, 'but –'

'I see it,' said Erik. 'We have found a pit of vipers.'

'Sigrun warned us about this.'

Erik's eyes narrowed. 'She has not betrayed us – yet. But I shall believe her only when I have spoken with my son.'

'You may not get the chance.'

Biarki had risen to his feet, and the gleam in his eye was more than firelight. He raised his drinking horn high above his head – then dashed it down on the table. It shattered, spilling ale in a widening puddle across the boards.

'You! That is enough!'

The skald stopped in mid-sequence. 'My lord?'

'You heard me, Thorfinn. Your words touch my honour.'

Hialti gripped his arm. 'The man meant no harm! Leave him be!'

'It is true, *jarl* Biarki. I meant only to praise you –'

Rolf banged a ring-decked arm on the table. 'Be silent, Thorfinn! Biarki, you are my right hand. There is none here who doubts your courage.'

'Then hear this,' roared Biarki. 'Hear this, all of you! I myself shall seek the truth! I shall seek out Greniandi – and if it still lives, I shall crush out its life and bring the proof back here to Lejre!'

All along the king's bench other men rose to their feet, shouting Biarki's praises or offering their support. To Brockman's horror, Erik stood up as well.

'Biarki! Boðvar Biarki!'

There was something in his voice that commanded attention. Gradually the noise around them died away as all eyes turned to Erik.

'This does you little honour. What need do you have of other swords than your own?'

The young man's eyes sought and met Erik's, and Brockman saw them widen, as if in recognition.

Now we're really screwed.

'You are a stranger in this hall,' said Biarki. 'Do you also doubt my courage – or my loyalty?'

'Neither,' said Erik. 'I come to bring you help.'

'Help? What help can you offer?'

'To take you to a place I have found. The place where Greniandi has hidden itself.'

What the holy hell . . .?

'You have seen it, stranger?'

'I have seen it. I will take you to it now – unless you fear the night.'

'I fear nothing. Bring my armour and my sword!'

The hall erupted into chaos. Around the high-seat, Rolf's retainers were bringing a magnificent full-mask helmet studded with gold, and a ring-mail byrnie with the king's raven emblem picked out in fine links of silver. Hialti brought Biarki's sword, its hilts bound with gold wire and studded with gems. The blade glittered with a familiar sheen ...

Pattern-welded. Almost like the halberd ...

'What is your name, stranger?' Biarki's voice was haughty and imperious, and there was a terrifying half-recognition in his eyes, but Erik met his gaze with an almost insolent ease.

'I am called Erik.'

'Erik?' The young man frowned. 'It seems to me I should know you. You have been here before?'

'Once. Once, long ago.' Erik's voice was clear and firm, but now there was the hint of that tormented, tortured look Brockman had seen as Erik described the hunt in the forest. Surely Biarki *must* remember it ...

'You have horses?'

'We have no need of horses. Our path lies through the forest.'

'As you wish. Svipdag, give these men their arms. We shall see what they can do with them.'

The one-eyed man nodded grimly and forced a passage to the door through the noisy throng that was already gathering there. Brockman found that he was unnaturally alert, aware of every slightest detail in the scene around him. He saw the glint of firelight in Svipdag's single eye as the big man forced his way through the crowd with their weapons. He saw eyes that sought them out, faces that showed curiosity, indifference, or a thinly concealed hostility. There were enemies here – deadly enemies – and there was no way to tell them from friends.

Erik's gambling with our lives.

The immediate risk was appalling, but there was sense in what Erik had done. By playing on Biarki's perceptions of honour he had ensured that they left at once, and alone. With night already falling, most of Kialar's creatures would be held within the stockade, duty bound to guard their king. There might be alvar-haunted beasts in the woods, beasts that would follow them, or even attack them – but three well-armed men had little to fear from beasts.

As long as we make it to the door.

After fifteen years of work on isolated sites, Brockman hated crowds. Now, as they forced their way to the door, he felt a surge of near-panic. Each glint of metal was a knife, drawn and ready to thrust. Each face in the shadows seemed to bear the telltale alvar nimbus – and each face in the light seemed to stare at him with undisguised hostility. Briefly he saw Sigrun among the other women, seemingly unmoved, emotionless – and then they were out, and his breath was a mist in the icy wind from the fjord. Another crowd was already milling around the gates to see them leave. The cart they had seen before was jammed at the centre of the crush, the oxen wide-eyed with fear as they were forced onward by the human tide around them.

Damn it to hell! This time they can't *miss . . .*

Erik paused for a moment – then the ghost of a smile crossed his face. He walked purposefully forward, pushing aside the few ragged thralls who blocked his path, and vaulted over the tailgate into the empty, cradle-like structure that formed the body of the cart. The driver started as Erik sprang onto the bench at his side, took the reins from his hands, and scrambled forward along the trembling harness-shaft. The noise of the crowd drowned out what he was saying, but the oxen quietened almost at once. As Erik urged them forward, the crowd parted in front of them, and the gates swung open onto the great causeway. Beyond it the forest rose like a wall between daylight and darkness. With a grin Erik leapt down from the driver's bench, beckoning the others to follow.

Biarki strapped on his helmet and wrapped a dark cloak around his byrnie. 'Now, stranger,' he said, 'we shall see if you speak the truth.'

Within the forest night had already fallen, but a patch of daylight lingered ahead of them. Erik walked unhurriedly, using the shaft of his halberd as a staff. Evening frost was crusting the snow with ice, and in their smooth-soled leather boots the walking was treacherous.

The clearing was a wide slash through the ancient trees – the mark of a fire, perhaps, as the ground was clear of all but the lowest growth. Erik stopped, leaning on his halberd.

'Now we may speak,' he said. 'Now that we have no shadows around us but our own.'

Biarki threw back his cloak, drew his sword, and brought it to the guard in a single, sweeping motion. 'What do you seek?'

'I would speak with you, Boðvar Biarki.' Erik spoke in English, ignoring the drawn sword. 'I would remind you of things that others have made you forget.'

A breeze whispered among the branches; then the forest seemed to hold its breath. The young warrior hesitated, but his expression was impossible to read. The ornate helmet hid everything but his eyes. 'I – understand what you say. I know ... how to speak – this way.'

'You learned it long ago,' said Erik. 'When you were a child.'

Biarki shook his head, searching for half-forgotten words. 'No,' he said at last. 'There is nothing before the boat. I remember *nothing*!'

'There was a house,' said Erik. 'A small house, out on the land. There was a room that was yours – and a tapestry that hung there.'

Biarki hesitated. 'You're lying – as only alvar can lie. You try to trick me ...'

Again the branches whispered, making flickering patterns of light and darkness at the edge of Brockman's vision. For a moment the young man's eyes were drawn away from Erik.

'*Think!*' said Erik. 'Deception has many faces. Trust your own memories!'

'I have dreamed these things,' said Biarki, slowly. 'But the alvar can read dreams – and bring them.' His sword remained unwaveringly at the guard, but his face was a study in concentration.

'There was a man,' said Erik, slowly. 'Your father ...'

Biarki shook his head, as though trying to dispel a persistent illusion. 'My father was Bjørn of the Uplands. He – died. Before I was born. There was a house, and a hanging. A great house, and a tapestry. With – warriors.'

'No, Biarki. A small house, like none that are here. A house with many chambers. And your *own* name was Bjørn. Your father it was who first called you "Biarki" –'

'My father gave me magic – he left this blade to guard my dreams and my waking.' He looked at it strangely. 'It is thirsty ...'

'And what of your mother, Biarki? Had she no magic?'

Biarki grinned. 'They say my mother sent me here. In a boat. Without oars. And at my side, my father's sword.'

'And she followed you, your mother?'

'Why these questions? Who are you?'

'Who are *you*, Biarki? Who are you that a creature from the half-world dares not face you?'

'Don't talk that way of Greniandi. It's bad luck.'

Once again a soft wind passed through the clearing, moving the branches on either side like the passing of some invisible host. Again Biarki's glance was drawn away from Erik.

'What does Sigrun say of Greniandi?'

'She calls him Vaknaði: the Watchful. Why do you speak of her?'

'I think,' said Erik, 'that Sigrun is a woman about so high, with hair that was once red-gold and lustrous, and with ice-blue eyes not unlike your own. I think, too, you have forgotten that she is more alv than human – and that she is your mother.'

The young man's eyes narrowed, and his sword snapped up, ready to strike. 'Who are you, stranger?'

'Have you forgotten me, also?'

'No. I saw you once before, at the place they call the gate stone. Now take me to Vaknaði, or die where you stand. I have a promise to keep – and no time for stories.'

'I know,' said Erik, stepping directly into Biarki's path. 'Better than you, perhaps.' His halberd swung to the guard almost too quickly to see, its blade menancing the younger man at neck height. 'I shall not harm you, boy, but I *will* have your attention.'

Biarki smiled savagely. 'You want to fight, old man? I'm glad. Naegling thirsts for blood, and yours will do as well as another's.'

Erik's eyes widened. 'Naegling?'

'My father's sword. By your looks, you've heard of it.' With a movement almost too fast to be seen, he struck at the shaft of Erik's halberd – but Naegling sliced empty air, and the halberd's shimmering blade was already lunging at Biarki's unprotected midriff. The younger man leapt backwards, turning his blade for a second stroke, but this time a quick flick of Erik's wrist rammed the halberd's shaft against Biarki's arm. Naegling dropped from his hand and thudded point foremost into the snow.

Erik smiled lazily and raised the halberd in a mocking salute. 'Will you hear me now, son of Sigrun?'

Biarki shrugged, and reached slowly for the swaying hilt of his sword. Erik made no move to stop him. He grasped it and tugged it smoothly from the earth. 'I'm listening.'

'There is a story,' said Erik. 'One you have not heard since you were a child in your father's house.'

'More stories?'

'True stories. When you were a child you told your father how you spoke with shadows. To him this seemed no more than a child's dreaming. Only you and your mother knew the truth – that the shadows were real. That you spoke with the alvar face to face, as no man has ever done before you.'

Biarki was not looking at him. His eyes were fixed on a point behind Erik's left shoulder.

'Only such a one,' said Erik, 'would see the *einheriar* as you do.'

Brockman's eyes widened. Now that he knew what to look for, he could almost see the wraith-like forms of the liosalvar that had passed out of twilight after the battle by the stone; but here, in the fading light, they were as insubstantial as dust motes in a sunbeam, all but lost against the glitter of the snow.

Biarki scowled. 'This is sorcery. King Rolf kills sorcerers.'

Erik nodded. 'Their heads make poor ornaments for a royal hall. So it is only to Sigrun that you speak of such things.'

'Why should I speak to her?'

'Beacuse she is your mother. But her father is Kialar, lord of the svartalvar – and a deadly enemy to all humankind.'

'Is this another story?'

'Kialar is as real as you, or I, or the *einheriar* you choose not to see. He is the dark lord of the twilight, who plays with your fate as you might play with a chess piece.'

Brockman shivered. The clearing seemed somehow colder and darker. The snow no longer glittered – it was chill and stark beneath a colourless sky. Biarki appeared unmoved.

'How can you know these things?'

'Because long ago I was Sigrun's husband, and your father.'

For a moment the young warrior stared at Erik, as if struggling to remember something lost almost beyond recall. Then he laughed softly.

'Must I believe that?'

'It is true, Biarki. Your first sword was my gift. Not the blade you hold now, but a child's plaything.'

The ghost of a memory stirred in Biarki's face.

'It was I who told you of the dragon, Biarki. Every night we would hunt it, together. Every night, unwittingly, I made you ready for the task Kialar had planned for you. But now –'

'Now?'

'The story must change. Your mother has taught me what I never dared to hope. We are not Kialar's tools; we can choose our own destiny. He thought of me as the unresisting anvil, of you as the sword he would forge there. Turn that sword against him, and we can save the worlds of time.'

'What are you saying? What do you want?'

'Vakna of The Watcher. Let it live.'

'What possible reason ...?'

'Kill it, and this world – your world – will vanish into shadow. You and I, anything human or half-human, will become no more than pawns in Kialar's game, to be swept from the board before the last battle.'

'I don't understand.'

'The Watcher guards the frontier between our world and twilight – between time and chaos. Without it, this world lies unprotected at Kialar's feet.'

Biarki frowned. His eyes pierced Erik – cold, gun-metal blue, like the trued steel that lay somewhere far on the other side of the gate stone. 'It killed my companions. It dishonoured my lord. Do you understand that, stranger?'

Unthinkingly Erik reached out to clasp Bjørn's shoulders and saw his son step back, hand on sword-hilt.

'Look inside yourself!' said Brockman. 'You've got both worlds in your blood. Surely you can understand what he means.'

Biarki made no reply. There was bafflement in his eyes.

He can't see it. He can't see beyond this place, because he's taken it as his own. And that could kill us all ...

'I don't know you,' said Biarki. 'And you – you say you are my father. But the words – the words are wrong.'

Erik's face twisted with the ghosts of human emotion. 'Then,' he said, 'I must stop you as best I can.'

The halberd scythed towards Biarki before the younger man had time to react – yet he was already reacting, trained to read the thoughts of an enemy in the very movements of his eyes. The ancient blade rang against an upraised sword and screeched along the edge in a shower of sparks. Biarki ducked low under the arc of the halberd, lunging at Erik's midriff, but the older man sidestepped and ran backwards, changing his grip on the shaft of his weapon to present the blade to his opponent. Biarki struck at the halberd, deflecting the blow, leapt to avoid the backswing, and lunged forward a second time. This time Erik used the shaft itself to block Biarki's sword, and the clearing rang with the concussion of seasoned wood against forged iron.

'What the hell are you doing?' yelled Brockman.

Erik ignored him as he turned his halberd almost too quickly for Brockman to see and thrust its butt end into Biarki's chest. The younger man staggered back half-winded, grinning savagely.

'You fight well, for an old coal-biter.'

'Save your breath,' growled Erik. 'You will need it.'

'For God's sake! He's your son!' Brockman had drawn his sword, but dared not come between the two fighters: the slightest distraction might be the death of either one. But for them, nothing existed beyond the arena of trampled snow that confined their strange battle. They were circling each other now, warily testing strengths and weaknesses – but Erik's breathing was faster, misting the air in great clouds, and sweat stood out on his face.

Damnation! He doesn't understand human limits. If he carries on like this, Biarki'll kill him.

Hesitantly, Brockman stepped forward.

'Keep away!' growled Erik. 'Keep away, or by the Tree itself I'll kill you first!'

Again Biarki lashed out with the sword, and again Erik turned the blow with his halberd-shaft; but this time a sliver of wood fell away. As the older man stepped backwards the smooth leather of his shoe slipped on a patch of crusted snow. The halberd swung from its defensive line, and Biarki's blade thrust into Erik's unprotected side.

Blood spattered the snow, and dribbled down the sword as Biarki turned his father's desperate defensive swing and struck again. This time the sword rang out against the blade of the halberd – and snapped it cleanly in two. The severed tip turned lazily over and over in the air to fall a few inches from Brockman's feet.

Biarki grasped his swordhilt with both hands, crouching forward as he advanced on Erik.

'Well, old man?'

Erik cast aside the broken halberd and stood unflinching, clasping the open wound in his side. 'There is a saying that fate goes as it must, Biarki.'

The younger man nodded. 'Then yours is kind. You can't hurt me, old man, and I must fight another battle.'

'Greniandi?'

'Yes. If I live, we'll fight again. Next time I won't hold back.'

'You cannot find the creature alone.'

'No? Listen, old man. Can you hear a sound like a heart, beating? I hear it, and it is Greniandi. It can't hide from me – not as long as it lives. This is *my* fate: to seek out Greniandi and destroy it.'

'Wait!' said Erik. 'Would you leave your king in the hour of his greatest need?'

Biarki had already turned away, but now, for a moment, he seemed to hesitate.

'What are you saying?'

'Jorvard is coming to Lejre with a great host. He means to fall on Rolf and destroy him. He means to take the kingship for himself –'

'Jorvard? That worm? He'd never dare. Not with more

234

strength than all of Fyn could muster –'

'He has it. He brings the powers of twilight in his train. The alvar themselves.'

Biarki laughed. 'With *this* tale you would keep me here? Your friend the skald has served you badly this day.'

'None the less, it is true. Without you, Rolf and all your companions will fall – and *then* where is your honour?'

'The king shall have my help – as soon as Greniandi is dead. If you know so much, you know the oath I have sworn to him – that nothing, not even death itself, shall keep me from fighting at his side in his greatest need. And now goodbye, old fool.'

Without a backward glance, Biarki broke into a loping run, heading for the faint path that led to the gate stone. Brockman stared after him irresolutely. 'I could follow him – try to stop him.'

'*No!*' Erik's hand gripped his arm with bruising force.

'You're letting him go? You were going to kill him!'

'I think – I think that at the last, I would have failed. Perhaps Sigrun is right. Perhaps there is nothing that can stop him – not even death.' The older man stumbled and fell to his knees, blood oozing from the jagged tear in his jerkin. He bared his teeth. 'In Tyr's name – why are humans – so damnably *weak* . . .?'

'You begin to understand,' said a voice from the shadows.

Erik looked up. His face was a battleground of emotions, masked with pain. 'Sigrun? Why – why are you here?'

'You do not know?' She stepped out from the shelter of the trees and knelt by his side in the snow, gathering her heavy cloak around him, brushing the draggled hair from his face. 'Because I am Biarki's mother – and your wife. That is my doom, and it is as potent as my son's.' She picked up the fallen halberd, and Brockman saw that the blade had broken cleanly, leaving a short, leaf-shaped point. For a moment she seemed to hesitate. Then she handed the weapon to Erik.

'I will care for him now,' she said. 'Someone must follow Biarki, and see what befalls him.'

Brockman looked meaningfully at Erik. 'You trust her?'

Erik smiled faintly. 'Never. But she is right. Follow him. See what he does. And tell me – tell *us* – what you see.'

Brockman hesitated. Then he started to run.

Within minutes his side was a raging agony. The pain half-blinded him, but still it seemed that the air around him was moving strangely, as if it responded to the winds of another world. The scarecrow branches of the ancient oaks broke the low rays of the setting sun into fantails of shadow and half-light – and by that other-worldly light he seemed to see spectral shapes drifting in and out of reality. It was as though the forest itself ran with him.

Biarki's tracks were clear in the snow: he had been moving at a slow, loping run, and the weight of his ringmail and his weapons left deep footprints. They did not lead towards the stone.

Twilight came. Ice caked in Brockman's hair and eyebrows, and gathered in rings around the sleeves of his stolen jerkin. His breathing grew harsh and laboured, and in the fading light the landscape around him seemed to change, mimicking the silence and emptiness of the world beyond the stone. Now conifer sentinels brooded amid the wintry ruins of oak and ash, and the ground rose in isolated crags and slow scarps. The snow lay more thickly here, and Biarki's tracks were criss-crossed with the trails of hunting animals. A raven launched itself from a storm-shattered oak, creaking its warning to the world.

The ground fell away at Brockman's feet.

The shallow cliff jutted out from the edge of the hill in soft-edged promontories that formed a vast amphitheatre. Trees clung to its margins, but its base was a spreading, white expanse, level, unchanging, and still – a frozen lake, muffled into silence by a gleaming shroud of snow.

To Brockman's right a pulpit of rock rose like an ebony silhouette against the sky, tipped with a coronal of gnarled and twisted trees. High above it shadow-shapes were circling, dark against the darkling sky, as a gibbous moon crept above the trees and the lake became a shining level of glittering sliver.

Then came a cry that echoed round the cliffs – an inhuman cry of loss and anger and despair.

The Watcher . . .

Suddenly it seemed that a thousand eyes were watching – that the cliffs had truly become an arena, crowded with invisible spectators. High on the rock pulpit, clear in the light of the rising moon, two figures circled one another in a slow dance of death. A pattern-welded blade flashed black and silver against the stars, swinging in a shimmering arc. A misshapen arm clawed out to meet it. Sparks glittered and fell, and moments later Brockman heard an echoing reverberation, as if metal had met and tested metal. Biarki struck a second time, but the blade could not pierce the alien flesh – Brockman saw the sparks flash again near the Watcher's jaw, and the glittering reflections in its strangely human eyes. Then its arm coiled around Biarki's midriff.

Brockman gasped. There was no way that mere human flesh could resist the grip of the Watcher. In seconds Biarki would be crushed to pulp . . .

Naegling struck again and yet again in a flurry of red-gold sparks, but the edge would not bite. The creature's claws were raking its opponent, but they seemed to make no impression at all. With a howl of frustrated fury it struck at the sword – and tore it from Biarki's hand. Brockman watched with horrified fascination as Naegling arced into the sky, hung poised for a moment at the peak of its flight, and then tumbled end over end down towards the lake.

He almost missed the noise in the undergrowth behind him. Only blind instinct made him turn – and even then he was barely quick enough to save himself.

He felt the wind of the axe as he threw himself aside, reaching clumsily for his sword and struggling to release it from the sheath. His attacker, a big man encased in chain-mail and a mask helmet, laughed. He feinted with the axe, grinning as he pushed his victim back towards the cliff-edge. It was unpleasantly like the encounter with the berserk in Rolf's hall, but this time there was no Hialti to help him. Brockman swung his sword experimentally. It was so perfectly balanced it felt like an extension of his arm – but he had no skill with it at all.

So who's making rules around here?

Almost without thinking, he drew back his arm like a pitcher on the mound and hurled the weapon with all the strength in his body.

He was only half-successful. The sword struck his opponent hilt-first – but it struck forcefully, on the jaw, and the man was totally unprepared for it. He dropped his axe.

Brockman grabbed the axe and struck out blindly. His first blow glanced ringingly off the man's helmet. His second bit deep into the unprotected neck.

Brockman had battled the inhuman alvar. He had seen men die at Erik's hands. But nothing had prepared him for this.

The man was still alive. There was nothing unnatural about it – his injury was appalling, but not quite fatal. Blood was bubbling from his nose and mouth, and frothing along the edges of his wound as he tried to scream through a half-crushed larynx. He clutched at his throat, struggling with the strap that secured his helmet.

Gritting his teeth, Brockman knelt down and undid the strap. With exaggerated care he lined up the axe and struck again, shutting his eyes at the last moment. There was a soft thump, and then he felt the blade strike frozen earth with a gentle rasping sound.

He wanted to be sick, but his stomach was empty.

Once, in a long-lost world, the thought of avenging Sarah had almost dominated his life. Now Anja and

Kristine were dead, and the battle against their murderers had already begun – a just battle, a battle against evil and darkness . . .

Except I don't want to fight it. I'm not cut out to kill people.

He opened his eyes.

The man was dead, but he could not have been alone – and if there was a human force in the forest, it could only belong to Jorvard, Rolf's ambitious and unscrupulous under-king.

In which case we're close to the end.

He knew what would happen next – or, at least, what the legends said would happen next. Jorvard would attack the hall at Lejre, driven by the jealousy and ambition of his alv-born wife. Rolf and his household, desperately outnumbered, would come out to meet the attack. And Biarki . . .

Biarki!

Brockman stared wildly around him, but the rock pulpit was empty – there was no trace of either Biarki or the Watcher. The ice-bound arena below was silent and empty – except for Naegling, its blade half-buried in the snow, shining in the light of the rising moon.

CHAPTER
9

Kialar ferr austan, koma muno Múspellz
Stynja dvergar fyr steindurom, veggbergs visir
Dreka hann drepa, en draugar risar

Kialar drives eastward as the final day is dawning,
Gibbering at the gate stone the hosts of darkness
gather –
The dragon is destroyed, and dead men walk
abroad . . .

Völuspá – The Prophecy of the Seeress

Brockman crouched low in the sparse shelter of a
hawthorn thicket, hidden by its canopy of snow. From the
first the forest had seemed an alien place – a frozen
jungle, only half-asleep under the blanket of winter,
pulsing with hidden life. Now it was moving.

He had felt it first as he searched back along his own
trail from Lejre. By then the moon had been high in the
sky, and the cold even more intense. A wind had risen
from the north, driving ragged clouds before it like
trailing, battle-torn banners. Leafless branches had
clacked one against another, scattering powdery snow as
they passed their messages back and forth across the
forest. And all the time he had known that somewhere –
somewhere close by – Jorvard and his army were
marching on Lejre.

His encounter with the scout had been a matter of

chance. He had seen no more of Jorvard's men. But he soon heard them.

After the wind had come a stillness – the stillness of deepest winter, when frost turns the earth to iron, shatters mountains, and flows in sullen rivers down to silent, frozen seas. In that unnatural silence he had heard the advancing army all around him: the faint jingle of ringmail, the creak of leather harness, the susurrus of a thousand booted feet sweeping through deep snow, and the myriad betraying sounds of armed men on the move. There were other sounds as well – as if the trees themselves were moving . . .

Now he crouched in hiding, held in the iron grip of the winter darkness, with Biarki's sword clutched to his chest. Naegling was warm in his hand. The hilts, bound with leather and gold wire, nestled against his fingers as if made for him to carry. The blade seemed almost new-forged, untouched as yet by the long centuries that had scarred and tempered the ancient halberd. The patterns of black and silver along its length glittered even in the ghostly half-light of this last, endless night. It had defeated the lord of the liosalvar, and left him for dead. Perhaps it could be used against Kialar.

If the Watcher's gone, it may be the last chance we have.

Somewhere far away a wolf howled to the moon. Others joined it in a strange, mournful chorus – but the sound came closer with each passing minute. Off to the left a tree branch cracked and broke as something tall and heavy brushed past it. A bird croaked harshly somewhere above his head.

Can't just sit here and wait for the wolves. Time to be moving.

It was harder than he expected. Every joint seemed stiff, every muscle ached, and his right leg was almost locked with cramp. The cold had reached every part of his body – he had taken the armour and helmet of the man he had killed, and the thigh-length ringmail byrnie was a layer of ice where it overlapped his woollen trews. The

241

metal of his ill-fitting helmet was cold enough to burn his fingers. His woollen cloak gave some shelter from the wind, but the boots had no warmth in them at all. The woollen leggings were soaked through, and he could scarcely feel his feet.

Can't feel that damned rib, either. Guess I should be grateful.

In the shelter of the hawthorn copse he had missed the subtle change of light and colour around him. Glittering silver had grown pallid and grey, and cloud-rack covered the sky. Now snow was falling – thin, powdery snow like the white pollen of a nightmare spring. Already his own tracks were disappearing, and there was nothing else he could use to find his way back. But the wind was returning – and with it came a sound like a thousand murmuring voices. There were words, too – not words he could understand, but a slow, repetitive chant. It was far away, and sometimes it disappeared altogether, but it was real. The voices reminded him of the skald in the hall at Lejre, singing of long-dead kings and their vanished champions – but this song had a sinister, rhythmic undertone.

Battle-chant, maybe. Whatever it is, I wish to hell it'd stop.

Snow whirled from the skeletal branches of the trees, forming elusive and transitory patterns like the faces and limbs of an invisible army. Were the *einheriar* with him still, or was this nothing but illusion? He had no way of knowing. His grasp on reality seemed ever more slender.

Who said only death is real?

The thought stopped him in his tracks.

Anja ...

For a moment he seemed to see her face in the dancing snow – a pale, moonlit face, eyes wide with passion as he held her in his arms. He remembered the perfume of her hair, and the rich scent of her body after their lovemaking. He remembered the strong and certain knowledge that here, at last, he had found a spirit so close to his own that love was inevitable. He remembered every quirk of her lips, every movement of her eyes, every changing note of her voice – and each memory was a knife carving out her epitaph on his own flesh. Anja had died pointlessly, needlessly. If he had moved a little faster, if she had listened to him, if Kristine had escaped the fire ...

He laughed, bitterly. He was caught up in a last, hopeless battle against Kialar and the svartalvar – but if Kialar won, the laws of cause and effect would pass away. In Brockman's world Anja was dead, and there was nothing he could do about it. In Kialar's world he might be able to change the tapestry – cut a thread or move it, link it with another, create a new reality where she was still alive ...

No. She died fighting that, and I won't betray her now.

He could see the look in her eyes as she refused to shoot at the children. In that moment he had known that he never wanted to lose her – and known, also, that both of them were marked for death.

And now she's gone. Like Sarah. But I survived before. At least I know that I can do it.

Now, he knew, the anger would follow. For months after Sarah's death he had found it impossible to talk to anyone. Hatred had poured out of him, till friends and family backed away and left him in the isolation he needed and loathed. He remembered the fear and incomprehension in their eyes; and the calm acceptance in Kristine's.

You knew so much. Why couldn't you save her, Kristine? Why couldn't you save yourself?

The answer was slow to come.

Kristine had accepted death the way she accepted life – on equal terms, and without fear. She had understood his anger only because she had passed beyond it. And Anja ...

He had seen Anja tearful and vulnerable. He had seen her angry and afraid. But all that mattered was that single moment in the hayloft when she had known she was going to die – and known that her only chance of survival was to betray everything she cared about.

She had passed the test.

And me. What do I believe in?

Maybe I believe in Anja. Maybe it's like Mom used to say – that now I've got two people to live for. And just one life to do it in.

The wind blew harder, in gusts that rocked high branches and scattered frozen clumps of snow across his path, obliterating the last remnants of the trail. He cast about for some familiar feature or landmark, but in the darkness of the deep forest he had no chance of finding them.

He was lost.

Bad timing, Brockman. Those wolves sounded hungry. Only human sounds I've heard lately are those voices. If they were voices. Or human, come to that . . .

He stopped for a moment, willing his fear to die, listening as the sounds of his own breathing and heart-beat slowed and quietened. At first all he could hear was the wind, racketing among the bare branches of the oaks, sighing through conifers, sweeping across deserted clearings. Then, once again, he heard the distant chanting.

He followed it, bowing his head against the rising wind, holding the cloak tightly around his body. He felt small and insignificant. He knew more of what was happening than any man alive – but there was nothing he could do about it. His life, or death, would change nothing at all.

Snow gathered on his boots, slowing him even further. The ringmail was burdensome and uncomfortable, and the helmet moved irritatingly as he walked, making it difficult to hear the voices on the wind.

But there was another sound as well.

Someone was following him, moving with a slow, deliberate pace that almost, though not quite, matched his own. Again he ducked into cover, cursing silently at his own fear, searching among the treacherous shadows for his pursuer.

Nothing moved. The sound had stopped as soon as he did.

He stared again into the trees. For a moment he seemed to see a half-human shape, tall as a tree, with a misty cloud rising from its mouth. Then there was only a spindly conifer, and powdered snow flying in the wind. He crouched in silence for another sixty heartbeats, hearing nothing except the music of the wind, and the distant murmur it carried.

Getting jumpy now. Starting to imagine things.

The trees were thinner here, and in places he could see the landscape beyond them. His search had taken him back to the Roskilde Fjord – but the night had brought a subtle change. When he left Lejre with Erik there had been ice-floes in the channel. Now the fjord was frozen from shore to shore. A high, ghostly cloud was moving across the moon, and its dark shadow was sweeping slowly across the ice ...

The cloud passed. Moonlight flooded over the distant hills and spilled onto the ice. But the shadow remained – and its edges glittered in the new light.

It was a forest made of spears.

At least a thousand men, in tight formation, were marching towards Lejre. Behind them were disciplined lines of horsemen and archers – and bringing up the rear were the slow, labouring silhouettes of horses and oxen dragging heavy carts laden with weapons, arrows, and provisions. It was Jorvard's army.

And I'm the only one who knows they're here ...

His grip on Naegling tightened. He knew how the story was supposed to end – what the legends said would happen. But what had *really* happened? What was Kialar trying to change, and why?

Jorvard's plan was clear enough. Lejre, on its island fortress, was all but impregnable – except from the sea. So Rolf's ambitious rival had taken an army through the heart of the forest, in the depths of winter, to mount an attack from the fjord itself. With this overwhelming force he would crush the household troops before any word could reach the outposts on the mainland.

Rolf doesn't have a chance. Lejre's full of Kialar's people. And while they're fighting in the stockade, Jorvard can take the place at his leisure.

With Lejre gone, Jorvard could pick off Rolf's supporters piecemeal. They would die as Anja had died; and once again Brockman was helpless to prevent it.

But there was more. In the forest he had felt otherworldly forces at work – now, watching Jorvard's implacable advance across the ice, he felt them again. The shadow he had seen was more than a trick of the moonlight. The army carried darkness with it like an advancing tide. Even the sky seemed to be changing.

Then, at last, he understood.

The Watcher was dead. The gate stone was open and unguarded. The twilight world was spilling into time like blood from a savaged throat.

For a moment he hesitated. There was nothing in the world of time that could stand against such an army. He was looking at the end of everything he knew and cared about. There might never be another sunrise – and if there was, he would never live to see it. He felt small, and insignificant, and very afraid.

But there was something he had to do.

Lejre slept beneath a sky that was drifting, imperceptibly, into nightmare. Plumes of woodsmoke coiled up from the vents under the gables of the great hall. Horses whinnied faintly in the stables, as if their sleep had been touched by the approaching shadow out of twilight. Flickering points of red and gold marked the watchfires of Rolf's garrison – but their light revealed no sign of preparation.

Brockman leaned against a tree to catch his breath. He had skirted the edge of the forest, slipping back among the shadows of the trees whenever the changing lie of the land might expose him to Jorvard's scouts. He had little doubt that there were others in the woods tonight, left to ensure that no word of Jorvard's treachery reached the island.

He was bone-tired. It had been a long, hard journey through the drifting snow, and the ringmail weighed heavy on his back. For a while he had thought of throwing it aside – but when every shadow might hide an enemy, he needed its protection. Sweat soaked his shirt, moulding it against the cold leather of his jerkin, and trickled down his back.

So what do I do? Make a run for it, and risk an arrow in the back?

Perhaps there were others who had seen the approaching army, and were even now on their way to Lejre? But they, too, might be killed before they could bring their message to the king.

At least they'd speak the goddamned language . . .

He smiled wearily. If he used Danish, he could make himself understood. *'Jorvard, han kommer!'* would probably be enough.

But I wouldn't live long enough to say it.

It was only with Sigrun's help that he and Erik had entered the hall – and only a mixture of cunning and blind luck that had brought them out alive.

So what do I do? Sit here and watch it happen?

Once before, in another world, he had faced an irresistible enemy, and seen everything that he loved destroyed in a few blinding seconds. Now he seemed to be the last hope of Lejre. He had no choice, and he knew it – but he would have to run, and run fast, to escape Jorvard's outriders.

And right now I'm in no shape to try it.

Just a short rest. That was all he needed . . .

When he opened his eyes again, he knew at once that time had passed him by. His mouth was dry and foul-tasting. The chill wind from the fjord cut through him like steel, and every limb was stiff and cramped. He could almost feel the tide out of twilight surging past him, sleeting through the old forest like the last winter of the world.

No more time. Got to run ...

But he was already too late. There was a sound on the wind that he recognised: the sound of burning timber mingled with human voices and the clash of weapons. And as he stumbled to his feet he saw that treachery had already come to Lejre.

A roaring column of black and gold clawed skyward from the heart of Rolf's fortress, throwing wild and twisting shadows over the buildings below. The main hall was scarcely damaged, but the guest hall beyond it was burning fiercely. In the ever-changing light Brockman caught brief glimpses of a savage running battle within the compound, and new fires rising from isolated buildings. There was little he could see, but much he could imagine. He remembered the deep shadows within the hall, even while the hearth burned high. By now there would be darkness enough for the alv-haunted shells that had once been human beings to murder Rolf's remaining *hirðmenn*. But there was something wrong ...

Rolf's people weren't expecting an attack. Half of them should have died in their sleep – but they're still fighting ...

In the flickering firelight Rolf's men would surely have little chance to tell friend from foe, or to understand that yesterday's comrade might now be a deadly enemy – yet it was clear that Kialar's strategy had failed.

As if someone was telling them who to kill ...

Even as he watched, a small group of heavily-armed warriors burst through the gate, stumbling down the slopes on either side of the causeway and out onto the frozen expanse that lay beyond. Two stragglers threw up their arms and fell to arrows from the palisade. The rest were safely out of range, but they had nowhere to run except the forest – and the only path they could follow had perils of its own.

Brockman watched them stumble and slide across the thin mantle of ice that covered the marshy inlet; and one by one he watched them fall, plunging into the clinging mud below as the treacherous surface gave way beneath them.

So the alvar blew it. They started too soon. Looks like most of those fires are already dying down. Or are they . . . ?

There was something strange about the light.

Dawn was hours away: the hills on the farther shore of the fjord were no more than a darker line against the night sky. The moon had set long since. Torn streamers of cloud and smoke raced across the heavens – but in the gaps between them, a pallid silver light shone out.

As if there were too many stars . . .

It was true. The last battle would be fought under the skies of the twilight world.

The murmur of a thousand voices drifted towards him on the wind, and as he looked out towards the fjord he saw a dark line across the ice – a line that once again flickered and changed to a bristling hedge of spears.

The enemy was in sight.

'Well met, Peter Brockman.'

He whirled in his tracks, with Naegling poised to strike – and looked into the mocking, gold-flecked eyes that had once belonged to Erik Larssen.

'You! I thought you were dead!'

'I was well tended.'

'Sigrun?'

Erik nodded impatiently. 'What has happened? How do you come to carry Naegling?'

'It was struck out of Biarki's hand.'

'The Watcher?'

'Yes. Can't tell you how it came out. I had a run-in with one of Jorvard's men.'

Erik stared down towards the icebound fjord. 'No need to ask. The Watcher is destroyed. But Biarki – you looked for him?'

'I tried, but he could've been anywhere, and I was right in the middle of Jorvard's army. Had to lie low till they passed me. Where's Sigrun?'

'She has done what she promised. Rolf still lives, and

Lejre still stands. Kialar's wolves went hunting too soon, and now they are hunted themselves. As for me, I shall do what I can here.'

For a moment Brockman's fear returned. The coming battle would be like none the world had ever known. At the farm and at the stone he had glimpsed a small part of Kialar's power; here its full force would be unleashed on a defenceless enemy. He was only a man, an ordinary man with no skill in weapons. He was tired, and cold, and hungry, and such strength as he had was almost gone. But Erik was looking at him with something like expectancy.

Brockman took Naegling from his sheath and held it out to Erik hilt-first. 'You'll need this.'

Erik shook his head. 'I have the halberd. Keep Naegling for yourself.' He looked searchingly at Brockman, with an irritating half-smile. 'Unless you have other plans?'

Damn it, stop reading my mind!

'This will be no battle for the faint-hearted, Peter Brockman. Twilight is unleashed on your world. There will be things that no man should see – but you, you have already seen far worse.'

'I killed Jorvard's man hand to hand. I'm not sure I could do it again. I'm not even sure I want to.'

'Your arrows pierced the hell-horse itself and laid it low. At the stone you faced Kialar's *einheriar* and tore their *fylgjar* from the flesh. I know you are no coward, Peter Brockman. Naegling has fallen into worthy hands.'

'I wish I believed that.'

'Then believe this. You have the same choice as Rolf himself. You can die afraid and alone, fleeing Kialar's shadow – or you can die among your own kind, fighting the evil that he brings. Which is it to be?'

What would Anja have done?

Jorvard's army was a dark line across the ice. The horizon bristled with spears that glittered in the alien light of another world.

It's like a cancer eating into time. There isn't any choice. It has to be destroyed, here and now ...

'I'm with you,' he said.

And I wish to God I wasn't.

The battle began before they could reach the ice.

Rolf's men, many still half-armed after the treacherous attack in the compound, had mustered on the quay to meet the threat from the fjord. They had taken precious minutes to move off, but their way was clear, and the ice firm beneath their feet. For Brockman and Erik the way forward had been barred by the treacherous ice on the marsh – they had seen what happened to those who tried to cross it. To reach the firm ice on the fjord itself they had to cross a wooded peninsula, thick with tangled undergrowth. By the time they emerged on the far side Rolf's *hirðmenn* were already closing on the enemy.

Brockman, struggling to match Erik's slow, loping run, heard rather than saw the moment when the wave of Jorvard's advance broke over the hedge of spears that opposed it. For an instant it seemed that the ice would shatter under the impact as it echoed and re-echoed among the surrounding hills, and the roar of battle-cries from both sides shook the stars. Rolf's slender line was engaged along its full length, yet somehow his men were holding their ground. At the centre, the king's raven banner was even bearing forward into the front ranks of the rebels. Brockman found himself cheering hoarsely – and then four horsemen on the near flank of Jorvard's army wheeled clear of the main force and galloped towards them over the ice.

'Save your breath,' growled Erik. 'You will need it.' He hefted the halberd in both hands, testing the balance of the damaged blade. Even now its reach made it a potent weapon, while Naegling would be a poor defence against a mounted attacker.

One of the horses stumbled, careened sideways on the

ice and hurled its rider to the ground. He did not get up.

'It seems the gods are with us,' said Erik, as the other three cautiously dismounted.

'Tell me that in ten minutes.'

Jorvard's men were seasoned fighters, and well-armed. Each wore a mask-helmet of black iron, a ringmail coif, and a knee-length ringmail byrnie – and each carried a round, wooden shield, a spear, and a sword.

Erik stood his ground, letting the men come to him over the frozen mud that fringed the lake. One of them stumbled before he could reach the firmer, rising ground along the shore – and Erik struck at lightning speed. Without ringmail to slow him he could move twice as quickly as his opponents, and the first man took the leaf-shaped tip of the broken blade in his throat before he knew what had happened to him. The second, behind him, parried Erik's thrust with his spear, striking out with the edge of the shield. The third turned towards Brockman, lunging with a dark, long-bladed spear.

Brockman feinted with Naegling – and the sword seemed to come alive in his hand. It cut cleanly through his attacker's spear-shaft, and its return swing tested the banding of the man's helmet. He stumbled backwards, warding off another stroke with his shield while he reached for his own sword. Again Brockman hammered at the faceless mask of the helmet, and the man went down, lifting his shield to defend himself. Brockman kicked it aside, and thrust Naegling two-handed into his opponent's open mouth. It rasped against bone – and jammed in place.

Gritting his teeth, he planted his boot against the fallen man's face and tugged at the hilt with both hands, wrenching the blade free. Erik was still battling his second opponent, warding off spear-thrusts with his halberd. With a reverse almost too fast to see he hammered the butt end into the man's stomach, then swung the blade around to strike at his neck. Erik's opponent threw himself to the left, feinting with the spear, but Erik stepped aside, crossed his arms for a clean downward thrust, and took out the man's throat with the edge of the blade.

He stepped back from the writhing body of his victim with an expression that mirrored Brockman's own revulsion.

'I had not understood,' said Erik. 'Here there is only the true death.'

Brockman scowled. 'Doesn't stop us killing each other.'

Out on the ice, the long battle-line swayed backwards and forwards, shield pressed against shield while the din of swords, spears and axes against wood and metal echoed around the hills. Windblown snow veiled the battle in drifting clouds of white. At the centre, Rolf's banner swayed over the heart of Jorvard's army as the king and his champions carved a blood path through the rebel ranks. Behind the lines on either side the wounded and the dead lay in tangled heaps, their blood purpling the ice in the haunted half-light of the shadow-world.

'Come,' said Erik, taking a sword from the outthrust hand of his dead attacker, 'we must do what we can.'

'Wait,' said Brockman. 'Look over there.'

At the edge of the trees a huge, dark shadow moved silently across the snow. As it reached the battle-line it reared up on two massive legs, and uttered a roar that came up clearly to the watchers on the shore.

Damnation, I saw that – I saw it in the forest . . .

For a moment it seemed the Watcher had returned. The creature was almost ten feet high, and nothing could stand against it. Brockman saw one man lifted bodily, flung down on the ice, and trampled where he lay. Another thrust at it with a spear that snapped on its hide like a rotten twig, only to be grasped in its arms and crushed to death. In the half-light the shadow-creature was nothing more than a looming darkness, but there was something familiar about it . . .

It's a bear – a gigantic bear . . .

'It is Jorvard's doom,' said Erik softly. 'Kialar's

253

scheming rebounds against him; there are other powers than his in the twilight. Come – there is work for us here.'

Below them the enemy battle-line was breaking into disarray as the shadow-creature scythed through Jorvard's troops. Behind it the men of Lejre surged forward, turning the flank of the rebel host, moving inexorably towards the raven banner at the heart of the battle. As Erik and Brockman stumbled across the ice and mud at the edge of the fjord it seemed that nothing could stop Rolf's advance.

Further out the footing was treacherous. A thin, frozen crust covered a deeper layer of soft, yielding snow that overlay the uneven pack-ice. The unnatural half-light drained all colour from the scene: living flesh took on the pallor of the dead, and the vivid banners and pennants of Rolf's army became nothing more than tattered shadows, punished by the rising wind. Dry, powdery snow whirled all about them, half-blinding them. Then they were in the thick of the battle, and there was no more time for thought.

At the forefront, Rolf's men had overlapped their shields to form an impenetrable wall, bristling with spear-points, that drove hard through Jorvard's demoralised army. The noise of clashing weapons, war-cries and death-cries numbed the senses – to Brockman the advance seemed to become a roaring wall of sound breaking across Jorvard's army like a tsunami. Scattered arrows flicked past them, but there was little real opposition. The bear was out of sight, and even the sounds of its passage were lost in the roar of battle, but its handiwork was all around them. At every step Brockman saw the shattered bodies of Jorvard's followers. Many were still half-alive, faces contorted with pain, hands clawing in the crimsoned snow, crushed and twisted limbs trembling in spasm or a last, desperate struggle for life.

Before long he stopped looking down.

His sense of time disappeared. The battle on the ice

had become an endless, weary effort to force the shield-wall forward over the bodies of the fallen. Sometimes an enemy spear would find a weak point, or a stray arrow would strike true, and another man would push forward to fill the gap in the front rank. Sometimes, just for a moment, Brockman would see the faces of the men they were fighting, distorted by fear, hatred, and the sheer physical effort of holding back the crushing force of the shield-wall. By now the bear was nowhere to be seen, and resistance to the advance was stronger. Even so, Brockman caught a glimpse of the king's raven banner.

They were winning. In a little while Jorvard's army would be driven back against the immovable barrier of its own baggage train.

Then something heavy smashed against the side of his helmet.

Half-dazed from the impact he turned, unsteadily, to face his attacker – and saw a thing that had no right to be alive. Shattered stumps of bone had torn through the flesh of the left arm. The face was a ruin – a single, empty eye protruded from a gashed and bloody socket. The byrnie had been ripped wide open; dark shapes oozed from the lips of a jagged belly wound. Yet the sea-axe in the man's right hand swung threateningly, ready to deliver a second blow.

Naegling lashed out to sever his hand, but the axe was already falling, and Brockman ducked clumsily out of its path. His attacker stepped sideways, using the force of the first blow in a return stroke that clipped Brockman's helmet a second time. Again Naegling lunged forward, piercing the tear in the man's byrnie – to no effect. Brockman leapt desperately to avoid a low cut at his ankles. This time his downward stroke took his enemy at the wrist, severing the sinews. The axe dropped from his attacker's hand as Naegling's backswing severed the ruined head from the body. For a few moments the headless corpse thrust against him, limbs flailing. Then it pitched forward into the snow, and lay still.

Beyond it was nightmare.

All across the ice the bodies of the slain were writhing with the same unnatural life he had first seen in the forest clearing. Empty eyes moved in pallid, bloodless faces that glimmered with the telltale nimbus of the alvar. Mutilated hands reached out for weapons half-buried in the snow. Behind Rolf's triumphant household an army of the dead was rising from the ice.

'*Draugar*,' growled Erik. 'The walking dead. Kialar's vileness knows no bounds.'

'Can't you do something?'

'We shall see.' He sheathed his sword, and lifted his halberd in the same gesture that Brockman had seen at the stone. The blade flickered with red-gold fire – then dulled to blue-silver as if nothing had happened.

Erik cursed savagely. 'The ways of time are strange to me, Peter Brockman. I cannot match Kialar's powers.'

'Damn it, there must be *something* –'

'There is nothing! I have sipped at the well of knowledge, for fear of the darkness in its depths. Kialar has drained it – he and all the svartalvar – and they have paid the price it demands. Now those same forces that have twisted and perverted their flesh are turned against us, Peter – and I have no knowledge, no understanding that can counter them! The king is surely doomed.'

And we're helpless. Just like we were at the farm. All we can do is fight on till they kill us.

All around them the broken and mutilated bodies of the fallen stumbled towards them, gathering such weapons as they could find. Some were feeble, unable to stand against the slightest blow. Others fought with demonic energy. Brockman's world became a ringing net of iron, where blows might fall from any side, and each moment brought him face to face with new horrors. Again and again Naegling sang against ringmail, or juddered against bone as the blade struck hard and deep. Again and again he faced a broken and mutilated corpse, its sightless eyes glittering with the parasitic *fylgja* of the alv who controlled it. On either side, Rolf's men encountered the haunted husks of their former companions – and fell before their onslaught. Brockman heard Hialti's voice raised even above the din of battle, calling on his companions to repay the gifts that Rolf had given them. He was standing back to back with Svipdag, hammering at a *draug* with a sword so blunted that it was little more than a club. Svipdag hewed grimly with his axe, and each stroke was the death of a man, but although the bodies of Jorvard's warriors lay piled about him like a rampart, there were too many for him to conquer them all. A dozen blades were striking at his shield, denting and twisting the metal banding at its edge, thundering against the boss, booming on the timber shell, until it split, and fell, and hungry spears stabbed through the gap to seek the one-eyed warrior's lifeblood. For a glorious moment the axe struck out, shattering a dozen spearshafts like so many matchsticks, but a dozen more struck home, driven by the full weight of Jorvard's shield-wall, tearing Svipdag's ringmail aside to pierce the grizzled doorkeeper through and through.

Hialti, feeling the spearpoints against his own back, roared in fury, lashing out with demonic energy at the living corpses ranged against him. The blow shattered the mutilated skull of his nearest foe – but it was his last stroke. Moments later he fell, pinned on the same spears that had killed his comrade, and the tide of battle swept across them. For a moment Brockman glimpsed Hialti's crushed and broken body – and then the horrors out of twilight were all around him, and he must strike, and slash, and parry without end and without rest. He no longer knew what he was doing, or why – his arm was an unbearable weight that moved with a will of its own, carrying his body with it. Then, finally, a heavy blow rang against his helmet, and he sank into a merciful oblivion.

He awoke to the sounds of battle – but they were fainter, and farther off. His back was stiff and cold, and something hard was digging into it. When he opened his eyes he saw Erik standing a few yards away, leaning on his halberd as he stared out between the trees into the starlit night beyond.

'The battle,' mumbled Brockman. 'What happened?'

'I brought you away.'

'You – ran?'

'You would rather I had left you?'

'There must be *something* you can do!'

'I can do nothing by dying. Kialar is lord here. It is the triumph of the true death.'

Brockman struggled to his feet, supporting himself against the tree. His head was still ringing as he stumbled across to Erik's vantage point. Out on the ice, the nearer wing of Rolf's army had folded back on itself, trapped between the rebel lines on the one side and Kialar's horrific sending on the other. Few had escaped. At the centre, the raven banner of king Rolf was falling back towards Lejre – but all along the battlefront the ice flickered blue and silver with the pallid aura of elf-shot.

'Kialar has unleashed his power,' said Erik quietly. 'He grows impatient. It may yet be his downfall.'

'We should *be* there,' said Brockman bitterly.

'Your death would serve no purpose. And mine would destroy what little hope is left. Be patient, Peter Brockman, and watch.'

On the ice, strange shadows flickered in the silvery light from the battlefront.

Svartalvar. In their own, true shape.

He stared at Erik with something approaching hate. The knot of men around Rolf's banner were still fighting hard – but now they were almost totally encircled.

'They'll be cut off,' said Brockman. 'There's no way they can make it back to the gates.'

'No?' Erik pointed towards the heart of the rebel army.

Something was stirring it like fire beneath a cauldron. An incandescent corona of blue shone out from its centre, and in that vivid and unnatural light Brockman saw, once again, the great bear. Its strident roar cut through the din of the battle, and none who faced it could stand against it – but now it was battling the full power of twilight, battered by a host of weapons, beset by *draugar*, punished by crackling bolts of elf-shot. For a little while it vanished altogether in a glittering column of fire.

Then came a noise like the death of a forest – a crescendo of tearing, echoing sound that rose above the noise of battle and reverberated among the trees. Brockman wanted to shout, but the words would not come out.

The ice! My God, look at the ice!

From the heart of the firestorm, dark lines crawled outwards in a fusillade of crackling concussions. Between them, short-lived islands and archipelagoes of ice tipped and turned, spilling friend and foe alike into the chill waters of the fjord. In the intense cold none could live more than a few minutes, and most were weighed down by their armour and equipment. Warriors clawed at one another as they struggled over the corpses of the newly-drowned and the threshing bodies of their comrades in the desperate hope of finding solid, unmoving ice. Banners teetered and fell, dragging men down in their sodden toils. For an instant Brockman saw the great bear ramping on its hind legs, hurling Rolf's enemies to their death. Then it was gone – and with it the greater part of Jorvard's unnatural army.

'Too late,' murmured Erik. 'Too late – but none has fought more bravely.'

For a while he watched as Rolf's few surviving *hirðmenn* held off the overwhelming rebel force with a tight shield-wall, reinforced with the piled bodies of their attackers. Then, at last, Rolf's raven wavered and fell. A great cry of triumph echoed from hilltop to hilltop – and then the empty, dreary silence of the deep winter night flooded back, like the waters of the fjord closing over the dead. Slowly, the scattered remnants of the rebel army gathered under their dark banners, picking their way over the ice towards Lejre. In their wake came shadows, slinking out of the forest – winter-starved scavengers, drawn by the smell of blood.

Not all of them were animals.

'Fate goes its own way,' said Erik at last, 'for all that Kialar or I can do. The king is dead, and all his champions with him – and I have seen the end of all I cared for.'

'So we've lost. Lost *everything*! Am I still supposed to be patient? What am I waiting for? *Tell me!*'

Erik fixed him with wide, gold-flecked eyes. There was a kind of madness in them. 'The Watcher is dead. My son is dead – and with him all who can challenge Kialar's dominion. Soon the hunters will come – Kialar's vile shadows – seeking out such enemies as remain. You, who struck down the hell-horse and defied their leader face to face. My *liosalvar*, or what remains of them – and the fool who was once their leader.'

'You're beginning to sound like the old Erik. He had a good line in self-pity. And you haven't answered my question.'

Erik raised the halberd. 'You *dare* –?'

'I dare. If you're as no-account as you say …'

Erik laughed. It was an utterly human sound, as human as his despair.

'Truly, Peter, you are a worthy companion! Will you join me in one last madness?'

'So there *is* something –!'

'I cannot be sure, Peter. At best it is a desperate throw. None can know what will come of it, and I least of all. But I shall need a *hirðmann* – such a *hirðmann* as my son was to his king.' Hesitantly the man who had once been Erik stretched out his hand.

Brockman clasped it. 'I know I'm going to regret this,' he said, 'but if there's any kind of a chance, then I'm with you. I'm with you all the way.'

Under the skies of twilight, the forest was changing.

Naked, winter-barren trees cast a network of shadows

like a thousand gnarled and grasping hands. Within those shadows dark shapes moved and whispered, and wary eyes shone silver in the light of a million stars. To Brockman, each crunching step through the wind-frozen snow-crust seemed to betray their progress to a silent army of watchers. It was like a child's puzzle-drawing, where a simple picture might conceal a dozen half-visible outlines – or a child's nightmare, where each shape might become another, more terrifying pursuer. All around them the *einheriar* flickered at the edge of vision, baffling the eye. Branches studded with iron-hard thorns clawed across their path, catching at their clothing and their flesh. Eyes glittered out of a copse – the dead eyes of a wolf, impaled on a gently swaying branch like a butterfly on a pin. Icicles rang one against another in a thin, unearthly music. And windblown snow cast a pallid, disguising veil over a landscape that was slipping out of time's dominion.

'It is *larnviði*,' said Erik. 'The Ironwood. In our world it circles the mound – now it spills into your world through the gate stone.'

'Anything live there?' asked Brockman.

Erik nodded. 'Creatures fouler than your darkest dreams.'

'So what the hell are we doing here?'

'We must find the stone again – but I cannot be sure of the way. The land is changing.'

'How about the *einheriar*?'

'They cannot help us.'

'For Christ's sake why not?'

'Because they are lost – just as we are!' snarled Erik – and thrust Brockman violently to one side. A black and leafless branch, heavy with thorns, swung past the place where his head had been.

'Move,' snapped Erik. '*Quickly!*'

Everywhere the strange, twisted trees of the Ironwood were writhing with a hideous vitality, hunting down any life different from their own. A red squirrel leapt from branch to branch, desperately seeking some avenue of escape. Again and again it slipped past a slowly-moving thorn or a twisting tree-limb until, at last, a solid hedge of dark spikes barred its way. With a final, desperate leap it sought the shelter of a tall oak, stranded in the midst of the alien foliage like an island in a storm – but the branch was too far away. It vanished into the twisting shadows below with a squealing cry of terror. All around them trees were turning, seeking them out. Again and again they struck with sword or halberd, carving a path that closed behind them as soon as they had passed. The trees pressed in on all sides, smothering them in creepers, lashing at them with thorn-laden branches, grasping at their ankles with gnarled and writhing roots ...

Red fire streamed from the tip of Erik's halberd. A questing branch caught the full force of the blast, withered, and fell away. Others turned aside. Slowly, a path opened before them – but behind them the trees had become a solid, impenetrable wall. At the same time the flickering half-presence of the *einheriar* vanished from the edge of Brockman's vision.

'We are hard by the stone,' said Erik. 'The gate into twilight stands open – or *larnviði* would never yield to the pitiful power I can bring to your world.'

'You're right,' said Brockman. 'Look over there.'

The clearing had changed beyond recognition. The ancient woodland was gone, swept away by the unnatural forest spilling out of twilight. The mound was all but overgrown. Even the stone was ringed with a hedge of thick-set thorns and brambles; but the few that had touched it were already withering and dying.

Two figures huddled in its shelter.

One was a woman, bare-headed, her hair pale silver in the starlight. The other, cradled in her lap, was a man: a young, bearded man, his body torn by a dozen terrible wounds.

For a moment Brockman seemed to see the living image of the peasant Pieta in Egerød church, down to the very clothes on Biarki's stricken body, and the grief in Sigrun's face. With a vile oath Erik unleashed a storm of fire against the trees that barred his way. They crumbled away in a shower of white ash and dying embers.

Sigrun looked up. Her face was pallid and empty – the face of a woman who had wept until there were no tears left. 'You come too late,' she said. 'He died in my arms.'

'No,' said Erik. 'He died on the ice, defending his lord.'

She stared at him. 'I don't – understand . . .'

Erik knelt by the body of his son, brushing flecks of snow from the bloodstained face. 'Your father was right to fear him, Sigrun. Even the Watcher fell before his power. You found him here?'

'Yes.'

Erik nodded. 'Yes – by the stone; but on this side. In your world, Peter. And in your world only his body could die. The part of him that belonged to time.'

Brockman frowned. 'What are you saying?'

'There was another part of him,' murmured Erik, 'a part that belonged to twilight. His *fylgja* sought out the bear that was his emblem and his name. He died as he had lived: with honour and fame, fighting the enemies of his king.'

'Honour and fame,' said Sigrun in a hoarse whisper. 'Are they worth a single moment of your son's life? Are they worth the true death?'

'To me,' said Erik, 'they have no worth. To Biarki . . .'

'It's true,' said Brockman. 'Don't you see? For him there was nothing else! You've seen these people, lived among them – you *know* there's nothing worse for a warrior than surviving the battle that killed his lord!'

She stared at him with something like hatred in her eyes. 'Then help *me*, Pe-tare! What should *I* want? What should *I* ask for in this terrible world of yours?'

'There is a task for you,' said Erik quietly. 'For you and your daughters.'

'For *Skuld* –?'

263

'There will be other daughters, Sigrun. Peter – give her the sword.'

'You have to be kidding.'

'No. It belonged to our son. It is rightfully hers.'

Brockman bit his lip, and unbuckled the leather harness that supported the sheath. For a moment he hesitated, fingering the familiar-seeming hilt. Then he held out the sword to Sigrun.

'Take it,' said Erik. 'Keep it safe. It is the one hope that remains.'

Sigrun pushed it away. 'Keep it yourself. I wish I had never seen it.'

'You have not understood,' said Erik. 'Without Naegling, I would be dead – and Biarki would have died for nothing. You must take it, now; or from this moment on the tapestry of time will be unseamed, and its threads will fall like winter leaves.'

Brockman shook his head. 'I don't get it. What's so important about –'

'This,' said Erik, gesturing with the halberd. 'Can you not see? This *is* Naegling. This is all that remains of Biarki's sword. Time has done its work – after so many centuries even this blade could no longer hold against the new-forged weapon in Biarki's hand. But without Naegling I could never have come here.'

Sigrun hesitated, staring up into Erik's face. Then she reached out, took the proffered sheath, and clasped it against her chest like a lost child. 'What must I do?'

'A wise woman told me how it should be. Its hiding place must be a woman's mystery, and its use a man's, until its time comes again. You will keep it safe?'

She nodded, but now there were tears in her eyes. 'Where will you go?'

'I have my place, as you have yours.' His voice was strangely tender, and for a moment he cupped her cheeks between his palms, meeting her eyes with a gaze that held love as well as power. 'We have learned much, Sigrun. But not enough, I think. There is still the game.'

'And – when it ends?'

'For me it has no end. My path is harder even than Biarki's. I must go; and you must decide where your heart lies. When your father returns, remember your son. Remember me, and remember what I have sworn to become. I think you will know what to do.'

For a long moment her eyes met his, and Brockman saw the very core of her humanity. Then she bowed her head over the body of her son and wept uncontrollably.

Erik turned away. His face was hard, and the old bitterness lingered in his eyes. 'Come,' he said. 'We must see what can be saved.'

Brockman hesitated. Once before he had stood at the boundary of time and twilight and seen the endless, barren hills of the alvar world like ghostly images overlaying reality. Now there was nothing to see except the sprawling horror of the Ironwood – but he could *feel* the presence of the boundary.

Erik reached out a hand. 'You gave your word to follow me. Will you break it now?'

Sounds like a great idea.

'No,' he said. 'I'm coming . . .'

They walked onward into darkness.

Soon the Ironwood and the circle of stones lay far behind. Above them the myriad paths of the mound vanished into a slow whirlpool of mist and cloud, blotting out the jewelled skies of the twilight world. Its pattern was familiar now. Brockman had seen it traced in fire as they escaped the Watcher and the battle around the stone, as though the air itself had been marked by the labyrinth of energies that had created the mound. Now, in the unnatural silence of the twilight world, he found himself remembering the fresco in the side chapel at Egerød – the dance of death.

Its origins were as old as man. On Stone Age sites all across Europe, spiral carvings symbolised the journey from time into eternity. He could imagine primitive *shamans* chipping them out with flint chisels, or painting them in caves deep below the earth, safe from the destroying years. And there had been dance-mazes, too – spiral labyrinths marked out with stones, where men and women linked hands to dance into eternity. It was the memory of that dance the Egerød painter had captured – as if a story from the very birth of humanity had been passed on, unchanged and unchanging, to find its expression in his flowing masterpiece. But always, even in the legends, there was the dark shadow, the monster in the labyrinth, the guardian, the Watcher; always a silent, lonely dancer, beyond the circle yet somehow at the heart of the dance; always the spectre that was death in life and life in death, the pursuer and the goal, the hunter and the victim. The Egerød painter had known it, too – yet instead of the traditional corpse or skeleton he had shown a demonic figure with curved, dagger-sharp teeth, and its arms hung from strange, peaked shoulders ...

As if he'd seen the Watcher. The rest I can almost understand, but that –

Brockman stumbled, almost falling over a dark, curving shape that lay full across the path – something as huge as a wind-felled tree, as dark as a fallen rock. In the twilight it seemed like the outgrown carapace of some vast crustacean, split open by the growing body and cast aside. He had seen fossil skeletons like this, backbone curled, limbs extended, as though the creature that formed them had died in indescribable pain ...

The corpse of the Watcher lay coiled in its final agony, its head thrown back, its jaws agape, its eyes empty, dull and lifeless, its single arm stretched out towards a slab-shaped rock at the side of the path.

Like Erik in the churchyard. As though we'd come full circle.

Erik stared at the Watcher's corpse, grim-faced and silent. Then, with a whispered oath, he knelt alongside its outstretched arm, running his finger over the face of the rock.

'What is it?'

'Something strange, Peter. There are marks here. Like the signs of your kind.'

'What are you saying?'

'The words. I know them. I have seen them in your world. But they should not be here.'

Brockman knelt by the stone, but it was almost impossible to see the markings. As he touched them and traced them out, he could see pallid dust gathering on his fingertip. 'It's like they've just been carved!'

'You understand them, Peter?'

'Not as such. I know they're runes – but there's something familiar about them.'

'Because you have seen this stone before. In your world it was part of the farm at Egerød. A stepping-stone –'

'Oh, come *on*! How could *that* stone be here? And *those* runes said that Erik – that you –'

He hesitated. At the farm, Erik had never mentioned carving the inscription on his first journey – and he had had no other opportunity. 'Look, are you telling me –?'

'Look carefully at the runes, Peter. Trace them out again. I think you may understand what they say.'

ᛁᚲ · ᚦᛖᚱ · ᚱᚢᚾᛁᛉ · ᚠᚨᛁᚺᛁᚦᛇ ·

ᛏᚱᛟᛗ · ᚺᚱᛖᚲᛁᚨᛋᛏᛁᚷᛁᛁ ·

Brockman narrowed his eyes as he struggled to match the runes to his memory of the inscription, but it was impossible. 'It's like there's something missing. I can't make sense of it.'

'It says "*Ik þar runar faihiðo. Troð drekijastiginn.*" "I carved these runes. Take the path of the dragon."'

'But that's not the same as what we found! There's nothing about Biarki! Nothing about –'

'None the less, Peter, these are the signs that were made. Perhaps their meaning is other than we thought.'

'But who –?'

Erik grasped the outstretched hand of the Watcher. Its massive claws were unsheathed, even in death – and the straight, chisel-like tip of the longest claw was still coated with dust . . .

'That's crazy. How could a – a *creature* like this know anything about –?'

'I have told you, Peter. The Watcher belongs to both worlds – to time and to twilight. Who can know how long it has lived, or how much it has learned?' He stood up slowly, staring at the stone and the hand that pointed to it. Then, in a swift and practised motion, he ran the halberd shaft through his hands and swung it downward in a long, glittering curve. A single, clawed finger-joint leapt skyward, turned end over end in a slow arc, and fell in the grass twenty paces from the stone.

'What the hell –?'

'I have need of a tool, Peter.' He gathered up the severed joint and picked out a small, rounded pebble that fitted easily in the palm of his hand. 'Good. And now there is work to be done.'

'Don't tell me. You're going to change the inscription?'

Erik knelt down in front of the stone, running his fingers across its surface. 'The runes are well spaced. There is room for more.'

'But what does it mean *now*?'

'I think I know.'

'Mind telling me?'

Erik did not answer. His whole attention was focused on the stone. Methodically, line by line, he carved out the new symbols that had brought his human self out of time and into the twilight world.

ᛗᛖᚱᛁᚲ · ᛞᚠᚱ · ᚱᚾᛁᚱ · ᚠᚠᛁᚻᛁᛗᚱ ·

· ᛗᚴᛏᛁᚱ · ᛒᛁᚠᚱᚲᛁ ·

ᚻᚠᛁ · ᛏᚱᚮᚻᚱᚮᚱᛗᚲᛁᚠᛋᛏᛁᚷᛁᛁ ·

Damn it, what did it mean? What was the Watcher trying to tell us?

Erik blew the last dust from the stone and sank back on his haunches. He looked at the severed claw with a strange, thoughtful expression, then laid it by the mutilated hand from which it had come.

'So. It is finished. And now, Peter, we must go to the end appointed for us.'

There was a finality in his voice that froze Brockman's blood. 'The end? What do you mean?'

'Look around you, Peter.'

With a start he realised that he, like Erik, had been concentrating on the stone with a fierce intensity – but now, too late, he realised that there had been a faint, flickering movement just at the edge of vision, as if the shadows around them had come alive. In the deeper darkness beyond the path, steel glittered in the light of the stars.

Alvar! And all we've got is a broken halberd and ...

Unthinkingly he reached for his sword, cursing as his hand touched the empty scabbard. Ahead, a line of alvar moved out to block the path, demonic in their fantastical armour, with pikes, spears and halberds charged and ready. Others stepped out of the darkness at their backs. Erik smiled faintly, and the humanity seemed to ebb from his face. Again Brockman saw the mark of immeasurable age, the accumulated wisdom and cynicism of a time beyond time.

'*Velkommen*,' said Erik. '*Velkommen, mine einheriar.*'

'What the hell –?'

He felt Erik's hand touch his arm. 'These are friends, Peter. Their *fylgjar* were with us in the forest. But you are right to be wary – if Sigrun has made the choice I expect of her, our enemies will not be far behind.'

Brockman looked warily around him. There were fewer than thirty of the liosalvar warriors, and most were on foot. He preferred not to look at the surviving mounts too closely.

'This is it? This is all we've got?'

'Not quite all,' said Erik quietly. 'There will be others, on other paths. And there are – powers – I can call upon.'

'What the hell does *that* mean?'

Erik did not seem to hear him. He was gazing back along the path.

'So,' he said. 'It begins. She has acted with honour – as I knew she would.'

'What –?'

Brockman bit off his own question. The Ironwood was moving.

Blue fire glittered among the writhing, tangled branches. Armour and weapons reflected its light. There were other highlights, too – unsheathed claws, glistening slime-covered flesh, bony carapaces and white, staring eyes. The powers of darkness poured back into twilight, their shadowy banners cracking and flapping under the eternal stars.

'It is Kialar,' said Erik. 'He has come to make an end.'

CHAPTER
10

But when I waked, I saw that I saw not;
I, and the sun, which should teach me, had forgot
East, west, day, night; and I could but say,
If the world had lasted, now it had been day ...

John Donne

'There is something I must give you,' said Erik. 'It has little worth, but it is all that I have – or almost all.' He grasped the pendant at his throat and tore it from its chain. 'Take it.'

'I won't be needing it,' said Brockman. 'After this, there's no place to go.'

'Still, it is yours,' said Erik. 'You were a good *hirð-mann*, Peter – and I have no gold. This silver must take its place.'

Reluctantly, Brockman stretched out his hand. 'If it makes you any happier.'

'There is one more gift,' said Erik. 'Once it belonged to my son. Now I give it to the only son I have left.'

He took the halberd in both hands and presented it with an almost formal gesture.

'No,' said Brockman. 'You know how to use it – you keep it.'

Erik looked at him levelly, his eyes glittering gold and silver. 'Only cold iron can protect you now; take it and be grateful.'

'But you –'

Erik shook his head. 'Do not concern yourself with me – the time has come when I must leave you.'

'*Leave!* What the hell –?'

Erik's face hardened. 'You dare to question me?'

'Damn right I do!'

'Good. Then you shall command here, Peter. Use Naegling well – and try to remain alive.' The ghost of a smile twisted his lips. 'Remember what I told you: in this place there are other powers than Kialar's.'

'Name one –'

But Erik had gone, as if the shadows and the darkness had swallowed him up.

Brockman swore obscenely. By now Kialar's forces were streaming out of the Ironwood in a tide of nightmares. In the black and silver pallor of twilight the svartalvar host was a Doré engraving come to vivid and terrifying life. But for the first time Brockman sensed the power that still remained in Naegling's broken and truncated blade. It glimmered with a light of its own – a warm, red-gold light like a hearth-fire in winter that brought colour and comfort to the chill, alien landscape of twilight.

What the hell. I could have died at the farm. And this time I've got a chance to fight back . . .

He glanced over his shoulder. The few remaining liosalvar had formed a disciplined line, weapons levelled at the guard. Kialar's forces were advancing – but slowly, and with difficulty. The lower slopes of the mound were a wilderness of boggy grasses, tumbling streams, and scattered, broken rocks, and the svartalvar were beginning to lose order. What had started as a fearsome shield-wall was already gap-toothed and ragged.

Good. Let the bastards come to us . . .

The gaps were widening as walls of rock and treacherous paths broke up Kialar's formations. In some places groups of svartalvar reformed into tighter, more compact wedges – but others, eager for an easy victory, were running ahead of their companions. Twenty were already within range, scrambling across a wall of broken boulders . . .

A wave of fire arced over Brockman's head and burst into billowing coronals of flame among the approaching svartalvar. Beyond them a boulder exploded into red-hot fragments that tore through twisted limbs and misshapen bodies like shrapnel. All along the slope, scattered bolts of blue flame flickered towards him – but none found their mark. After the next burst from his liosalvar all that remained among the fire-blackened rocks below was a huddle of burned and shattered bodies – and a twisting, blue-silver mist that danced over the corpses like smoke in a rising wind.

Fylgjar. Living souls . . .

Brockman wanted to cheer – but two svartalvar wedge-formations were already coming into range, and this time he could see that Niord's warriors would have no easy victory. Again their fire streamed over him and down the slopes of the mound, but now it met a solid wall that deflected and scattered it like a breakwater. And now the coruscating blue fire of the svartalvar came in a single, answering wave.

Instinctively, Brockman raised the halberd to defend himself – and saw sizzling bolts of elf-shot scatter to right and left as it intercepted the enemy's fire. A shimmering red-gold afterglow hovered around the broken blade like a mockery of the alvar nimbus. Once again liosalvar fire turned the landscape to blood – and this time it left gaps in the nearer wedge. Brockman saw a long, webbed hand beating desperately at the blackened, eyeless ruin of a monstrous head before it was trampled into the ground by its own kind. Bolts of svartalvar fire shimmered and died all around him – but now, as he parried them with the halberd, the blade glowed white with power.

Almost unthinkingly, he thrust the halberd towards the advancing wedge in the gesture that Erik had used.

Light blinded him. Sound deafened him. It was as though the force of each fireball, each bolt of energy, had been gathered, magnified, and concentrated into a single, searing blast. When he could see again the svartalvar wedge had disappeared. Flames flickered along the path where grass smoked and burned, and this time there were no lingering *fylgjar*. Cold iron had brought the true death to the svartalvar – and further down, Kialar's followers crouched behind boulders and rock-faces, seeking what shelter they could find.

It was never *this powerful before. It's as though it needed to be broken. . .*

Another wave of red flame exploded to the left, as more of Erik's followers joined the battle, but there was no way of linking the scattered liosalvar groups without exposing them to a deadly fusillade. Even so, the attacking fire had become nothing more than scattered, random bursts. Kialar's people had learned to fear the power of iron.

Which is great – except there's too many of them. They'll take us out one by one. And there isn't a damned thing I can do about it.

The light around the halberd blade flickered palely now, and there was no fresh energy to feed it. It had turned a massacre into a siege – but that could only delay the inevitable end.

The battle became an endless, wearying series of isolated outbursts. There was no movement on the slope except the half-seen, flickering presences of *fylgjar* locked in a silent battle of their own. In the unchanging starlight, the landscape appeared to be frozen in a single unending moment. Motionless shadows created a perpetual, bewildering series of illusions as Brockman's mind struggled to interpret them. A dark rock pinnacle became the image of Biarki's final incarnation, a raging bear rearing up on its hind legs to strike out at its enemies. Scattered, shapeless boulders seemed to flicker with motion like the corpses of Jorvard's followers rising from the ice around Lejre. Tufts of pale grass, glittering with dew, haunted the periphery of his world like the advancing scouts of a hidden army. Far to the right, an isolated crag stood out as starlight shone through a gap in the cloud, and for a moment Brockman seemed to see the Watcher in all its power ...

The crag moved.

There came a cry – a single cry, filled with triumphant intensity. It came from all around him, echoing back from star-studded sky and twilit hills alike. It was a hunting howl that filled the universe with fear as the earth parted with a soft sigh beneath the feet of a being as powerful as time itself ...

Beyond hope and beyond understanding, the Watcher roared out its challenge to the svartalvar host. At first, Kialar's creatures held their position, unable or unwilling to believe what they saw. Then a blinding tide of blue fire washed over their attacker. Brockman held his breath, blinking away crimson after-images. Surely nothing could resist such power –?

Another wave of energy roared up the slope. A rocky promontory cracked and fell in a welter of tumbling boulders. The bodies of fallen svartalvar vanished in silent explosions of flame. And then, out of the chaos and the devastation all around it, Brockman saw the dark figure of the Watcher breasting the flames like a swimmer. It scythed into the panic-stricken ranks of the svartalvar, striking to left and right with a mindless, methodical savagery. A few stood their ground, hurling silvery bursts of elf-shot at their age-old enemy. Most turned and ran, leaving weapons and armour scattered across the battle-field. None could stand against it – every living creature in its path was destroyed. Behind it, mist rolled down the slopes of the mound in a silent flood, blotting out the scars of the battle and veiling the burned and broken husks of the slain. A frosty cold sucked the last heat from Brockman's body – and below him, in a world of silver starlight and elf-shot, he saw the dark outline of the Watcher's bestial head, and the long, snaking arms striking down Kialar's followers with merciless, irresistible power.

Cautiously, the liosalvar followed in its wake, picking off scattered groups of surviving svartalvar. Kialar's main force was already withdrawing towards the Ironwood – but the paths they had come by were closed against them. The wood had become an impenetrable wall of inter-locking thorns and branches. All along its length blue fire sparkled and died, but the svartalvar could not prevail. As quickly as they burned out an opening, new branches snaked inwards to close it again. Brockman saw a disciplined wedge-formation cut its way deep into the wood, only to vanish under a sprawling, writhing mass of darkness. And as Kialar's minions battled to escape, the Watcher gathered its own harvest.

Brockman had seen the grisly trophy over Rolf's high-seat, claws gleaming in the light from the long-fire. He had seen the contorted body on the path. He *knew* the Watcher had been destroyed. Nothing else could explain how twilight and the Ironwood had spilled into his world . . .

But there was something Erik had said – something that might be the beginning of an answer . . .

'It shares the nature of the gate. It is touched by the passing of your world. There comes a time when it must renew itself.'

As he struggled to understand, he seemed to hear Kristine's voice.

'I think it is Erik that he fears. The father of such a one as Biarki must surely have great power.'

And in the forest Niord had spoken with Erik's voice.

'I am becoming such a weapon as Kialar has forged. Alv and human. Time and eternity. Twilight and sunlight together. One being . . .'

Brockman was running before the thought was complete – running into the starlit arena where the Watcher rampaged among Kialar's stricken army. Stones and pebbles skittered down the path, and his own breathing was a storm in his ears. He knew the creature must hear him, that any moment now he would see it –

. . . the high-peaked shoulders, the long-jawed head, the narrow eyes protected by thick ridges of bone . . .

276

But Brockman knew that Erik had seen something more – something trapped within the monstrous eyes as Sigrun's *fylgja* had been trapped in the dying prison of her human body ...

... the light of understanding, even of reason, a mind like his own, suffering pain like his own ...

The wail of a dying svartalv echoed among the rocks of the mound, to be answered by the Watcher's earth-shaking roar. A mass of twisted metal and mangled flesh sprawled wetly across the path at Brockman's feet. He looked up to see the Watcher's curved, dagger-sharp teeth glistening in a lipless grin beneath its wide-set, flaring nostrils; a monstrous, distorted shape that was utterly alien – yet somehow familiar ...

'*You?*'

The face changed. Brockman saw what he had glimpsed once before, and found impossible to believe. For an instant, no more, he saw the tired, blood-spattered face of Erik Larssen. There was only a ghost of his humanity left. The grim set of his mouth spoke of Niord's fanatical determination – of the will that had made him fight on when all was already lost. Only a lingering softness around the eyes spoke of Erik's forgotten vulnerability, and the weariness of immortality wasted in an endless, meaningless struggle for power.

For the last time, Erik's eyes met his – and then, once again, the great head was a mask of horror. The Watcher roared, and turned away.

Trembling, Brockman pressed himself against the rock.

Kialar had guessed the secret of the Watcher – that it drew its power from time and twilight together. Again and again he had struggled to create a weapon that might destroy it, struggled to unite time and twilight in a single, living being. Finally, after a time beyond measure, he had succeeded – and created the very thing he sought to destroy.

Erik's strange union with Niord had made him a part of both worlds, linking the knowledge of both worlds together in a single mind. Now, driven by his human hatred of Kialar and by blind, merciless alvar logic, he had achieved his final destiny. What was it Erik had said?

'I have sipped at the well of knowledge, for fear of the darkness in its depths. Kialar has drained it – he and all the svartalvar – and they have paid the price it demands.'

Now Erik had taken the dragon's path to the deepest knowledge of all – and he, too, had paid the price of ultimate power with his own body and all but a lingering ghost of his humanity. He had explored the powers at the heart of the mound – and taken on the mantle of the Watcher, to turn the darkest powers of twilight against the lord of darkness himself.

Naegling and the Watcher – both destroyed, both renewed, both more powerful than they ever were before. Did Erik know that? Or was he just guessing – hoping?

He thought of Erik's enigmatic words to Sigrun. *Remember me, and remember what I have sworn to become. I think you will know what to do.* To Brockman it had meant nothing at all, but she had understood – and done exactly as he asked. She had sent her father's hosts into twilight to meet the full force of Erik's new-found power.

'Sigrun has acted with honour – as I knew she would.'

Not the betrayal Brockman had imagined, but a wiser, more human choice – a final sacrifice for the husband she would never see again.

'No time for dreaming,' said a voice from the shadows. *'This is a time for dying – Brock-mann.'*

Blinding, blue-white elf-shot shattered the darkness, and Naegling blazed with new energy as Brockman parried the blast with a speed born of desperation. In its glare he seemed to see a tree that moved like a man, face helmeted with bark, head crowned with two living branches, before Naegling spat a river of white fire.

Kialar laughed aloud; from behind him.

'You fight well – for a human.'

Brockman threw himself to one side as the svartalv's second blast scorched the ground where he had stood. He fell clumsily, taking his full weight on his left hand. He heard the bones snap before he felt the pain, and the halberd slipped from his fingers.

Illusions, damn it. Illusions and trickery . . .

The ground exploded under his feet, and he rolled helplessly down the steep slope of the mound towards the writhing mass of thorn-decked branches that was the Ironwood, his ears ringing with Kialar's mocking laughter, the halberd tumbling and sliding after him . . .

There was a dark shape between him and the wood. Across its surface, crystals glittered in the starlight. He crawled towards the stone, pressing himself against it as if it could somehow shelter him from his terrible pursuer. It felt cool and grainy against his hands as he turned to face Kialar for the last time.

'Now, Brock-mann . . .'

Brockman grimaced with pain. He scrabbled for the pendant with his left hand. The broken bones grated as he clasped it, and its sharp corners dug into his flesh. With his right hand he caught up the halberd in a hopeless attempt to ward off Kialar's final blow. He saw the svartalv's arms drawn back like branches in a gale, twisting and writhing like the living gibbets of the Ironwood. He saw the gnarled, twig-like fingers move in a pattern of death –

And then there came a roar that shook the earth and sent shuddering vibrations through the stone at Brockman's back, and the eyes of the Watcher erupted out of shadow like twin beacons of flame. For an instant, as the deadly claws scythed towards him, Kialar hesitated. Then he threw out his arms in the final gesture of the sending.

The pendant glowed white-hot in Brockman's hand, searing his flesh to the very bone. Pain sleeted through every nerve and struck at his heart with a shattering hammer-blow. The vision of twilight disappeared in a blinding white glare – and he fell, helplessly, knowing that he was already dead . . .

For a long count of seconds he was blind, dazzled by coruscating after-images. The shock had thrown him flat on his face, and even when his vision cleared he lay still, shaking with pain and reaction, too shocked to understand what had happened or why. His trembling fingers touched frost-brittle grass. His cheek was moist with dew. It seemed, for a moment, that nothing had changed, that he lay in the shadow of the stone and the shadow of death ...

The pendant burned with power as it fell from the charred and broken fingers of his left hand – but as it touched the earth, its glowing aura shimmered and died. Behind him was the stone. And before him ...

I don't believe it. It's another trick. It has to be.

The farmhouse stood exactly as he first remembered it, the single eye of the kitchen window bright with light. Dark shapes stretched across the churchyard to make a strange shadow mirror where a woman stood in silent contemplation.

Anja ...

Shock blocked out the pain of his ruined hand. The battle was over. Kialar's power had penetrated the barrier between time and twilight – and hurled him back into his own world. But here, somehow, Anja was still alive; and there was another familiar face at the window.

His own.

For a few seconds he struggled with the paradox. He had come back a few hours – or perhaps a day – too soon. And if that impossibility were true, then he had also been granted his dearest wish: a chance to change what had happened at the farm. But surely this could only be another of Kialar's mocking illusions ...

He clasped the pendant in his right hand, feeling its edges bite into the flesh. This was no illusion. Now there was no need for Anja or Kristine to die. Now he could warn them about the children, about the hell-horse, even about the burning –

But only if there was time.

When am I? What day? What time?

That, at least, he could see. The church clock stood at ten minutes past two. And he could see another shadow from the kitchen, a taller figure moving in a way he had learned to recognise.

Erik. It's Erik, telling us what happened to him in twilight . . .

He struggled to remember exactly what had happened that night, and when. Erik had spent at least an hour talking to them, and Brockman had no way of knowing how much of that hour was left. Unless . . .

He crept closer to the kitchen window, skirting the flood of light from the oil-lamp, straining to hear what Erik was saying. Instead he heard Anja's voice. She sounded frightened, almost ashamed.

'What do you mean?'

Erik's answer was quiet – too quiet to be heard outside. He could hear only Anja's side of the conversation.

'I am sorry, Erik. There is something I must fetch from my room.'

Cautiously, Brockman peered over the window-ledge – and saw his own face looking back at him. It was a hard face, cut with sharp lines of grief, thin-lipped, narrow-eyed, but softening, changing, at the edge of a new beginning that was about to be cut cruelly short. At any moment, he knew, the gate stone would open behind him and the Wild Hunt would sweep over the farm. He *had* to warn them, now . . .

No. It isn't going to work. I can't just charge in . . .

They would be confused, incredulous. Erik had been duped before – he would never believe that a second Brockman was anything more than another illusion, sent to lead him astray. And his own younger self would think the same.

Besides, he dared not change the past too much. Unless he and Erik were driven into twilight, unless they

281

truly believed that nothing was left for them in their own time, the Watcher might never be created – and all they had fought for would be lost.

But the wind was already rising. The Hunt was on its way. Whether or not he warned them, he *had* to find shelter for himself – and quickly.

How the hell can I get in? Have to try the other side, away from the kitchen.

Climbing the churchyard wall one-handed was no easy task, especially in the dark, but a network of old ivy made it barely possible. After a few desperate minutes he dropped heavily onto the grass on the far side. The blind windows of the farmhouse stretched away to the right. To the left, dark trees swayed gently in the rising wind. The first window was firmly secured. So was the next. In desperation he tried them all, but the faint hope he had begun to cherish was already fading into oblivion. There was no way in, and nothing he could do. At any moment the storm out of twilight would sweep over the farm, and his last chance would be gone …

'Hr Brockman?'

He started violently. Kristine Hansen was watching him with a faint smile, as if he were a clever child who had stumbled on the solution of a simple puzzle.

'Come in, Hr Brockman. It is a cold night.'

He hesitated. 'Look, I don't know how to tell you this, but –'

'I understand, Hr Brockman. There is little time. How long before the storm?'

'The storm – you *know*?'

'How long, Hr Brockman?

'Just a few minutes. But –'

'And will the alvar burn the farm? Come, don't look so startled.'

'Yes. It was – will be – about an hour before dawn.'

'And then, perhaps, you will escape with Erik?'

'Yes – but you and Anja …'

'Come into my bedroom, Hr Brockman. I think you

282

will not be discovered here.'

She reached out a hand to help him across the ledge. The room was almost in darkness, lit only by an oil lamp burning in the next room. In his confusion he tried to support himself on his left hand, and almost fell against her. There was more strength in the wiry body than he had expected: her touch was gentle, yet firm and re-assuring.

'*Åh*, your poor hand.' He felt her touch on his ruined fingers, saw her shake her head as she grasped the extent of his injury. 'This shall be cared for – but for now I must go back, or it will seem strange to the others. There is pain?'

'No. I mean, mostly I don't seem to feel it.'

She nodded. 'I shall return as soon as I may.' She was already moving towards the door when he remembered the excuse she had made for leaving.

'The pills –!'

She turned back with a self-deprecating smile and took the bottle of pills from its place at her bedside. 'Thank you, Hr Brockman. I think that I am getting old.' At the door she paused for a moment and turned back. He saw a warmth and concern in her eyes that reminded him more forcibly than ever of his own mother. 'You can manage without a light? Just for a little while?'

He nodded.

'You have great courage, Hr Brockman. Hold to that for just a little longer.'

She closed the door gently, leaving darkness and a faint, lingering scent of lavender.

She expected to find me here. But why? How?

He sat gingerly on her bed, trying to fathom it out. The sight of Anja had filled his body with a strange, pulsing energy that made nonsense of the pain from his wounds and the muscle and mind-sapping fatigue of the battle. He felt wonderfully alive, alert for every tiny change in the light from the window, every slightest noise. From the kitchen he heard the unbelievable sound of Anja's voice – and the angry, overconfident sound of his own. But behind them he could already hear the slow, rising note that heralded the storm.

There was a crash of breaking glass from the kitchen. The wind became a keening, turbulent whine, and somewhere far away he heard the thin cry of a svartalv captain, calling on its followers. An answer came, and then another, bloodless and remote – and then, in a deep, booming counterpoint, the terrible roar of the hell-horse . . .

The Hunt had come.

The wind became a gale that beat against the side of the house and roared through the loft space over his head. He heard it sweep through the kitchen, scattering plates and pans – and heard the voices there as silence returned. A little later the kitchen door opened. Footfalls echoed across the wooden floor of the dining room and paused outside his door.

'Wait here a moment, *pigebarn*. I must fetch the key from my room.'

Kristine – and Anja. Going to fetch Naegling from its hiding place. I can't believe she's just the other side of this wall . . .

He stepped back quickly as the door opened. Kristine did not even look at him. Instead she walked carefully across to a loose rug on the floor, moving it aside with her foot. Then she took a key from the drawer of her dressing table and rejoined Anja in the dining room. He heard the main door to the courtyard slam shut as they went out to fetch the halberd.

Damn it, she was trying to show me something . . .

Frowning, he knelt down by the rug, but in the darkness he could see nothing at all. The old floorboards were polished, but warped and uneven, and the cracks between them felt wider than they should be. A chill draught blew upwards into the room, and the air smelled damp and stale. He touched cold metal – a circular handle of coiled and twisted iron. Three feet further on he found more metal, and the slick smoothness of fresh oil.

A trap. That's what she meant. There's another way out!

He heard the two women returning, and once more he stepped back from the door – but this time it did not open. Again he heard the voices in the kitchen as Naegling was taken from its wrappings – and then the faint crunching of gravel as the two teenage lovers walked past his window on their way to the churchyard.

Got to remember what happened – and when *it happened. Can't risk anyone coming in and finding me. Let's see – when I heard the kids I went to Erik's bedroom. Then I stayed a while in the kitchen – damn it, the others were searching the house!*

The thought had scarcely formed when he heard the dining room door open, and footsteps approaching across its wooden floor. He looked desperately for a hiding place, but there was nowhere that would serve – even standing behind the door he would be discovered in seconds. And in the battered remnants of his sixth-century clothing and armour he could hardly pass for his younger self. The door was already opening ...

It was Kristine. She shut the door behind her like a conspirator – or a child. He had the feeling that somehow, despite the terror of the Hunt and the threat that hung over them all, she was enjoying this as she enjoyed everything else in her life.

'There are some children outside,' she whispered. 'I cannot think they mean any harm.'

For a moment he was shocked. He could only remember how Kristine herself had suggested that the children might be unwitting hosts for the alvar ...

Because someone had told her.

'Don't be fooled,' he said. 'The alvar have taken them in their sleep. The kids don't know what they're doing – but they could kill you as soon as look as you.'

'*Herre Gud!* I must tell the others!'

'Yes – but do it carefully.' He grinned. 'You know how to make them believe you.'

'Hr Brockman, you are a very impudent young man.'

'I'm sorry. It's supposed to be part of my charm.'

Outside, he heard other footsteps crossing the dining room.

Anja on her way to the parlour. With – me. I'm glad I can't see myself.

'You were right, you know.'

'Right?' She was pretending to look puzzled, but there was a mischievous twinkle in her eyes.

'About us. Me and Anja. Even if you *did* talk me into it.'

He heard the smile in her voice as she answered. 'There was no need. From the beginning I saw that you made a fine couple.'

'So you just oiled the wheels a little.'

'I am an old woman, Hr Brockman. I know how these things are done.'

'Thanks – I think. The trapdoor –?'

'There is a passage. To the church. Another family secret.' She paused, staring out of the window. 'Strange – there is a boy just outside. He has a – a coloured light. He looks so young –'

'He is. But I can't vouch for the alv inside his head.'

'What should we do? They are only children, Hr Brockman.'

'Don't try to reason with them – or fight them. It wouldn't help, anyway. Just keep the windows shut. Bolt them if you can. And don't go outside unless you have to. Kialar's people have a weapon. Like lightning, only quieter and nastier. You can't stop Kialar, but you can give me some time. With a little luck, we could all come out of this alive.'

'Hr Brockman?'

'Yes?'

'You have changed. You are a kinder man than you were. God grant we can escape from this without those poor children coming to harm.'

'Amen. You'd better go.'

Moments later he heard raised voices in the parlour – his younger self and Erik arguing about who should go outside, and Kristine desperately trying to prevent them.

No wonder she was so adamant about it.

A few minutes later he heard the courtyard door slam a second time. Soon Erik and Anja would be opening the doors to the drive. Nothing had changed – events seemed to move with a momentum of their own that had nothing to do with his presence or anything he said. Kristine had given her warning, and been ignored.

Perhaps, after all, there was nothing he could do for Anja – except join her in death.

Elf-shot re-echoed around the courtyard. The children had attacked, just as before – and a few moments later there was a babble of voices as Anja was carried into Erik's room, just on the other side of the wall. Now, for the first time, he could hear what was being said – and what he himself was saying.

After a little while he tried not to listen. He sounded arrogant, stubborn, and more than a little stupid. Besides, there was something slithering across the gravel outside the window.

Of course. Kialar's sending.

Again he heard Kialar's mocking imitation of Erik's young son – and now, remembering the battle in twilight, he found his own right hand gripping the halberd, itching to use it. When he heard Erik strike at the alv he felt nothing but sympathy.

The voices died away. Anja was back on her feet, and Kristine had taken them back to the kitchen – well away from her secret guest. Vaguely he heard the fire on the mound, and something that might have been his own cry of horror at the illusions Kialar had sent against him. Then, unmistakably, Kialar's voice.

'*Son of Lars, I weary of waiting! You hear me, son of Lars? You shall not escape – you, or the others.*'

He could not hear Erik's replies – but he heard the cry of the hell-horse, and although he knew what it would do he flinched as it struck the churchyard wall. For a few moments there was confusion in the house. He heard his own shouts, and Erik's, as they battled the hell-horse.

Then the door swung open, and Anja rushed in.

The sight of her stopped his tongue. So much had happened since those endless seconds on the staircase that he had remembered her almost in the way he remembered Sarah – as a bittersweet moment locked in the past. Yet here she was, alive, with the scent of their last lovemaking still faint on her body. He could see her, smell her – even touch her.

Slowly, still unbelieving, he stretched out his hands. He was vaguely aware of pain, but all his attention was on Anja – her face, the light in her hair . . .

'Peter! What *happened* to you? Your fingers! Your –'

Her eyes widened as she took in his ringmail, his clothes, and the blood, grime and sweat of his battle in twilight. Behind her, Kristine shut the door and clasped her granddaughter's shoulders.

'There is no time to explain, *pigebarn*. It is Peter – but he has passed through the stone.'

She stared at him, trying to understand. 'Like – like Erik?'

'Not quite,' said Brockman. 'I – got myself lost in twilight. You might say I've come back before I left.'

She bit her lip, staring at his hand, struggling to come to terms with what was happening. 'You mean that – you know what is going to happen?'

He hesitated. It would be so easy to lie, to give her an excuse for acting differently.

No. I believe in her. I have to tell her the truth.

'Yes. I know. Unless you do something pretty damn desperate, those kids'll set fire to the farm.'

'You are saying I must harm them?'

'There's no other way to stop them. If you don't they'll probably kill you – and the rest of us.'

'It makes no difference, Peter. I will not hurt my own patients, not even for that.'

'Thank God. I love you, Anja Kristiansson. There's a trapdoor in this room – a way out. You and Kristine use it, first chance you get.'

'But Erik? And – and you?'

'They – we'll get out. Our own way. It's important, Anja. Now for God's sake close these shutters!'

Anja started as if she had woken from a dream. Outside, the crack of breaking stone and the crash of shattered timber rose even above the keening howl of the wind. He could still hardly believe that wooden shutters had kept out the supernatural power of the hell-horse, but now at least he knew that it was vulnerable.

He knew. But Anja and Kristine had no idea.

'Anja. Don't be scared of that thing out there. It looks like something out of a bad trip, but your bow could kill it.'

'Yes!' said Kristine. 'There is a painting – in the church –'

Anja was staring at him. 'There is something about you – something different –'

'No time now.' He took her arm and pushed her towards the door. 'Get those other shutters. And for Christ's sake don't let on that I'm here.'

'Come, *pigebarn*,' said Kristine. 'We must hurry.'

'Yes,' said Brockman. 'But hurry back, as well.'

For a long time he heard nothing but the noise of the storm-wind raging through the roof-space overhead. Kristine had managed to keep Erik out of the bedroom, but he dared not leave the room. The churchyard was too far away for him to make out what was happening there – all he could hear was a rhythmic crash as the hell-horse beat against the wall.

Then a deafening, animal roar echoed through the house.

She's hit it. Can't be long now before Kialar brings in the firebrands.

He was wrong. It was an eternity before the first, thin strands of smoke appeared between the planks of the ceiling. He could hear Anja's footsteps overhead, running back towards the stairs, then her shouts and Erik's as they struggled to battle the fire. Again his sense of time played him false. When he had been up there himself, in the thick of the action, it had seemed only a few minutes before Anja pulled him away. Now he realised that his struggle with the advancing fire had slowed its progress for nearly half an hour. His plan had almost worked.

But now the upper part of Kristine's bedroom was filling with smoke, and he could already see the glimmer of flames between the planks of the ceiling. At any moment Anja would rush down the stairs ...

God, if there is a God, don't let her die now! Don't let all this be for nothing!

He was so concerned for Anja that he forgot his own danger. It was only when he heard a crash from the parlour that he realised the roof was fully alight, and burning fragments were already raining fire into the body of the house. The smoke was catching at his throat – he had to crouch down to breathe freely.

Soon, Anja – got to make it soon!

The door opened, and he saw a woman's silhouette against the sinister light of rising flames.

'Anja?'

'No, Hr Brockman. I am sorry. She tries to help with the fire ...'

'Damn it, that's what killed her before!'

'Hr Brockman – you do not *know* that she died. Now come. Help me open the trapdoor.' Kristine knelt down awkwardly by the ring in the floor, setting her lamp near the wall as she fumbled to lift the trap.

'I'll do it,' said Brockman, tugging at the handle. 'Try to get Anja –'

There was another crash. Flames raced down the wall in a red-gold flood, and the room was suddenly filled with smoke. He heard his own voice cry out Anja's name – and then she was crouching in the door, gasping for good air, stumbling into the room as fragments of burning wood fell all around them.

'Down, Kristine!' he yelled. '*Now!*'

Above them the ceiling was already sagging as charred and overloaded beams started to give way. At any moment it would fall.

'Anja! You next!'

A beam cracked, showering sparks, ash, and flakes of blackened wood. The air was unbreathable, thick with dark smoke. Gasping, he lay full length on the floor and slid feet-first down the ladder, closing the hatch after him. Seconds later something heavy crashed down on top of it. The roof had fallen in. There was no way back. But as he reached the foot of the ladder Anja flung herself into his arms, and for a moment he had no thought for anything else.

Kristine coughed discreetly. 'Enough now, *pigebarn*. You will have time enough to love him. Come, Hr Brockman – follow me.'

Kristine's lantern revealed a tunnel that looked almost as old as the farm, roofed with massive timbers and sloping gently downwards into darkness. In its confines the roar of the fire and the thunder of falling timbers seemed louder than ever.

'Be wary of the mud, Hr Brockman. The tunnel is sometimes a little damp.'

'You *knew* about this place? From the start?'

'It has been here since four hundred years. Of course I knew.'

'Then why –?'

'I was waiting, Hr Brockman. Waiting for you. Now come – we must take sanctuary.'

The tunnel was not a long one, but further in Brockman had to stoop below roof-timbers raised by the smaller men of another century. Sometimes Kristine's lantern would show up markings on the wood: there were Roman numerals, left by the carpenters to show how the timbers fitted together, and other, stranger markings. He saw curious stick-like figures surrounded by runes and symbols, but there was no time to look at them closely or to understand what they might mean. The noise of the burning echoed strangely in the confines of the tunnel, till it seemed to be coming from all around them. It was as though the fire pursued them, anticipating their every move. He half-expected to find the church itself on fire, if they ever reached it ...

The ground under Brockman's feet began to slope upwards. He could feel a draught against his face as air was drawn through to feed the hungry flames destroying the old farm. But there was a darkness at the end of the tunnel, and a damp, musty smell.

The door was old – far older than the tunnel itself. The great wrought-iron hinges had been forged by a master smith into writhing, many-limbed dragons ramping clear across the door, holding together ancient timbers sprinkled with green moss and white fungus. The handle was a single casting, a grinning demon's head with a metal ring hooked through its nose. Kristine took a big iron key from somewhere inside her dress, slotted it carefully into a hole in the mouldering timbers, and turned it with an obvious effort.

The door creaked open. There was a faint light beyond it – a reddish, fiery light that Brockman recognised. It came from a grating above their heads. There were steps, but the grating itself would have to be levered out from below. Without thinking, Brockman gripped the halberd in both hands. He felt a grinding agony of broken bones, and as he glanced downward the light of Kristine's lantern showed him, for the first time, just how badly he was hurt.

The fingers of his left hand were charred and blackened stumps. His wrist and palm were a swollen, purplish mass of burned skin, bruised flesh and shattered bone.

He passed out as he finally felt the pain.

Cool air moved over his face. There was an echoing sound of birds, as if they were singing far away, in another world. There was a multi-coloured light, tinted with grey. There was pain, too – but it was muted now, and his ruined hand was bound with torn strips of linen. His right hand was tight shut, clutching the pendant as Erik had done that night in the churchyard, long ago – or yesterday.

He looked up into Anja's face.

'It is morning,' she said. 'The battle is finished.' She held out a gilded goblet filled with water, feeding it to him in small sips. After a while his eyes focused. He was lying on one of the pews, beneath the painting of the hell-horse . . .

'The kids!' he murmured. 'What about the –'

Anja put a finger to her lips, and pointed.

In one of the side-chapels, Kristine had gathered the children around her. He could hear her voice, low and almost hypnotic, but the words were lost in their own echoes.

'What's she doing?'

Anja smiled. 'What she does best – telling them a story. They are tired, and a little frightened, and they do not know what has truly happened. I think they will believe what she says.'

'What about the farm?'

'The – how do you say? – fire brigade are here. I have told them stories, also – that the children made a fire to warm themselves, that there was an accident. That Erik –' she hesitated.

'Don't feel bad about Erik. He's found something he has to do – something no one else can do. And Sigrun – I mean Eleanor –'

'Eleanor? You have seen her?'

'Yes. She learned to love him, Anja – the human way.'

'And – you?'

He smiled. 'What do you think?'

'I – don't know. There is something about you. When I saw you in *Mormor*'s bedroom, it was like – like you were not the same person.'

'You're right. I'm not. I've been given something no other man ever had.'

She frowned, brushing back a stray lock of hair with her hand. 'I don't understand.'

'It isn't so hard. When I escaped from the farm with Erik, I thought you were dead – you and Kristine both. I had to think about you like I thought about Sarah. I wasn't going to see you again – ever – so I had to decide what you meant to me.'

'But –'

'No. Let me finish. It's important. When Sarah died all I could feel was anger. I couldn't let go. With you I didn't have to. It was like you were already part of me. When there was a choice to make, I could think what *you'd* have done, and know it was right. Last night you made a choice – to risk death rather than give up a trust.'

She reached out to touch his hair. 'That was not so difficult. You trusted me with the truth. And you also, you are a man to be trusted – and a kinder man than the one who came to my window.'

'There's blood on my hands, Anja. Could you live with that?'

She touched his bandaged hand. 'Can you, Peter?'

'Probably. But I could always use a little help.'

Anja laughed. It lit up her whole face with a radiance, a pure joy, that he had never seen in her before.

'Then you shall have it, Peter, and willingly. But what will you do?'

'I don't know – yet. But I will. Soon. You'll wait?'

'Yes. And you, you will also wait. *Mormor* is calling me.'

'Go ahead. Those kids need you more than I do.'

She squeezed his right hand and walked across the church to join her grandmother. Still smiling, Brockman stared up into the vaulted roof. More than ever, the crowded paintings spoke to him in a voice that was somehow familiar. Everywhere there were tiny details, half-hidden figures, that added a new meaning to each

294

scene, a meaning he could almost understand ...

'Hr Brockman? May I sit with you a while?'

He nodded, momentarily startled. His mind had been far away in another time, and he had not even heard Kristine's approach.

'How're the kids?'

'Kids?'

'I'm sorry – the children.'

'I think they will take no harm from what has happened. In my family we are used to telling stories.'

'I can believe it. But you're also damned mean with them. Most of last night you were handing them round in episodes – and there's one you still haven't started.'

She looked at him quizzically, with a slight movement of her eyebrows. 'I cannot think what you mean, Hr Brockman.'

'I can, Fru Hansen. How did you know I'd be outside the farm?'

For a little while she did not answer – she simply looked around her at the paintings that filled the church with their vitality and their strange, quirky beauty.

'When I was a little girl, Hr Brockman, I did not live here on the farm. My father had a business in Copenhagen, and we lived in a big house in the middle of the city. But my mother was often ill – and when she was, I would be sent here, to the farm, to my grandmother.

'I was very young, and to me this was a strange and exciting place. But most of all I loved to come here, to the church, and to see the paintings, and to make stories about them.

'One morning my grandmother found me here, looking at the men in their armour fighting each other. She asked what I was doing, and I told her. She did not laugh, Hr Brockman – she understood how to talk to children. She said that there were many other stories about the paintings, and that some were very old. After that, we would come here every day – and each day she would tell me a new story.

'I still remember them, Hr Brockman. I remember them all. But until now I had never understood that all those stories were true. And that the strangest, the most mysterious, that was the truest of all.'

Brockman frowned. 'You mean – you knew about me because of a *story*?'

'Yes, Hr Brockman. Because of a story. A story that has passed down my family from mother to daughter, from grandmother to granddaughter, for longer than anyone can remember . . .'

'Going to tell me?'

She smiled, her eyes dancing with laughter. 'Do you need that I should tell you?'

'Humour me.'

'As you wish.' She made herself comfortable on the pew, smoothing out her skirts, glancing up for a moment at the fresh daylight that streamed through the window above their heads.

'I remember like it was yesterday. It was Christmas Eve, and I sat by this very window, in my prettiest dress – my Sunday dress. We were come to the church early, to look on the paintings. And my grandmother said: "There is something you shall know, my little Kristine. Today we have come to church by the path, just like good Christian people – but there is another way. In my bedroom, under the old rug, there is a part of the floor that lifts up, and underneath it is a tunnel."

'I was curious. I asked who made the tunnel, and why. And she told me that on another Christmas Eve, very long ago, an old beggar woman had come to the farm. She was thin, and pinched, and dressed in rags, but there was something strange about her eyes. She scratched at the window, asking for just a crust and a cup of water, but the farmgirl was afraid to answer. Then the farmer's wife came and scolded her. "It is Christmas," she said. "The birthday of our Lord!" So she opened the door, and set the old beggar woman in by the fire in the kitchen.

'In the beginning the woman said nothing, though she

was glad to take broth and small ale. The farmer's wife was busy with the Christmas meal, and when the meat was ready she gave the old woman a piece with some new-baked bread and butter.

'"That was kind," said the woman, "and more than kind. That I am happy about, for good things will come to your family if you are always kind to strangers."

'"I do not wish rewards," said the farmer's wife. "But I will not see folk go hungry when there is food enough for everyone. Our Lord tells us to feed the hungry."

'"Your lord is a good man," said the woman, and then the wife knew that this was no Christian, but one of the alvar come to call. "But now I shall tell you a thing. One day – not now, but long from now – there will be a time of great danger. *Helvedsmund* will open, and hunters out of the twilight will come to burn this farm and all who are in it. If any are to live, there must be a way of leaving it that is hidden from all but your own family. On that day a man they know will come to them tired, and hurt, and wearing strange clothes. They may think him a ghost, or a nightmare. They may think the Good People have taken him. But he will speak only the truth. They must do all that he says; and when he tells them to go, they must leave at once by the secret way. Remember this. Tell it to your children, and your children's children. One day they shall thank you as I thank you now."

'And with that, she was gone, as if she had never been.'

Brockman said nothing. He was thinking of a younger man, hardened and sceptical, who had refused to believe something that was outside his experience – and the same voice talking to him, gently showing him the way.

'*There is something every child knows – that the oldest stories, the stories told not once but a thousand times, they have a heart of truth.*'

'Anja's right,' he said. 'You tell one hell of a story, Fru Hansen. You know, I was never much with words. Always had my nose in a comic – when I was a kid, I mean. Mom hated it. Said they were all garbage. Probably right – but the art excited me. *I* wanted to draw like that. Spent hours copying the best panels line by line, working out how they were done, *why* they were good ...' He smiled. 'When I met Sarah the first time, I couldn't talk to her. I didn't speak Hebrew, and her English was *lousy*. We were sitting in this café in Haifa. I took her napkin and grabbed a pen from the waiter. Drew a little comic strip. Her and me, like something out of *True Romance*. Funny thing was, it worked ...'

Gingerly, he slid his legs sideways off the pew and put his feet on the floor, levering himself up with his right hand. Every bone and muscle was aching, and his legs trembled, but he had no time to think of his body. He was staring up into the ceiling, marking out the composition of each painting in his mind, seeing how image followed image, each contributing something new, yet each telling a complete story in itself ...

The Watcher. The hell-horse. Niord and Kialar. Sigrun and Biarki. And the style. No wasted lines. Good, strong colours in big areas. Like comics – you have to work fast, before the plaster dries.

Funny. In a way I knew the moment I saw them. Even then, I think I knew ...

'There's something I have to do,' he said. 'It'll take me a long time. Maybe the rest of my life. But it's important, and I can't do it alone.' The old woman bent her head. There was no need to explain – she had already understood. 'Fru Hansen – where will you go now?'

She smiled. 'I shall live here. Now that the farm has gone I can set a smaller house on the same ground – somewhere I can be comfortable on my own. It is not right for Anja to spend her life caring for me – and I have so many things to remember, and so many things to be thankful for. Have I answered your question?'

'Yes. Yes, you have.' He fingered the pendant, feeling the sharp edges bite against his hand. 'But it isn't only my choice.'

'You are thinking of Anja?'

'Yes.'

'She loves you, Hr Brockman, and she trusts you. You must do as you did last night. You must tell her the whole truth – what you mean to do, and why. When she understands your choice, she will follow you wherever it takes you. But there are two things I would ask of you.'

'Anything.'

'I would ask you to remember the love you feel for her now – and speak of it with her every day. And I would ask that sometimes you remember me.'

He smiled. 'Fru Hansen, there's no chance in the world that I'll ever forget.'

In that spring after the second King Christopher was driven from Denmark, and his son, prince Erik, died in battle, two strangers came to Egerød. The man was one-handed, and carried many scars. He seemed older than his years and there was the look about him of one who had seen much. The woman was younger, but her beauty was of a strange kind, so that some whispered of alvar and the twilight world.

The man named himself to Master Erland the priest as one Peter Eriksson, and gave himself out as a church-painter. Master Erland doubted the man, but gave him permission to show his skill in a small corner of the church – an alcove out of sight of the nave. He watched the painter make up his colours, and saw how the woman helped him, holding the boards for him when his own blackened and misshapen hand would not serve him. He worked in swift, bold strokes, sketching out his drawings in a few lively lines, then colouring them with a skill born of long practice. In a single day Master Erland saw the dance of death appear before his eyes, with such vivid-ness that his dreams were haunted by it.

The painter desired no payment, and asked for no other reward than bed and board for himself and the woman. In return, he said, he would paint the church as no church had ever been painted in the history of Denmark.

Master Erland was uncertain, and spent long hours in thought and prayer. But he could find no harm in the man, and supposed him to be some penitent lately returned from the wars. The woman he found quiet and biddable, and greatly skilled with the sick of the parish. The children of the farm came to love her, and through her the man. He spoke little, but loved to make drawings for them while his wife told them of places and people beyond their knowledge – strange stories that were passed on from house to house, and from village to village, till at last none could remember how they had begun.

The year turned through summer to a chill autumn and a bitter winter. Day by day the paintings grew – and to Master Erland each new figure, each detail, was a kind of miracle. He had seen the churches of his neighbour priests, and spoken with them of others further afield, but he knew of no paintings like these. There were men and women with faces that seemed ready to speak, and bodies that seemed almost to move in the changing light of a winter evening. There were devils with the heads of beasts, and the wings of bats or dragons, who struck down sinners with blazing tridents, or battled among themselves in the dark corners of the church.

But the wall above the altar remained empty – and if Master Erland asked when the painter might begin work there, the man would stare at it thoughtfully, and say:

'Another day.'

When Eastertide came round again, the church was alive with the painter's work. Saints, disciples and apostles crowded the ceiling. Armies battled up the nave. But still the great wall above the altar stood empty.

Then, on the eve of Easter itself, Master Erland saw a light in the church. He tried to gain entrance, but the great doors had been barred against him, and the lesser doors were locked fast. All night the light burned unceasingly, and shadows flickered along the windows. The next morning he found the doors flung wide, and the painter's tools scattered about the church. In a single night the wall above the altar had been transformed into a great Judgement, where the father creator called the just to the summit of the heavenly mountain, while devils drew down the souls of the faithless to eternal torment.

But there was something strange about this Judgement that made it unlike any that Master Erland had seen before. For here, the devils issued from a gateway like the ancient heathen earthwork in his own churchyard, but raised up on twisting, painted pillars like those of his church – and the scenes within it were rendered in rare and costly hues of red-gold and sapphire blue that would not have disgraced the palace of a pope.

Of the painter and his woman there was no trace. Some said they had seen two figures on the road, walking towards Copenhagen. Others said that word of his skill had reached the bishop, who had summoned him to work on the great cathedral at Roskilde. But the farmer's little child, who had loved the woman's stories, told how the mound in the churchyard had opened for them – and how they had walked into the light of it side by side, their faces bright with joy.

CITY OF BARABOO

Barry B. Longyear

'Who can resist a circus?'
Joan Vinge, author of *The Snow Queen*

Cargo: One Circus
Destination: The Stars

Shakedowns, breakdowns, catastrophes, cataclysms – the show must go on. And the circus had never failed to raise a laugh in a world badly in need of one. But by 2142 John J. O'Hara's Greater Shows were showing a loss. Time to close them down.

But if Earth had run out of room for a circus, out there in the galaxy was a whole new situation. There were plenty of other planets where an appreciative audience would be willing to pay for a top-rate, razzle-dazzle show.

Or at least, that's how John J. O'Hara saw it.

'An impressive Ringmaster with an unusual show!'
Roger Zelazny

FUTURA PUBLICATIONS
AN ORBIT BOOK
0 7088 8100 9

A SPELL FOR CHAMELEON

Piers Anthony

Xanth was the enchanted land where every citizen had a special spell only he could cast. It was a land of centaurs, dragons and basilisks.

But poor Bink alone had no magic. And unless he got some – and fast – he would be exiled. Forever . . .

The Good Magician Humfrey was convinced that Bink did indeed have magic, magic as powerful as any possessed by the King or by Magician Humfrey himself.

But no one could fathom the nature of Bink's very special magic. Bink was in despair. This was worse than having no magic at all . . . and he would still be exiled!

Don't miss . . .
THE SOURCE OF MAGIC
CASTLE ROOGNA
CENTAUR AISLE
OGRE OGRE
NIGHT MARE
in the Xanth series

FUTURA PUBLICATIONS
ORBIT FANTASY
0 7088 2466 8

THE RINGWORLD ENGINEERS

Larry Niven

In the decade since its first appearance, RINGWORLD has become the most talked-about locale in Known Space and made the name of Larry Niven synonymous with ingenious, inimitable SF.

THE RINGWORLD ENGINEERS sees the return of Louis Wu (now hooked on electrical ecstasy as a wirehead) and the aging kzin warrior Speaker-to-Animals, while introducing the Hindmost, puppeteer mate of mad Nessus. Together the bizarre crew seek to avert tragic cataclysm in the Ringworld System.

THE RINGWORLD ENGINEERS confirms Larry Niven's reputation as one of the foremost living writers of SF.

FUTURA PUBLICATIONS
AN ORBIT BOOK
0 7088 8074 6

CIRCUS WORLD

Barry B. Longyear

When the circus ship City of Baraboo crashed on
Momus, the troupers of O'Hara's Greater Shows turned
a rockpile world into a showcase of razzle-dazzle and built
a new civilisation based on showmanship.

Then the Varilian Council of Warlords decided that the
circus world was a prime spot for a garrison and brought
in an armada to 'liberate' Momus . . .

FUTURA PUBLICATIONS
AN ORBIT BOOK
0 7088 8091 6

LUCIFER'S HAMMER

Larry Niven and Jerry Pournelle

The chances that Lucifer's Hammer would hit the earth
head-on were one in a million.

Then one in a thousand.

Then one in a hundred, and then . . .

'TERRIFYING . . . It's the best end-of-the-world story
since ON THE BEACH . . . superb detail, shudderingly
believable.'
Frank Herbert

'A blockbuster of a read . . . Niven and Pournelle are two
of the best storytellers around, with that rare ability to
put you, the reader, there, terrified out of your wits as
one sledgehammer twist follows another.'
Gordon Thomas author of THE VOYAGE OF THE
DAMNED

FUTURA PUBLICATIONS
AN ORBIT BOOK
0 7088 1362 3

PROTECTOR

Larry Niven

PHSSTHPOK THE PAK had been travelling for most of his 32,000 years – his mission to save, develop and protect the group of Pak breeders sent out into space some 2½ million years before . . .

BRENNAN WAS A BELTER, the product of a fiercely independent, somewhat anarchic society living in, on, and around an outer asteroid belt. The Belters were rebels one and all, and Brennan was a smuggler. The Belt worlds had been tracking the Pak ship for days – Brennan figured to meet that ship first . . .

He was never seen again – at least not in the form of Homo sapien.

FUTURA PUBLICATIONS
AN ORBIT BOOK
0 8600 7848 5

THE BLUE SWORD
The Chronicles of Damar

Robin McKinley

Damar. A land of mountains and plain, of fertile valleys and great forests, of streams as clear and sparkling as the air its people breathe. A frontier land, squeezed between the Homelanders' stuffy empire and the demon-ridden kingdoms of the North. A land of mystery and legend, of Hillfolk with strange powers they can barely control, to whom honour is a living thing, and courage an essential of humanity.

The Blue Sword is the first in a series of fantasies set in that enchanted land. It tells of Harry (Angharad) Crewe, and how she came by mysterious ways to Damar and its kind. There she came under the protection of fire-haired Aerin, fabled queen of long ago, and learned to wield Aerin's Gonduran, the Blue Sword, Dragon-killer, against the legions of the North. And so became herself a legend, to Damar's weal, and demons' woe.

Winner of the John Newbery Medal 1984

FUTURA PUBLICATIONS/AN ORBIT BOOK
FANTASY
0 7088 8155 6

THE LONG ARM OF GIL
HAMILTON

Larry Niven

Armed for death in the outer reaches of the galaxy, Gil
Hamilton is the global police force's top operative. He can
reach into a man's brain for the truth . . . or for the kill.

But Gil's peerless intuition, devastating psychic powers
and phenomenal courage will be tested to the limit.
Because around every corner there lurks and enemy.

THE LONG ARM OF GIL HAMILTON – three
fabulous novellas from the famed KNOWN SPACE
series.

FUTURA PUBLICATIONS
AN ORBIT BOOK
0 7088 8070 3

All Orbit Books are available at your bookshop or newsagent, or can be ordered from the following address:

Futura Books,
Cash Sales Department,
P.O. Box 11,
Falmouth,
Cornwall TR10 9EN.

Alternatively you may fax your order to the above address. Fax No. 0326 76423.

Payments can be made as follows: Cheque, postal order (payable to Macdonald & Co (Publishers) Ltd) or by credit cards, Visa/Access. Do not send cash or currency. UK customers: please send a cheque or postal order (no currency) and allow 80p for postage and packing for the first book plus 20p for each additional book up to a maximum charge of £2.00.

B.F.P.O. customers please allow 80p for the first book plus 20p for each additional book.

Overseas customers including Ireland, please allow £1.50 for postage and packing for the first book, £1.00 for the second book, and 30p for each additional book.

NAME (Block Letters) ....

ADDRESS ....

....

☐ I enclose my remittance for _____

☐ I wish to pay by Access/Visa Card

Number ⬚⬚⬚⬚⬚⬚⬚⬚⬚⬚⬚⬚⬚⬚⬚⬚

Card Expiry Date ⬚⬚⬚⬚